A FIERY
FRIENDSHIP

GABRIEL GALE'S

AGES OF OZ

A FIERY
FRIENDSHIP

Written by LISA FIEDLER

Illustrated by SEBASTIAN GIACOBINO

MARGARET K. McELDERRY BOOKS
New York London Toronto Sydney New Delhi

MARGARET K. McELDERRY BOOKS
An imprint of Simon & Schuster Children's Publishing Division
1230 Avenue of the Americas, New York, New York 10020
This book is a work of fiction. Any references to historical events, real people, or real places are used fictitiously. Other names, characters, places, and events are products of the author's imagination, and any resemblance to actual events or places or persons, living or dead, is entirely coincidental.
Text and logo copyright © 2017 by Polymorph LLC
Illustrations copyright © 2017 by Sebastian Giacobino
Back cover texture copyright © 2017 by Thinkstock
All rights reserved, including the right of reproduction in whole or in part in any form.
MARGARET K. McELDERRY BOOKS is a trademark of Simon & Schuster, Inc.
For information about special discounts for bulk purchases, please contact Simon & Schuster Special Sales at 1-866-506-1949 or business@simonandschuster.com.
The Simon & Schuster Speakers Bureau can bring authors to your live event. For more information or to book an event, contact the Simon & Schuster Speakers Bureau at 1-866-248-3049 or visit our website at www.simonspeakers.com.
Also available in a Margaret K. McElderry Books hardcover edition
Book design by Debra Sfetsios-Conover and Irene Metaxatos
The text for this book was set in Sabon LT Std.
The illustrations for this book were rendered digitally.
Manufactured in the United States of America
0418 OFF
First Margaret K. McElderry Books paperback edition May 2018
10 9 8 7 6 5 4 3 2 1
The Library of Congress has cataloged the hardcover edition as follows:
Names: Fiedler, Lisa, author. | Giacobino, Sebastian, illustrator.
Title: A fiery friendship / Lisa Fiedler ; illustrated by Sebastian Giacobino ; Gabriel Gale, creator.
Description: First edition. | New York : Margaret K. McElderry Books, [2017] | Series: Ages of Oz | Summary: When her mother is imprisoned for practicing forbidden Magic, thirteen-year-old Glinda must save the future of Oz from the four Wicked Witches.
Identifiers: LCCN 2016032878 | ISBN 9781481469715 (hardcover : alk. paper) | ISBN 9781481469722 (pbk) | ISBN 9781481469739 (eBook)
Subjects: CYAC: Fantasy.
Classification: LCC PZ7.F457 Fi 2017 | DDC [Fic]—dc23
LC record available at https://lccn.loc.gov/2016032878

TO MARIA AND NICK MAKRINOS,
THE PARENTS I ALWAYS WANTED
—GABRIEL GALE

FOR MY DAD, BUDDY, WHO REMEMBERS
ALL THE BEST MOMENTS, IF ONLY IN HIS HEART
—LISA FIEDLER

A FIERY
FRIENDSHIP

GABRIEL GALE

Greetings, Reader.

I, Gabriel Gale, am one of a fortunate few who can claim the honorable title Royal Historian of Oz. I have been to the Land of Oz many times. It is a land in a realm called Lurlia—a place constructed by the will and talent of Fairies and Fairyfolk. And it is much, much closer than you think.

I realize the idea of crossing realms might be difficult to believe, but the best and most interesting things generally are. What is important for you to understand is that I *know* Oz, backward and forward as they say, meaning that I have studied its history and I have seen its future. I also happen to have a very *personal* connection to the subject. But that is a discussion for another time.

I have shared all of my Ozian knowledge with a colleague who is being credited as the "author" of this book, but that is merely a publishing formality, since neither she nor I nor anyone else can "write" history; history *happens*. Our job is to remember and reveal it, without (as people often do) reinventing it. In the case of Oz, there is no need to take such liberties, for no amount of reinvention could possibly compare with how it actually happened.

And continues to happen.

At the time when this story begins, Oz was in a state of great and lingering unrest. I would say the turmoil had gone on for centuries, but in Oz time does not reckon itself in such terms. Four ferocious Witches led the four separate countries of Oz, and every citizen, be he Winkie or Munchkin, be she Quadling or Gillikin, was taught to hate anyone who lived beyond the borders of his or her own country. War was always a possibility then, and there is upheaval still in this wondrous place today—trouble, danger, Wickedness. I have already lent my energies to the fight, for I believe that Glinda's call to arms from long ago remains our call to arms today.

Know this: before you have finished reading this letter, a hundred thousand Magical things will have occurred in Oz. Some of them Good, and some of them Wicked. That is the part that never changes.

In conclusion . . . whatever you've heard about Oz is the *story*.

What I am about to unveil to you is the *truth*.

And so we begin, when Glinda the Good was a mere thirteen years of age. It is (according to Earth's calendar) the cusp of summer in the late 1700s.

And the time . . .

. . . is midnight . . .

1

WICKEDNESS
ON THE LAWN

If Glinda Gavaria had known how long it would be before she would ever again sleep the deep, peaceful sleep of the innocent and unaware, she might have elected to ignore the voice outside her window and simply remain in bed.

But the murmurings that awoke her from her slumber were impossible to ignore:

> *"Wax and wane, shrink and swell,*
> *sister to all, who loves us well*
> *Fairy of brilliance, Fairy of night,*
> *lead us to wisdom, set us to right."*

As Glinda's senses unfurled into wakefulness, her eyes opened to a room awash in shimmering moonlight. Into this luminous glow, she called out softly, "Mother?"

Her mother's voice came back to her, though not precisely in reply:

"Beloved Moon Fairy, you gaze upon us from heights unattainable, ruling the sky with hopefulness and grace."

It was a moment before Glinda realized her mother's words had not come not from the parlor where she often sat up late, sewing by the fireside; they had come from outside on the back lawn.

She tossed aside her bed linens, causing Haley Poppet to slip from the covers and land in a cottony heap on the rough wooden planks. Stepping over the rag doll, she padded to the window and peered out at the tiny yard.

There beneath the ruby maple tree stood Glinda's mother, Tilda, bedecked in a flowing cape of fabric so sheer it might easily have been spun from rainwater and cobwebs.

Tilda tilted her head toward the uncommon brilliance of the midnight sky; her russet-gold hair swung back in a cascade of shining ringlets, revealing the delicate chain of platinum she always wore around her neck. Dangling from this was a glittering red stone cut in the shape of a teardrop. Glinda had never seen her mother without it, and there in the moonlight it seemed to gleam more brightly than ever before.

"I know it is a great risk to summon you, Princess Elucida," Tilda confessed, her eyes skyward, her arms outstretched. "But I find myself in profound need of your guidance."

She's summoned the Moon Fairy? thought Glinda. This smacked of that which in Quadling Country was an undertaking most strictly forbidden:

Magic.

Ages ago, all forms of mystical pursuit had been outlawed. Only the Witch Aphidina and those to whom she'd granted her express permission were still allowed to engage in Magical activities.

"I'm dreaming," Glinda whispered, shaking her head in disbelief. "That is the only possible explanation. I *have to be* dreaming."

For where else but in a dream would her mother invoke Princess Elucida, Fairy of the Moon? As far as Glinda knew, Elucida existed only as a character in an ancient piece of Ozian folklore.

"My daughter has come of age, Moon Fairy, and the time has come for her to know. If I am to prepare her for all that is to come, I must see now with my own eyes what peril awaits." Tilda held out one upturned hand. "Despite the danger of this errand, I ask that you share with me that which only you can see."

The response came swiftly: a trembling moonbeam gathered itself from the glow and settled gently upon Tilda's open palm; an unbidden thrill shot through Glinda at the sight of it. Even in a dream, such potent Magic was wonderful to behold.

Tilda closed her fingers around the streak of light, coaxing it into a glimmering ball. Then she lifted her willowy arms to the sky, and as she did, the graceful movement was reflected in the looking glass above Glinda's dressing table, giving the bizarre impression that her mother was both inside and outside at the same time.

The effect was so entrancing that suddenly Glinda wanted nothing more than to be outside in the moonlit yard beside her mother, though whether to prevent the Magic or to join in it she wasn't entirely sure. The beauty and mystery of the act drew her to it, even as the threat of punishment caused a knot to form in her chest.

Glinda ran through the parlor, past the spinning wheel and the dying fire on the hearth, into the kitchen with its heavy oaken door. She reached for the iron handle and pulled.

But the door did not budge.

She tried the window. Also locked tight. Pressing her face to the glass panes, she watched as her mother bowed her head.

"I accept your secrets and your wisdom," Tilda murmured, her fingers going to the red stone at her throat. "And I ask that these be made visible." Then she tossed the shimmering ball of moonsparkle into the middle of the yard.

A sudden breeze swept through the yard, rustling the branches of the ruby maple, rippling the grass beneath the swirl of Tilda's gossamer cape. Glinda watched, astonished, as the moonlit yard began to transform into something unfamiliar. The curtain of the night seemed to crackle and splinter, as if the very atmosphere were breaking, twisting itself into a wavering phantasm.

Where the moonbeam had landed, four dark figures were now assembled on the lawn, facing one another like points on a life-size compass. Their faces were featureless smudges, and in them Glinda sensed an undeniable ugliness, if not of countenance, then surely of character.

The sinister foursome encircled three equally hazy shapes, though these were made not of darkness but of fear. They formed a trembling triangle within the outer circle.

It was clear that these interlopers were unaware of Tilda standing just inches away. Somehow, Glinda understood that they did not exist in the *now* but in a realm somewhere beyond. Their presence revealed a moment yet to come, an event still in the making. This was a vision of the future; and Tilda, with the Moon Fairy's aid, had called it forth!

A flicker of motion near the ruby maple caught Glinda's eye; a fifth specter was materializing like a shiver along one's spine. But this newcomer did not join the circle; instead, it hid behind the tree, where Tilda could not see it.

Glinda knew instinctively that this fifth being was a

darkness beyond all imagination; a vile intrusion, an invasive tagalong, riding the glittering coattails of Elucida's Magic. It was as faceless as the others except for the presence of two glowing orbs where its eyes belonged, pustules of red light that seemed to glare out of the future. Not quite eyes but eerily eye-like things, trained on Glinda's mother, who continued to study the four ghastly figures in the circle.

With a flutter of her fingers, Tilda uttered the word, "Identities," and as she did, the gloom began to fall away from the figures, one by one.

The first to appear was Daspina, the Wild Dancer of the West, rising from the murky depths of her own shadow. Her nimble body was clothed in a swirling gown of yellow, adorned with rows of snake scales. On her feet she wore a pair of Silver Shoes, and as though unable to resist the urge to dance, she swayed and shimmied in her place to some raucous music only she could hear.

Across from her, on the eastern point of the mock compass, Ava Munch, the Royal Tyrant of the East, emerged like a spring zephyr with a winter chill. Known for her extraordinary beauty and her even more extraordinary ruthlessness, Ava carried herself proudly, cradling in her hands a Silver Mask. On her regal frame she wore a gown of opulent blue silk that matched her lapis-colored eyes.

In the northern position loomed Marada, the Brash Warrior. Fully turned out in heavy armor, she was tall and muscular, short on grace but long on ferocity. Her face seemed to fight its way out of the blank darkness, presenting itself with a scowl on her thin purple lips. Covering her hands were a pair of Silver Gauntlets, which glinted in the moonlight.

Glinda's stomach lurched at the sight of them, the diabolical Witches from the North, East, and West. A feeling of dread filled her as she turned to watch the transformation of the fourth lifeless smudge—the one that occupied the southern point of the circle.

This last visitor revealed herself from the ground upward, as if she were a weed growing out of the soil. First came the slim skirt of a red satin gown, climbing into a slender torso over which was draped a gleaming vest of finely woven Silver Chainmail. Proud shoulders sprouted next, then an elegant neck. Her head appeared, adorned with a tall headdress. Finally, Glinda saw the exquisitely angular face.

The most familiar face of the whole horrid quartet: Aphidina. The Witch of the South.

But that was impossible. Aphidina was known to despise the three other Witches, denouncing them as her sworn enemies. Aphidina, who was known by all to be fair and generous and wise, would never deign to associate with such evil.

Aphidina was a worthy queen.

And the others . . .

. . . were just plain Wicked.

Glinda felt a coldness creep over her. She was about to call out to her mother to cease this dangerous escapade when her gaze was pulled skyward by a silent spark bursting forth from the midpoint of the moon. It traced a downward path through the sky like a single, illuminated teardrop, sparkling against the velvety blackness of the night. As it drew nearer, Glinda saw that it, too, was a living creature.

"Elucida, Princess of the Moon," she whispered.

Closer and closer she came, this delicate, sweet-faced Fairy with translucent wings. Wings, Glinda realized, that were beating frantically in search of escape! Kicking and thrashing, Elucida struggled to halt her quickening descent. Glinda could see the panic on her face as she clawed at the night sky, desperate to fight her way back up to the moon.

But the force that dragged her down was far too great; she was trapped, dangling as if from an invisible noose, above the Witches' heads. The light that spilled from her luminous skin poured over the three cowering shapes in the center of the circle, as if to save them from this vicious ritual, but even Elucida's moonlit brilliance could not dispel the darkness that held them there.

Daspina attacked first, swinging her hips and arms in graceful time as she sang, "Dance, Moon Fairy, dance—dance until you are so lost in your own distraction that you've forgotten there is anything to accomplish!"

Elucida's body began to jerk and jitter, writhing without rhythm or reason until she was spent from exhaustion.

Still dangling, the Fairy spun a quarter turn to face Marada, who said nothing except to emit a growl. Clasping her gloved fists above her head like the victor of some unholy battle, she stomped her spurred sandals in the grass as if she were on the march. With every thunderous pound of the Warrior's feet, the fragile Elucida became more and more entangled in heavy iron chains.

When Marada had finished, the Fairy spun again, so that now her pleading eyes were locked on Ava Munch's. Raising the mask to her face, Ava spoke in a voice like breaking glass: "Displease me not, nor irritate, or sudden death will be your fate," and as she chanted, a powerful blue force radiated through the eye slits of the Silver Mask—a Magical gaze so hateful and so terrifying that the Fairy cried out and began to shrivel. As she did, Aphidina took hold of her, turning her to face the southern point on the compass. Although her grasp was tender, the Fairy winced in pain.

"Fear nothing," said Aphidina, her words as soft and serene as falling orchid petals. "For this is Quadling and all is well. Here you are as safe and as free as I allow you to be."

From its hiding spot behind the tree, the fifth figure flung its arms into the air and made a seizing gesture. The four Witches did the same; moving as one, they threw their eager arms toward Elucida, capturing their prize in a violent four-pronged embrace. Daspina snatched her tiny fluttering feet, Marada gripped her hands, Ava grabbed her face. And Aphidina, cackling with a sound like dying leaves, reached out her long, long fingers to crush the fragile, fluttering wings.

Glinda had not known light could shriek in fear, but Elucida cried out in such terror that the sound seemed to swallow the remaining glow from the sky, threatening to plunge the whole backyard—perhaps even the whole of the Lurlian realm—into total and endless darkness.

From behind the tree, the dark haze of the fifth figure folded its smoky fingers into a fist, and Glinda felt the monster's invisible stranglehold around her own throat; she tried to shout for her mother, but her voice was trapped in the stranger's grip. Lungs clenching, arms flailing, she slammed her fist against the window hard enough to shatter one of the panes.

The noise startled Tilda, who spun away from the ghostly vision of the Witches to meet Glinda's eyes through the glass. Swinging her weightless cape, she summoned another gust of wind and the vision vanished in an explosion of darkness, taking the fifth figure with it in a blaze of failed light.

The chokehold ceased and Glinda fell to the kitchen floor, gulping for air.

In the yard, her mother waved her hands in a motion that was sweetly hypnotic and began to sing:

"Do not worry, do not weep,
dream your dreams and sleep your sleep.
Stars belong around the moon
and what belongs is coming soon.
Sleep your sleep and dream your dreams.
What is, is not quite what it seems . . ."

Glinda's eyelids drooped, then closed. She found herself once again curled beneath the coverlet of her bed with her rag doll tucked softly into the crook of her arm, though she could not remember walking back to her room.

Perhaps she had been there beneath the blankets all along.

Dreaming.

From the looking glass above the dresser, Tilda's reflection whispered, "Only the truest among us will see through the darkness to bring forth the brightest of light."

"I don't understand," said Glinda, her words rolling into a yawn.

"You will, my darling. And what you will know, above all, is truth."

With that, Glinda drifted back to sleep to finish her dream; a dream filled with questions waiting to be asked, tainted by the grim awakening of doubt.

2

REGRETS WILL NOT BE TOLERATED

Glinda awoke to a sky filled with dazzling sunshine.

This did not suit her mood in the least. Because today was to be the Day of Declaration at Madam Mentir's Academy for Girls. Today Glinda would choose her future.

As she made her bed, her mind prickled with the fading memory of a frightful dream. Stepping into her slippers, she took herself to the kitchen, where her mother was arranging flowers in a pewter vase.

On closer inspection Glinda saw that the clippings were not yet flowers, only buds. Little knots of life, which would bloom into plump roses in the coming weeks. For now they were only the promise of the flowers they would soon become. She wondered why her mother's hands trembled so; perhaps the stems had thorns.

On the sideboard sat the Declaration Day invitation, scarlet lettering engraved on creamy pink card stock.

Madam Mentir's Academy for Girls

STRONGLY RECOMMENDS

THAT YOU ATTEND THE ANNUAL

CELEBRATION OF DECLARATION DAY

IN WHICH

THE CONCLUSIVE CLASS SHALL CHOOSE

THEIR FUTURES

Schedule of Events

AT THE HOUR OF TEN: BESTOWING OF THE SCROLLS

AT HALF PAST THE HOUR OF ELEVEN: FAREWELL TEA

REFRESHMENTS GENEROUSLY ARRANGED

BY OUR MOST POWERFUL AND GRACIOUS

BENEFACTOR

APHIDINA, WITCH OF THE SOUTH

Conclusives & Guests

BE PROMPT. DRESS WELL.

REGRETS *WILL NOT* BE TOLERATED.

"Mother, I need your advice." Dropping onto the kitchen bench, Glinda reached across the table for a popover, still warm from the tin. "Today I must declare and choose what I shall do with myself for the rest of my life."

"So says the invitation," her mother replied absently, placing a stem in the vase; it was much too long and needed to be clipped, but Tilda made no move for the shears that lay upon the table.

"Is something wrong?" asked Glinda, nibbling the crispy edge of the popover. "You seem distracted."

"Do I?" Tilda reached for the last bud, but abandoned it to take up a scrap of linen fabric instead, then a needle threaded with black string. Without a word of explanation, she began to stitch the shape of a circle.

"I have some concerns," said Glinda. "About my future."

"As do I," Tilda murmured, her needle dipping and rising expertly until the tiny image of a winged being had appeared on the fabric within the circle.

Glinda waited for Tilda to expound, but she didn't. *"Mother!"*

Startled, Tilda looked up from her sewing. "I'm sorry, darling," she said, setting aside her work. "You were saying?"

"I was saying that I've been thinking about Declaration Day. I had a dream—at least I think I did—though I can't quite catch hold of it in my memory. Even so, I do believe the dream was trying to tell me something. But it's all a bit fuzzy."

"Fuzzy?" Tilda went to the fireplace to remove the tea-kettle, only to realize that the water had not yet begun to boil. Glinda furrowed her brow and watched as her mother returned the kettle to the fire; it wasn't like Tilda to be so distracted.

Pouring herself a cup of buttermilk from the pitcher, Glinda said, "It's common knowledge that Aphidina inscribes the scrolls in *advance*, and in order to graduate with her kind favor, every girl's Declaration must match the future the Witch has written."

"Yes," Tilda muttered. "That is the grand tradition."

"And of course," Glinda went on, reaching for the abandoned bud and slipping it into the vase, "everyone also knows what happens when a girl misdeclares."

"I suppose everyone does."

"But doesn't it seem tremendously unfair that we are only allowed to choose from four possible careers? Why only four? And why *those* four? Chambermaid, Seamstress, Governess, and Nurse. Why must our options be so limited? What if I wished to become—oh, I don't know—a dancer? Or a dealer of rare coins? Or a botanist?"

Tilda frowned, preoccupied. "*Do* you wish to become a botanist?"

"Not really," said Glinda with a shrug. "But I did earn highest honors in Horticultural Expressionism for Girls."

The teakettle whistled, but Tilda made no move to fetch it. Once again she reached for the fabric scrap.

Glinda noticed that there were now four faces embroidered around the circle, though she didn't recall seeing Tilda add them. With a sigh, she got up, removed the kettle from the fireplace, and poured her mother a steaming cup of tea.

"Now that I think of it," Glinda grumbled, "why is it that at Madam Mentir's, the title of almost *every* course ends with the qualifier 'for Girls'? Does educating female students somehow require a specific approach?"

Secretly, Glinda had always marveled at the subjects her friend Leef Dashingwood was exploring at Professor Mendacium's Institute for Intellectually Promising Young Boys: Intro to Cartography, Essential Metallurgy, and the Basics of Sword Forging. Glinda would have given *anything* to sit in on a sword-forging lecture! In fact, not long ago, just before his unexpected departure from Mendacium's Institute, Leef had loaned Glinda one of his reference books, *The Particulars of Pointy Combat*. At first she'd been excited about studying something that hadn't been assigned to her. After further contemplation, however, she determined that it might not be wise to take such a risk, since at Madam Mentir's, reading outside the classroom was profoundly frowned upon. She'd returned the book to Leef without ever getting past the illustrations in the first chapter.

"Why do you suppose Aphidina takes such an interest in what we are taught?" Glinda asked, gulping down another bite of popover. "And in what we are *not* taught as well?"

"That's an excellent question," Tilda replied. "In fact, all questions are excellent questions, if they are asked at the proper time, and under the appropriate circumstances."

Her eyes darted to the window overlooking the backyard. "Unfortunately, this is not that time and these are not those circumstances."

Glinda scowled, propped her elbows on the table, and dropped her chin into her hands. "Governess, Nurse, Seamstress, and Chambermaid," she lamented. "I just don't feel . . . *appropriate* for any of these vocations. Or maybe it's that the vocations are inappropriate for me. But I do have to choose *something*. I must declare my path, accept my scroll, and determine my future."

"That's exactly what you must do," said Tilda, an anxious tremor in her voice. "Trust me, child. This is not the time to be contrary."

"Isn't it?" Glinda leaned against the back of the bench and folded her arms. " If I'm meant to declare myself, then shouldn't I actually *declare* myself? Why shouldn't I exercise a bit of independent thought?"

"This is not the time for such flights of fancy," said Tilda firmly. "For one thing, I do not relish the thought of watching you experience the consequences of misdeclaring!"

"Neither do I," Glinda agreed. "So I suppose I'll just do what everyone expects of me and declare myself a boring old Seamstress."

For the first time since Glinda had come to breakfast, her mother smiled. "A boring old Seamstress? You? Never!"

"Oh, Mother! I'm sorry!" Glinda felt her cheeks flush with shame. "I didn't mean to imply—"

"It's all right," said Tilda, reaching out to stroke Glinda's red hair. "I take no offense. It is simply my occupation. And as you seem to be discovering for yourself, an occupation can only ever be what one *does*, and not, in the truest sense, who one *is*."

Glinda had never thought much about who her mother was. She only knew that as a girl, Tilda had been apprentice to an old woman called Maud, who was said to have been the best Seamstress Oz had ever known. They had not seen her in some time, but when Glinda was small, they had often gone along the Road of Yellow Brick to visit Maud in her cottage on the outskirts of Quadling. Maud had come to visit at their house only once—Glinda remembered that occasion fondly as the day Maud had given her the gift of Haley Poppet.

As Glinda drank her buttermilk, she tried to remember the song Maud had sung that day: *Count by one, a quest begun, Count by two, with hearts so true . . .*

Tilda stood and carried her tea to the kitchen window to again gaze out at the yard. As Glinda's eyes followed her, she noticed the glistening glass panes—for some reason she was expecting one of them to be broken.

An image flashed in Glinda's mind, a piece of the dream: *her mother in a sheer, sparkling cape, dark figures gathered on the lawn, the splintery web of a broken windowpane . . . a red gown and headdress . . .*

"I've only just remembered," she began with a shudder. "Last night, in my nightmare, I saw—"

Before she could finish, there was a knock on the kitchen door.

"That will be Ursie," said Tilda, referring to Glinda's classmate and best friend, with whom she had walked to Madam Mentir's every day for the last six years. "You'd better hurry along and get ready for school."

Since there was no point in delaying the inevitable—whatever the inevitable might turn out to be—Glinda rose from the bench and headed to her bedroom. As she did, she gathered up a handful of her long rusty hair and began to twist it into a braid. Then a thought struck her that had her deftly weaving fingers halting mid-twist.

"Perhaps I shall leave my hair down for today," she said.

Tilda looked stricken. "All the girls at Mentir's wear their hair in plaits or pinned up," she said. "And on Declaration Day of all days, you must follow suit!" She closed her eyes and shook her head. "What I mean to say is that it's a lovely thought, my darling. But I doubt Madam Mentir would allow you to accept your scroll with your hair unbound."

With an exasperated huff, Glinda went to dress for school.

And Tilda tossed the linen scrap with its hasty black stitches into the fire.

3

INCENDIARY COMMAND

Aphidina's castle was a thing of stalks and vines, of pollen, pods, and petals—a suitable dwelling place for the Haunting Harvester Witch of the South.

Ages ago Aphidina had stood upon the most fertile spot in all of Quadling Country and thrown a handful of enchanted seeds into the dirt. In a voice blooming with dark Magic she demanded of the land a palace.

And the land had given it to her.

The castle had grown up around her from the rich Lurlian soil—a living edifice of stems and creepers shooting off here, trailing there, climbing and clinging and bending toward the sun in a magnificent melding of agriculture and architecture. Like nonliving castles, this one had windows and sweeping staircases, larders, sculleries, and a frightful dungeon deep within its root system, all protected almost to the point of impenetrability by Wicked enchantments. Every spring season, fresh buds would burst forth from the palace and burgeon into hallways and ballrooms and chambers for reflection. Sometimes rooms died off and needed to be pruned away to allow for the growth of new ones. But Aphidina didn't mind. She enjoyed redecorating.

Deep in the heart of the castle was the Witch's audience chamber, where one day long ago a throne had pushed itself up through the cracks in the floor. It began as a stumpish thing with dull gray bark and gnarled branches prickling with cones. But in time the throne had grown into an appropriately elegant seat for Her Witchliness of the South. It had a tall back and smooth limbs for armrests, whereupon the Witch might strum her fingers and think her Wicked thoughts.

It was upon this throne that Aphidina was sitting when the candles began to flicker. She flinched in her fancy chair. The Harvester knew a visitation when she saw one.

She was here. She who ruled all.

Mombi. The Krumbic one, who could turn Good Magic to dark.

And today she had turned herself to fire.

Aphidina understood that Mombi could have just as easily arrived as a stallion with a tail of braided snakes, or a horned salamander with burning coals for eyes. She could be anything, but she could not *have* everything. Not yet.

That was what Aphidina and the others were for—to get it for her.

Through the snapping of the candlelight, the announcement came without preamble: *"The Grand Adept has revealed herself at last."*

Aphidina's cold green eyes locked on the flickering flames. She was not overly fond of fire.

"Her name is Tilda Gavaria, and she is a mighty Sorceress, to be sure."

"This is extraordinary news," was Aphidina's cautious reply. After a moment's hesitation she asked, "And where was she found?"

"She is a citizen of Quadling Country."

Aphidina's jurisdiction. Her lips twisted and her long fingers fussed with the chainmail vest she wore over her gown of poppy-red satin. "My deepest apologies. But if I may ask, how precisely did you locate this Tilda?"

"I sensed the expansion of a mind," the fire hissed.

"You felt someone *learning*?" Aphidina couldn't help being impressed. "I was not aware that you could do that."

The flames sputtered. *"It has not happened in quite some time. The Foursworn have been cautious. So cautious I had begun to think they'd given up."* There was a pause, in which the fire grew even hotter, as if from the force of its own excitement. *"Last night I felt Gavaria requesting information from the Moon Fairy, who sent a vision in reply. A vision of the future, and to this I attached myself, like a virus."*

"Contamination is an excellent skill," Aphidina noted. "What did you discover?"

"That the Ritual of Endless Shadow can indeed take place." Something like a chuckle, but uglier, crackled beneath the fire's voice. *"I saw a fusion of Magic and sacrifice in which you and your sister Witches—"*

"They are *not* my sisters," Aphidina muttered petulantly.

"—drag the Moon Fairy from her celestial perch, plunging the world into perpetual twilight."

The Harvester felt the chainmail pressing heavily against her chest as she resisted the urge to gasp. She knew that the Ritual of Endless Shadow was Mombi's greatest goal. For eons it had been beyond her grasp, but today Mombi's long-abandoned thirst for the moon had been reignited.

All because of Tilda Gavaria.

"A question, My Incendiary Liege: you said that the ceremony 'can' happen. Am I to understand that it is not a certainty?"

The flames writhed upon their wicks. *"A vision of the future is a prediction, not a promise. Do you know what that means, Aphidina?"*

"Yes." Aphidina pretended to smooth her satin gown, when in fact she was just wiping the sweat from her palms. "It means there is work to do."

The fire flared in agreement. "*We must hunt down Gavaria if we are to find the Elemental Fairies and collect the Gifts of King Oz.*" A plume of angry black smoke billowed out of the flames. "*A task you should have accomplished the first time I assigned it to you.*"

At this, the Witch stiffened. There had been no mention of the Elemental Fairies or King Oz's Gifts for centuries, although Aphidina suspected that not a day went by when this Krumbic nightmare didn't wonder about them.

"*I need not remind you that of all the Magic in Lurlia, the power contained within your sisterhood is the only power that can destroy those odious Elemental Fairies.*"

"Again, *not* my sisters," Aphidina murmured, "and no, you need not remind me of that."

The more important fact of which she also did not need to be reminded was that, other than the power of the Krumbic one herself, "those odious Elemental Fairies" were the only things standing between Aphidina and her doom; it was cold comfort that the same was true for the other three Wickeds. She supposed this was what one might call a cosmic balance, or a "fair fight." But of the many things the Harvester hated, fairness was the one she detested most.

"*I believe,*" the fire crackled on, "*that one of the Fairies—your own nemesis, in fact—is rather close at hand.*"

Aphidina gave a little croak of horror. "How close?"

"*Extremely,*" the candlewicks sputtered, sending a

shower of sparks sizzling through the air. These rained down around Aphidina's throne, igniting into a ring of flames encircling the Witch and licking at her feet. *"Gavaria has the Fire Fairy in her possession. We need only arrest her and she will deliver him directly into our hands."*

"A most fortuitous coincidence," Aphidina said, all but gagging on the words. "But you know it is altogether possible that the Fairy might destroy *me* before I extinguish him."

"That is a risk I am willing to take," the fire crackled. *"Though I strongly advise that you do not allow such a calamity to occur. If you can destroy this Fairy and steal the Gift, then there will be no need to perform the ceremony beneath the moon."*

"Your concern for my well-being is humbling," Aphidina drawled, drops of perspiration forming on her brow; more trickled down her spine. She wondered if the dampness might have an adverse effect on her Silver Chainmail.

A flash of motion near the doorway caught her eye. A sense of something that had not been there before, the sprouting of a new chamber perhaps, or the dying-off of some long-forgotten room.

"I shall have the Sorceress Gavaria arrested as soon as possible, Your Combustibleness," she said, though she was not looking forward to gathering the mass of muck and swamp gas she called a bounty hunter. Sometimes she regretted having created a thing of such repugnance in the first place; Aphidina preferred to look upon beauty and elegance whenever possible, and Bog, while effective, was ugly.

Aphidina quickly crooked a finger at her handmaiden, a tiny girl blossom she'd cultivated herself from a bulb in a clay pot.

The girl flower had eyes the color of spring grass, and on her head instead of hair grew delicate pink and white petals. She was obedient, lovely to behold, and smelled delightful. Indeed, the only evidence that she'd been brought forth from Wickedness was the ridge of thorns that grew down the middle of her back. As she neared the sweltering circle of fire, she wilted a bit.

"Daisy," said Aphidina, her skin beginning to blister, "summon the prison wagon back from its rounds."

"As you wish," said Daisy, and the flower girl ran off to see it done.

"I will send the bounty hunter to apprehend the Foursworn Sorceress Gavaria the moment the wagon returns," Aphidina promised the fire.

At Aphidina's feet, the fire roared up in a conflagration of anticipation. Tongues of flame curled themselves into fireballs and shot out from the circle to explode in every corner of the room. If this was Mombi happy, it was nothing short of spine-chilling.

A long moment of broiling silence passed in which the Harvester took a deep breath of scalding air and mopped at her forehead. Drawing her sizzling toes up under her gown, she inquired, "Majestic Malevolence, will you be taking the flames with you when you go?"

But Mombi was already gone; unfortunately, the circle of fire remained, blazing around Aphidina's throne. She recognized it for the warning it was:

CAPTURE THE SORCERESS.

DESTROY THE FAIRY.

DO.

NOT.

FAIL.

The Witch sighed and slumped in her chair. Had the roar of the fire not been so great, she might have heard the faint sound of boot heels retreating along the corridor that led away from her throne room. She might have even noted the slight disturbance in the air of the audience chamber, caused by the whipping retreat of a heavy cloak.

But Aphidina was too intent on watching the encroaching blaze to realize that her order to arrest the Sorceress had been overheard.

4

UNBEARABLE DISCOMBOBULATION

As Glinda walked through town with Ursie Blauf, her mind was filled with thoughts of Declaration Day.

Around the girls were the familiar redbrick buildings, with their red-painted porches and profusions of flowers in shades of vermilion and scarlet. The only hue bolder than the flora was the vibrant red coats of Aphidina's army.

As always, the soldiers milled about in great numbers, lounging in the doorways of private homes, marching in platoons down quiet lanes, and lingering in the bustling town square. Glinda had never wondered at their presence before, for it was a fact known to all that the army was there only to ensure the comfort and safety of the Quadling populace. Today, though, she asked herself this: If Quadling were as safe as it was said to be, what need was there for soldiers?

Ursie had just announced that she'd be declaring herself a Governess at today's ceremony. Glinda could picture it as plainly as if it had already happened. Ursie would call forth a scroll from the enormous, ancient urn set on a riser in the middle of the school's Grand Drawing Room, and it would more likely than not say *Governess* upon it. Then one of the instructors would shake Ursie's hand, wishing her a "steady future," as opposed to the more hopeful blessing of "good luck."

"My sister is a Governess. And my mother was a Governess," Ursie was explaining. "Seems a good fit, since I don't despise babies much. I'm positive 'Governess' is what my scroll will say."

Glinda nodded, envying Ursie's certainty.

"Will you choose Seamstress?" Ursie asked. "Like your mother?"

Glinda's reply was a faltering smile.

Turning the corner, the girls stumbled upon two strapping soldiers politely escorting Master Abrahavel J. Squillicoat, the apothecary, out of his shop while three more set about boarding up his windows.

"Nothing to be concerned about," the larger of his captors assured the chemist, as pleasantly as if he were merely ordering a cough elixir, as opposed to removing him bodily from his place of business.

The second officer smiled a charming smile. "This is Quadling and all is well," he said. "Here you are as safe and as free as Aphidina allows you to be."

Glinda stopped short. She had heard that phrase before.

A burst of light from the sky, a shadowy compass . . .

"Step aside, please, miss," the first soldier advised.

Glinda leaped out of the way, but not before meeting Squillicoat's gaze. Despite his tranquil demeanor, she was surprised to see the glint of panic in his eyes as the soldiers whisked him away, cheerfully promising him a pleasant walk to the outskirts of Quadling.

"I always liked Master Squillicoat," said Ursie with a frown. "He blended a poultice that all but saved my life when I caught a case of the Insidious Splotches back in Fledgling year."

Glinda and Ursie continued on, quietly thinking their own thoughts until they reached the town square.

"Ursie," Glinda began cautiously, "have you ever really, truly believed the legend of Elucida the Moon Fairy?"

Ursie lowered her eyebrows and gave Glinda a sideways look. "Have you?"

"I'm not sure," Glinda confessed. "But I think I might have dreamed about her."

"A Moon Fairy sounds lovely," said Ursie. "Almost as delightful as the legend of the elusive Sea Fairies. Such stories are far more interesting than the things we learn at Mentir's, like 'fireflies hate the taste of roses,' and 'icing on tea cakes should always be spread from left to right, and never right to left.'"

"Fireflies love roses," Glinda corrected absently. "It's poppies they dislike."

Just then shouts rang out across the square. Glinda and Ursie turned to see a gang of children, hooting and clapping.

"Now what?" said Ursie.

The children seemed to have someone or something surrounded. A mournful howl rose up from the center of their circle, and Glinda dashed toward the uproar.

What she saw caused her heart to clench. There, curled on the ground, was an enormous, quivering bear, his black eyes shining with fear.

"Hit 'im again!" snorted the tallest boy in the group. "With a rock this time!"

There was a sickening *thunk* as the stone found its mark and again the bear groaned in agony.

"Dopey bear," hissed a pointy-faced girl with wispy mud-colored hair. "Can't even walk a straight line without toppling over himself."

"Bumbling oaf!" shouted a chubby boy; he had freckles all over his doughy face and up and down his plump arms. Grabbing a stick from the ground, he commenced to poke it into the bear's silky fur.

The bear whined and cried out, as much in shame and sadness as in pain. He attempted to disengage himself, but succeeded only in growing even more discombobulated.

Somebody spit on him, and the bear covered his face with his giant paws, only to be kicked hard in his backside by a gangly boy with bile-colored eyes and buck teeth.

"Stop it!" came Glinda's shrill command. "STOP IT this instant!"

The shout was so fierce that the baiting ceased immediately; sticks and stones fell to the ground as the tormentors turned in search of their accuser.

Glinda felt their bitter eyes upon her.

"What are you doing?" Ursie whispered. "Are you trying to get us clobbered? Those are Field Waifs!"

Glinda had never been this close to a Field Waif before. They were the children of Quadling Country whom Aphidina had deemed more inclined to physical labor than academic pursuit. Rather than being sent off to Mentir's or Mendacium's to struggle through six years of cognitive enlightenment, they were instead graciously allowed to serve the Witch in a capacity more suited to their constitutions—as farmhands. By her kind decree, these Field Waifs toiled in the Perilous Pasture, sowing and hoeing and harvesting crops from sunup to sundown, and all without ever being expected—or permitted—to open a book. They had a reputation for being a surly lot, with a deep dislike for any child who was not a field laborer.

As if to prove it, the bile-eyed boy was pushing up his sleeves and stalking toward Glinda. She blanched but forced herself to look the delinquent in the face.

"You were hurting him!" she said. "He can't help it if he's clumsy."

"Still ain't no business of yours," said the pointy-faced girl.

Sizing up the young thugs, Glinda quickly determined that she was both outnumbered and out-nastied. Deciding that cunning was her only option, she gave the pointy girl a knowing look.

"Perhaps it isn't," she said. "But you should know that this bear is not just any bear."

"What bear is he, then?" the chubby boy asked, dribbling a string of saliva.

"He is Major Ursa," Glinda said, the fictitious distinction rolling off her tongue so easily it made her smile. "A high-ranking member of Aphidina's Royal Animalian Guard." Aphidina did not *have* an Animalian Guard, but Glinda was reasonably sure the Waifs did not know this. "Oh, and did I mention, he is the Witch's particular favorite?" Putting on a reverential voice, she genuflected before the bear and said, "Good morning, Major."

By now the bear had drawn himself up to all fours and was licking his wounds. His teeth were like razors. And his claws! One swipe could have removed from that chubby boy the majority of his fat freckly flesh. But for all the animal's size and might, Glinda understood that he was not a swiping sort of bear.

"How nice that the Witch has sent you into town today," she went on, her smile urging the bear to play along. "Is your mission to search out and arrest any poor-mannered miscreants who might be causing trouble?"

The bear stopped licking, made a wuffling sound, as though to say, *Sure, why not?* and nodded his enormous head.

Whether the girl and the chubby boy understood that *they* were the poor-mannered miscreants to which Glinda was alluding was hard to say, but they did take a nervous step away from the "major." Bile-eyes wasn't quite so easily convinced.

"If he's a major, then why's he lettin' us bash him without bashin' us back?"

Glinda gave the boy a cool look. "Members of the Animalian Guard do not 'bash' children." She shook her head. "I wonder what Aphidina would think if she knew what you've done to her beloved friend."

"She's gonna tell the Witch on us!" shrieked the sharp-faced girl. "Run!" She bolted, shouting for her friends to do the same. They ran after her.

The clamor of the Field Waifs fleeing caught the attention of a nearby soldier. He waved to the uniformed driver of a wagon across the square; the driver cracked his whip and the horses took off after the Waifs. Then the soldier approached Glinda and Ursie.

As he drew nearer, Glinda saw that he was in the process of some bizarre transformation. Where his nose should have been was a gnarled tree knot, and the fingers with which he gripped his musket were thick vines. Hanging down from under his hat was not hair but a straggle of green ivy.

"What were those little blighters doing away from the pasture?" the soldier demanded of Glinda.

Glinda could only stare. She had never seen anyone in such a state before.

"They were just up to their usual shenanigans," Ursie assured him, averting her eyes. "No harm done."

When the soldier marched away, Glinda fell to her knees beside the bear. She stroked his head and used the cuff of her red school dress to wipe the blob of Field Waif spittle from his fur. Then she untied her braids and used the two ribbons to bind his wounds.

"I'm sorry they hurt you," she murmured in his ear.

The animal rolled his shoulders in a bearish shrug, causing him to totter. "It's truboo," he said, his voice like honey. "I um clum-ubsy. I wumble-wobble when I walk and clumsy-umsy when I talk."

Glinda gave him a scratch behind his ears; then she and Ursie hurried on toward school. To her surprise, the bear followed, tumbling along behind.

Squillicoat's sudden eviction, Field Waifs, the changeling soldier . . . Glinda had witnessed these sorts of goings-on her whole life, but today was the first time she'd ever been troubled by them. She felt as if she was now seeing things as they really were, rather than how she had been taught to see them.

An image of four smoky figures flashed in her mind.

"Ursie," she said before she could stop herself, "I'm not so sure that Queen Aphidina is really what she seems to be."

Ursie's face brightened with interest, and, if Glinda weren't mistaken, relief. "I'm so glad to hear you say that, because—"

Fwummpppff!

Behind them, the bear tripped and rolled over himself like a big furry acrobat. Glinda quickly went to help him right himself.

"Thumk clu," said the bear, nuzzling her cheek.

Returning to Ursie, Glinda prompted, "Because why?"

But they had reached the academy campus, and Ursie shrugged. "Never mind," she mumbled.

Glinda turned to the bear. "You'll have to stay out here," she told him. "Will you be all right?"

The bear snuffled happily and replied, "Yumsy," which Glinda took to mean *yes*. Then he waddled over to a butterfruit tree and curled up at its roots.

Glinda and Ursie approached the knotty hazel hedge,

which marked the campus boundary. Beyond it the academy stood proudly, the red-shingled rooftops of its turrets piercing the sky, its rusted weathervane pointing ever southward in homage to Aphidina. There was a rustle and a *swoosh* as the snarled hedge opened itself to allow them entrance.

Sweeping through the gap in the hazel branches, Ursie gave a wistful sigh. "Wouldn't it be nice if *we* were allowed to use Magic?"

Glinda's eyebrows shot upward in surprise.

"Think about it, Glin. We're surrounded by Magic, inside and out. Magic is our greatest truth, but only those whom Aphidina allows can use it. It's not fair, and what's worse, it makes everything feel like a lie."

As they made their way up the gravel footpath toward the school's front steps, Ursie glanced around cautiously. Then she took both of Glinda's hands in hers. "I have a secret," she breathed, her eyes sparkling. "A secret about Miss Gage."

Miss Gage, who had come to the academy at the start of this year to teach seminars on How to Hear the Stars Twinkle and Lullabies as Literature, was Glinda's absolute favorite teacher. She was nothing like the rest of the faculty at Madam Mentir's; occasionally Glinda had wondered if Miss Gage had been hired by mistake.

"A secret? Tell me!"

"It was something I discovered months ago," Ursie

confided, "in a homework assignment for Lullabies. We were given an old cradlesong to memorize, remember?"

Glinda nodded.

"Well, as I was chalking the lullaby onto my slate, I made a mistake. So I erased what I had written."

"And . . . ?"

"And the dust from the chalk rose up in a little cloud, and I could see the very words I'd just rubbed out, floating in the air. Then the letters rearranged themselves and spelled out a message."

Glinda's eyes went round. Nothing like that had ever occurred in any of *her* homework assignments. "What did the message say?"

Again, Ursie looked around before leaning in close to whisper what the chalk had told her:

"Lullabies are sweet enough,
  but you are made of stronger stuff,
For Oz we'll soon begin the fight,
  when those who yearn for truth unite."

Glinda's skin tingled. "What does it mean?"

"It means," said Ursie, skipping up the broad steps to the academy's grand entrance, "that there might just be something to look forward to."

With that, she turned and pushed open the front door.

Glinda hurried after her, wondering why Miss Gage

would risk sending Magical communiqués under the guise of lullaby homework. That was just asking for trouble.

With a deep breath, Glinda followed Ursie through the imposing doorway and into the school's stately entry hall. There, serenely descending the sweeping staircase in the foyer, was Miss Gage.

And she was looking right at Glinda.

5

MADAM MENTIR'S
ACADEMY FOR GIRLS

Miss Gage held Glinda's gaze for a long moment. Then, from her pocket, she removed a small mirror in a filigree frame and examined her reflection.

The staff scurried about the entry hall in preparation for the day's event, hanging decorations and placing bowls of red zinnias on gleaming side tables. A custodian ambled past, carrying the ceremonial urn brimming with scrolls.

Glinda saw her classmates gathered in one corner, fussing with their hair ribbons and shoe buckles. As a class they were known as the Conclusives, and they'd been together here at Mentir's since their first day as Fledglings, six years before. All had gone to great lengths to look their best for the festivities; they had starched their pinafores and polished their boots, and with the notable exception of Glinda, every girl's hair was neatly braided or pinned up. Blingle Plunkett's golden tresses had been swept into a twist with cascading tendrils framing her delicately featured face.

When Blingle spotted Glinda and Ursie, she waved them over. It was not so much an invitation as it was a direct order.

Glinda had always thought Blingle would make a fine replacement headmistress should Madam Mentir ever retire, or inexplicably disintegrate into a pile of red powder and disappear in the wind, which was exactly what had happened to Headmaster Mendacium earlier that semester!

"Glinda Gavaria!" Blingle gasped. "What happened to you? Your hair is an absolute catastrophe!"

"Nothing happened to me," said Glinda, wishing she could twist *Blingle* into a tendril. "I gave my hair ribbons to a clumsy bear."

Blingle scowled. "That doesn't even make sense, Glin-*duh*."

"It makes perfect sense," said Ursie. "And what business is it of yours how Glinda wears her hair anyway? Honestly, Blingle, you always act as if you're so much older than we are, and so much more important."

"I am important," said Blingle. "Just ask Minx." Her eyes narrowed as she gave her best friend a poke. "What do *you* think, Minxie? Am I important?"

"Oh, yes, Blingle," yelped Minx. "You are colossally important!"

It came as no surprise to Glinda that Minx agreed with Blingle, since the one time Minx had *disagreed* with her, Blingle had "accidentally" cut off six inches of Minx's beautiful chestnut-colored hair. It had been chalked up to a "freak sewing class mishap," but Glinda suspected that the "accident" had been both intentional and premeditated.

"Important and wise," chirped D'Lorp Twipple, who had dimples and a tendency to hiccup. "Not to mention sophisticated and kind."

"Just like Aphidina," added Trebly Nox, who, like the others, would never forgo an opportunity to flatter Blingle . . . whether Blingle deserved it or not.

A derisive snort came from the direction of the stairs, and Glinda turned to see Miss Gage slipping the filigree mirror back into her pocket.

Now Madam Mentir's harsh voice rumbled through the entry hall like wagon wheels over cobblestones. "Glinda Gavaria! Approach!"

Obediently, Glinda dashed across the foyer and presented herself to the headmistress, executing a flawless curtsy. "Good morning, Madam," she said. "Happy Declaration Day."

"How can I be happy," the headmistress snarled, "when one of my Declarants has forgotten to braid her hair?"

Across the foyer D'Lorp let out a nervous hiccup.

Glinda kept her gaze on the floor. "I apologize, Headmistress. It was unavoidable."

"Well, I shan't have it!" Mentir boomed. "No graduate of this academy will be allowed to declare with her hair unbound. It sends the wrong message."

Glinda had no idea what sort of message the absence of braids could possibly send, but she refrained from saying so. A muffled giggle from across the foyer told her the Declarants were witnessing her humiliation with great interest and, in Blingle's case, deep delight.

"I am tempted," Mentir stormed, "to forbid you to declare!"

Glinda's throat tightened. "Forbid me to—?"

"That will mean no ceremony, no scroll, no future for you!"

No future? And all for the want of an appropriate hairstyle? Glinda couldn't believe what she was hearing. "Please, Madam," she choked out. "You can't forbid—"

"Silence! I am considering."

It was at this very moment that the Declaration Day guests suddenly began to assemble on the front steps. This was odd, as it was over an hour and a half prior to the time noted on the invitations. Glinda could see them through the diamond-paned windows, making their way up the front steps. Even *they* looked confused as to why they were arriving so early, as if they'd somehow come without meaning to. But there they were.

The gentlest of sighs came from Miss Gage. "Not yet half past eight and the families have begun to arrive," she noted calmly. "And all at once, no less."

Madam Mentir looked positively apoplectic. She clapped her hands sharply and addressed the class. "Conclusives, to the drawing room! *Immediately!* Your families, it seems, have elected to redefine punctuality. Now, line up according to height. Runts to the front, gangly ones fall in behind. During the ceremony, those of you who are pretty may smile if you choose. Plain girls, endeavor to look content; smart if you can manage it."

In a scuffle of shoe leather the Declarants hurried from the foyer. Reluctantly, Glinda lifted her face to meet the headmistress's scowl.

"Go to the toolshed and find a length of twine," Mentir commanded. "Use it to tie back that flame-colored hair." She clicked her tongue in disgust, as if having red hair was a crime Glinda had willingly committed.

"Thank you, ma'am. Thank you in large amounts."

Mentir took a moment to study Glinda's face. "And when the Declaration activities commence, you have my permission to smile." Then she dismissed Glinda with a grunt, composed her features, and strode to the entrance to welcome her guests.

As Glinda rushed from the foyer, she paused at the back door to glance back over her shoulder toward the stairs.

Miss Gage was nowhere to be seen.

6

A Thing of Cold, of Sludge, and Silt

The reflecting pool was the centerpiece of Aphidina's entry garden.

The crystalline body of water sat like a sparkling jewel, surrounded by a border of wildflowers, further encircled by the roundabout of fieldstone pavers that marked the beginning—or the end—of the bridge path, depending on whether one was entering or exiting the palace grounds. Entering was the more frequent occurrence, for other than Aphidina herself and those in her employ, few who were delivered here were ever given the opportunity to leave.

As Aphidina descended the outer steps of her palace, the train of her red gown trailed along behind her like the shimmering slime of a slug. Daisy shuffled along warily beside, petals fluttering, leafy arms pumping in her efforts to keep up.

"Did you send word to the wagon driver?" asked the Witch, barely tipping her fine chin in Daisy's direction.

"My Queen, I did as you asked. The driver has altered his course and is returning here as we speak." She paused to punctuate the news with a nervous smile, loosing a sprinkle of pollen from her plump yellow cheeks. "You will be pleased to hear that this morning has yielded a full cart."

Aphidina sniffed. "Pleased" was not at all what she was feeling at the moment, given that she was about to perform her least favorite task. The summoning of Bog, for a queen who valued elegance and beauty almost as much as she prized power, was a loathsome errand indeed. She wished she had created him differently. She wished she had made him lovely. But his purpose was to be mighty and merciless in equal measures and his appearance, horrendous as it was, was suited to his responsibilities.

Even if it did cause Aphidina's stomach to sour.

The Witch cast a longing glance toward her favorite feature on the entire property—the Grande Allée of Symmetrees. She would much prefer to be strolling that tranquil lane, bordered by two rows of towering trees, each individual specimen perfectly symmetrical to the one that grew across from it. These she had cultivated since they were saplings, and they, like everything else in her garden, were enchanted. She took great pride in the precision of them, the order and equilibrium—mostly because she was the one who controlled it.

A short distance from the reflecting pool, a high wall constructed of enormous Lurcher creatures enclosed the expansive castle grounds. The wall was interrupted by a towering gate of giant cabbage leaves, which opened and closed by Magical command. The leafy doors were guarded both within and without by her best changeling sentries.

Gliding to the edge of the reflecting pool, the Witch took a moment to admire the way it held the sky upon its surface so that the pink clouds overhead appeared to be also resting upon the calm sheen of the water.

What lay beneath the calm was quite another matter.

Aphidina raised her arms and, dipping one toe into the pool, chanted an incantation:

> "From the depths of muck and mire
>   bring to me what I desire,
> A thing of slime, a thing of cold,
>   of sludge, and silt, morass and mold
> Vanish clean and clear and blue!
>   Congeal Bog! You've work to do!"

Then Aphidina snatched her toe out of the water and leaped back.

At the edge of the pool, the gorgeous riot of snapdragons

and toadflax, columbines and zinnias wilted and withered. The water began to roil in huge burplike bubbles, bursting up from the deep bottom of the pool. And while the playful pinkish clouds in the sky remained as they were, those mirrored on the boiling surface did not; their reflections darkened to reddish black, drawing together into a storm mass from which jagged bolts of lightning flashed.

Blue-white bursts speared eerily into the fathomlessness, shedding light on the swampy swirl spinning up from the pool's floor. Mud sucking itself into itself to form a torso of massive muck muscles, spewing green slime that became arms and legs and a swollen headlike thing.

Daisy turned away.

Aphidina did not. This was her beast, her creature. And although the sight of him sickened her, she never ceased to be amazed by her own ability to bring about terror.

The water gushed back and fell away, leaching into its own banks until only a murky puddle remained at the bottom. From this Bog rose up, like a mudslide in reverse. Stink and stagnation; marsh gas and weedy rot. His breath was a gaseous heaving from his broad chest as he trudged out of the pool and through the flower bed, slopping right past Aphidina, who recoiled, knowing that his very presence would leave a stain.

"Open the gates," cried a sentry from outside. "The prison wagon comes."

A sizzle of Witchcraft—*swoosh!*—and the cabbage leaves

swung open into the garden. Aphidina could see the prison wagon making its way across the long moat bridge. In no time, it was through the gate, the horses at full gallop, the wheels grinding violently over the stones of the roundabout.

In a cloud of stench, Bog planted himself in the path of the team as if they were merely a litter of kittens scampering in his direction.

"Whoa!" the driver hollered, pulling back on the reins. "Whoa!"

The horses reared and whinnied, skidding to a halt a hairbreadth from the bounty hunter's muddy form. With a slurping growl, Bog stomped past them, yanking the driver from his seat and tossing him into the murky shallows of the reflecting pool.

He climbed onto the seat to take the reins.

"The prisoners!" the driver choked from the mud puddle.

Aphidina gestured wildly to the sentries, who ran to unload the captives—a gang of panic-stricken Field Waifs and a boy in blue—from the enchanted cart.

Aphidina locked eyes with the boy. His twinkling blue eyes inspired her; she could sow them in her garden—eyes like that, if properly planted, would yield a dazzling blue patch of delphini-winkles before midsummer.

But Bog was already punishing the horses with the crop, shouting insults and threats to the frightened team, and the sentries were forced to quit their task, leaving the boy and a few remaining Waifs in the cart.

"Ride with the muck!" the Witch commanded her soldiers.

Obediently, two sentries hurled themselves into the saddles of their waiting steeds and steered them into the wagon's wake.

"H'yah!" croaked Bog, cracking the reins. The wild-eyed horses sprang into motion.

Flinging herself out of the way, the Witch managed to aim one quick spell at the frightened Field Waifs still trapped in the prison wagon. "Straw and rags, rags and straw, here's what you get for breaking my law!"

She knew not what crime they had committed, but their unexcused absence from her pasture was more than enough to warrant a Magical punishment—especially since no Quadling citizens were present to witness her vengeance. "With vacant eyes and brainless heads, henceforth protect my flower beds!"

The dark charm settled over them as the wagon bombed past, taking the turn of the circular path so recklessly that Aphidina thought it might flip. But Bog steadied the tilting vehicle with a ferocious tug on the reins, and the wheels slammed back down to the stones. The Waifs and the boy in blue bounced hard on their wooden seats. The cart bolted onward, fishtailing through the gate and taking out one of the Lurchers as it did.

No matter; Aphidina would simply send a gardener to the Perilous Pasture to harvest another. She would repair the wall *and* plant the delphini-winkles. Because the blue-eyed boy would be back; Bog would see to that.

And this time, Tilda Gavaria, Sorceress of the Four-sworn, would be with him.

7

THE SCRYING MIRROR

Glinda slipped out the back door and hurried across the rear lawn to the toolshed. Sounds from within stopped her in her tracks: anxious pacing and hushed voices. She pressed her ear to the door to listen.

"If only I weren't obliged to take part in this ridiculous Declaration ceremony, which I myself pushed up an entire hour by mobilating the guests as a diversionary tactic."

Glinda immediately identified the speaker as Miss Gage. But what in the world did she mean by 'mobilating'? That was a word that had definitely not been taught in Approved Vocabulary for Girls.

"Now tell me," Gage went on, "why have you sought me out?"

"I have come seeking help from the Foursworn."

This second speaker was a girl, though it was clear to Glinda that she was not a Conclusive, or for that matter, even a Quadling. Her accent was stiff and sharp, as if each word were being bitten off at the end. Glinda guessed it was the accent of the enemy Gillikin region, or perhaps Munchkin Country (it was said that Winkies warbled, as a general rule), since she'd never heard anything quite like it before.

"My name is Locasta," said the girl. "My father was a Revo—Norr of Gillikin—but he has been missing now for many months. . . ." Her voice broke and she trailed off, but when she began again, the resolve in her tone was even stronger. "Before he disappeared, he told me that if ever I found myself in trouble, I should come to Quadling to find you."

"I remember your father well," said Gage. "We met long ago at one of the earliest Minglings, when the cause was very new." The teacher paused. "*Are* you in trouble, child?"

"Not me," Locasta said. "My younger brother, Thruff. He has joined with the Witch Marada. He has been threatening to do it since our father disappeared, but I don't believe he's Wicked, just desperate and angry. I tried to explain to him about the Foursworn and the rebellion, but Thruff is extremely . . . stubborn."

"Are you sure about this?" Gage asked.

Locasta nodded. "He stood up to Marada at the Levying

and got himself hauled off to the castle dungeon."

"That's not quite the same as joining her ranks," Miss Gage pointed out.

"You don't know Thruff. I'm certain by now he's found a way to prove his usefulness." Here Locasta let out a disgusted sigh. "Or perhaps she tired of him an hour into their association and he's already dead. With Thruff, it could go either way."

"When was he captured?"

"Two weeks past," Locasta replied. "It has taken me that long to get to Quadling, as escaping Gillikin was a nearly impossible task. I had to make my way in secret, traveling after dark with only small bits of Magic to aid me."

There was a pause as Miss Gage considered Locasta's problem. "How can I be of assistance?"

"I require an introduction to the Grand Adept who dwells here in Quadling. Surely she is the only one who can assist me in saving Thruff. Can you help me?"

"I'll most certainly try," Gage promised. "But I am sorry to say I am not personally acquainted with the Grand Adept. The Foursworn, as I'm sure your father explained, operate under deepest cover. So for secrecy's sake, I've kept my distance." The teacher echoed Locasta's dreary sigh. "I will try to arrange a meeting. Here, take this with you. It's a scrying mirror. It will lead you to the old Makewright's cabin. Wait for us there." There was another anxious swish of skirts. "I must leave you now. They'll miss me if I'm too long absent."

"Truth Above All," said the girl.

"Yes," said Miss Gage, her footsteps approaching the door. "Above All."

Glinda quickly concealed herself on the far side of the toolshed, under the pink cloud of a cherry blossom tree, and peered around the corner just as the door swung open. Miss Gage rushed out and hurried up the path toward the academy's back entrance.

A second later the girl emerged.

Locasta Norr was like no one Glinda had ever seen. Her hair was a mass of long, curling ringlets, a dazzling shade of deep lavender, and her eyes were the highly charged purple of amethyst stones.

She *was* a Gillikin, of this there was no doubt, for the Gillikins were known to be smaller in stature than the willowy Quadlings (though taller than the Winkies, who were not nearly so squat nor bulky as the Munchkins).

Most peculiar was the girl's clothing. She did not wear a full-skirted gown, like Miss Gage, nor was she turned out in a simple cotton school dress with a ruffled hem and pinafore apron, like Glinda. Locasta sported a hooded tunic with blousy sleeves and tight cuffs; the tunic was pale violet and belted around the middle with a wide purple sash. And she was wearing *knee breeches*! Leather ones, tucked into sturdy boots that were snugly fastened around her calves with straps and laces.

It was when Locasta bent down to adjust one of these

straps that a small shiny object slipped out of her tunic pocket and into the soft grass.

Miss Gage's mirror.

Without even thinking about what she was doing, Glinda leaped from the shadow of the toolshed, picked up the fallen compact, and called, "Wait. You dropped this."

In the next second, Locasta had grabbed the front of Glinda's pinafore and slammed her up against the cherry tree.

"Who are you?" she demanded.

Glinda squirmed against the rough bark of the tree trunk. "Let me go."

"Not until you tell me what you're doing out here," Locasta snarled, tightening her grip.

"Not that it's any concern of yours," rasped Glinda, "but I gave my hair ribbons to a clumsy bear, and the head-mistress will not allow me to declare if I don't tie it up."

"She wants you to tie up a bear?"

"No, my *hair*! She wants me to tie up my *hair*." Glinda eyed the girl's own tangle of purple curls. "You have my apologies for overhearing your conversation, and I do hope you are able to correct the situation with your brother. Now, please release me! I need to get back inside."

Locasta made no move to let go. If anything, her hold on Glinda's pinafore grew tighter.

Glinda began to struggle. When Locasta laughed at her piteous attempts to free herself, a bolt of fury shot through

her, and with one mighty thrust Glinda sent her captor toppling backward onto the lawn.

For a long moment, the two glared at each other.

Glinda had never shoved anyone before, but the sight of Locasta on her backside in a pile of twigs and grass clippings, not to mention the look of complete astonishment on her face, was oddly satisfying.

It was then that she noticed the girl's wrists.

What she had first thought to be the cuffs of Locasta's violet tunic were actually rusted metal shackles, clamped around her wrists.

Locasta quickly shoved her hands in her pockets, concealing the manacles. "Don't you have a ceremony to attend?" she huffed.

"Yes, I do," said Glinda, holding out Miss Gage's mirror yet again. "But I would recommend you take better care of this. It was a gift, after all."

The Gillikin rolled her eyes, then stood up and slipped the mirror into her pocket. "I hope I never see you again," she said.

"The feeling is quite mutual," Glinda retorted. But Locasta did not hear; she had already broken into a run.

8

DECLARATION DAY

Glinda hurried across the lawn toward school. It was time for her to declare herself.

"Glinda!" someone called from the road. "Glinda Gavaria, is that you?"

Glinda turned in the direction of the voice and saw a young man in an army uniform approaching. His sturdy shoulders and cropped mane of shining, husk-colored hair were unmistakable.

"Leef Dashingwood!" said Glinda, relieved to see a friendly face after her ugly run-in with the purple-haired ruffian. "What a lovely surprise."

The young soldier closed the distance between them

with long, swaggering strides. This was the first Glinda had seen of Leef since his abrupt departure from Mendacium's; he looked quite smart in his cutaway coat of deep scarlet, its velvet lapels winking with bright brass buttons. But when Glinda's mind flashed back to the image of the changeling soldier in the square, she shuddered.

"What are you doing out here?" Leef inquired cheerfully. "Shouldn't you be inside enjoying the Declaration Day festivities?"

"The headmistress sent me out to find some twine," Glinda explained, her fingertips going to her still-unbraided hair.

"Looks more like she instructed you to prune the cherry trees," he teased, grinning as he removed a twig from her tangled hair and examined its froth of tiny pink blooms. "Some girls wear ribbons. This is far more original."

Glinda smiled. She hadn't realized how much she'd missed Leef's humor and easy company. But the sight of him dressed in Aphidina's war uniform was troubling, to say the least. "Where are you off to in your military trappings?" she asked warily.

"Aphidina's castle. I am to be presented to the Witch in the Hallowed Hall of Hollyhocks."

"We learned in Horticultural Expressionism for Girls that Hollyhocks are a symbol of great ambition," Glinda said, frowning at the idea of Leef bowing before one who consorted—even in a nightmare—with the Wickeds.

"Well, ambition is a good thing, isn't it? Although I would be lying if I said I wasn't nervous."

"Then don't go!" Glinda blurted this out before she could stop herself.

"Don't go?" Leef laughed. "Why would I ever elect to do that?"

"I just have a bit of a strange feeling about it, is all. Really, Leef, you don't *have* to be a soldier, do you? Surely the most intellectually promising boy in a school filled with intellectually promising boys could be anything he wished to be!"

"That's what Headmaster Mendacium said." A flicker of sadness darkened Leef's eyes. "Right after Aphidina invited me to leave school early and enlist in her army." He shook his head. "Just before he turned up powdered."

Only now did it occur to Glinda what a coincidence it was that the Headmaster's talc-y demise would occur on the heels of Leef's premature departure from the institute. Everyone knew that Mendacium had fervently protested the Witch's invitation, arguing that the boy was of promising intellect, after all, and deserving of a complete education.

Glinda's frown deepened, and without thinking, she reached out to place her hand on the arm of Leef's rich velvet coat. The gesture made him smile.

"Come to Declaration Day!" she urged. "Some of the girls are bound to misdeclare, which will surely make for a bit of excitement." She cringed. "The way things are going this morning, I just might be one of them."

"You? Never!"

His confidence in her only made her more eager to prevent his visit to the Witch. "Please, Leef," she said, gripping his arm, "skip the Hall of Hollyhocks and come see me accept my scroll!"

"I'm sorry, Glin," he said with a lift of his shoulders. "I cannot ignore Aphidina's request."

Glinda sighed. "No," she conceded. "I suppose you can't."

Faint strains of harpsichord music had begun to waft through the open windows of the Grand Drawing Room, and Glinda knew she should hurry back. "I really must go, Leef, but I do wish you the very best of luck."

"And to you the same," he replied, twirling the cherry blossom between his fingers. "I trust you will be a grand success at whatever future you choose."

"Choose, or have thrust upon me," Glinda muttered.

"Even so, a future is a future, is it not? And we are lucky Aphidina is so willing to allow us to have one." Then Leef clicked his heels and gave her a gallant little bow. "Happy Declaration Day, Glinda Gavaria. And may your hair always bloom cherry blossoms. Though, in truth, you are more than unique enough without them."

Glinda blushed at her friend's kind words. "Thank you," she said.

"You're very welcome. Good-bye."

"Good-bye."

But Leef Dashingwood made no move to take his leave. Instead he just stood there, holding the flowery twig and smiling at Glinda.

Neither of them noticed the sudden flutter of a dark cape in the distance.

From across the lawn, the harpsichord music reached a dramatic crescendo, and Glinda was reminded that she had somewhere exceptionally important to be. Dipping a quick curtsy, she turned and hurried toward the school.

Leef watched her go, smiling after her as she ran up the garden path and into the building. Then he tucked the delicate cherry blossom twig carefully into the pocket of his coat and marched off to meet the Witch.

By a stroke of good fortune, Madam Mentir was facing away from the Grand Drawing Room's entrance when a flushed and breathless Glinda slipped through the towering double doors. She was sweaty and dusty from her tussle with Locasta and inexcusably late. Most of her classmates had already made their Declarations and had crossed to the far side of the expansive room; they stood now, shoulder to shoulder, each proudly holding her scroll, more than a few of them sniffling and misty-eyed. Only half a dozen girls had yet to declare, and these few were marching single file toward the copper urn in the middle of the drawing room.

Standing at the ready beside the urn was Mistress Misty Clarence, Dean of Disastrous Decisions, who had been present at every Declaration Day ceremony since the founding of Mentir's Academy. She was responsible for addressing misdeclarations, which made for a fair amount of suspense in an otherwise tedious ceremony. Judging by the bored look on Mistress Clarence's face, Glinda surmised that so far, everyone in this Conclusive class had declared as per Aphidina's expectations.

Smoothing her wrinkled pinafore, Glinda swung herself into the slow-moving line, lifting her chin and puffing out her chest in the hopes of looking as though she'd been there all along.

Ursie stepped forward, beaming. In the urn, the tightly rolled Declaration scrolls shuffled themselves, until one rose weightlessly out of the urn and floated across the space to hover over her head. "Ursie Blauf," she declared boldly. "Governess!"

Glinda watched as the scroll unwound itself in the air above Ursie; written on it in beautiful calligraphy was the word GOVERNESS.

There was a sprinkle of applause from Ursie's family as the scroll rolled up and placed itself in her hand. Ursie curtsied and took her place among the Declarants.

Next came D'Lorp, in the midst of a hiccuping fit.

"D'Lorp-*hic*-Twipple-*hic*. Seamstress-*hic-hic-hic*."

The same ceremonious floating and subsequent unrolling

occurred, rightly identifying D'Lorp as the Seamstress she planned to become. She hiccuped once more for good measure, then fell into formation with the others.

Next came a girl named Baloonda Quish, who until Miss Gage's arrival at Mentir's had been plagued with a heavy lisp. But thanks to the teacher's elocution lessons and the student's own diligence (in Baloonda's words), "the *s*peech *s*ituation had been *s*ucce*ss*fully *s*olved."

"Baloonda Quish," she said, her crisp diction ringing through the room. "I serenely and self-assuredly select Seamstress."

But when the scroll floating above Baloonda's head opened, it revealed the following: CHAMBERMAID.

The spectators emitted a collective groan of pity.

"It happens," crooned Dean of Disastrous Decisions Clarence, calmly gesturing for the crowd to settle down. "You all know it happens. If it didn't, I'd be out of a job." Then she pointed a finger at Baloonda's forehead and recited the following words:

"Much to learn and much to do
So back to Fledgling year with you
To better know for what you're meant
Repeat the years you poorly spent
You came, you saw, and yes, you tried
But now you must be Youngified!

The entire gathering watched as the consequence for misdeclaration, a process known as Youngifaction, was brought to bear upon Baloonda Quish: she began to shrink, not just in size but in *experience*, becoming younger . . . smaller . . . *emptier* as she reverted to the small child she had been on her first day at Madam Mentir's six years before.

Glinda was thankful that the sound of Baloonda's thirteen-year-old bones and organs squeezing themselves back to the proper size for a six-year-old could not be heard above the applause of the crowd. Essentially, Baloonda was being given an academic pardon, a second chance to please the Witch. She would return to Mentir's next fall as a Fledgling to have another crack at it—all of it. How lucky!

But as Glinda watched her classmate's backward transformation, she realized that what was even worse than facing another six years of Reading Only When Absolutely Necessary for Girls was that all of Baloonda's memories were being reclaimed as well. Joyful days spent playing on the school lawn leaked away, as forgotten as if they'd never happened! Every secret, every promise, every last daydream of the childhood she'd already lived would be erased. Stolen. Gone.

And Glinda, like everyone else, just stood there watching it happen.

Glinda's heart thudded when Baloonda's long braids began to reel themselves back into her scalp, slithering like

pretty snakes. A moment later there was a painful popping sound and a pair of wispy pigtails sprouted out of either side of Baloonda's head.

"What have you to say, Quish?" Mentir prompted as the CHAMBERMAID scroll tore itself to tiny bits and sprinkled itself around Baloonda like the world's saddest confetti.

The Fledgling-size Baloonda looked nervous but managed to respond. "Baloonda Quish humbly thank*th* Queen Aphidina in ab*th*entia, for allowing me *th*ic*th* more year*th* of ex*th*ellen*th* in education at Madam Mentir*th* Academy for Girl*th*."

The crowd applauded wildly. Someone cried out, "How patient and generous is Aphidina, the Witch of the South," and several others chimed in, "Hear, hear! Hear, hear!"

"Next!" Mentir bellowed.

Trebly all but skipped up to the urn and sang out, "Trebly Nox. Chambermaid."

In response to Trebly's declaration, her brother, Obblish, stuck out his tongue and sputtered a loud, wet raspberry. This earned him a frown from Madam Mentir and a good hard pinch from his mother, who scolded, "Obb Nox . . . *shush!*"

Next came Blingle, who sashayed toward the urn, batting her eyelashes at the spectators. "Miss Blingle Plunkett shall become a Nurse," she announced, as if she'd done it a hundred times before.

Blingle's scroll shot up from the urn and tumbled end

over end like a baton toward the Declarant. It opened above her head and agreed with what Blingle had said: NURSE. The scroll landed in her reaching fingers with a flourish, and Blingle curtsied exuberantly to the crowd before going to join the others.

At last it was Glinda's turn to step forward. She could feel the eyes of her fellow Declarants and their families upon her soiled dress and snarly hair. A gust of harsh whispers blew through the room.

"Glinda Gavaria," she said, her voice a whispery scrape in her throat. "Gov—"

Panicking, she gulped back the word and shook her head. "Um . . . I mean, Sea—" Again she cut herself off. "That is . . . Nur—"

But the word would not form. Not on her lips, and not in her heart. Nurse, Chambermaid, Governess, Seamstress . . . not one of them felt like a future that could ever belong to *her*.

Madam Mentir shot up from her chair, crooking a finger at the urn as she stomped across the room. A scroll leaped up and sailed toward Glinda to dangle above her head.

Like a guillotine.

The headmistress did not quit stomping until she was nose-to-nose with the errant Conclusive who still had not claimed a future. "*Declare!*" she commanded.

Glinda scanned the room, searching for her mother, and found her standing beside the harpsichord. Suddenly the only words in Glinda's head were those she'd heard once in a dream: *Lead us to wisdom, set us to right . . . Lead us to wisdom, set us to right . . .*

Enraged by Glinda's silence, Mentir again shouted in her face, "*DECLARE!*"

Still Glinda did not speak, and yet, to her shock, the scroll began to unfurl above her head. Resolved to settle for whatever future it gave to her, Glinda looked up at the opened Declaration scroll.

And found it blank.

9

STEADY FUTURE ONE AND ALL

Blank!

This was an unprecedented calamity, for in the entire history of Madam Mentir's Academy, no Declarant had ever received a *blank* scroll.

Glinda half suspected the floor would open up to swallow her whole. Or at the very least, she would be Youngified, like Baloonda. The mere thought of that made her so dizzy she thought she might drop. But Miss Gage was suddenly at her side, meeting Madam Mentir's chilling gaze as she reached up to harvest the empty parchment from the air where it still hung, bare and empty above Glinda's head.

"Possibility," the teacher announced, as confidently as if the letters were printed there in boldface type. "That is the future for which Glinda Gavaria is destined. No single word could ever be large enough in scope or meaning to define what our Glinda might become. For doesn't the absence of one word allow for the presence of *all* words?"

A murmur of agreement rippled through the gathering as Gage presented the scroll to Glinda.

"I have every faith that in time Glinda will arrange this multitude of as-yet-unwritten words into a life story of immense purpose."

It was a beautiful sentiment, but Glinda doubted Mentir would consider it an accurate interpretation of a scroll full of nothing.

"Possibility is *never* an option here at the academy," she snarled. Seizing the blank scroll from Glinda's grasp, she began to snap her fingers at it, harshly and in quick, measured time, one snap for each letter: *S* (*snap*); *E* (*snap*); *A* (*snap*); *M* . . . The letters appeared on the parchment one by one, as if each little *click* from the headmistress's fingertips was instead the touch and sweep of a well-inked nib. When Mentir had finished snapping out the tempo, Glinda's future had been scrawled across the scroll in dripping black ink: SEAMSTRESS.

"You wouldn't dare to insult your own mother by declining to follow in her footsteps, would you?" Madam Mentir challenged through her teeth.

Glinda shook her head and went to join her snickering classmates as Madam Mentir turned to face the class and address them in a stern voice.

"Your years here have been well spent. See that you squander nothing of what you have been so generously taught." Her flinty eyes bored into each graduate in turn as she curled her colorless lips into something that was not quite a smile. "In the name of Aphidina, Witch of the South, I wish you girls a steady future. Steady future, one and all."

The graduates rejoiced; they clapped and cried and curtsied, singing out to Madam Mentir in a sugary chorus of thank-yous, waving their scrolls in the air.

"Steady future," the Declaration guests chimed happily.

But to Glinda, the cheerful echo of the headmistress's words sounded less like a blessing . . . and more like a curse.

10

IN THE HALL OF HOLLYHOCKS

The Haunting Harvester had had a long morning. Krumbic fire, stagnated law enforcers, and now a visit, at her own command, from the most capable and ambitious young soldier in the entire Quadling army.

Leef Dashingwood.

Entering the freshly budding Hall of Hollyhocks, Aphidina felt the weight of the Silver Chainmail vest she wore. Unbidden came the memory of the moment it had become hers. *That* had been a day marked by colossally bad judgment, and the Krumbic one had never quite forgiven her for her greed, not to mention her failure. It was bitter consolation that her three rival Witches—Marada in the North,

Daspina in the West, and that fiend Ava Munch, who hid behind a Silver Mask in the East—shared in this guilt.

It was all the fault of the silver! Those glittering gauntlets, the shoes of sterling, the helmet with its shining mask, and oh, that sparkling chainmail, all there for the taking from the shadow of the fallen king . . .

"Dashingwood has arrived, Your Highness."

Startled by Daisy's voice, Aphidina realized she'd been gripping the chainmail so tightly the silver was cutting into the soft flesh of her fingers. "Present him," she rasped.

Daisy skittered aside, and there was Leef.

He could not have been more impressive if Aphidina had grown him herself.

She studied him as he swept into the Hall of Hollyhocks, stinking of Goodness and cherry blossoms and pride. When she had him pulled from Mendacium's—based on reports that he excelled at, well, *everything*—she'd worried that there was simply too much decency in the lad for him to ever be the kind of soldier she required. But once he was drafted into her elite ranks, his willingness to please and his need to be the best had made him as malleable as a birch sapling. He *believed* (as he'd been brought up to believe) in the supremacy of Quadling Country and the absolute right of Aphidina to rule as she saw fit. In short order his fierce loyalty to her unseen Wickedness had thoroughly trampled his ability to recognize anything else.

Even so, today she carried in her palm an enchanted

potpourri of dried bark, nipped buds, and root hairs—a changeling charm that would turn him into a walking twig—just in case.

As he marched toward her, his presence seemed to demand the respect of the whole flowery hall. The slender columns of hollyhock that made up the chamber walls stood taller to greet him, and he in turn threw back his shoulders and let them. There was a tinge of disappointment in his eyes. Perhaps he had expected more pomp, more circumstance? A brass band, medals dangling on stiff ribbons, sergeants at arms?

Too bad.

She could smell his ambition from across the hall, as pungent as a gardenia bed freshly fertilized with piles of aged manure.

"Welcome, Dashingwood," said Aphidina, closing her fist around her handful of Magic. "Stand there." She pointed to a spot in the center of the room, then said quietly, "Grow," and the floor around him broke open, spitting up hollyhock.

For all his promising intellect, the idiot actually beamed. "It is my great pleasure to make your acquaintance, My Queen," he said, clicking his boot heels and offering a bow. "I am, as ever, your faithful servant."

"Indeed you are," Aphidina crooned, for already the red and copper hollyhocks had climbed up to surround him like the bars of a cage.

With a smile that contained no mirth, the Witch approached the boy, her elegant fingers again grasping her chainmail vest.

"Leef Dashingwood," she said in a most casual tone, "I would like to talk to you about a friend of yours."

11

FORTUITOUS FOREWARNING

Glinda tried to enjoy the Farewell Tea, but the events of the morning hung about her like steady rain. After gulping down a celebratory glass of iced ragweed tea with Ursie, she slipped away from the crowd to conceal herself on the bench of a window seat and attempted to gather her thoughts.

Peeking out from behind the curtain, she caught sight of Miss Gage standing in a far corner of the room, with her back to the festivities. She appeared to be engaged in conversation, though Glinda could not make out to whom the teacher was speaking.

Her eyes remained on Gage's back until whomever it

was she'd been whispering to disappeared into the crowd with the nearly imperceptible flip of a dark gray cape. It seemed Miss Gage's second mysterious encounter of the day had concluded without incident.

But when the teacher turned around, her typically rosy complexion had gone ashen. Her troubled eyes scanned the room until they fell on, of all people, Tilda Gavaria, who was detained in conversation with the Blaufs. Mr. Blauf, a wagon wheel salesman by trade, seemed intent on selling Tilda a new set of hub rivets even though Ursie's mother reminded him repeatedly that the Gavarias did not own a wagon.

Miss Gage set out across the room in long, purposeful strides, momentarily waylaid by D'Lorp Twipple, who, in an emotional hiccuping frenzy, threw her arms around the teacher to bid her a choppy but heartfelt farewell.

Spotting Glinda in the window seat, Miss Gage waved over D'Lorp's hiccuping head. "Glinda Gavaria!" she called. "I was hoping you might introduce me to your mother."

This was the last thing Glinda wanted to do. Despite Miss Gage's skillful handling of the blank scroll debacle, there was no getting around the fact that just an hour ago she'd been colluding with a Gillikin hooligan in a toolshed. And what of the clandestine chalk-dust message she'd sent to Ursie?

Springing up from the window seat, Glinda hurried to

collect her mother from the Blaufs. "Mother, I'd like to go now, please."

Miss Gage had managed to disentangle herself from D'Lorp and was now hastening in the Gavarias' direction.

"It seems your teacher wishes to speak with us," Tilda said.

"I have nothing to say to her," Glinda insisted, tugging her mother toward the exit, while eyeing the approaching Miss Gage, who was pressing the first two fingers of both hands in an X over her heart.

Tilda stopped in her tracks.

Gage was moving more briskly now, dodging a serving maid with a tray of empty glasses.

Just as Miss Gage reached Glinda and her mother, Madam Mentir appeared from nowhere and stepped directly into her path. Miss Gage stumbled backward a step.

"Gage," snapped the headmistress, "summer school begins in a fortnight, and you have yet to turn in your lesson plans for Advanced Butterfly Collecting for Girls."

"Oh . . . well . . ." Miss Gage's eyes met Glinda's over Mentir's shoulder. "Can it wait just a moment? I've been so hoping to meet Glinda's mother."

"Glinda is no longer your concern," Mentir snarled without so much as a glance at the Gavarias. "She's declared. Concluded. She is a *was*." The headmistress flung out her hand and pointed to a doorway hung with red velvet curtains at the far end of the drawing room. "My office. This instant."

Miss Gage pressed her lips together and nodded. "Very well."

"I'm sorry we didn't get a chance to talk," said Tilda. "Another time, perhaps."

"Oh, yes, most absolutely," said Miss Gage, extending her hand for Tilda to shake. "Another time."

Tilda accepted the teacher's hand.

"Come along, Gage," said Mentir.

Tilda headed for the door so quickly that Glinda fairly had to run to keep up.

As she stepped for the last time through the doors of Madam Mentir's Academy, she felt the unsettling sensation of a pair of eyes boring into her back.

She turned, fully expecting to find Madam Mentir's withering gaze upon her.

But it wasn't Mentir. In fact, it wasn't anyone, as far as she could tell.

Then, out of the corner of her eye, she caught a flicker of gray—the swirling hemline of a cloak or cape. But before she could be sure, the towering front doors of Mentir's Academy closed behind her.

And Declaration Day was over.

Outside, Tilda pointed to the gravelly road at their feet and made a curving gesture with her finger. Next she tilted her chin upward to the rusted weathervane on the roof and blew softly and steadily until the arrow had spun a half turn. Then she grasped Glinda's hand, and they set out at a frantic pace.

"Come along, Glinda. We must hurry."

Clumsy Bear, who'd been napping under a tree, rolled himself to an upright position and wobbled along behind. Glinda would have liked to allow him to catch up, but Tilda hurried on without even sparing the animal a glance.

Without preamble Tilda said, "Tell me about your nightmare."

"My what?"

"Your dream. Last night, remember? You dreamed I was performing Magic out in the yard and then you saw a ghostly vision, yes?"

"Yes," Glinda replied.

"I want you to tell me about it." Tilda was walking faster, urging Glinda to do the same. "Tell me everything."

"But I can hardly recall it," Glinda protested. Then, with a thud of her heart, she asked, "Mother, how can you possibly know what I dreamed?"

"Because, my darling, it wasn't a dream at all." Tilda stopped walking and unfurled her fingers to reveal a small, wrinkled piece of parchment. "Miss Gage slipped this to me when she shook my hand."

Glinda looked at the scrap and realized it was a note. The message, written in Miss Gage's elegant script, read simply *Bog*. As she looked at it, first the words, then the parchment itself melted away.

"What does 'Bog' mean?"

"I fear you'll find out soon enough," said Tilda. Again she grabbed Glinda's hand and resumed her rush. Clumsy Bear struggled to keep up. "Now, tell me exactly what you saw in the yard."

Glinda frowned, picturing the distressing vision of the night before, which was suddenly abundantly clear in her mind. "I awoke and heard you reciting something. I saw you in the looking glass, but you were outside, alone under the ruby maple. And suddenly *they* were there. Four shadowy figures made of darkness. They were standing in a circle. And then a fifth one appeared."

Tilda's grip tightened around Glinda's fingers. "There was a fifth?"

Glinda nodded.

"That is disquieting in large amounts," Tilda murmured, more to herself than to Glinda. "The risk of my discourse with the moon was greater than I had imagined. Elucida would have never sent the vision if she had known it could be . . . infiltrated." She shook her head, and a long russet wave loosed itself from her tidy bun. "I'm sorry, Glinda. Go on, please. You were describing a fifth Witch."

"Witch? I never said Witch." But as the scene unfolded in Glinda's memory, she gasped. "You're right! The smudges *did* become the Wickeds! And Aphidina was with them!"

"I saw her," said Tilda. "But right now, I am more interested in the fifth Witch. The one I did not see."

"It . . . *she* . . . was not part of the circle," Glinda explained. "She was hiding, peeking out from behind the maple, like a shadow. I caught only a glimpse, but I remember she was different."

"Different? How?"

"She had . . . eyes. The others didn't at first, but this one did, like two red-hot coals. I think she . . . *it* . . . saw you!"

Tilda paled. "Miss Gage is right, then. I have been discovered. Which means we have very little time."

"Time for what?"

"To prepare for Bog's arrival." Tilda doubled her pace. "What you saw—the vision—will likely be realized in time. I cannot say for certain when, though I sense it is still a ways off. But it is impending and it is dangerous. Deeply and exceedingly dangerous."

Glinda felt ill. "Why? There have always been Witches. What is so dreadful about them *now*?"

"For ages, the Witches have been singular forces of darkness, content to inflict their Wickedness separately upon the four corners of Oz. But last night, Elucida showed us that they are planning to join together. I believe that fifth figure you saw is more threatening than all of them, and she will unite the four Wickeds in a confluence of evil that even the mighty Foursworn may not be strong enough to withstand."

"The Four *Who*?"

They had turned the corner onto their quiet little lane. Tilda peered about anxiously before crossing the dusty road, sweeping through the gate, and dashing up the slate pathway that led to their front door.

"I will explain when we are safely indoors," said Tilda. "If Miss Gage's hunch is correct, we must hurry to—"

"Mother, I don't think you should trust Miss Gage," Glinda interrupted. "I don't think you should trust her at all! She was talking to a Gillikin girl in the toolshed. An enemy of Quadling!"

Tilda shook her head. "That is what you have been taught, because that is what the Witches would have us believe." She pushed open the door, peeked into the parlor, then hurried inside, pulling Glinda with her.

"Even so," Glinda said, "I think Miss Gage is up to something."

To Glinda's astonishment, Tilda smiled. "She *is* up to something, my dear heart. She's trying to save my life."

12

STRANGE INHERITANCE

Tilda slammed the front door and bolted it. Then she rushed to the kitchen and locked that door as well.

"Does this have something to do with you using Magic?" Glinda asked.

Tilda checked the lock on the window. "It has everything to do with it."

"Magic is against the law. Against every law!"

"Tell me, Glinda, would you rather have a mother who is lawful . . . or one who is Good?"

"Aren't they the same thing?"

"Not always. And certainly not in Oz, not now." Tilda's next words came quickly but clearly. "It is time for you to know who I am. And who I am, who I have always been, is an exceedingly powerful Sorceress."

Glinda struggled to make sense of it. "So . . . *not* a Seamstress?"

"In many ways, I am a Seamstress. I put things together. Restore what has been tattered, mend what has been torn. But I am first and foremost an accomplished practitioner of Magic. A Grand Adept, as it is called by the Foursworn, and I am avowed to protect the incarnation of Good."

Glinda shook her head. "I . . . I don't know what any of that means!"

"It means that I have studied and mastered all four of the Magical Pathways that we Ozians are born to travel, and because of this I have risen in the ranks of the Foursworn, an ancient society that began when the kings of the four countries swore loyalty to the first King Oz, the rightful ruler of this land, who was brutally vanquished by the Wicked Witches."

Glinda frowned in confusion. "That's not what we were taught in Histrionics for Girls—" She cut herself off as understanding dawned. "Oh. I see. What we learned was Aphidina's made-up version, wasn't it?"

Tilda nodded, her eyes taking on a faraway look. "When the Wickeds stole King Oz's throne, they did so with abominable force. And on that day, we, the Foursworn, pledged our devotion and named ourselves the guardians of the perennial lineage of Oz." She blinked away a tear as she strode briskly to the parlor, where a small wooden chest sat waiting on the hearth. Glinda had not noticed it that morning, but now it seemed to take up the entire room. She watched as her mother carried it to the kitchen, then selected the plumpest rosebud from the pewter vase and placed it upon the trunk's lid.

"What's in there?" asked Glinda.

"A gift I have long planned to present to you, when you were ready to receive it."

Tilda disappeared into her bedroom and returned with an iridescent cloth—the gauzy cape she had worn last night in the yard. This she draped over the dining table before placing the chest on top of it. "Open it," she instructed.

Glinda frowned. "No."

"No?" Tilda blinked. "Glinda, this is no time to be petulant."

"I'm not petulant, I'm angry. You should have told me! You should have trusted me!" She swallowed a sob. "*I* trusted *you*! And you lied. About everything."

"I don't deny that," said Tilda. "And I'm sorry. But I kept it from you for your own safety. Revolution isn't the sort of secret one confides in a six-year-old. Or even a ten-year-old. It was much safer to let you just believe what Aphidina wanted you to believe. Until now." She nodded to the chest. "Bog is coming. I have bent the roads that will lead him here and slowed his journey by thickening the air and pushing the wind against him. But he will transcend my efforts soon enough, so we must hurry."

Glinda looked down at the Seamstress scroll still clutched in her hand. Then she looked at the battered chest and gasped as the rosebud that lay upon its lid burst into a luxuriant red bloom right before her eyes.

With a heavy sigh, she tossed the Seamstress scroll into the fireplace.

"Go to your room, please, and bring me Haley Poppet."

Glinda found this an odd request but did as she was told. A moment later she was back, and she placed the rag doll on the table. Tilda put the open rose back in the pewter vase among the rosebuds, then nodded to Glinda, who opened the chest.

Reverently, Tilda reached into the chest and removed three objects, which she arranged beside the doll: a slender book, a map, and a deck of cards.

Then she went to the windows and drew the calico curtains tight across them. "Some answers can only be found in the shadows," she said. "Thus is the case with your future. Your true and powerful *Magical* future!"

As the words pressed themselves into Glinda's heart, she understood that her life would never be the same. "What do you want me to do?" she asked.

"Look closely," Tilda instructed. "Don't just *look* . . . *see*."

Glinda studied the collection of items, all of which seemed perfectly ordinary.

"Do you see them, Glinda? Do you see them *eternally*?"

"I . . . I think so."

"Good." Tilda handed her the book. The cover bore but a single word: MAGIC.

Running her fingertip along the deckle edges of the handwritten pages, Glinda opened it and instantly recognized that the penmanship was her mother's. When Tilda had written it, Glinda could not imagine, but she sensed that the contents of this slight volume had taken more lifetimes than her mother's to create.

Opening to a page toward the back, Glinda read aloud:

"Lurl Ly Lee, Listen and Be . . .
Lurl Ly Lo, Question and Know . . .
Lee Lily Lurl, Time Shall Unfurl . . .
Lee Lolly Lawl, Truth Above All."

"I don't understand," she said. "It seems to be equal parts wisdom and nonsense."

Tilda shrugged. "A thing is not nonsense simply because you cannot understand it. Magic speaks in its own cadence, its own rhythm. That's what makes it Magic."

Fanning the pages, Glinda inhaled their papery scent. Enchantments and incantations seemed to waft into her head like an intoxicating fragrance—spells and directives, diagrams and encouragements. A language wholly new to Glinda and yet one she longed to understand.

The first section included a chart labeled simply *Pathways of Magic.*

WITCHCRAFT	*SORCERY*
MAKECRAFT	*WIZARDRY*

"These are the four Magical Paths," Tilda explained, "which the Witches' embargo forbids us to explore. It is a violation of our birthright, a denial of a most basic fairy need."

"Ursie called it a lie," Glinda noted.

"Ursie was right. The Foursworn's goal is for Oz to be governed by that which is its own intrinsic truth. Truth—"

"—Above All," Glinda finished, remembering Locasta's words in the toolshed.

Tilda nodded. "When the rightful ruler is restored, she will give us back this right, but for now you must remember that Magic is a part of you and that your proper pathway beckons you always. Do you understand?"

"I think so."

"We are all born predisposed to one of the Magical Pathways." Tilda smiled. "Some of us have the talent to master all four. The strength of a Sorceress's Magic is guided by her intellect; she deals in enchantment. Witchcraft is connected to emotion; it effects transformation through incantation. Wizardry relies upon illusion and ambition. And finally, the craft of the Makewright is both humble and noble, in that he or she creates ordinary objects from materials imbued with Magic, so that they may take on Magical qualities of their own."

"How does one know which sort of a Magician he or she is?" Glinda asked.

"The Magic knows," Tilda explained. "And your spirit reaches out for the Magic to which it is most suited."

Glinda hesitated, then asked, "Which am I?"

"That is not for me to tell you," said Tilda. "You and your Magic must determine that on your own, together."

"Magic sounds a great deal like friendship," Glinda observed.

"That is perhaps the best definition of it I have ever heard."

When Glinda closed the cover, the book disappeared.

Her eyes went next to the map, which depicted the four enemy countries of Oz surrounding the mysterious Center-lands. It was not etched on paper, like the maps Glinda had seen at school (all of Quadling, *only* of Quadling), for this one was fashioned of the finest fabric and thread, and was embroidered in painstaking detail—mountains, valleys, rivers, and roads. It was a marvel of both needlecraft and cartography, and she knew instinctively that this was her mother's handiwork.

Quadling was stitched entirely in shades of red, and in the appropriate locations Tilda had added tiny outlines of Aphidina's famed Perilous Pasture and the Woebegone

Wilderness. To the east, in brilliant blue, was Munchkin Country, which featured at its easternmost edge a crag identified as MOUNT MUNCH. The base of this tall hill abutted a vast, dull area called THE DEADLY SANDY DESERT. The name made Glinda shudder.

Winkie Country in the west was sewn in bright sunny yellows, except for a wide area of dull brownish gold labeled THE WINKIE WASTELAND. And finally, in the North was Gillikin, in bright purple thread. Pretty as the color was, there was an air of gloom about the place. The topography consisted mostly of mines and collieries.

"We never studied anything like this in Why Girls Never Need Trouble Themselves with Geography class," said Glinda. "It's a magnificent map." Her fingers traced the beautiful compass rose, stitched into the precise center. A tiny amethyst stone had been sewn into the heart of its star.

"Thank you," said Tilda. "But look again. Look deeper."

Glinda returned her gaze to the map and gasped when the rendering of Gillikin began to shimmer. The map seemed to be deepening, taking on dimension, as the flawless purple stitches loosened and pulled apart to reveal a maze of catacomb-like caverns—the mines. And below these was yet another stratum, a whole world hidden *under* the mines. A *layer* of Oz *beneath* Oz, winding and wending endlessly, it seemed, far deeper than even the fathomless mine shafts of Gillikin.

"Truly amazing," Glinda breathed. "What does it mean?"

"It means that nothing is ever *only* what its surface reveals," said Tilda. Then she pushed aside the map, and as she did so, it vanished in a pale sparkle of smoke.

Now she picked up the cards and shuffled the deck. Then she dealt them out in a perfect semicircle. Glinda was surprised to see that they were all face cards. The artwork, tinted in rich jewel tones, was masterful, detailed, and yet somehow whimsical.

"Look closely at these cards," Tilda instructed. "But don't just *look* . . . *see*. Secure them in the depths of your recollection, so that you may call upon their secrets whenever you have need of them. Do you see them, Glinda?"

Glinda nodded, for indeed, her memory seemed to be widening and deepening like a puddle during a heavy rain. More astonishing was the fact that, as Glinda gazed at the faces on the cards, she was certain the cards were *gazing back*.

"The Arc of Heroes," said Tilda, indicating the curved row of cards. "All those pictured here have served the Magical history of Oz. To them we owe our thanks and our allegiance. Study them carefully, take them into your heart."

Glinda's eyes went to the first card in the arc. THE KING UNITER. Confident and proud, he was drawn tricked out for battle in gleaming armor.

And then . . . he *wasn't*. His Silver Gauntlets, Shoes, Chainmail, and Masked Helmet were suddenly gone from the illustration, as if some unseen hand had simply blotted them away. Glinda felt a stab of panic to see the king left so vulnerable.

"King Oz," said Tilda, bowing her head reverently. "He is the strength of our past, and she is the hope of our future."

Glinda moved to the image on the second card, which was identified in flowing script to be A QUEEN ASCENDING. But depicted upon the card was not a grown-up, rather a very small child dressed in a simple green frock. She had burnished golden hair and eyes that twinkled like two large emeralds. Her lips were pink, like tourmaline gems, pouty now but promising to bestow smiles soon enough.

Suddenly the vibrant illustration began to fade, its colors paling, its outlines vanishing until it was just a pencil-gray ghost of itself. At the same time, from deep within the pulpy fibers of the card stock a new picture slowly began to *rise up*—a queen *ascending*! This new image passed through the original, borrowing a curve here, absorbing bits of color there, and what emerged was a drawing of the same girl, just slightly older, in a regal gown of snowy white. On a banner beneath her feet were written these words: THE RICHES OF CONTENTMENT.

"She is Princess Ozma," Tilda explained. "The manifestation of the Oz spirit in its female form, for balance in the land comes only when both male and female are trusted to guide and govern in turn."

Glinda couldn't help smiling at the princess on the card; she felt as though she'd just made a friend.

"Hurry," Tilda coaxed.

Glinda quickly memorized the next three cards in the arc, but when she came to the sixth, she had to pause. Its beauty took her breath away.

The card bore the name LIGHT OF NIGHT. Here was a Fairy all silvery and long-limbed, the legendary Princess Elucida, who ruled the moon. She had a playful face with high cheekbones and upward-tilted eyes the color of midnight, framed by sleek black hair cropped to her pert chin. Glinda gave a little yelp when Elucida's delicate wings began to flutter, producing a gentle breeze.

Glinda studied the seventh card: THE PRIESTESS MYSTE-RIOUS. The drawing was of a Fairy of advanced years who wore a stern expression but whose eyes hinted at a kind spirit and unfathomable depths of wisdom. In sketching her, the artist had manipulated dimension so skillfully that the Priestess Mysterious appeared to have been drawn not *upon* the surface of the card, but just *beneath* it. Glinda had to squint to appreciate the details of the sword the priestess held high above her head. Its hilt was adorned with glittering jewels.

The final card in the neatly dealt arc featured a bearded man in ragged attire—THE LONELY TRAVELER.

"I show these to you," said Tilda, "because in this life we must play the hand we are dealt." She indicated the bowed formation of the cards. "Remember, a hero's path is neither straight nor simple."

Then she gathered up the beautiful cards and tossed them into the air. They wafted downward, briefly taking on the shape and color of maple leaves as they fell; Glinda reached for them, but before she could catch one, they had vanished.

A sound in the distance—the thunder of hoofbeats—had Tilda leaping to her feet.

She removed the gemstone pendant from her own neck and draped it around Glinda's. The stone was brilliant and berrylike; Glinda knew it to be a red beryl, rare and precious. Her fingers clutched the stone as if by their own volition.

"You cannot begin to imagine what a treasure you have in your grasp," Tilda whispered. "See how prettily it's been cut, how the facets shine like *fire*? Do you see the gleam contained within its depths?"

"Yes," said Glinda, hastily reaching to remove the chain. "But it's far too valuable for me. I shouldn't be the one to wear it."

Tilda took hold of Glinda's wrists. "You are the one who *must* wear it," she said in a tone that brooked no argument, "until this treasure can be secured in its rightful place."

Glinda swallowed hard and let the pendant drop back into place around her neck.

Just then a horrible rushing noise filled the sky above the house, and a fluttering of darkness pressed itself against the windows. Through the slender gap in the drawn drapes, Glinda saw pairs of flashing eyes, thrashing talons, and ferociously snapping beaks.

"Birds?" cried Glinda, clutching her mother as the swarm flung itself at the window glass. "What are they doing?"

"Spying for the Witches," said Tilda. "The Wickeds enchant the more menacing breeds—vultures, hawks, ravens—and use them to learn secrets. Say nothing more, just listen." Tilda lowered her voice to a whisper as tears welled in her eyes. "This is the day a mother dreads more than any other. The day her child must step away from innocence and learn that the world contains dark corners and treacherous cliffs. But if you look for it, there is also friendship and loyalty to be found; true hearts and mingled minds, and those determined to see Goodness triumph."

"I don't know what you're talking about," Glinda sobbed, grabbing Haley Poppet from the table and using her cottony face to wipe the tears from her own cheeks.

Tilda went to the parlor window and threw the curtains open. Outside, the avian commotion was growing more furious. Hundreds of pointed bills were now pecking at the fragile windowpanes. It was a wild, Wicked rhythm. Not a beat, but a beating. Chinks and fissures, like a thousand colorless scars, began to appear in the glass.

"Mother, they're breaking the windows!"

Calmly, Tilda aimed her hand toward the shattering glass, made a graceful movement with her fingers, and said simply, "*De*struction, no; *in*struction, yes."

As soon as the words were spoken, Glinda thought she saw one of the fractures forming a word; a word written in her mother's elegant hand: *Fire.*

On a second glance, it was gone.

"Remember what you spoke of this morning," Tilda continued. "About thinking for yourself? You were right. The time has come for you to put your faith in your own ideas; allow them to burn as brightly as *fire.* For the only manner of *thought* that can truly *last* is *independent.*" She looked into Glinda's terrified face and repeated the last word slowly, drawing out each syllable for emphasis. "*In . . . de . . . pen . . . dent.*"

The birds fought harder, pecking, flapping, screeching. Glinda saw more words breaking across the shattering surface of the windowpanes: *Thought. Last. Independent.*

A crow cawed; the shrill call of a falcon pierced the air.

"Enough!" said Tilda, pressing her hands to her ears. In a brittle singsong she began to recite:

"From evil you've come, be deaf, be dumb!
To evil you'll go, but naught you'll know!"

Removing her hands from her ears, she pointed to the window. With a flick of her finger, the birds went silent and motionless—utterly still. "The spell will not last more than a minute," Tilda explained. "Wicked Magic of this caliber is difficult to thwart."

In the street, a horse whinnied.

Glinda dashed to the front window and looked out, pressing her palms to the shattered panes and peering through the veil of halted feathers.

Her heart froze. A wagon drawn by four colossal horses came barreling down the street and slammed to a stop in front of the house.

The sight of the driver tore a scream from her throat. His very existence was an impossibility, and yet there he was: a hulking beast of muck and mud, of gaseous marsh vapors and clots of slime. Growing out of his head was a reedy tangle of dead grass and long, lashing cat-o'-nine-tails. Dirty rivulets dribbled from him, splattering and oozing. It was clear that this brute had not been born or even built; he had been *dredged* from the foul sucking bottom of some stinking swamp.

"Bog?" choked Glinda.

"Aphidina's bounty hunter," Tilda confirmed. "He is going to take me away from here. And I am going to let him."

"No!" Glinda's chest began to heave. She pulled her hands from the window and felt her palms tingling where the broken glass had pressed against her tender skin. Outside, the muck monster was seeping down from the driver's box.

Glinda ran to her mother and threw her arms around her waist. "Can't you stop him? What's a little more Magic at this stage? Turn him into a wedge of cheese. Or make us fly!"

Tilda shook her head. "This may be my only chance to discover who this fifth Witch is and what she is planning. I need to get inside that castle."

"What good is learning the fifth Witch's designs, if you will be trapped in some awful dungeon . . . or worse?"

"I am deciding to go in," said Tilda, "and I have decided that I will come out. I would not allow myself to be captured if I was not certain that I could allow myself to be rescued."

Even in her frantic state Glinda could not help but think that her mother's attitude hovered somewhere between arrogance and recklessness. "How can you be so abundantly certain?"

Tilda smiled. "Because, my darling child . . . *you* are going to save me."

13

BOGGED

Glinda was positive she'd misunderstood. "*I'm* going to save you?"

"Yes. And to do that you must first go to Maud, the old Seamstress. You will find her in her cottage on the outskirts of Quadling. Do you remember the way?"

"I . . . I think so. I just follow the Road of Yellow Brick. Right?"

Tilda nodded. "Get to Maud and tell her I have been arrested by Aphidina. She will know what to do."

Nudging Glinda to arm's length, Tilda made sure the pendant was secure around her neck. Then she snatched Haley Poppet from the table and pressed the rag doll into Glinda's grasp. "Take good care of her," she whispered, though whether to Glinda or to the poppet, it was hard to discern.

Shouts rang out from the front walk. A horse snorted and stamped its giant hoof.

"Glinda," said Tilda in a level voice. "You must leave here. Now! Go out the back door and run as fast as you can."

But her words were lost in the thunderous noise of Bog's approach as the beast pounded up the front steps; one kick from his mud-formed legs shattered the door into jagged planks. As he stepped over the rubble and into the house, the last flame of the hearth fire sparked, flashing off the stone at Glinda's throat and blinding Bog with its brilliance.

The monster growled, blinking his popping eyes against the beam. With a mighty roar he tore the pendant from Glinda's neck and flung it across the room. The chain caught on the stem of the single blooming rose in the pewter vase and sent it clattering to the floor. Buds skittered across the wooden floorboards.

Bog reached with a seeping brown hand to grab Tilda by the front of her dress.

"Tilda Gavaria, you are charged with the treasonous offense of breaking the Magical Embargo."

Glinda let out a sob and fell to her knees amid the scattered rosebuds.

But Tilda did not deny the charge. Nor did she plead for mercy as the ferocious bounty hunter hauled her out of the house and dragged her down the path.

Glinda scrambled to her feet and ran after them, stumbling over the slate pavers as if she'd only just learned to walk.

By now, many of the vultures and ravens lay dead on the ground beneath the windows, victims of their own fury. Those that had survived awoke from their Magically inflicted stupor and lifted themselves away from the house to circle low overhead. Bog yanked a bulrush from his sludgy scalp and whipped it at the flock, dispersing them in a storm of shining wings and broken beaks.

The bounty hunter's wagon waited beyond the gate; it was a simple open tumbril cart with narrow benches and low wooden slats for sides. Inside, Glinda noted with horror, were the Field Waifs she'd encountered just that morning, though in Bog's wagon, they were far less boisterous. In fact, they were silent.

Two of Aphidina's soldiers flanked the wagon astride dust-colored horses. Though not as hideous as the wagon driver, they were terrifying just the same. One dismounted to tie Tilda's wrists.

When he was done, Bog hoisted her up and tossed her into the wagon with the other prisoners. Then, without warning, he jerked Glinda off her feet and threw her into the wagon as well.

Tilda's face went stark white. "You have no warrant for her!" she shouted. "She is innocent. Release her."

"She tried to blind me," the swamp monster replied in a splatter of muck. "That is Assault on an Agent of the Witch."

Glinda's heart knocked against her chest as she watched Bog glom himself back to the driver's box. She moved quickly to the side of the wagon, about to throw her leg over.

"I wouldn't if I were you," said one of the prisoners—not a Field Waif, rather, a charmingly compact boy with bright blue eyes.

"We're contained by an enchantment that can only be broken from without, to load the captives in," he explained, swinging his arm as though to reach beyond the slatted sides. Glinda gasped when his hand connected with an invisible force.

In the driver's seat, Bog cracked his whip over the backs of the team. "Yah!" he growled. "Yah, yah!"

The wagon lurched; beside it the riders spurred their horses. There was the sound of clacking wheels and the *clip-clop* of hooves as the wagon pulled away, picking up speed as it went.

Glinda turned frantic eyes to her mother, only to see that Tilda had curled down over her knees and was rocking back and forth in a steady rhythm.

"Mother?" Glinda rasped. "Mother, what are you doing?"

Tilda's only reply was to chant faintly into her bound hands: "*Lead us to wisdom, set us to right . . . Lead us to wisdom, set us to right . . .*"

As the wagon bounced and rumbled on, Glinda watched her mother, Tilda Gavaria, Grand Adept of the mysterious Foursworn, retreat into a world of her own.

Glinda crammed herself onto the wagon bench, between the pointy-faced girl and the bile-eyed boy, who both sat stiffly and motionless, staring straight ahead.

Keeping her eyes low, Glinda braced herself for their nasty taunts, but when not a single insult came, she cautiously lifted her gaze to the freckly boy, who was propped listlessly on the opposite bench.

Glinda had to swallow a scream. The boy was no longer a boy at all!

He was as chubby as before, but now his girth consisted not of plump flesh but haphazard clumps of crinkling hay filling out his dirty shirt. The hair poking from his scalp had gone from lank and greasy to dry and strawlike, and his face had flattened into burlap with a splattering of *painted-on* freckles around his dull, lifeless *hand-drawn* features.

Whirling to her left, Glinda saw that the same fate had befallen the pointy-faced girl! Mere hours ago she had been a living, breathing, poor-mannered child; now she was a pitiful patchwork things of rags and straw, slumped on the wagon bench. To Glinda's right the bile-eyed boy bobbed eerily in the wind, his gaze blank, his scribble of a mouth an angry line.

She turned to the boy who was sitting beside the freckled effigy on the opposite side of the wagon—the one who had warned her of the wagon's enchantment. He was holding an ax and looking at Glinda with raised eyebrows. Dressed in various shades of blue, he had twin-kling eyes and a charming smile. "Nick Chopper," he said, by way of introduction. "Of Munchkin Country."

"Glinda."

"Pleased to acquaint ourselves," said Nick. "Circumstances could be better, of course."

When the boy reached up to tip the blue conical hat he wore, Glinda noticed with alarm that his left hand was made of tin. On closer inspection, she discovered that his entire arm had been fashioned of tin as well, and so had both of his legs.

She eyed his ax. "Are you dangerous?"

"Only to trees," he said. "And myself. I came to Quadling to escape Ava Munch, the Wicked Witch of the East. Figured it was just a matter of time before I found myself at the mercy of her Terror Gaze."

"Her *what*?"

"Never mind. Better not to fill your head with such an image. Besides, Ava has other spells that are almost as bad." Nick flexed his metal arm so that it shone in the sunshine. "She put one on me and my ax. It's the reason I'm mostly tin. Every time I use my ax, I chop myself to bits."

"That's horrible!"

Nick shrugged, as though he'd become used to the idea of turning to metal. "At least I've been able to stay one step ahead of her Wickedness by replacing my missing limbs with tin ones. So as not to disappear completely."

To Glinda this seemed like small comfort indeed.

She slid a glance at her mother. Still chanting. Still rocking. She sighed and turned back to Nick.

"Why Quadling?" she asked. "Why not Winkie, or Gillikin?"

"There's a legend that says there's only one way to vanquish Ava Munch. It has something to do with the wind, although I can't imagine how a wind, even a stiff one, even a *gale*, could destroy a Witch as powerful as Munch. In any case, the folklore suggests that whatever it is, it's hidden somewhere in Quadling. I'm here because I'd be doing all of Munchkin Country a favor if I could find the thing to destroy our Royal Tyrant." He gave Glinda a sheepish look. "I suppose you think I'm a bit of a miscreant for wanting to destroy the Witch of the East."

A day ago, Glinda would have surely answered yes. But she wasn't sure anymore. "Wrong" suddenly seemed more difficult to pin down. And "right" was now completely up for grabs. Finally she shook her head. "She's done a horrible thing to you. She must be very Wicked indeed."

The cart sped onward until they had left the township far behind. The road wound along the edge of the Woebegone Wilderness. Although the dense, mysterious forest was not exactly forbidden, it was a place Glinda had intentionally avoided all her life.

Through the trees of the Woebegone, Glinda caught a glimpse of Aphidina's castle. It was by anyone's standards an architectural marvel, a cross between a magnificent edifice and an oversized root vegetable; part plant, part palace.

Spreading out around it was the Perilous Pasture, its soil the color of fresh scabs. Whatever the Witch had grown there had already been harvested, and judging by the size of the hole left in the ground, it had been a crop of something gigantic.

Nick was eyeing Tilda, who was rocking faster now. "Is she all right?"

"I honestly don't know," said Glinda, her voice catching in her throat. "I've never seen her like this before. I can't imagine what she's doing."

Nick considered his fellow prisoner as she continued to chant, her words coming more quickly, and louder as well. "If I didn't know better," he whispered, "I'd say she was summoning."

Without warning, the wagon wheels screeched to a violent halt, the horses snorting and whinnying as Bog jerked hard on the reins. Glinda and Nick were knocked from the narrow bench; Haley Poppet flew out of Glinda's pocket and went skidding across the splintery planks of the wagon floor.

Tilda stopped rocking abruptly.

"What's happening?" asked Glinda.

"Something in the road ahead," said Nick, pointing. "A girl!"

Glinda looked. Then she gasped.

Purple curls . . . knee breeches . . . wrist cuffs.

Locasta!

14

WITHIN AND WITHOUT

G it outta the road!" growled the seeping muck mass that was Bog. "Or I'll run ya over."

Locasta did not budge.

As the bounty hunter raised his whip to make good on his threat, a deep roar exploded from the woods and Clumsy Bear careened out of the forest, spooking the horses; they pranced and bucked, eyes wild, nostrils flaring.

"Control your mounts!" Bog commanded, but no amount of spurring or snapping of riding crops could calm the frightened horses. One reared up, throwing his rider into the trees. The other gave a panicked *neigh* and bolted, his soldier clutching the saddle for dear life.

Clumsy went straight for the driver's box, hurling his furry self as if he'd been shot from a cannon. Bog's muddiness was no match for the ballast of a full-grown bear. The attack sent him flying out of his seat like a rag doll.

Rag doll! Glinda tore her eyes from the commotion to search the wagon floor for Haley Poppet, only to find that Tilda was already tucking the doll into Glinda's pocket with her bound hands.

With Bog pinned under the weight of the tremendous bear, Locasta approached the wagon. Her blazing amethyst eyes went directly to Glinda. *"You?"*

"Yes, *me*!"

"Who *are* you?"

"She is Glinda," said Tilda. "My daughter."

Locasta frowned at Nick Chopper, who gave her a wink and tipped his pointed hat.

"Are you a Sorcerer?" she demanded. "A Wizard?"

"Woodcutter," said Nick. "Sorry."

Locasta rolled her eyes and turned an anxious expression to Tilda. "I need to get you to the Makewright's cabin . . . now!"

"There's powerful Magic trapping us in," said Nick. To prove it, he swung his fist, then jerked it back with a wince, rubbing the burn from his knuckles.

"Mistress Gavaria," cried Locasta, "can you uncharm the wagon?"

Hope surged in Glinda. "Of course she can! She's a

powerful Sorceress." She reached for the rope that tied her mother's hands, frantically pulling at the knot. It held tight.

"Let me try my ax," Nick offered, putting the lethal edge to the rope. Still the binds would not be severed.

"Glinda," said Tilda, her tone urgent. "Remember what Nick said. The Magic of this wagon can only be breached from without."

"If that's so, then we have no chance of escaping!" Glinda's trembling fingers again gouged hopelessly at the knot.

"Think," said Tilda. "Think of what you must do."

"Why can't you just *tell* me what to do?" Glinda shrieked.

"Because this must be *your* Magic. Now, just *reflect* upon how you discovered me in the yard last night and find the answer *within* yourself! Or perhaps, *without*."

Glinda covered her ears to muffle the splat of Bog's fists pummeling Clumsy. Closing her eyes, she saw herself awaking into the gleam of moonlight. Her mother was outside in the yard, and also in the room, somehow, but not really. Tilda's image had been reflected in the looking glass above the dresser. Within and without.

"The mirror!" Glinda turned to Locasta. "Miss Gage's mirror!"

Locasta reached into her pocket and withdrew the delicate compact.

"Open it," Glinda commanded. "Hurry! Now hold it so my mother can see herself."

Locasta obeyed, aiming the reflective surface at Tilda. Glinda could see her mother's image captured in the silvery circle. Just as she had imagined Tilda both inside and outside in the dream, it was now as if Tilda were at the same time inside and outside the Magical prison wagon.

Locasta saw it too. She quickly tilted the mirror downward so that Tilda's hands were reflected. Tilda pressed her palms together, her fingertips pointed at the invisible boundary that separated the three captives from freedom. Slowly she began to pull her hands apart. In the mirror, her reflection did the same.

"It's working!" Glinda cried, sensing a gap beginning to form in the invisible wall. "Mother, just a little wider, and we'll all fit through. . . ."

But the ropes would not allow Tilda's hands to open any farther.

"Mistress Gavaria, please!" Locasta implored. "You must squeeze through the space. You must escape."

There was another gurgling huff from Bog, and a growl from the bear. Clumsy was weakening, and Glinda could see that it was only a matter of seconds before Bog freed himself.

Tilda gave Glinda a mighty shove that sent her through the gap in the Magic; she landed on her hands and knees at Locasta's booted feet. Tilda did the same to Nick, who rolled to the edge of the road, clutching his ax.

"No!" screamed Locasta. "Not her! *You! * We need *you!*"

But Tilda had already lowered her hands, closing the broken place in the invisible perimeter.

Nick pointed to the bounty hunter. "Bog's freed himself," he warned. "Better get going!" Then, with a farewell wave of his ax, he ran across the road and disappeared into the woods on the far side.

From behind the boundary of Wicked Magic, Tilda looked from her daughter to the girl with the purple curls and whispered, "Unite." Then she began to sing:

"As fire seeks a place to burn,
In seeking strength, no stone unturn,
A perfect fit must be achieved
For this bright flame to be conceived.
Wisdom waits, where shadows fall.
A friend, like truth, can conquer all."

"You have to go!" Tilda instructed. "Both of you. Run! *Run!*"

"You heard your mother," Locasta cried. "Let's get out of here!"

But Glinda could not bring herself to move.

With a roar that rivaled the bear's, Locasta scooped Glinda up and tossed her over her shoulder like a sack of Quadling cotton. With one last, frustrated look at Tilda, Locasta took off into the cover of the Woebegone Wilderness.

On the opposite side of the road, Clumsy Bear stood

wobbling on his hind legs, his sweet face filled with sadness as he raised one paw and waved good-bye.

Bog slopped back to the driver's box and bellowed, "H'yah!"

The horses lurched forward. Glinda watched the wagon barrel along the road until the trees of the Woebegone swallowed up her view.

The bear, the bounty hunter, and her mother were gone.

15

THE WOEBEGONE

Glinda thought her ribs might splinter as she bounced and jostled on Locasta's shoulder. "Put me down!"

"Why?" Locasta panted. "So you can run back to the road and let that smelly mud bucket make you his lunch?"

"Put. Me. *Down!*"

"Shut up!" Locasta commanded, and ran faster.

"But I don't want to come with you to the Makewright's cabin!"

Locasta stopped running and dumped Glinda onto her backside in a pile of rotting leaves. "And I don't want you to come with me!" she shouted, standing above Glinda with her hands planted on her hips. "Not that you'd care, but I came a very long way to seek your mother's assistance. Then she goes and summons *me* and that stumbly fur ball to rescue *you*!"

"It is a bit ironic," Glinda allowed.

"No," Locasta shot back with a scowl, "what's ironic is that instead of a Grand Adept, I'm stuck with a little schoolgirl dressed up in ruffles"—her scathing gaze fell on Haley, peeking out above the hem of Glinda's pocket—"who still plays with *dolls*!"

Her glare lingered on the poppet until the scowl gave way to a grin, then a chuckle. The next thing Glinda knew, the purple-haired girl was doubled over, clutching her sides in an effort to catch her breath.

"There's no need to laugh at me!" Glinda snapped.

"Oh yes there is!"

"And I don't *play* with her. I simply"—Glinda searched for the accurate word—"*cherish* her."

Locasta laughed harder.

Just then a sudden gust of wind encircled Locasta, lifting the long, plum-colored curls off her shoulders and scattering leaves.

"Where did that come from?" asked Glinda.

"Who knows?" Locasta was still almost breathless with laughter. "Maybe we've stumbled into a fairy lair and that's what happens when the Wards of Lurl decide to tickle the lesser spirits of the air. Or maybe it's just a windy day!"

"Oh," said Glinda, aching to ask what a Ward of Lurl was but fearing the question would just earn her more ridicule.

"Let's go," said Locasta. "The Makewright's cabin is just through those trees on the other side of the Whoa! Be Gone Wilderness."

It was Glinda's turn to chuckle. "It's not 'Whoa! Be Gone,' it's 'Woebegone,' as in sad and miserable."

"Yeah, well, you say it your way, and I'll hear it mine," Locasta retorted. "Maybe you need to start listening to the world a little more carefully, Glindy."

"Glinda."

"The point is, I know a warning when I hear one. 'Whoa! Be gone' means 'Stop and turn back.'"

Glinda stood up and brushed the dirt from her backside. "Which is exactly what I'm going to do. There's no reason for me to join you at the Makewright's cabin. I need to get to Maud's cottage, like my mother said."

"Who's Maud?"

"She's a Seamstress."

Locasta cocked an eyebrow. "Are you having some kind of hemline emergency?"

"You wouldn't understand," said Glinda. She looked around in an effort to get her bearings. "Do you happen to know the way back to the road?" she asked tightly.

"I don't," said Locasta. "And even if I did, I wouldn't tell you."

Glinda's eyes narrowed, and she stared at the girl in disbelief.

"Oh, don't look at me like that! I'm trying to help you. You just escaped the bounty hunter, remember? You're a fugitive now. If you set foot on that road, you'll be scooped up by the Witch's soldiers in no time."

Glinda hadn't thought of that. "Then how am I going to get to Maud's?"

Locasta folded her arms across her chest. "Sounds like you've got a problem."

Ignoring the Gillikin's superior look, Glinda glanced from one unremarkable tree trunk to another as she tried to remember the direction from which they'd come.

"What are you doing?"

"Getting my bearings. So I can find my way out."

Locasta snorted. "What part of the word 'fugitive' do you not understand?"

"I have to get to Maud's!"

"Suit yourself," said Locasta. "I certainly have no need of your company!"

"And I have no need of yours!"

"Good luck with your Seamstress."

Glinda began marching north.

Or perhaps it was east.

She turned and took three long strides west.

Or perhaps south.

This was not good. Around her the Woebegone Wilderness

spread out in all directions. Indeed, it did seem to be shouting from every crust of lichen and dying fern, "*Whoa! Be gone!*"

If only she could.

Defeated, she dropped her gaze to the forest floor. Her only hope was to go with Locasta to the Makewright's cabin.

"All right," she said, her eyes trained on the mossy ground. "I shall go with you to the Maker's lodge."

When no reply came from Locasta, Glinda choked down her pride and tried again. "I will try not to be a bother if you'll . . ." She sighed, digging the toe of her boot into the dirt. "If you'll please just let me come along with you."

Again, silence.

Glinda felt her fists clenching. *She's going to make me beg!*

With an apology poised upon her lips, she snapped her head up to look Locasta in the face.

But Locasta was nowhere to be seen.

Glinda's chest seized with panic. She was lost and alone in the Woebegone Wilderness!

With no other thought in her head beyond escape, she took off, barreling through the brushwood, dodging pricker vines and hurdling swampy puddles. She had no idea where she was heading.

She ran until her boot caught on a stone and she crashed forward, landing so hard it took her breath away. There she lay, facedown in the dead leaves, wishing for a trail to follow. And as she did, she recalled what her mother had said:

Magic is a part of you . . . your proper pathway beckons you always.

Glinda stood up slowly, allowing the words to calm her, and took a step. As she did, up from the mossy floor of the wilderness sprang a road.

A Road of Red Cobble.

16

INTERROGATION BY SLUG

The candlelit room was like a thicket of prickly weeds and briars that tore at Tilda's clothes. Stalks wrapped around her ankles and held her fast; one slick vine snaked into her hair. Her wrists remained bound by Bog's enchanted ropes.

She had been dragged through the castle by the bounty hunter and flung before the Haunting Harvester. Bog stood beside the Grand Adept now, drooling muck and dripping mud in puddles on the floor.

Upon her throne, Aphidina cocked her head and raised her fine brows, studying the prisoner intently. "Well done, Bog," she said.

Tilda felt him swell a bit; his pride had a foul stench, but she did not allow herself to gag or even wrinkle her nose.

This was as close as any Foursworn had been to a Wicked since the day the Witches had seized power from the king. She knew it. The Witch knew it. Even Bog, whose brain was swamp gas, knew it.

Aphidina rose from her throne, clad in a gown of apple-red silk. In Quadling Country, only Aphidina and her favorites were permitted to wear such sumptuous fabrics. Rumor had it that when her silkworms had exhausted themselves, she ate them, dried, for breakfast.

Her gown was embroidered in a floral pattern that bloomed before Tilda's eyes, the flowers stitching themselves from bud to blossom in an ever-changing design.

Aphidina circled the hostage slowly, squinting her green eyes, unbothered by the fact that the train of her exquisite gown was trailing through the muddy puddles of Bog's sweat. She completed her tiny orbit and stood scowling into Tilda's face.

The Grand Adept could smell the dank, mulchy odor of the Witch's breath. She forced herself not to recoil. On Aphidina's left cheek was a small black mole—a beauty mark—which was in stark contrast to the porcelain whiteness of her skin. When the mark began to slither, Tilda realized it wasn't a mole at all but a plump, wet slug, inching its way toward the Witch's mouth and leaving a silvery trail of slime along her cheekbone as it went.

"Do you know why you are here?"

"Of course," said Tilda. "I am here because you fear me."

The Witch hissed and posed a second question: "Do you know that I can turn you into a stinkweed or a root vegetable with a flick of my wrist?"

Tilda might have dared her to go ahead and try, but at that moment the slug slid between the Witch's lips and disappeared into her mouth. Aphidina's head gave an eerie bob, her chin dropping to her chest.

Behind Tilda, Bog flinched. And with good reason.

For when Aphidina's head twitched upright again, Tilda saw that the Harvester's bright green irises had disappeared and had been replaced by miniature swirls of dark smoke. In her mouth, her tongue had turned to flame. Now the strange eyes trained themselves on the spot just below Tilda's collarbone.

"*Where is the Fairy Ember?*" demanded a voice that wasn't Aphidina's.

Tilda felt her lips quirk up in a smile. Now they were getting somewhere.

"Where he and the others have always been," she replied. "Safe from your quartet of Wicked underlings. I should think you would be grateful for that."

"*Why would I ever feel gratitude to you, Foursworn?*"

"Because while the Fire Fairy is hidden, this Haunting Harvester through whom you speak is safe from him."

When Aphidina's body flinched, Tilda knew her remark had struck a chord.

"Yes, I know that yours is the voice of a power far more malevolent than that of the Witch of the South. You are the fifth Witch, the one who found your way into the Magic of my midnight vision." Here Tilda smiled. "How unsure of yourself you must be to feel the need to skulk as you do, keeping to the shadows and allowing others to take your chances for you. Or perhaps you are simply a coward."

"*I am neither unsure nor afraid,*" the voice assured her. "*And if you had even an inkling of the havoc I intend to wreak upon Oz, you would understand why I choose to protect myself. I must, for I am the only being potent enough to execute that which must be done.*"

"And what exactly is that which must be done?" Tilda inquired.

Searing heat rolled off the Witch's body in waves. "*You are too curious by half,*" said the voice. "*And I am too shrewd by twice that. You will not get the answers you seek!*"

Aphidina's form lurched toward Tilda, her head bobbing downward so the fiery eyes could examine her empty throat.

"*Where is the stone?*"

"What stone?"

"*I saw it! Did you think I would not guess its significance?*"

"Congratulations to you on your powers of deduction," said Tilda. "And to think, it only took you a few measly centuries to figure it out."

With a roar and a puppetlike jerk of her arm, the Witch shoved Tilda to the floor. This put the shell of the Harvester nose-to-nose with Bog.

"*She wore a pendant of red stone,*" she said in a shrill voice. "*Did you take it from her? Do you dare to steal from me?*"

The muck thing trembled. "No, Highness. I did not touch it!"

"*Then where is it? She had it last night beneath the moon.*"

"There was a child," Bog stammered, his words spattering brown droplets that ran down Aphidina's blank face. "A girl! She wore it. It near blinded me!"

"*And where is she?*"

"I arrested her, but she escaped."

"*Failure!*" The flaming pupils flared as the Witch's body shook in a spasm of fury. "*To sand, mud!*" she proclaimed. Instantly the moistness that was Bog went dry, caking into a stinking pillar of silt. It held his monstrous shape briefly, then burst in an explosion of smell.

Again Aphidina's body convulsed as she bent to face Tilda, still sprawled on the ground. More corms and roots and wild vines slithered up from the dirt floor to secure the Grand Adept.

"*I will have that pendant, and the Fairy who resides in the depths of it*," the voice promised. "*I will yank it from your daughter's neck if I must, and along with it, her head.*"

Tilda felt a shiver in her soul but managed to give the voice a cool smile. "That is doubtful," she said. "For she is among allies. Mighty ones."

This earned her a slap to the mouth from the Witch's flapping hand. "*Is that what you think, Foursworn? That I and my Wicked Ones will not be able to hunt down a little girl and whatever pathetic Good Magician she will run to in your absence?*"

Tilda rose to her knees and squared her shoulders. "That is exactly what I think," she lied.

This time Aphidina's hand delivered a fisted punch, straight to Tilda's belly.

Tilda swallowed her howl of pain and glared at the Harvester, hoping to determine the identity of the evil being the slug had delivered to speak from inside her.

But as she peered into Aphidina's eyes, the smoke that had obscured the irises billowed and shrank away.

The Witch blinked; her piercing green eyes had been restored. When she opened her mouth, Tilda saw that the tongue of flame had vanished.

Struggling to regain her wits, the Witch Aphidina touched her blistered lips and looked down at the muddy hem of her gown. The embroidery of her dress had ceased to bloom and, worse, the blossoms that had opened seemed to have died on the vine, fading and withering until they were nothing more than a haphazard pattern of colorless knots.

Tamping down her panic, Tilda gave the Witch a condescending snicker. "If *I* had embroidered such flowers," she assured her, "they would never have shriveled."

Aphidina hitched up her gown and stamped her foot, and Tilda found herself plunged into the hollow interior of what seemed to be an enormous cocklebur pod.

And she wasn't alone.

17

THE MINGLING

A road of cobblestones, as red as a summer sunset and as solid as steel, had pressed itself up from below the ground at the toes of Glinda's boots, unfolding into a lane that extended only a yard or two ahead.

It didn't offer much in terms of distance, but was an option she hadn't had just a heartbeat before. And so it seemed only logical that she should choose it.

She placed the heel of her right boot onto the red pathway and took a step, then another. And another. With her fourth step, she would reach the end of the road.

But the moment she came to the last cobble, another several yards of cobblestones pushed their way up from the ground, stretching forward even as the ones upon which she'd just stood seeped silently back into the dirt, disappearing behind her without a trace.

Glinda tiptoed to the end of this second section of cobbles and sure enough, a third segment rose up from the forest floor. It was clear that as she went along, each new segment would extend just a bit farther than the one before it, as if with every yard she traveled, the road was coming to trust her—and she it—more and more.

Glinda quickened her steps and the road kept up with her. Nothing could stop it! It wound around broad stumps and under bent saplings; it even made a bridge of itself to carry her across a narrow creek.

As her boots tramped out a steady rhythm, the cobblestones erupted onward until they delivered her into a clearing, bordering a small lake. Her heart leaped at what she saw on the far side: the old Makewright's lodge, abandoned and forlorn.

She had to look twice to be sure, for the ramshackle structure was nearly hidden under the lush greenery of climbing wisty-mysteria vines; its roof sagged precariously under a heavy growth of ivy.

And then she spied something else.

In the clearing that separated her from the lake and the Makewright's cabin, the air had begun to dance. Shadows of light darted to and fro, first transparent, then nearly dimensional, then gone again in the flutter of an eye. The flickers were fusing to themselves, and what was mostly mist melded to become solid at last.

What materialized before her was a gathering of fairyfolk. Not just Quadlings, but Gillikins, Winkies, and Munchkins as well. A more bizarre and unexpected congregation Glinda had never witnessed. She counted a dozen in all, and from the looks of things, they were preparing for combat. Most brandished swords; others wielded crude slingshots or clubs, while a few carried bayonets or pistols with carved ivory handles.

And beneath them was the Road of Red Cobblestones, sprawling wider to accommodate their numbers.

Her first panicked thought was that an all-Ozian war had broken out, but she soon understood that the mood of this assembly was not a hostile one. If anything, there was a great sense of alliance.

One of the Winkies—dressed head to toe in a shade of yellow that put one in mind of dill-o-daffles—noticed Glinda gawping at the edge of their circle. Raising his hand, he called for his comrades to stop thrusting, parrying, and clanging their weapons.

When the metallic clamor had ceased, the Winkie turned to Glinda and asked, "Are you new?"

Glinda cocked her head and frowned. "In what sense of the word?"

A Gillikin smiled and twirled his purple mustache. "What he means is, do you intend to become a member of our corps? Have you come to train for battle?"

"I don't think so," Glinda answered. "And if I may, sir . . . what battle?"

The participants exchanged serious looks.

"The battle against the Wicked Witches, of course," said a Munchkin (this Glinda deduced from his cobalt-colored breeches and matching vest). "There has long been war on the horizon. On all of our horizons."

"There is only one horizon," Glinda pointed out.

A Quadling grinned and twirled his sword. "Precisely."

"We Revos intend to be ready when it happens," said a Winkie woman.

"What is a Revo?" Glinda inquired.

"A Revolutionary. And we are a Revo Mingling. Although we hail from so-called enemy countries, we are all of a mingled mind-set. Which is to say that we are aligned in our ambitions to topple the Wicked regime. For ages, we've operated in secret under the auspices of a secret society called the Four—" The Winkie paused and cocked her head. "Perhaps I shouldn't be telling you this."

"It's all right, Samiratur," a Munchkin said. "If she can see us, that means she possesses the true heart of a rebel. If the road itself has deemed her worthy, then so it must be."

Glinda could not deny that she'd been brought to this spot by a path of red cobblestones that rose and fell like ocean waves. But how could a road—and a hidden one at that—measure one's worthiness?

"If the Road of Red Cobble has led her here," observed a Munchkin lad, every bit as charming as Nick Chopper had been, and with the same bright eyes, "it is for good reason."

"And what is more Good than reason?" the Quadling propounded. "Or more reasonable than Good?"

The Winkie, Samiratur, considered these opinions. She looked quite fetching in her loose yellow trousers and blousy shirt, with a pleated cape hanging from her shoulders to just below her waist. "My friends are correct," she said at last. "We need not keep our secrets from you." She turned and nodded to the mustachioed Gillikin. "Go on then, Fwibbins, tell her what we do."

"From time to time, we gather along the Road of Red Cobble to teach and learn the ways of warcraft," Fwibbins explained. His hands were scarred and rough with calluses. His wrists were bound in the same ugly, rusted shackles Locasta wore.

"Have you ever tried your hand at swordplay?" asked the Quadling. "Or even held a blade?" He was holding a narrow, gleaming blade in his hands, and he seemed well versed in how to use it. Glinda had seen an illustration of such a sword in Leef's *Particulars of Pointy Combat* reference book; she seemed to recall that the accurate name for this weapon was "spadroon."

When Glinda shook her head, a Munchkin girl stepped forward and smiled; Glinda saw that her teeth were not

uniform in size, and every third tooth was adorned with a twinkling blue stone. The girl and her Munchkin compatriots were much smaller than the others, squat and roundish. But there was nothing diminutive about their energy. Glinda sensed a collective spark in these spunky souls that belied their tiny stature.

The girl's sword was called a saber, and it was curved in a way that made Glinda think of fine calligraphy.

"You may use my blade," the Munchkin girl offered.

Glinda recoiled. Seeing a sword in a book was one thing. Up close was quite another. "I believe, given the choice, that I would prefer to wield my wits rather than a weapon," she said.

A purr of agreement rippled through the Mingling.

"It would be a far better Lurlia indeed," said the Quadling with the spadroon, "if only we could attack with blades of thought. Not to injure, but to enlighten."

"Yes," said Glinda, picturing such a marvelous weapon: a sword of smarts, a blade of brilliance forged of vision without vengeance. The image came to her so clearly it was as if this sword of light were hovering before her eyes. Instinctively she reached for it, then realized it was just the sun's rays filtering through the trees.

"Perhaps it is not the armament, but she who is armed that matters most," said Samiratur.

Again the Munchkin girl held out her sword.

Glinda hesitated, took the saber, and examined it—the

weight, the curvature, the way its handle fit so comfortably in her grip. She eyed the edge of the blade. It was so sharp it almost wasn't there. But her admiring of the saber was interrupted by a sudden pounding in the distance, like the thudding of enormous feet.

"Aphidina's hybrids," Samiratur cried, her face paling. Or perhaps not so much paling as disappearing, fading from view. "Seems she's had a bumper crop, from the sound of it." As the footsteps drew nearer she turned her face, which was becoming less substantial with every passing second, to Glinda. "You must take cover."

With that, the Mingling dwindled to a flickering of light. The last thing Glinda saw was the tip of the Munchkin girl's saber, glinting into nothingness.

Then, from behind her, a hand clapped firmly down upon her shoulder.

Glinda opened her mouth to shriek, but a second hand clamped over it, trapping the scream inside.

Whirling around, she found herself blinking into a pair of crackling purple eyes.

"Not a word," Locasta warned, her voice a chilling whisper. Ducking down behind a large stone, she pulled Glinda with her.

Through the trees Glinda spotted the source of the pounding: a tremendous creature in a thousand shades of green approaching the clearing, creeping like ivy on a trellis, making its way through the forest. As it moved, its gigantic feet instantly took root in the moist soil, forcing the beast to rip them out of the ground with every step. New shoots spun out from its neck and knees and belly like lariats, lashing and whipping.

"What is it?" Glinda's voice was a hushed croak.

"A Lurcher," Locasta answered grimly, "grown by Aphidina in the Perilous Pasture. She plants ordinary seedlings, then fertilizes them with the ground-up bones of her most ferocious Quadling soldiers. That's what causes them to grow so mean, or so I've heard."

Glinda's mouth went dry. "She uses the bones of dead soldiers?"

Locasta slid her a look. "I never said 'dead.'"

The Lurcher was stomping nearer. Glinda could hear the swish and slither of new growths slicing through the air. She could feel the vast green shadow falling over her.

And that was when she saw the snow.

18

BENJAMIN CLAY OF
NEW YORK COLONY

Snow.

In late spring? A moment ago it had been clear and warm. "What's happening?" Glinda asked. "Why is it snowing?"

"I don't know," said Locasta, raising an arm to block the whipping of icy flakes against her face. "This isn't my Magic."

"*Your* Magic?"

Locasta did not reply; she was tracking the approach of the hideous vine creature, who moved with slow, steady power. The roar that ripped from deep within the gnarled body was the sound of growth—fast, ferocious, *unnatural* growth. Lurching with every step, it trudged onward even as the blustering winds pushed against its reedy chest.

The snow fell harder. Glinda's coppery hair lashed at her face, its frozen tips biting at the skin of her cheeks and forehead. Locasta's plum-colored curls were so coated with ice and snow that they looked completely white. Glinda could feel the snow deepening around her booted ankles; in the next heartbeat it had reached as high as her knees.

"It's a blizzard!" Locasta hollered above the charge of the wind. This was no exaggeration; the storm was blocking out everything but the Lurcher on the march. "They sent the blizzard to destroy the vine creature!"

"*Who* sent it?" Glinda shouted.

"The Wards of L—!"

A green shoot snapped down from the Lurcher's shoulder and wrapped around Locasta, binding her arms to her sides. Then, with a jerk, it snatched her off the ground and swung her into the sky like a kite. The plant monster was so unspeakably tall that Glinda could barely make out Locasta's tiny form, whirling above its head.

With frantic eyes, Glinda considered her surroundings— behind her were the dense trees of the Woebegone; ahead, the clearing and the lake.

As she struggled to come up with a plan, a violent shiver ran through her. It was clear that the temperature had plummeted in the short time since Locasta had been captured. In fact, it was so cold that she could see the shallow edges of the lake frosting over with a thin layer of ice.

A thought came to her, but she would have to act quickly.

Placing herself in front of the Lurcher, she waved her arms in the air to get its attention. When it stared down at her, she thought her heart might stop. But she did not run.

Reaching down, the Lurcher slapped at her with a giant twiggy finger, but she was ready for it and ducked, backing up toward the lake, one step, then two, until her boot heels touched the edge. When the beast made a second grab, Glinda turned and dove deep into the icy water. Her lungs seized in her chest, the cold bit at her like razor teeth, and the huge green fronds that grew up from the muddy floor swayed and swirled, whooshing around her face, wrapping themselves in her hair. If she became entangled in the plants, she would drown.

If she didn't freeze first.

Kicking as hard as she could, she broke the surface, breathing in frosty gulps of snowy air, treading the frigid water.

The Lurcher spun out a wiry vine to capture her, but Glinda dove. When she splashed up again, she taunted, "What's the matter, b-b-beast? D-d-don't you know how to s-s-swim?"

The Lurcher grunted. Icicles now hung from its face like translucent fangs.

"What's to be s-s-scared of?" Glinda jeered through trembling blue lips. "It's n-n-not over your head!" Quaking

with the cold, she rolled onto her belly and began to swim toward the opposite shore with long, furious strokes; her wrinkling fingers sliced into the water, which was thickening to ice.

Enraged by her insults, the Lurcher gave chase, stomping into the lake, where its giant feet sank instantly into the soft bottom and took root; the depth of the mud made it impossible for it to free itself.

Exactly as Glinda had hoped.

But what she hadn't planned on was the swiftness with which the lake would freeze.

The undercurrent caused by the beast's struggle tugged at Glinda, pulling her down. Blue-blackness surrounded her; a slow descent into the watery chill. Above, the clear surface was hardening to an opaque ceiling of ice. The moment she felt her toes squish into the muck of the lake bottom, something wrapped around her ankle in a slick, leafy embrace. Another frond encircled her waist.

And lifted her!

The water plants were carrying her back up, pushing her higher and higher until she broke through and her knees found the safety of the frozen surface.

She saw the enormous Lurcher trapped from the waist down in the unyielding ice. Glinda could hear the sickening crunch as stems and stalks broke away, spinning on the wind into the pearly expanse of sky.

The shoot that held Locasta turned brittle and brown,

and she dropped to the ice with a thud. Slipping and sliding, Glinda scrambled across the ice to take hold of Locasta's tunic; teeth chattering, fingers burning with cold, she dragged her to the bank. Together, they squinted into the whirling whiteness and watched the falling snow bury the Lurcher.

Then, as quickly as it had blown up, the wind died down, calming to a mere breeze. The snow ceased to fall, but for one last glistening flake, which wafted down from the now-placid sky to land softly on the tip of Glinda's nose.

It was over.

Locasta grinned, shaking the icy coating from her hair. "You knew he'd get stuck," she said, impressed. "Good thinking."

"I'm not so sure about that," Glinda muttered, eyeing her dripping-wet school dress. In her pocket, Haley Poppet was soggy but safe.

"Well, you saved my life. So thank you."

"You saved mine," Glinda reminded her.

"Then we're even." Locasta grinned. "And at least now I can boast that I've seen the Wards of Lurl in action."

"I have no idea who you're talking about," said Glinda, rubbing the chill from her fingers, "but if their goal was to stop the Lurchers, they could have accomplished *that* with no more than a good frost."

Locasta shrugged. "When it comes to weather conditions, the Wards tend to favor excess. Floods, droughts, twisters."

"Who—or what—exactly are the Wards of Lurl?"

"Seriously?" Locasta stopped brushing the snow from her shoulders. "Do you even *live* here? You don't know anything about Oz at all."

"I know only what my mother taught me," Glinda admitted. "I can't begin to imagine what *your* mother taught *you*, but—"

"*My* mother taught me nothing!" Locasta hurled back. "Because *my* mother was taken away by the Wicked Warrior Witch, Marada of the North, when I was small and Thruff was a tiny little baby wrapped in a purple blanket. My father's gone too, in case you were wondering, but I don't know where. He was a miner who worked all day and all night in a deep, dark pit to feed me and my brother and our five older sisters. Oh, did I mention that Marada took them, too?"

Glinda dropped her eyes to her boots in the swiftly melting snow. "No," she said. "You didn't mention that."

"Well, she did!"

A gentle breeze fluttered up, blowing the last of the cold from the air and lifting the damp ringlets from Locasta's face. And then:

"I beg your pardon. . . ."

Both girls spun in the direction of the muffled voice and found that it had come from deep within a snowdrift—a snowdrift with two stocking feet sticking out of it!

"I require a bit of assistance," said the voice.

They dropped to the ground and dug until they had freed a boy from the snowy trap. He scrambled to his feet and stood before them, looking dazed. He, like the girls, must have been caught unawares by the storm.

"Thank you for digging me out."

"You're welcome," said Glinda.

The boy's gaze moved beyond them to the lake, where the top of the vine creature's head stuck out of a giant drift, gray-brown now and shriveled. While he studied the Lurcher, Glinda studied him. He looked to be about her age, and he wore a fine suit of clothes, similar to the sort the boys at Professor Mendacium's wore for formal class assemblies: breeches snug at the knees, and a satin waistcoat over a shirt with ruffled cuffs and collar. His calves were clad in white stockings, but his shoes, it seemed, had been lost in the squall. Glinda imagined his poor toes must be frostbitten.

She slid a quick glance at Locasta, who was also looking the boy over. His dark hair was tied at the nape of his neck with a leather cord, but a few stray locks had come loose from the binding. Overall Glinda sensed great intelligence and humor in the lad.

When he turned his attention from the frozen vine beast to Glinda, she thought she saw a jolt of recognition in his eyes. But that was impossible, since he was clearly not a Quadling. His eyes moved to the purple-haired Gillikin, where they lingered for a long moment.

"Where am I?" he asked.

"Quadling Country," Glinda replied, at the same time that Locasta said, "Oz."

"Oz," the boy repeated, turning slowly in a circle, his shoeless feet squishing in the slush as his eyes drank in the wondrousness of the Woebegone. Then, with a triumphant cheer, he began jumping up and down and laughing with unabashed glee.

"I knew I would find it," he cried out.

"I've heard about people jumping for joy," Locasta whispered to Glinda. "But I've never actually *seen* it happen. Certainly not in Gillikin Country."

"He is awfully happy to be here," Glinda observed.

"Hah!" said Locasta. "I'm sure when he hears about the Wicked Witches, he'll want to go right back to wherever he came from."

Locasta allowed him another moment of celebration, then cleared her throat loudly. "I am Locasta of Gillikin Country," she said. "And this Quadling *child* is Gondola Gap-Toothia."

"It's *Glinda*!" Glinda ground out. "*Gavaria*."

The boy offered a courtly bow to each young lady in turn. "It is an honor to make your acquaintance," he pronounced. "I am Benjamin Clay, lately of the New York colony. You may call me Ben."

Locasta raised an eyebrow. "Where is this New York you speak of?"

Ben laughed and shook his head. "It is in the newborn country of America, which is in a world called Earth."

"Oh," said Glinda, feeling foolish, because she'd never heard of any of those places. "Have you come here for a reason?"

"Not one that I'm aware of," Ben answered. "But it's exciting just the same."

"You can come with us to the Makewright's lodge," Locasta announced. "If the Wards have sent you, then you must be honorable. Or at least not dangerous."

As if in agreement with Locasta's assessment, a loud squawk came from high in a nearby tree.

"There you are!" said Ben. With a frenzied ruffling of feathers, a tremendous bird swooped down to land gracefully on Ben's outstretched arm. He gave the creature a pat on his regal white head. "I call him Liberty."

"And I wish you'd stop!" These words were spoken in an emphatic baritone—by the bird. "I'm sorry to tell you, Benjamin, but I have always resented that name."

Ben's eyes went round. "Liberty, did you just . . . *speak?*"

"I did," said the bird. "And believe me, it's been a long time coming!"

The next thing Glinda knew, the boy from New York, with an expression of genuine shock upon his face, had collapsed in the snow.

Liberty let out a sassy chirrup, which Glinda strongly suspected was laughter, and Locasta dropped to the ground for a second time to dig Benjamin Clay out of the snow-drift.

As Locasta dug, Glinda gazed across the clearing where the Makewright's cabin stood, ramshackle and forlorn.

Suddenly it was the only place in the world she wanted to be.

19

THE ELEMENTALS
AND THE WICKEDS

Aphidina could not get the taste of the slug out of her mouth.

Nor could she purge the sting of Mombi from her guts. How dastardly and impolite of that Krumbic demon to inhabit a Witch's body without an invitation.

But it had always been this way. Mombi cared nothing for the comfort of the Four whom she herself had Wickedly nurtured to Magical maturity.

After her distasteful encounter with the Good Sorceress Gavaria, the Harvester, in an effort to soothe her anxious mind and aching innards, had gone out to walk the palace grounds and admire all the things that grew from the soil she herself had enchanted. Ordinarily, the sight of such tainted beauty cheered her.

But not today. Today was ugly and exhausting and overgrown with weedy thoughts that seemed to grow denser and more poisonous the more she tried not to think them. For example, the fact that she owed not only her power but her Magic to Mombi. That was a debt she would be forced to pay for all eternity. Although, if the Elemental Fairy of Fire had his way, Aphidina's "eternity" might be brought to a close far sooner than she ever expected.

As she strolled the front garden, the Witch took some dark joy in the sight of the Field Waif scarecrows that had been brought back in the wagon. Eventually, they would be delivered to the Perilous Pasture and mounted on sticks, but for now they lay in a lifeless pile beside Bog's reflecting pool. The boy in blue—whose eyes she had hoped to sow in her flower garden—had escaped the bounty hunter, which angered her immensely. But that was a fit she could pitch at another time. Today she had the missing Fire Fairy and the Grand Adept's missing brat to fret over.

As the scents of chrysanthemum and honeysuckle washed over her, Aphidina's mind trailed backward like pollen on the wind to her earliest memories. She possessed no pleasant girlhood recollections or tender feelings of being small and sweet and vulnerable. She, and the three others like her, had been collected (and by "collected," what she actually meant was "stolen") by Mombi long before they had time to learn sweetness, or anything else.

Aphidina shivered with the sudden need to recall the part of her history she had not lived—to remember it just as it had been told to her, the part that had come long before she even existed but was entirely responsible for making her what she was.

And although it was a pathetic beginning to be sure, it was *her* beginning, and it gave her solace even as it caused her skin to crawl.

Because it all began with a disgusting thing called love. . . .

The world called Earth, where the Primal Fairies embarked upon their existence, had given way to a new kind of being. Humans, they humbly called themselves, and because the Fairies loved them and wanted them to be happy, they chose to bequeath that world to them and all of their descendants.

On the day before the first tomorrow, the Primal Fairies took their leave to bring forth a new home.

Lurline, Queen of the Primal ones, was named the Architect of Worlds, and was elected to oversee the flurry of creation. To do this, she borrowed from Earth four essential graces. One was Water. One was Air. One was Fire. And the last was a piece of the Earth itself. Lurline commanded these elements to transcend their inanimate natures and become the Elemental Fairies and proclaimed them Ember, the Fairy of Fire; Poole, the Fairy of Water;

Ria, the Fairy of the Air; and Terra, the Fairy of Lurl.

Glistening and filled with light and poetry, the Elemental Fairies set to work. Terra carved out valleys and burst into mountains. Poole trickled into streams and begot rivers, which swelled into oceans. Ria filled the sky with motion and called it wind.

But the birth of a world is large work, and sadly, as with any ambitious endeavor, there was unforeseen and unavoidable waste: the unfelt heat from the fires, the breezes that did not blow, the water that went stagnant, and the stone and sediment that were not reliable enough to form sturdy Lurlian ground all understood that they were unwanted and as such felt slighted and ashamed. Shame soon hardened to fury, then hatred. And because it is the nature of a thing to be the enemy of that which has forgotten it, the waste turned itself to Wickedness, and thus was born the one true threat to peace, the one great adversary of Good.

Because Lurlia was a gentle place, the Wickedness could not find a single Fairy willing to harbor it. And so the waste burrowed deep into the realm and waited, wrapped in its own misery, for another forgotten thing to come for it.

And another forgotten thing did; tens of thousands of sunsets and moonrises had colored the sky before the Shadow arrived, but when she did, she felt the anger of the waste and knew that she could use it to her advantage. She collected four beings—all of whom were young and frightened and forgotten as well—and she tempted them with promises of power, if only they would obey.

And because they had nothing to lose, they agreed.

From the depths of the waste where Wickedness grew thickest, the Shadow gathered up as much evil and enmity as she could hold in her hands, and with it she anointed the four frightened ones, making of them a great dark power, and in so doing making them the sworn and eternal enemies of the Elementals who had unknowingly supplied the source of their Magical prowess.

Aphidina was initiated by Fire, Marada by Lurl, Daspina by Water, and Ava Munch by Wind.

These were the ones the Shadow named Wicked, and there were only four.

Only, but enough.

20

THE MAKEWRIGHT'S CABIN

The door to the Makewright's lodge swung open even before Locasta reached for the handle; she motioned for Glinda to enter first. Ben left Liberty on a low-hanging branch; then he and Locasta followed Glinda inside.

The moment she set foot upon the wide, gleaming planks of the floor, Glinda was overcome with a sense of welcome.

Welcome, and Magic.

It was a humble place, this home to the old Maker's craft, where promise and possibility expressed themselves in gears and cogs, hinges and nails. Wood shavings lay curled on the floor like the letters of a proud man's signature. Glinda smelled candle wax, and hickory smoke.

A deeper breath detected scents of sawdust, tree sap, and warm clay.

"It's probably been empty for ages," Locasta explained. "Maybe longer. Since the Magical Embargo at least. It's a secret to all but the Foursworn and therefore very safe."

The old Makewright's furnishings were spare, but inviting. Against a far wall stood a bed with four unadorned posts; this was covered with a lightweight patchwork quilt, and although Glinda understood that it had not been slept in for quite some time, she thought perhaps the downy pillow bore a slight indentation at the center, as if someone had lain his head peacefully upon it just the night before.

Most impressive was the long trestle table that dominated the center of the space. Plain and unpolished, its battered surface held a truly mystifying array of tools and instruments, only a small number of which Glinda could identify.

She wandered across the room, where a nightstand held a pile of well-worn books. To her amazement, one of these was the selfsame book of Magic her mother had produced from the mysterious chest, the book that had disappeared from Glinda's hands.

"What exactly is a Makewright?" asked Ben.

"One who fashions and creates ordinary objects and imbues them with a Magical purpose," Locasta said. She lifted an eyebrow. "Don't you have Magic where you come from?"

Ben laughed. "Hardly. Although"—he shrugged—"sometimes I feel as if we used to have it. Sometimes I can feel it shouting from under the rocks and between the raindrops." He blushed. "That sounds mad, I suppose."

Locasta shook her head.

"Sometimes I'll hold an object in my hand," Ben went on. "A garden trowel or the plunger of a butter churn, and suddenly I'm overcome with the sense that the object is waiting for me to do something, to give it something it doesn't have but wants. Ability, perhaps. Or life."

"Sounds like you've got a bit of the Makewright in you," said Locasta.

A brass gadget on the table had caught Benjamin's eye. With great reverence he picked it up and began to examine it.

"What is it?" Locasta asked.

"A theodolite. And a fine one it is."

"What does it do?"

"It measures." Ben ran his hand over the device, which was essentially a spyglass fastened to a wheel. "Calculates vertical and horizontal angles. Quite useful for mapping. I'm an apprentice surveyor, you see." He bent a grin at Locasta. "Among other things."

"What sorts of other things?" asked Glinda, returning to the trestle table.

"I dabble in poetry. I'm not entirely hopeless at fencing, and I've been told I sit a horse better than most lads of my age." When his eyes fell upon a wedge-shaped chisel and mallet, he smiled. "Oh, and I'm a bit of a sculptor as well."

"Truly?" said Glinda. "You sculpt?"

"I've tried my hand at it a few times, with satisfactory results." He gave them a modest shrug. "If mapping is about recording what *is* there, then sculpting is about seeing what *isn't* there . . . yet. My tutor taught me about a famous artist called Michelangelo, who said, 'I saw the angel in the marble and carved until I set him free.' I suppose it's the idea of something beautiful hidden deep within something as abrasive as stone that intrigues me."

"Beauty buried within something abrasive," said Glinda, sliding a grin at the Gillikin girl. "Hear that, Locasta? Maybe there's hope for you after all."

She had to duck quickly to avoid the ball of yarn Locasta flung at her.

"The problem," said Ben with a wistful look, "is that my father doesn't see much value in things like art and poetry. He is a gentleman farmer."

Locasta gave him a curious look. "Does that mean he's polite to his vegetables?"

Ben smiled. "No, it means he is a man of great wealth and education who also happens to farm. And survey. Mostly he hobnobs with the important political figures of New York, Philadelphia, and Boston." Ben's smile vanished. "He is determined that when I come of age I will become a great statesman."

"I take it you're not the political sort?" Locasta said.

Ben shook his head. "Politics is not art. Governing is not poetry. I am as committed to the cause of liberty as anyone, but for myself I'd much prefer to create things of artistic beauty and leave the forming of a nation to others."

Glinda had an image of Ben standing beneath a scroll that read STATESMAN and understood the look of frustration on his face. Although the forming of a new nation did sound rather exciting to her.

They turned their attention back to the Maker's table, which also held crimpers and calipers, a brass drafting compass, and bolts of some heavy dull-colored fabric, twine, and straw; there were irons and pliers and shears.

"Oh, my," said Glinda. There were hollow bamboo rods of varying lengths, a scattering of square nails, and several coils of rope. A sharpened quill poked out of a squat bottle of red ink, and beside that was a journal with a leather cover.

Her attention was pulled from the journal by a soft whirring sound, like a cat purring. Locasta was fiddling with a mechanical object that consisted of an open iron drum perched upon a small pedestal with a crank attached. A nudge from Locasta's fingertip sent the tub part spinning.

"It's a zoetrope," came a familiar voice from the opposite side of the room.

Glinda jerked her head around to see Miss Gage. In all the ruckus, she'd completely forgotten that the teacher had arranged with Locasta to rendezvous here.

Gage was seated in a red upholstered chair. Angled

toward it, to encourage conversation (or perhaps conspiracy), was a wooden chair with finely turned legs, painted cherry red. Between these stood a kidney-shaped table stained a deep magenta. How Miss Gage had entered the cabin and placed herself in the chair without Glinda seeing, Glinda did not know, though she suspected it had something to do with Magic.

"It's been a day, hasn't it, dear Glinda?" said Gage. "I'd venture to say you've learned more in this one morning than you have in the whole six years of your education combined. Horticultural expressionism, indeed!"

Noting Glinda's damp clothing, Miss Gage made a wringing motion with her hands and said, "Dry."

Glinda was not at all surprised to feel the moisture vanish from her dress.

"Hello again," said Locasta, making her way to the teacher and handing her the silver filigree mirror. "Thanks for this. It was more helpful than I'd ever imagined."

Slipping the mirror into her skirt pocket, Miss Gage smiled at Ben. "I see the Wards of Lurl are up to their old tricks. And you are?"

"Benjamin Clay of the New York Colony, at your service."

Miss Gage inclined her head politely, then turned to Glinda and indicated the cherry-colored chair, inviting her to sit.

"The most horrible thing has happened," Glinda blurted. "My mother has been arrested for performing

Magic. She spoke to the Moon Fairy, and received a vision of the future."

"I'm sorry to hear that," said Gage. "But if Tilda Gavaria risked a Magical discourse with Elucida, I'm sure she had a very good reason."

"Who are you, exactly?" Glinda asked. "You are much more than just a professor of lullabies."

"I am a Sorceress, and a member of the brave and noble Foursworn."

"Are you a Grand Adept?" asked Glinda.

"Not yet. At present my abilities are a mere shadow of your mother's."

This reminded Glinda of Locasta's comment about the snowstorm not being a result of "her" Magic, and she turned to the Gillikin with wide eyes. "Are you a Sorceress, too?"

Locasta shook her head. "I practice Good Witchcraft. Or at least, I will, with a little more training."

"What do the Foursworn do?" asked Ben.

"Our goal is to restore Oz to its own deepest truth," said Gage, "by overthrowing the Witches and returning the rightful Oz ruler to the throne."

Ben nodded as if he had some experience with this sort of thinking. "And who exactly is this rightful ruler?" His gaze moved curiously to Glinda, who gasped.

"It isn't *me*!" she assured him, then turned to Gage with a gulp. "It *isn't* me, is it?"

Miss Gage shook her head. "The next rightful ruler is Princess Ozma, the Queen Ascending, and she will be the very embodiment of Truth Above All. Just like King Oz was before her." Gage's eyes twinkled. "And as she was before him."

Glinda remembered her mother's cards, the images of the armorless king and the girl dressed in green, then white. "I don't understand," she confessed. "How can she be before and after King Oz?"

"It's all quite complicated in its simplicity," Gage allowed. "The Oz spirit is never-ending and ever repeating. I'm sure your mother intended to explain it to you."

"She started to," said Glinda, wiping a tear from the corner of her eye. "Then Bog arrived."

"I only know bits and pieces of it myself," Locasta admitted. "My father had begun to explain it to me, and then—" She frowned away the thought. "Maybe it's time Glindorf and I both heard the rest."

"It's *Glinda*!" Glinda protested.

"I know," said Locasta, grinning.

Miss Gage drew a deep breath before she spoke. "It's slow work, enlightening the hearts and minds of those who have been so oppressed by fear and illusion. The bringing about of war is nothing if not an exercise in patience and preparation, but we are determined. Our revolution *will* happen." Her eyes darted to Glinda. "In fact, it might even be happening now."

Glinda felt a cold shudder race up her spine. Her mother, it seemed, had chosen her words carefully when she'd talked about "protecting" the Oz lineage, for she had mentioned nothing about *overthrowing* the Witches in a *war*! But it was clear now that restoring the Oz spirit to the throne would require a great battle indeed.

"War," she said, testing the weight of the word on her tongue. "It's such a brutal thought. It's hard to believe my mother would involve herself in such an undertaking."

"The Good do not *seek* war," Gage explained. "War comes looking for them in the form of Wickedness, poking and daring, baiting and bullying until Good can no longer allow it to go on. In the eyes of the Good, war is an unavoidable response to the reprehensible and intolerable. But it is never a lightly offered invitation."

Glinda thought back to Clumsy Bear, surrounded by those heartless Field Waifs. He'd howled in pain and protest but had endured their attack without lifting a paw. It was Glinda who had seen the injustice, the Wickedness of the moment. And it was Glinda who had brought it to an end.

War.

"Only a small number of us remember the world when King Oz was our liege," said Miss Gage with a wistful sigh. "Life for all was as it was meant to be when Oz ruled."

Ben gave her an odd look. "Miss Gage, if *you* can recall the time of King Oz . . . well, I beg your pardon, but how old *are* you?"

Miss Gage smiled. "Older than I appear."

"I guess time in Oz works differently than it does at home," Ben noted.

"It must," Gage allowed, tapping her chin in thought. "I know little of where you hail from, except that Earth forgot its Magic long ago. Here in the Lurlian realm, age and time and Magic dance around one another in such a way that years can tease themselves into becoming days, or, in some cases, shrink to mere minutes. Seasons buckle and spin, afternoons yawn and stretch themselves into ages, or curl into moments. Time is variable, like a tall man with hunched shoulders, or a tiny girl standing on tiptoe. It ambles, it sprints, it leans near or away, sometimes with great purpose, other times for no reason except that it can."

"Speaking of time," said Locasta, "since we don't want the Grand Adept to spend a single moment more than she has to in Aphidina's dungeon, maybe we should discuss how we're going to get her out."

"I'm going to save her," said Glinda, surprised at how confident she sounded.

Locasta blinked. "You?"

"Me and Maud," Glinda amended.

"Who's Maud?" asked Ben.

"She's an old friend, a Seamstress who dwells at the edge of Quadling. My mother said Maud would tell me how to rescue her from Aphidina's castle."

"*You?*" Locasta repeated with a huff. "Why *you?*"

Glinda planted her hands on her hips. "Well, I *am* her daughter."

"I know that. But this doesn't exactly sound like a job for a girl in ruffles. Or an old Seamstress."

"Are you saying I'll fail?"

"I don't know," Locasta snapped. "Let's ask your dolly if she thinks you're up to the challenge."

"How dare you—"

"Girls!" cried Miss Gage, in her best teacher voice.

Glinda and Locasta frowned and fell silent.

"Now," said Gage, her forehead creased in thought, "Locasta is right about this presenting a challenge. There is only one being in all of Oz who has the power to defeat Aphidina."

"Let me guess," said Ben. "It isn't Maud the Seamstress?"

Gage shook her head.

"Then who?" asked Glinda and Locasta in unison.

"His name," Miss Gage replied in a solemn voice, "is Ember. He is the Elemental Fairy of Fire."

"I've never heard of an Elemental Fairy before," said Glinda.

"Not many Ozians have. The Witches have been very careful to keep their existence from the masses." Rising from her chair, Miss Gage went to the table and gave the zoetrope a little spin. "It hasn't been difficult to do, since

Ember and the other three Elemental Fairies have been in hiding for ages."

"Hiding?" said Glinda. "Why?"

"Because the reverse is also true: the Wicked Witches are the only beings who can destroy the Elementals."

This news was met with a long, grim silence.

"So Ember is Aphidina's nemesis," Glinda said at last. "And she's his."

Gage nodded. "For lack of a better term, yes. The Foursworn leaders, Grand Adepts all, intended to loose the Elemental Fairies when the time to revolt against the Wickeds was at hand. But until that time, they've chosen to keep the Elementals safely concealed."

"Seems like a waste of perfectly good power to me," Locasta observed. "If I were in charge, I'd have let the Elementals clobber the Witches a long time ago, whether the fairyfolk were ready for it or not!"

"Then it's a good thing *you're* not in charge," Glinda muttered.

"Perhaps there's more to the Elementals hiding than just avoiding the danger of the Witches," Ben suggested.

"Perhaps," said Gage, "though only the Grand Adepts know for sure. In any case, the capture of Glinda's mother has certainly hastened the course of action."

"Gotta start somewhere, right?" Locasta's eyes were bright and eager. "So why don't you just tell us the location of Ember's hiding place and we'll take it from there?"

"I would," said Gage with a heavy sigh, "but that, too, is a secret known only to the exalted Foursworn leadership."

Glinda felt a rush of despair, and again, silence settled over the cabin. Then something occurred to her, and her eyes flew open wide. "Maud knows where the Fairy is!" she exclaimed. "She must! Why else would my mother tell me to find her?"

"Now *that* makes sense," said Locasta. "Maud must be a Foursworn Grand Adept, just like Tilda. If she knows where Ember is hiding, she can lead Glinda to him, and Glinda can unleash him on the Witch! Problem solved."

"Except," said Glinda, "as you yourself reminded me back in the Woebegone, I am a fugitive. I'll never make it to the outskirts of Quadling without being seen by the Witch's bird spies or her plant minions."

"Actually, I don't believe traveling to Maud's will be an issue," said Gage, and to Glinda's surprise, the teacher-Sorceress smiled. "That's what the Road of Red Cobble is for."

21

THE COUNTING SONG

W hat's the Road of Red Cobble?" asked Ben.

"A secret and Magical road as true to Oz as the Foursworn itself," said Gage. "It moves those who travel it at precisely the speed they need to go, and because it is invisible to Wicked Magic, as long as you walk upon it, neither the Witches nor their underlings can see or touch you. And since they don't know of its existence, they won't even know to look for you there. Only those connected to our cause will be able to detect your presence."

"I wish I could build a road like that," said Ben. "Where is it?"

"Everywhere and nowhere," Gage said simply. "It's an

ever-changing safe passage upon which only the just and worthy may tread."

"It found me in the forest," Glinda said. "It brought me to a Mingling of Revos."

"And it brought me to the clearing to find you," said Locasta.

"See? Then it has already proven itself to you." Gage sighed. "Although it does have its quirks."

"What kind of quirks?" asked Glinda.

"That is hard to say," Gage admitted with a grin. "The road reserves the right to behave as it sees fit, depending on the behavior of whoever happens to be traveling upon it at the time. I've been told it always has good reason for doing—or not doing—whatever it decides."

"Sounds like an excuse for teaching lessons," Locasta grumbled.

"It does," said Ben with a shrug. "But isn't that what journeys are for?"

"What happens when I leave the red cobblestones?" Glinda asked.

"If danger is nearby, it may find you," said Gage.

"Well then," said Locasta, "we'll just have to be very sure we keep to the road at all times."

"We?" Glinda whirled to gape at the Gillikin girl. "*We* must keep to the red road? Who, may I ask, is *we*?"

"You and me," said Locasta, as if daring Glinda to argue. "I'm going with you."

"No," said Glinda with an emphatic shake of her head. "You're not."

"Yes," said Locasta with an equally emphatic nod. "I am. A lot is riding on this, and not just for you. For Oz! So it's settled. I'm going with you."

"It is the opposite of settled!" cried Glinda, trying to imagine how utterly *explosive* it would be to travel all the way to the outskirts of Quadling with Locasta traipsing along the road beside her. "When my mother told me to seek out Maud's guidance, she never said anything about taking someone along with me!"

Locasta strode across the room and put herself toe-to-toe with Glinda. "But when she pushed you out of that wagon, she said, 'Unite.' Don't you remember?"

Glinda did remember, but she had hoped Locasta wouldn't. "You actually think she was talking about *you*?"

"I was the only one there!"

Glinda snuck a glance at Ben, who was standing beside the trestle table, busying himself with the Makewright's collection of treasures. He was examining the lengths of bamboo, weighing them in his hands, calmly, industriously. If she were going to take anyone on this journey, she would much rather it be this intelligent, well-mannered stranger from New York than the fiery ruffian from Gillikin.

"Glinda," Miss Gage prompted, "why don't you want Locasta to join you on this journey?"

"Because she thinks I'm a silly schoolgirl in ruffles, and

she only wants to come along to annoy me and make fun of me."

Locasta rolled her eyes and flung her arms in the air. "I don't want to come along so I can make fun of you, you dunderhead! I wanted to come along so I could *protect* you! But now you can just forget it. Go by yourself. See how far you get!"

With her purple eyes flashing, she stomped to the door and crashed out into the fading light, a strange mellifluous sound floating in her wake. It took Glinda a moment to realize that it was a sound of Locasta's own making.

Locasta was humming.

Although Glinda was fairly certain she didn't even know she was doing it. It was a soft, sweet melody, which was surprising, coming from Locasta.

What was even more surprising was that Glinda recognized the tune.

Locasta returned to the cabin just as Ben finished tinkering with the bamboo sticks. He'd lined up ten pieces of graduated length and employed a small knife to cut a piece of rope. This he used to bind them together.

"What is that?" Locasta asked.

"I'm not sure," said Ben. "It appears to be some manner of musical instrument, but I haven't a clue how I was able to construct it. It was as if something . . . or someone . . . guided me in assembling it."

"The Makewright's enchantment," said Miss Gage. "His energy still resides here—an overlay of being, you might say, a happy sort of existential remainder. I believe the Maker's Magic just assisted you in making that pan-flute."

"Is that what it is?" Ben held the instrument to his lips and hesitated, as though waiting for further instruction. Sure enough, a breeze came up to fan the pages of the Makewright's Journal; it opened to a leaf on which a collection of musical notes had been carefully dotted across a staff.

"Can you read music?" Glinda asked.

"Well, I couldn't before. But something tells me I'll be able to now."

"Go ahead," Locasta urged. "Play."

Ben took a deep breath and released it gently into the longest of the bamboo tubes. The little flute produced one clear note. With his sparkling eyes on the Maker's Journal, he began to move the pan-flute side to side against his lips. The result was a melody, simple and pure.

And familiar.

It was the song Locasta had been humming. Which also happened to be the song that had swirled into Glinda's memory that very morning.

"I know that tune! It's the song Maud sang—" The recollection was returning to her so vividly it was almost as if it were happening all over again. Glinda saw herself as a small child on her own back lawn. It was the day Maud had given her the gift of a handmade rag doll— Haley Poppet—and it was also the first time her mother ever suggested she try her hand at embroidery. Glinda had struggled at first, but Maud was patient and showed her how to correct her mistakes. She'd spent the afternoon practicing her needlework in the dappling of shade cast by the ruby maple tree while Tilda, Maud, and Maud's apprentice, Gremil, expertly stitched letters onto a piece of starched linen, the shadows of the leaves playing upon their work.

Glinda quickly described the memory to the others. "How do you know that song?" she asked Locasta.

To this, Locasta gave a curt shrug and murmured, "Just something my father taught me," with her eyes trained on the toes of her scuffed boots.

"Did Maud's song have words?" Miss Gage inquired.

Glinda nodded and began to sing along to Ben's flute music:

> *Once upon a Wicked deed*
> *Two times two invoked a creed*
> *Sworn to honor, these brave four*
> *A rightful ruler would restore*
> *Count by one, a quest begun*
> *Count by two, with hearts so true*
> *Count by three to set them free*

Count by four, at peace once more
Good will rise and Wicked fall
For Oz, forever: Truth above all.

As the final note swelled from the pan-flute, filling the lodge to its rafters, Glinda felt the warm tickle of coincidence around her heart. "I haven't thought of that little song in ages," she said, "and yet this is the second time today it's come to my mind."

"That has to mean something," said Ben.

"Two times two, sworn to honor." Glinda considered the lyrics. "Do you think that might refer to the Foursworn?"

"It must," Miss Gage agreed. "Perhaps Maud's counting song is actually a prophecy, or a prediction."

"Or a dire warning," Locasta added with a grimace.

"'Count by one, a quest begun,'" said Glinda. "Perhaps the 'one' refers to me, since I'm going off on a quest in search of Maud and the Fire Fairy."

"That seems like a reasonable analysis," Ben concurred.

Glinda repeated the next line slowly. "'Count by two, with hearts so true.'"

"Your 'one' became two when Locasta rescued you from Bog," Gage observed, her face bright with discovery. "And Tilda encouraged you to unite—that's certainly two by two in my opinion."

Glinda and Locasta exchanged looks. Neither was thrilled with the idea of being a duo. But there they were.

"It seems we're going to Maud's together," said Glinda, mustering a smile.

"Seems we are." Locasta returned the smile. More or less.

"Count by three," Ben said. "Do you think the Foursworn knew I was coming?"

"I believe they did," said Glinda. She turned to Miss Gage. "I suppose that makes you the fourth."

"Oh!" Gage laughed. "That seems unlikely, doesn't it? You three are so young and I'm . . ."

"Old enough to remember King Oz," Ben finished.

"Yes," said Gage. "Old enough for that. I suspect the fourth traveler will be someone more like the three of you. A Magician more recently come to his or her craft."

"So there is to be a fourth someone," Locasta mused, knitting her brow.

Through the window, Glinda glimpsed a flutter of gray. *Liberty, probably*, she told herself, *just stretching his wings*. Or perhaps a low-hanging cloud.

Gage nodded to the Makewright's table and said, "Benjamin, let's you and I see what might come in handy on this 'quest begun,' shall we?"

Ben beamed and reached for the theodolite.

As Glinda watched them sort through the Makewright's tools and gadgets, she felt Locasta's critical eyes upon her, taking in the fancy boots, red ruffled school dress, and matching pinafore.

This appraisal went on so long that Glinda squirmed and adjusted a ruffle. "What?" she demanded at last.

"Oh, I was just wondering," Locasta drawled, her mouth bending into a grin. "For this quest of ours . . . that's *not* what you're planning to wear, is it?"

Miss Gage lit a fire on the hearth (without the aid of a flint), while Ben helped Locasta measure off several yards of fabric from a bolt on the Maker's worktable. It was of a nubby texture, oat-colored and perfectly serviceable.

Glinda hated it.

"I don't see why I can't just wear my academy uniform," she grumbled, her fingertips stroking the soft sheen of her school dress.

"First of all," Locasta said, smoothing a length of material across the tabletop, "Madam Mentir is one of the Witch's minions, so as far as I'm concerned, that is the uniform of the enemy." She made a crease in the fabric, indicating where Ben should cut. "Second of all, it's ugly."

"It's not *that* ugly," Glinda protested. "Is it?"

"Hideous," Gage concurred, her eyes on the fire.

"The color's not bad," said Ben, using the Makewright's heavy shears to cut the desired yardage from the bolt. "But other than that . . ." He wrinkled his nose and shook his head. "Sorry."

Glinda sighed. "Well, at least let me help with the sewing. After all, I was very nearly declared a Seamstress.

Before Miss Gage's Possibility speech, that is."

Locasta's response was a wag of her eyebrows. "Sewing? Who said anything about sewing?"

"Oh." Glinda's cheeks went pink. "Right. I forgot. Magic."

When Ben finished cutting, he stepped aside and gestured to the fabric. "Have at it," he said to Locasta, his eyes gleaming with anticipation.

Locasta swung her purple curls behind her shoulders and took hold of the fabric's edge; then she began to twirl, dipping and lifting the material so it swelled like a cloud, spinning it above her head, then behind her back, then up again, snapping it toward the ceiling. It moved like a banner in a breeze, and Locasta ducked gracefully under it, or stepped over it, or let it wrap itself around her, only to unfurl it again, chanting to the rhythm of her dance:

> *"Apparel come, apparel be*
> *From fabric now apparel see*
> *Believe, believe . . . and there's a sleeve*
> *Be swift, make haste, to form the waist*
> *A sash, a cuff, a hem . . . enough!"*

Abruptly, Locasta stopped dancing. She was holding a perfectly formed oatmeal-colored tunic blouse with a loose red sash and neatly folded cuffs.

"Astounding," breathed Ben.

"Nicely done," said Gage.

Locasta lifted an eyebrow at Glinda, who was examining the flawless tunic. "Well?" she prompted. "What do *you* think?"

"*I* think," said Glinda allowing the tiniest of smiles, "that I'll be needing a pair of trousers, as well."

22

FIRST LIGHT.
THEN DARK.

They rose at first light.

The sky outside the windows shimmered with a pastel gleam, which Locasta, a miner by trade, likened to a handful of opals spilled on silk. Then she set to work on dancing Glinda a pair of pants.

Ben, with his hair mussed and his eyes still sleepy, padded softly to the trestle table. It was only then that Glinda realized he was still in his stocking feet.

Locasta noticed too. Tossing the newly conjured trousers unceremoniously at Glinda, she pulled a pair of boots from beneath the upholstered chair. "I found these last night. I suppose they were the Makewright's. Seems fitting, since you've got the gift of manufacture."

Ben looked pleased at her assessment. "Thank you," he said, slipping first one, then the other foot into the ancient boots. "I do fancy myself a bit of a tinkerer as well as an artist; an inventor of sorts. I often spend my afternoons in the smithy's shop, or visiting with the apothecary, learning whatever I can." He stood up, testing the boots. "It may not be the same as imagining new laws or drafting declarations of an independent nature, but I do think what I know can make just as much of a difference."

After they'd eaten a breakfast of warm bread, hearty porridge, and birch-bark tea, Ben collected the items he and Gage had chosen for their journey: the theodolite, some rope, a lantern, and the Makewright's leather-bound journal. These were loaded into a knapsack that they found hanging on a peg near the door. Glinda was positive it had not been there the night before.

Then Ben, in his borrowed boots, went outside to allow Glinda some privacy to change her clothes.

The tunic Locasta had fashioned hung on the post of the Maker's bed. The trousers, still tingling a bit with the Magic that had brought them, were in Glinda's hand.

"Must I?" she asked.

"Glinda Gavaria is no longer the schoolgirl she once was," said Gage with respect. "Today she sets out as a seeker of truth."

"And she's not going to do that in ruffles!" said Locasta,

tugging at the bow that secured Glinda's pinafore. "Time to retire this awful thing!"

Glinda removed Haley Poppet from the dress pocket and laid her gently on the Makewright's pillow. The doll's button eyes gazed back at her serenely, as though she knew she was being left behind but minded not at all. The golden thread that secured Haley's back caught a ray of sunlight through the window and sent a warm glow across the cabin.

Glinda shrugged off the pinafore and slipped the rumpled red school dress from her shoulders.

As Miss Gage quietly folded Glinda's clothes and placed them beside Haley on the pillow, Glinda reached for the tunic and pulled it over her head. Then she stepped into the trousers.

A perfect fit. Magic, it seemed, had a knack for sizing.

Ben appeared in the doorway, his boots tapping anxiously. Glinda couldn't tell if the excitement was entirely his own, or if it was a bit of enchantment lingering in the Makewright's shoes, urging him onward. "Ready?"

She allowed herself one last glance at the pinafore and the poppet before turning away from the bed. "Ready," she said.

Miss Gage placed her hand on Glinda's shoulder. "One thing before you go. I'm sure your mother would want you to know, to see with your own eyes, why our pledge to protect the royal lineage of Oz is so infinitely important. Ben, will you please bring the zoetrope to Glinda?"

Ben did as he was asked, and Glinda accepted the strange contraption as if it were a precious gift. Examining it, she saw that inside the drum was a band of parchment on which was drawn an array of austere black-ink illustrations. The barrel also had several narrow slits cut into it at regular intervals.

"Try the crank," said Ben.

Glinda gave the handle a tentative turn. The drum moved, but only a little.

"There's a better way," Locasta said with a knowing air. Plucking the Magic book from the nightstand, she held it in her upturned palms; from nowhere a breeze fluttered up and opened the book to a page labeled, *For the Purpose of Magically Animating Items of a Mechanical Nature. Part I: Zoetropes.*

"Well, that's specific," Ben observed, grinning.

"Locasta, you read the spell aloud," Gage directed. "As the zoetrope revolves, Glinda, you look through the cuts in the side."

Glinda placed the gadget on the curved table and hunched down so that the slits were at eye level.

Locasta read:

> *"Roundiling, spindiling, outside and indiling*
> *Story unfold-a-ling, story be told-a-ling*
> *History, mystery, tell all of this to me*

Whirl-a-ring, swirl-a-ring, past is unfurl-a-ring . . ."

Glinda jumped when the crank turned of its own accord and the barrel began to spin, picking up speed as Locasta repeated the spell at a jauntier tempo.

"Roundiling, spindiling, outside and indiling . . ."

The pen-and-ink renderings leaped to life, moving, changing . . . *being*. As the drum whirled, the pictures transformed from spare sketches to intricate, vibrantly hued miniatures featuring a man bedecked in silver armor. His proud bearing and regal manner were unmistakable. He was King Oz.

As Glinda marveled at the moving images, it became clear that they were telling her a story. A true and terrible story.

As it revealed itself to Glinda, her heart began to pound. . . .

THE ZOETROPE'S TALE

The king has invited the best and the brightest of his land to a celebration in the Reliquary, the most artful wing of his Emerald Castle, which sits at the highest point in the Centerlands of Oz. He has just unveiled seven newly commissioned masterpieces, all dear to his heart.

Glasses are raised, toasts are made, and compliments extended. The Goodness innate in the

Land of Oz brings joy to its inhabitants, and tonight they revel in it, pledge to sustain and increase it, vow to defend it for time beyond time. Goodness and truth, they all agree, are the only foundations on which to build a land (a toast to the Elementals here) and with which to nurture a civilization (a cheer to everyone else here).

Among those in attendance are an elderly Quadling Seamstress who reminisces with her dear friend, a Munchkin lady; she laughs a sweet, breathy laugh and carries a delicate scalloped fan of blue, which she flutters flirtatiously for the benefit of the dapper Winkie gentleman who wears a yellow cape and neatly creased pocket handkerchief. Also present are the four magnificent Elemental Fairies. One is brilliantly bright, another is sturdy and solid, the next is a marvel of fluidity, and the last a miracle of weightless, life-giving power.

A King from afar and his princely young Son are engrossed in conversation with the King's Mystic. Several knights and their ladies mingle about as well, all of whom are steadfastly loyal to King Oz. Most prominent among these is Sir Stanton of Another Place. His physical strength is rivaled only by the breadth and depth of his intellect. There is not an ounce of Fairy Magic in him (having been brought to Oz by the mystic Wards of Lurl by way of an avalanche), but he is respected by the king nonetheless. When a waltz strikes up, Stanton invites a young lady—the Seamstress's apprentice—to dance and soon discovers with great delight that she is, thought for thought, as wise and as confident as he.

A tumult begins outside the walls of the Reliquary; through the lavish stained-glass windows the guests spy the source of the commotion. Four she-beings have arrived, unexpected, uninvited . . . un-everything, really; nothing in them aligns with what it means to be of Oz. They have swooped down from the dark sky like a storm, or a pestilence.

They proclaim themselves Witches, and the Witches who are guests at the party take umbrage to this, as they would never willingly associate with such hoydens. In Oz—up until this very moment— Witchcraft has been a pure and gentle art form.

The four trespassers taunt the king, croaking insults and dares from the Reliquary terrace. The words of the unwelcome ones are so ugly that the partygoers hardly notice how stunning in appearance these Witches are. All anyone sees is their fury, for it is great; unmatched.

What it is, is Wicked.

King Oz calls upon his four Regents Valiant— Lord Quadle, Sir Wink, the Viscount Gilli, and the Archduke of Munch-Kindred—who put down their crystal glasses. These five brave leaders go outside to confront the intruders.

Perhaps—

Perhaps—

Perhaps—

The zoetrope squealed to a stop and the spell book slammed closed with a *bang*.

"This *can't* be good," Locasta muttered as the lively drawings ceased their dance. Surrendering all motion and color, they stilled once again to become static black jottings; jottings that now began to blur, seeping and spreading into shapeless inkblots—liquid bruises marring the pale parchment. The warmth of the lodge gave way to a deep chill, as if the Goodness of the Makewright's enchantment was cowering before a sinister presence.

"What's happening?" asked Ben.

Miss Gage's face was taut with concern. "I don't know."

Nerves prickling, Glinda kept her eyes on the blotches as they narrowed into thin rivulets, dripping into the bottom of the drum like heavy black tears.

In the bottom of the zoetrope, the inky puddle began to swirl, faster and faster, until it had lifted itself out of the drum and into the air; there it expanded into a billowing black cloud.

Glinda covered her face with her hands, but it was too late; the dark mist had filled her mouth with bitterness;

her tongue and throat burned. Locasta erupted into a fit of violent coughing, and Ben squeezed his eyes closed against the stinging, churning cloud.

"Quickly!" cried Gage, pushing through the dark haze to snatch the knapsack from the table. "Everyone out of the cabin. Now!"

Dizzy and gasping, Glinda followed the teacher, but as she stumbled toward the door, she could feel the memory of King Oz's celebration melting into the smoke, as though the cloud were trying to steal it away, erase it from her mind.

Locasta scuttled at their heels, with Ben close behind. The four burst out the cabin door and into the bracing dawn. Seeing their urgency, Liberty sprang off his branch and followed, for Miss Gage was running now, toward the farthest boundary of the Maker's land. There she stopped, pressing the knapsack into Ben's grasp as he, Glinda, and Locasta sucked in great gulps of the clean, fresh air.

None of them noticed the tiny green lily shoots pushing up through the rosy soil at their feet and bursting into bloom.

"You must get to Maud's cottage as fast as you can," said Gage as the Road of Red Cobble swelled up from the ground before them.

"Astonishing," said Ben. "It's almost as if it were expecting us!"

"You'll be safe on the road," Gage reminded them. "It

knows where you need to go, and you'll be protected as long as you tread upon it! Now hurry. You must get away from here!"

"What was that?" Glinda asked, ignoring the flowery trumpet blossoms now fully open beneath her feet; the sinister feel of the smoke still clung to her.

"I think the better question is 'Who was it?'" said Gage, her eyes darting back to the cabin. "And the answer is that I have no notion at all, which is why you must be off." She gestured anxiously to the road.

The three travelers leaped onto the cobblestones; Ben and Locasta lit out at once, but Glinda paused to cast a wary backward glance at the Maker's lodge. She could see the black ink cloud pressing itself feverishly against the windows, like a beast trying to escape. Her gaze lingered until a sudden breeze swirled in, loosing the new-grown lily petals from their stems and lifting them into a pink-and-white whirl, obscuring her view.

"Get to Maud's!" Gage repeated.

Glinda nodded as the petals whipped away in the wind. "Truth Above All!" she cried.

And then she ran.

23

MIST IN THE MORNING

The Road of Red Cobble rose and fell, winding away from the cabin, along the outer edge of the Woebegone. The stones of the road were as sturdy and promising as they'd been yesterday when they'd led Glinda to the Mingling in the clearing.

This, at least, was comforting.

As they meandered through the quiet countryside, she realized that Gage had been right about the road's ability to hasten (or slow) a journey; while she and her friends were moving at an utterly ordinary speed, the world around them was whipping by at a truly incredible velocity, as if the Road of Red Cobble had convinced time to warp itself into a more expedient passage from here to there.

Magic, as a mode of travel, certainly had its advantages.

"This must be what it feels like to fly," she noted, smiling up at Liberty, who circled lazily above their heads.

"It's a wonderful sort of freedom," the eagle said.

"You say 'freedom,'" Locasta sneered. "I say dark Magic. In Oz, flight is discouraged, except in the most extreme emergencies. Only the Wicked Witches use it."

"Not that she's calling *you* a Witch, Liberty," Glinda clarified as the bird sailed down to land upon Ben's shoulder.

"I should think not!" he chirped. "Although, as long as we are on the subject of calling me things, I'd like to propose an immediate alteration."

"You want to change your name?" Ben looked crushed. "Why? My father named you for the mood in the colonies, but for me, it's more reflective of that feeling of personal expression. In either case, Liberty is a fine name."

"Liberty is not a *name* at all," the bird countered. "It is a *concept*. A laudable one, yes, but it seems to be the *only* concept anyone in the New York colony ever wishes to discuss." He gave his tail feathers an indignant shake. "In the tavern, on the farms, in the square . . . 'Liberty, liberty, liberty!' That word is bandied about constantly."

"Oh, I see," said Glinda with a sympathetic grin. "Every time you hear it, you assume someone is calling your name."

The bird nodded his sleek white head. "I'm forever

turning this way and that to see who's addressing me. It's a wonder I haven't suffered a case of whiplash."

"Maybe you should change your name to that, then," Locasta teased. "Whiplash. Whip, for short."

"I have a better suggestion." Liberty puffed out his chest. "I'd like to go back to the name my mother gave to me when I was but a fuzzy little eaglet in the family nest."

"Fair enough," said Ben. "What was it your mother called you?"

In reply, Liberty let out a long, shrill screech that had them all covering their ears.

"*That's* what she called me," Liberty said in a kind of half chuckle, half tweet. "After all, *she* spoke Eagle!"

"Very funny," said Ben, rubbing his ears.

"I think it's safe to say that the name loses something in translation," Locasta pointed out.

"The closest interpretation in your tongue," said the bird, "would be Feathertop."

"Feathertop," said Glinda. "I like it. It suits you."

"Well, I'm a bird, so . . ."

"Very well," said Ben. "Feathertop it is."

Satisfied, the newly christened Feathertop sprang from Ben's shoulder and returned to the sky.

Glinda watched him go, the talking eagle from a world she had never even dreamed existed, the chatty companion of a human boy who could channel an enchantment and turn it into a flute! It was all so bizarre she actually

had to remind herself that just yesterday—*yesterday!*—
she'd been walking to school with Ursie Blauf, worrying
about arriving at Declaration with her hair unbraided.
How mind-boggling it was to know that this very morning, as she set out from the Makewright's lodge, her fellow
Conclusives would be starting their new lives as members
of the Quadling workforce. Glinda felt a tug at her heart,
imagining Ursie installed somewhere as a Governess.

From the bottom of her heart, Glinda sent up a wish for
Ursie's happiness. Then she laughed.

"What's got you tickled?" asked Ben.

"Oh, I was just wondering what my friend Ursie would
think if she knew that I was setting out on a quest with a
fiery-hearted Gillikin girl and a boy from another world."

"I'm sure she'd be utterly dumbfounded," said Locasta,
who was several steps ahead of them, moving at such a
vigorous clip that even the red road was having difficulty
keeping pace. "I know *I* am."

"Well, I for one cannot imagine anyone more suited to
the task," said Ben.

Glinda sighed. "That's because you haven't known me
very long."

"In point of fact," said Feathertop, returning to hover
above them, "he's known you much longer than you think."

Locasta stopped walking. She looked first at the bird,
then at Ben. "What are you talking about?"

"I've seen this place, this . . . *Oz* . . . before." Stuffing his hands into the pockets of his knee breeches, he met Glinda's eyes and shrugged. "I've seen *you*."

Glinda blinked at him, astonished.

"I think you're going to have to elaborate on that," said Feathertop.

"One day last autumn I went out with my father to help him mark off the boundaries of a particular tract of farmland. I was feeling awfully pleased with myself, as this was the first time my father had allowed me to use his theodolite. It meant he had great faith in my abilities and trusted that my measurements would be accurate enough to effect a fair and proper sale."

Glinda couldn't help but smile at the pride in his voice.

"As I was looking through the eyepiece," Ben went on, "thinking how beautiful the foliage was in all its autumn glory of ginger gold and crimson, suddenly there was . . . well, for want of a better word, a shimmer. The scene I was viewing wavered, as if the air were breaking. Can you picture such a thing?"

"I can," said Glinda, remembering the vision of the five shadowy figures two nights past. "Quite vividly."

"At first, I thought the lens of the theodolite had simply clouded over, but even after I polished it, it was like looking through the mist that rises from the lake on fall mornings. Through the blur of the lens, I saw a village. It was a town, but not my town, and even stranger was the fact that it seemed to be moving at a different speed, not faster or slower, just—*other,* and *elsewhere.* It seemed to be right there before me, and yet miles and miles in the distance. Days and weeks and months away, but *now,* as well. I saw people going about their business, and I called out to them, but they couldn't hear or see me. They were like ghosts, gliding straight through enormous boulders, passing through the trunks of trees. It was a moment before I realized that the trees and rocks were in the realm that is New York, and these strangers *were not.*"

"They were here," said Locasta. "In Lurlia."

"Yes," said Ben. "We were sharing the same patch of the cosmos, experiencing the same whisper of time, only from entirely different perspectives. I have since determined that our separate realities—Earth's and Lurlia's—have always been intersecting, but somehow, in that moment, the theodolite made it visible to me."

"Magic," said Glinda.

"Yes," said Ben, reaching out to take Glinda's hand in his. "And in that Magic I saw you, in your pinafore and red dress, on the lawn of a big white building with towering turrets."

"Madam Mentir's Academy," said Glinda. "My school."

"I told my father what I'd seen."

"Ooh!" Locasta winced and cocked an eyebrow. "How'd that go?"

"Not well, I regret to tell you. He was frightfully concerned; thought perhaps I'd caught a fever. He took me straight home and put me to bed with a tonic. It made me sleepy, and as I drifted off, I heard the sound of wings beating just outside my window. Right before my eyes closed, I caught a glimpse of a gigantic crane . . . the largest I'd ever seen, with brilliant red plumage and wise, gentle eyes."

"Pastor!" guessed Locasta. "He is one of the mystic Wards of Lurl. He must have enchanted your theodolite, and then he brought you here to Oz."

"At first I couldn't imagine why," said Ben. "But when I saw the contents of the Makewright's workshop, I knew my skills and interests could come in handy on this Magical quest, far more than they ever could at home, where my father will not rest until he's made of me a barrister or a statesman."

"Interesting," said Locasta. "I wonder if the Wards of Lurl will ever send you home."

"I certainly hope not," he said.

The sun was in the midpoint of the sky when Locasta turned to Glinda and said, "When we get to Maud's, I think you should let me do the talking."

Glinda's eyes flew open wide. "You? Why you?"

Locasta gave her a smug look that said, *Isn't it obvious?* To Glinda, it wasn't obvious at all.

"Just because you have a little more experience with Witches and Magic than I do, I hardly think you should be the one to deliver my mother's message to her oldest friend. The Grand Adept sent *me*. I'm the one who is supposed to save her."

Locasta let out a bark of laughter. "And I'm the one who saved *you*! So I should be the one to explain everything to Maud."

"Absolutely not!" Glinda shot back. "*My* mother, *my* friend, *my* quest, *my* responsibility! *I'll* do the talking."

Locasta opened her mouth to retort. But as she did, the red road halted, and the section of the path beneath their feet quickly sank away, vanishing back into the dirt.

Glinda felt a twinge of alarm. "I thought the road was going to take us to Maud's."

"Quirks," said Locasta. "Remember? It's probably trying to teach us a lesson. And if you ask me, it's telling us to 'let Locasta do the talking.'"

"And *I* told *you*," said Glinda through her teeth, "my mother trusted me to enlist Maud's assistance!"

"All right, let's not start that again," said Ben, maneuvering himself between the two girls and holding up his hands. "We have to get to Maud's house without the road." He gave Glinda an expectant look. "Which way to the cottage?"

"I'm not certain," she said. "It's been so long since we've come. And on those occasions we'd travel the Road of Yellow Brick."

But the red road had led them on an entirely different course, and now it had chosen to disappear at a very nondescript crossroads in the Quadling outskirts. No signposts, no landmarks. Only a lone, smiling scarecrow propped on a stick in a field of new corn. But of course, he wasn't talking.

"I remember," said Glinda, "that we would follow the yellow bricks as far as a narrow brook, which we crossed by way of a footbridge, and then we walked the rest of the way on dirt trails lined with red geraniums. But without the yellow road as a starting point, I'm really not sure which way to go. I don't see the brook, or the footbridge."

"Feathertop," said Ben, "fly as high as you dare, and tell us what you see."

The eagle obeyed, soaring skyward, looping around the area once, then swooping back. He called down with a whistle, which Glinda took to mean, *Follow me.*

"Still think flying is Wicked?" she said to Locasta, who replied with a snort.

As they traced the short path of the eagle's flight, Locasta glanced over her shoulder. "Careful," she warned. "Without the road underfoot, we aren't protected."

Moments later, they rounded a bend and were standing before Maud's cottage. The sight of the place did Glinda's heart good, familiar and pleasant behind its whitewashed fence laced with climbing rosieglories and razzleberry vines. Everything about it said, *Welcome.*

"Do you think she'll remember you?" Ben asked.

"You're extremely forgettable," Locasta pointed out.

"She'll remember me," said Glinda.

They hurried up the flagstone walkway to the cheerfully painted front door.

"Liber . . . I mean, Feathertop—" Ben gave the eagle's head a friendly pat. "Why don't you wait out here?"

As Feathertop perched comfortably on a fence post, Glinda knocked on the door.

From inside the house she heard a shuffle of footsteps, then the metallic clunk of the bolt sliding from its hold. The door swung open, and Glinda gasped.

She had expected to be greeted by her mother's cherished friend Maud, or perhaps Maud's longtime apprentice, Gremil. Instead she found herself staring into the smiling face of someone else.

"Glinda! What a lovely surprise! Hello."

"Hello," said Glinda with a gulp, ". . . Blingle."

24

THE TRAPESTRY

How deliciously chummy of you to visit me on my first day as the Seamstress's apprentice," Blingle crooned, inviting them in with a sweep of her arm.

Glinda hesitated on the stoop. "Apprentice?"

Hadn't Blingle declared herself a Nurse at yesterday's ceremony? A little knot of concern began to form in Glinda's belly. Squaring her shoulders, she entered the cottage.

"You're certainly keeping peculiar company," Blingle observed, casting a glance at Locasta and Ben. "As if that Ursie Blauf weren't bad enough."

Glinda bristled. "Where's Maud?" she asked.

"Oh, you know Maud," said Blingle. "I'm sure she's just

hanging around somewhere, tying up loose ends." Then she laughed, as though she'd just made a brilliant joke.

Blingle eyed Locasta's plum-colored curls. "A Gillikin! Well, you don't smell nearly as repulsive as I imagined an underground laborer would."

This had Locasta lunging for the apprentice, but Ben caught her before her hands found their way to Blingle's throat.

"Speaking of peculiar," Blingle went on, "that is surely an *interesting* ensemble you're wearing." She frowned, suddenly agitated, as her eyes raked Glinda up and down. "Where is it?"

"Where is what?" Glinda asked.

Blingle shook her head, and her expression softened. "Never mind. Please, make yourselves at home." She sounded like she owned the place.

Looking around Maud's house, Glinda noticed a cross-stitch sampler hung in an oval frame against the white brick of the fireplace. The sampler consisted of basic *X* stitches forming simple block letters spelling out an ancient piece of poetry:

> *A hero is he who, as in a myth, rallies on fields*
> *of battle.*
> *His spirit ever steadfast as words he wields*
> *and takes the lost one in hand, leaves with a*
> *heavy heart.*

So solemn is this affair, yet remember:
A righteous fight
can soon ignite
To yield the light
When those far too long
Independent
At last unite.

It was the sampler Maud and Tilda had made together on the day Maud had given Glinda the gift of Haley Poppet. Glinda recalled how the sun had dappled their work with shade patterns cast by the ruby maple. Her mother had encouraged her to stitch a word or two, but her first attempt at the *I* in *Independent* had come out snaggled, so Maud had shown her how to unravel it and try again.

Looking at the piece now, Glinda noted that Maud had since embellished it, enclosing the poem within a perfect circle of bold green stitches. Beneath the circle was a kind of zigzag flourish. It took only a second for her to recognize that the additional stitches formed a hidden word: *Oz.*

Turning back to Blingle, she asked, "Where's Gremil?"

"I sent him to the kitchen to fix my lunch," said Blingle, with great disinterest. "I must say, I do hope he's aware of the rules for frosting tea cakes."

Locasta's face registered disbelief. "Rules? For tea cakes?"

"Of course," said Blingle. "They must always be frosted right to left."

"Left to right," Glinda corrected.

"In Gillikin Country we don't *have* tea cakes," Locasta informed them. "But if we did, I'm sure nobody would much care which way the frosting went!"

Blingle dropped herself into Maud's rocking chair, plucked a soldier's coat from the basket beside her, then selected a needle from the pincushion. Its point gleamed as she dipped it into the heavy red velvet and jerked the thread through.

In all the times Glinda and Tilda had come to Maud's house, Glinda had never seen the old Seamstress attach so much as a single button to a military uniform. But today the basket beside Blingle's chair was practically overflowing with them—coats and jodhpurs, shirts and sashes.

It was terribly strange. And terribly, terribly wrong.

"Is that company I hear?" came a voice from the kitchen. A second later, Gremil entered the room carrying a tray of cakes and tea. He was a slender youth with a mop of rusty hair and big bright eyes of golden green. Gremil stopped in his tracks at the sight of Glinda.

"Nice to see you, Gremil," she said as carelessly as she could, taking the tray from Gremil's trembling hands. "It's been quite some time, hasn't it?"

"I'm so very happy you've come," said Gremil. But he did not sound happy at all.

Now Ben pointed to a wide, hand-stitched tapestry hanging on the parlor wall. "Did Maud make this?"

"No," said Gremil, lowering his eyes. "I did. It was commissioned, you might say, a while back. Over time, I've been *compelled* to add more details."

"Compelled?" Locasta repeated. "Like, forced?"

Blingle's rocker gave a loud creak. It sounded like a warning. "Please, do have a closer look at that *trapestry*," she said.

"I believe what you meant to say was *tap*estry," Ben noted.

Blingle pursed her lips and kept sewing. "I know what I said."

Ben and Glinda crossed the room to stand before the handsomely embroidered piece. "It's quite intricate," said Glinda, awed by the piece. "I've never seen such precise needlework."

In the rocker, Blingle yanked her final stitch into a knot and bit off the thread. "Yes," she purred. "You might even call it *captivating*."

"And such costly materials," Ben noted.

"Costly, indeed." Gremil's tone was grim. "You cannot even conceive of its worth."

Glinda leaned closer to admire the luster of the piece, which was awash in colorful yarns and jewel-toned threads. With one very significant exception.

In the corner of the tapestry was a lone figure embroidered in plain, bleached string. Glinda knew instantly that this was not Gremil's work; while the stitches were neat and clean, they were far too severe, lacking the grace and fluidity he would have learned from Maud's loving hand.

The pale image was of an old woman; Glinda thought she might be familiar, but the absence of color made her difficult to recognize.

Ben reached out to trace the woman's colorless threads.

"Don't touch that!" Blingle snapped.

Startled, Ben drew back his hand.

As her eyes wandered over the crewelwork, Glinda's unease deepened. At the far edge of the scene she spotted a dark-haired girl sewn with her back facing out, as if she were searching for something in the infinite distance. As Glinda stared, the figure slowly turned her head, revealing her profile.

She's moving, Glinda thought. *The embroidery is moving!*

The puzzled look on Ben's face told her he'd seen it too.

The girl did not look like any Quadling child Glinda had ever met; she was dressed in a hooded gray cloak and heavy brown boots that laced up above her knees.

To Glinda's shock, the girl lifted her hand as if to point at something outside the tapestry; the movement created a slight ripple in the fabric, and Glinda imagined she felt the ripple in her own flesh, which was now tingling with goose bumps.

Pulling her gaze from the girl, Glinda examined the rest of the tapestry, which featured a depiction of the main street that ran through town. She saw the smithy's barn, and the baker's kitchen; even the apothecary's shop, with a tiny stitched replica of a shingle hanging above the door: MASTER ABRAHAVEL J. SQUILLICOAT—APOTHECARY it read. Inside the shop was sewn an image of the kindly old druggist at his post behind the counter. Minuscule as it was, Glinda could see that the resemblance to the actual Master Squillicoat was uncanny.

He was holding an almost imperceptible piece of chalk (half a stitch in size, at most) and a slate that looked just like the one on which he'd written out countless recipes for his tinctures and potions.

The memory hit Glinda like lightning—just the day before, Squillicoat had been dragged away from his shop. The soldiers had promised him a pleasant walk to the outskirts. And now, here he was in a handmade tapestry on Maud's cottage wall.

With a racing heart, she reached out to touch her fingertip to the apothecary's distinctively hooked nose.

In the tapestry, Squillicoat blinked.

Then, just as the dark-eyed girl had done, the apothecary raised his hand and extended his tiny stitched index finger.

"What are they pointing at?" Ben whispered.

"I think," Glinda whispered back, "they're pointing at Blingle!"

Glinda slid a sideways glance at her former classmate and was alarmed to see that with every to-and-fro motion of the rocking chair, Blingle seemed to be wavering back and forth through her own lifespan—when the chair tilted back, she appeared as her familiar, youthful self, but with each forward pitch she transformed, if only for the space of a heartbeat, into a wizened old hag, her skin leathery, her hair a dull and frazzled gray.

Without warning, the old-then-young-then-old-again Blingle sprang up from the rocker and stretched her arms out in front of her. As Glinda stared, Blingle's craggy fingers narrowed one by one until all ten had turned into long, pointed sewing needles.

> "Baste and darn, darn and baste
> A stitch for the Witch is never a waste.
> Sew and mend, mend and sew
> Into this crewel so cruel you'll go!"

As the Wicked chant filled the cottage, Ben and Locasta began to shrink in on themselves, growing thinner and thinner until they were no wider than a length of string. Two of Blingle's finger needles released themselves to fly across the room like darts, each catching one of the threads that were formerly Glinda's friends and plunging them into the tapestry! While these dove in and out of the fabric, Blingle chanted louder:

> "Wizardry wondrous, Wizardry bring
> Eight more lengths of Magic string!"

Long strands of colorful threads appeared, dangling from the eyes of Blingle's eight remaining needle fingers. She aimed one disfigured hand at Gremil, sending orange, green, and lavender threads snapping in his direction, twisting with her wrath. The enchanted strings encircled the apprentice, binding his arms and legs.

Frantically, Glinda grabbed for the threads, but a long pink length shot out from Blingle's hand to lash her like a whip. Then a red string spun forth and wrapped itself tightly around her ankles. A yellow one bound her wrists.

Glinda struggled to break free of her colorful bindings, but the Magic was too strong. She jerked her head around to examine the tapestry on the wall. It was as horrifically beautiful as it had been just seconds before—a shimmering mural, a textile masterpiece.

There was just one difference.

Two additional figures were now embroidered there.

Ben and Locasta.

Trapped in the cloth.

25

LOOSE ENDS

W asn't that fun?" Blingle taunted, her gray hair returning to its golden richness, her haggard skin softening
once more. Only her hands were different—amid the eight
shiny needles were two knuckly stubs, all that remained of
the fingers she'd sacrificed to sew Ben and Locasta into the
trapestry. "My liege Aphidina will be so delighted by my
success, don't you think? She sent me here this morning,
expressly to collect you, and now I have."

"How did the Witch know I was coming to Maud's?"
Glinda demanded.

"Our Witch has ways and means, and her ways are
mean indeed." Blingle looked down her pert little nose and

lowered her voice to a mock whisper. "Don't tell anyone, though. It's a *secret*."

"So you're a Witch, then?"

Blingle gave an indignant sniff. "I am a Wizardess. Wizardry is the Magical calling that relies upon ambition, achieved through illusion."

"What have you done with Maud?" Glinda asked through gritted teeth.

"Nothing," Blingle spat. "Her fate was sealed long ago."

Glinda glanced at the prisoners stitched into the tapestry. "What of my friends?" she asked. "And the apothecary?"

"I assume they'll remain there until the Witch can think of a use for them," Blingle replied with a toss of her hair. "My stitches, and Gremil's too, are hexed so as to be reversible when need be."

"And who is the dark-eyed girl? The one in the cloak."

"She is absolutely nobody. I found her skulking around the cottage shortly after I arrived this morning. I was appalled, of course. I mean, honestly! Who wears a cloak nowadays?" Blingle gave a delicate hoot of laughter. "She knocked on the door expecting Maud and found me instead. Imagine her surprise! I'd stitched her into the tapestry before she even knew what was happening. Perhaps I'll just take a blade to her and rip her out altogether. I'm certain no one will miss her."

Glinda looked at the girl in the trapestry. The girl looked back at her.

"Now then," said Blingle, "all that remains is for me to send word to Aphidina that I have carried out my task with exceptional results." Sashaying to the door, she opened it, leaned out, and called, "Bird!"

"Bird?" Glinda echoed.

"Well, of course," Blingle trilled, utterly disgusted by Glinda's stupidity. "How else would I get the news to the Witch?" Again she shrieked, "*Bird!*"

An avian creature came swooping into the cottage.

But unlike the feathery snoops who'd descended upon Glinda's house yesterday, this bird was not a crow, nor a raven, nor a vulture.

This bird, to Glinda's immeasurable relief, was an eagle.

When Feathertop saw Glinda bound in thread, he let out a screech of outrage. His sharp gaze went to the Wizardess. "I take it this is *not* Maud?"

Glinda shook her head.

With a loud ruffling of feathers, the eagle dove for Blingle, who screamed and swatted at him with her needles. But Feathertop did not retreat; wings thundering, he caught the dangling threads in his beak, dragged her from the cottage, and took to the sky.

Glinda watched through the open door until they had disappeared over the tree line. Then she turned a frantic expression to Gremil. "Can you untie us?" she asked. "Magically?"

"I'm a Makewright," Gremil told her. "A Maker's Magic does not work that way. What's wanted here is a bit of Sorcery—an enchantment." He looked eagerly around the room until he spotted the sewing basket. "Perhaps you can enchant the sewing shears."

Glinda followed his gaze to the basket filled with military togs. Tucked into it was a pair of heavy scissors. "But I don't know how."

"Maud taught me that our earliest Magic is born from our emotions," Gremil explained. "Right now you are coursing with feelings. If you can choose the proper words and speak them with enough resolve, Magic might indulge you, and infuse your spell with the mystic influence you require."

"I'll try," she said, focusing on the shears in the sewing basket. "The proper words. Must they rhyme?"

Gremil surprised her with a smile. "It couldn't hurt."

Glinda thought hard for a moment, then closed her eyes and began to chant:

"Scissors snip and scissors slice,
Please be helpful, please be nice.
Nip and clip this horrid thread
Before my friends and I are—"

She gulped back the final word with a shudder. "No! I take that back. What I meant to say was . . ."

"Nip and clip this thread away,
So Gremil and I can save the day."

When she opened her eyes, the scissors were rising up from the basket, opening and closing. They remained there hovering above the military togs, but as they moved, Glinda felt the binds around her wrists and ankles begin to fray and fall away in pieces.

When she was free, she rushed to the basket, grabbed the shears, and cut away the threads that held Gremil. Then she ran to the tapestry.

"How do I release them?"

"It is the Wicked Witch's Magic that traps your friends," said Gremil, his voice grim. "I am sorry to say I know only how to sew her enemies into the scene, and not how to get them out." He let out a long sigh. "Some time ago the Witch came to Maud with a finely woven piece of linen. She required a prison, though she did not call it that. But when she described to us the manner of textile piece she desired, we knew it would be as much a jail as any made of iron bars. Aphidina said the linen was Magical, woven on her own evil loom. She told Maud that she would henceforth be sending citizens to us and it would be our duty to embroider them into the enchanted cloth."

"And Maud couldn't refuse to do it?" asked Glinda.

"If she had, surely the Witch would have suspected she

was a member of the Foursworn. She did try to disqualify herself by telling the Witch that her eyesight was failing and her fingers were no longer nimble enough for such tedious work. I thought she'd convinced her, because Aphidina accepted her excuses with no show of anger at all. She merely said that she hoped Maud would reconsider, left the fabric, and went on her way." Gremil's face wilted in shame. "The next morning I arrived to discover that Maud was missing. It was hours before I found her . . . where Aphidina had trapped her in the fabric."

Glinda remembered the colorless image embroidered there amid the brightly colored ones. No wonder she had seemed familiar . . . it was Maud!

"I thought the Witch would spare her once I agreed to do the work," Gremil continued, "but Maud remained there in the tapestry. The message was clear: if I refused to persist in this horrid work, the Witch would do away with her completely."

Glinda went to the tapestry and found Maud, who wasted no time in trying to tell her something—she was making a frantic plucking gesture with her tiny thumb and forefinger.

"I don't understand!" said Glinda, trying to make sense of the gesticulations. "You're . . . pulling? Tugging?"

Maud's embroidered head bobbed in the affirmative as she continued to enact the plucking motion, more fervently now.

In her mind, Glinda was suddenly a child again, sewing in the shade of the ruby maple. Maud was showing her how to fix the lopsided letter *I* by unraveling it with a firm tug upon the *loose end* of the thread. Not by *tying*, but by *tugging* it, just as she was miming now.

"If I find the right knot, can I *unravel* the Magic?" Glinda guessed.

Maud clapped her hands, indicating that this was correct.

"But there must be a million knots. How will I know—?"

With a proud flourish, Maud pointed to herself.

"Of course. You were the first prisoner in the trapestry. Your image contains the first stitch, the one that started this Wicked Magic." Folding back the edge of the tapestry, Glinda found the only knot formed of bleached, colorless thread, the knot that secured Aphidina's first evil stitch.

She gripped the scissors, preparing to cut. But she couldn't bring herself to do it.

"What's the matter?" Gremil asked.

"Blingle said that Aphidina would leave the prisoners in the cloth until such time that she had use for them," Glinda said. "She said *your* stitches and Blingle's are reversible. But *you* didn't sew Maud. Aphidina did."

She turned back to the tapestry to see Maud speaking to the stitched image of Abrahavel. The apothecary shook his head, but the miniature Maud seemed adamant. Finally, with a look that was both grim and grateful, Abrahavel agreed to what Maud was asking him to do. Using his chalk, he scrawled something onto the slate. The word revealed itself in a sloppy backstitch: UNRAVEL.

"No!" said Glinda. "I won't do it. Just give me a moment. I'll think of something else."

"Glinda," said Gremil, "Maud is as keen to defeat the Witches as your mother is. She has devoted her whole life to that goal, and now is her last chance to act on her dedication. Let her contribute this much to the rebellion."

Glinda's throat felt tight. She shook her head. "I can't."

"But you must."

Maud was smiling at Glinda from within the tapestry; although her pale stitches were stark and stern, her expression was sweet and sincere.

And brave.

"Are you certain?" Glinda whispered to the cloth.

Maud nodded.

Once again Glinda folded the fabric over and found the one dull knot, the one Aphidina had tied with her own cold and bony fingers. She slid the blades of the shears around it.

Snip.

Then she reached for the loose end and pulled. Stitches began to fall away, beginning with Maud's colorless ones. In her wake a hundred thousand brilliantly hued stitches released themselves as well, unraveling the schools and the town and the landscape until at last Ben, Locasta, and Squillicoat were standing before Glinda in Maud's cottage.

They were free.

But Maud was no more.

Glinda wasn't sure how she made it to the rocking chair. Perhaps Ben carried her. Perhaps she crawled. Such was the depth of her heartbreak.

The dark-eyed girl in the charcoal cape had taken it upon herself to remove the sewing basket from beside the rocker and toss the military uniforms into the fire.

Maud was all Glinda could think. Her mother's friend and mentor, a courageous Foursworn rebel, was *gone*. Maud, the only one who could help her rescue Tilda from the Witch's prison by pointing her to the whereabouts of the Fire Fairy, had unraveled.

When Feathertop returned to tell them of his dealings with Blingle, Glinda felt as though she were listening from the bottom of a deep, dark hole. The Wizardess, the eagle explained, struggled viciously until they were well above the treetops. It was as if she'd been too angry at first to even recall that she had Magical abilities, but the moment she did, she threw a hex upon him, which forced him to open his beak and release her.

"The presence of power does not guarantee the absence of stupidity," Feathertop mused. "Naturally, she fell like a stone, tumbling through the blue sky. I lost sight of her after that."

"If the Witch dispatched Blingle here," Locasta noted,

"that means she either made a very lucky guess, or she knew Glinda was on her way."

In the rocker, Glinda trembled. Locasta was right; the danger of the quest was now undeniable. Aphidina was in pursuit.

Gremil and the dark-eyed girl, who had quietly introduced herself as Shade, went to the kitchen to see what might be had for supper.

Locasta talked with Squillicoat, who shared what news he had of the Revolution; in turn Locasta explained what had happened to Tilda. Ben fiddled with Maud's spinning wheel, pausing occasionally to ask Glinda if she was all right.

She wasn't.

Later, following a satisfying meal of sizzled asparagumtion spears on a bed of saffrompy rice, Gremil said it was time for him to go. He would set out on the Road of Red Cobble to seek the nearest Mingling and begin his training as a Revo.

The others wished him nothing but the best. Glinda could only manage a nod of farewell.

It was not until midnight, after the others were all fast asleep, that Glinda rose from the rocker and tiptoed to the fireplace to fetch the cross-stitch sampler from its frame.

Using a spool of golden thread from the sewing basket—the same thread, she was certain, that Maud had used to stitch up the back seam of Haley Poppet—Glinda began to sew, centering her careful stitches beneath Maud's Z-shaped flourish. When she was finished, three new words had been added to the old sampler, their letters a twinkling of gold against the white background:

TRUTH ABOVE ALL.

With a contented sigh, Glinda tucked it into one of the pockets Locasta had wisely and considerately danced into her trousers. "*Truth above all*," she whispered to the moonlight.

From the shadowy corner where Shade slept, she thought she heard the quiet girl return the wish.

Then Glinda closed her weary eyes and went to sleep.

26

THE GIFTS OF OZ

"Glinda . . ."

Someone was shaking her from a sleep in which she had dreamed of nothing but nothing.

"Glinda, it's time to wake up."

Her eyelids felt heavy as stones; she willed them open. Ben's large brown eyes looked back at her.

"There is word from Miss Gage," Locasta said, her lips quirking into a half grin. "But you've kind of got to see it to believe it."

Outside the Ozian morning was soft and sweet. And filled with butterflies.

Thousands! Millions, perhaps—hovering, dipping,

bobbing. Glinda imagined she was looking at a multitude of winged kisses come to life in the air behind Maud's house. Monarchs and fritillaries, painted ladies and cloudless sulfurs, floating, flying, and spinning like a pastel daydream.

Her mouth fell open. "It's beautiful."

"Wait," Locasta whispered. "It gets better."

Indeed, the kaleidoscope of butterflies had begun to move in what looked like an acrobatic ballet. They were arranging themselves into a figure, each bringing its own dainty geometry to the task.

The first few dove downward to the grass; the next several came to settle above them. A third battalion swept into the swiftly emerging image, belling outward in the shape of a long skirt. Another bunch fluttered above these, nipping inward to become a ladylike waistline. Torso, arms, and shoulders appeared, and finally, a very familiar face.

"Miss Gage!" Glinda exclaimed, recalling Madam Mentir's reprimand about unfinished lesson plans for a Butterfly Collecting class. Clearly, Miss Gage was putting her knowledge to better use.

The quiet beating of countless wings gathered itself into an airy adaptation of Miss Gage's voice.

"My dear Glinda, I am so very sorry about Maud. She was true to the Foursworn to her very last breath, and our cause burns brighter in the wake of her passing."

"But how will I find the Fairy and save my mother without

Maud?" Glinda asked, her voice cracking over the name.

"You must find a way," said Gage. "Readiness and hope are the order of the day."

In a flutter of color, the butterfly whose place marked Miss Gage's lips separated itself from the group to alight above the bridge of Glinda's nose, as if the teacher-Sorceress were pressing a gentle kiss upon her forehead; it left a pale, glimmering lip print on Glinda's skin.

"Take good care," Gage whispered, sending more butterflies to deliver Magical kisses to Locasta, Ben, Shade, and even Feathertop, who was perched upon Ben's shoulder.

The rest of the butterflies dispersed into the brightening daylight, slowly dissolving the fluttering portrait of Miss Gage as they did.

Watching them take to the sky, Locasta touched her thumb to the spot on her forehead where Miss Gage's lip mark still shimmered, then blew gently upon it and said,

"From affection, comes protection,
If we're parted, you'll be guarded,
Thanks to this, a shielding kiss."

As the words trembled in the morning air, a curlicue of silver light shot out from the kiss print. The twinkling encircled the four children and the eagle briefly before making a sputtering *ffffzzztttzzttt* sound. With a judder and a blink, the light vanished.

"Hmmm. Guess I've still got some work to do on that one," Locasta muttered.

With the kiss still tingling on her forehead, Glinda watched the last butterfly disappear into the blue. Just before she lost sight of it, she was sure she heard the wingy sound of Miss Gage's voice.

"Find the Fire Fairy, Glinda!" it called to her. "Find Ember."

Back inside the cottage, Ben set about brewing a pot of sweet razzleberry tea while Glinda and Squillicoat sat at the dining table.

"Do you have any insight as to the whereabouts of the Elemental Fairies?" Glinda asked the apothecary. "Ember in particular."

"I'm sorry to say I do not," Master Squillicoat replied. "Though knowing Tilda, I'd be surprised if she didn't let on more than you realize."

"You mean like a hint?" said Locasta. "A clue?"

The apothecary nodded.

"I suppose it's possible," Glinda conceded. "Although most of what she said sounded so strange and nonsensical that—" She broke off with a wince.

"What's wrong?" asked Locasta.

"My palms are stinging! It feels as if I'm holding fire, or broken glass or—"

Broken glass! Glinda's mind spiraled back to her mother's

capture—the birds at the windows, the glass panes splitting, the cracks taking the form of words.

She ran to the parlor window and pressed her hands to the panes. Recalling the words her mother had spoken, she whispered, "*De*struction, no; *in*struction, yes."

Crrrraaaacckkkk—fissures spread through the glass like a crystalline firework, splintering into Tilda's unmistakable script!

"How is this happening?" asked Locasta. "You aren't Magical enough to execute this kind of enchantment yet."

"It's not just Magic," said Squillicoat. "It's memory mixed with the Magic that exists in this cottage. We don't just remember with our minds, you see. We tuck memories away within all of our senses—touch, taste, smell." He nodded to the window. "Glinda has been carrying this particular memory in her hands. It seems she just needed a place to put it."

Glinda read the message in the broken window aloud, and Ben quickly jotted the words in the Maker's journal. "Fire, Thought, Last, and"—she waited for the final word to etch itself into the glass—"Independent."

These were the same words Tilda had gone to such lengths to emphasize just before Bog broke down the door.

Glinda's mother *had* given her clues!

"But what do they mean?" Locasta asked, strumming her fingers on the dining table so fervently that the teacups rattled in their saucers.

"My mother did say something about allowing my ideas to burn like *fire*."

"Fire, as in the Fire Fairy," said Ben. "Now we're getting somewhere. What else did she say?"

"That the only kind of thought that would last was independent."

Locasta frowned. "So what's the connection between those four words and the whereabouts of the Fairy? What could possibly be the link?"

Glinda's eyes flew open. *Link.*

As in chain!

A vision of a red stone on a platinum chain flashed in her mind, and she repeated the fourth word, just as Tilda had, rolling the syllables slowly from her tongue: "In . . . de . . . pen . . . dent. Can it be? Can it really be that simple?"

"Can what be that simple?" asked Squillicoat.

"I know exactly where the Fairy is hiding!"

"*Where?*" Locasta and Ben chorused.

"Here!" Glinda reached for the red beryl stone on its chain around her neck. "In. The. Pendant."

Everyone stared at Glinda, whose fingers were fumbling beneath the neckline of her tunic. When her hands came away empty, she wanted to weep. "It was here! Right here around my neck! She gave it to me . . . but then Bog came and it flared in his eyes . . . he broke the chain . . . he flung it."

"I believe she's finally lost her mind," said Locasta.

"No!" said Glinda. "Listen to me! There is a gemstone. A red beryl pendant. My mother gave it to me just before Bog broke down the door. I think she tried to tell me that the pendant is the answer to defeating the Witch."

"*Jewelry?*" Locasta scoffed. "You're suggesting we can vanquish a Wicked Witch with *accessories?* What else will we need for this brutal attack? A pretty parasol, perhaps, maybe a couple of hair ribbons?"

"I used my hair ribbons on Clumsy Bear," Glinda blurted, and immediately regretted it, as it earned her a disgusted eye roll from Locasta. Taking a deep breath, she willed herself to be steady. "What I am trying to tell you is that the Fire Fairy is . . . *in the pendant.*"

Ben's eyes lit with understanding. "Ember's hiding in the stone!"

"Yes!"

A silence fell over the cottage; four pairs of eyes went to the V neckline of Glinda's tunic as everyone realized at precisely the same second what the problem was.

Locasta, of course, was the one to put this realization into words. "You *had* the Fire Fairy. And you *lost* him?" Her eyes flared like purple flames.

Glinda's green eyes flared back. "I did not *lose* him. A mud monster *ripped him off my neck* and threw him across the room!"

"You should have gone back for it!"

"Did you not hear me say 'mud monster'?!"

"*I* would have gone back!"

"Calm down, Locasta," Squillicoat admonished. "In Glinda's defense, she did not know at the time what the stone contained. And since we cannot change what has already happened, we will simply have to trust that the stone is still in the house where the muck monster threw it after removing it from Glinda's neck."

Now Ben ventured a question: "Does anyone else think it odd that Tilda gave the stone to Glinda?"

"What are you getting at, lad?" Squillicoat asked.

"Well, if Tilda knew she was being taken to the Witch, why didn't she just keep the pendant with her and unleash Ember when she got there?"

It was an excellent question, which had the occupants of the cottage settling into a contemplative hush. A hush that was broken suddenly when Locasta began to hum, softly at first, then louder and with more gusto. It wasn't Maud's counting song this time, but Glinda recognized it nonetheless.

"That's the song my mother sang just before we ran off into the Woebegone!"

"Whoa! Be Gone," Locasta corrected automatically.

Glinda resisted the urge to challenge her. "Do you remember the words?"

Locasta nodded, then closed her eyes and, in a voice as sweet as fresh air, sang the words that Tilda had sung:

"As fire seeks a place to burn,
In seeking strength, no stone unturn,
A perfect fit must be achieved
For this bright flame to be conceived.
Wisdom waits, where shadows fall.
A friend, like truth, can conquer all."

When she was finished, Ben grinned. "Fire seeks a place to burn. Sounds like another clue to me!"

"The Fairy of Fire *seeks* a place. A perfect fit must be achieved." Locasta began to pace the cottage. "I think it's telling us that before Ember can burn, the stone must first be fitted into . . . *something*."

"Something my mother obviously did not have in her possession," Glinda concluded. "Which was why simply wearing the pendant to Aphidina's castle wouldn't have been enough to destroy the Witch."

"All right then," said Ben, and ticked off a list of tasks on his fingers. "All we have to do is determine *what* this object is, *where* it is, how to *retrieve* it from this place 'where shadows fall,' and finally, *fit* the stone into it."

Locasta gave him a weary look. "Right. That's *all* we have to do."

"Well, I didn't say it was going to be easy."

Glinda slipped her hand into the pocket of her breeches and closed it around the neatly folded sampler. Just feeling the stitches of the golden thread against her skin gave her hope. She noticed that the apothecary was tapping his chin thoughtfully.

"Master Squillicoat," she said, "do you have an idea?"

"I believe I do." He turned to Ben. "May I see that journal?"

Ben gave the book to Squillicoat, who allowed it to fall open in his hands. There, covering two full pages of the little journal, was a drawing of a beast with the head of a giant horned ram and the body of some pouncing cat-like creature. Glinda stared at the drawing, unsure whether she should be comforted or intimidated by the existence of such a beast.

"'The Queryor,'" Ben read.

"Never heard of him," said Locasta.

"'The Queryor,'" Ben continued, "'is utterly neutral, neither good nor bad—like curiosity itself. Formed of ongoing inquiry and the desire to challenge and question, he represents the general essence of wonder and exploration. One may appeal to the Queryor when faced with the most dire or elusive of questions.'"

"So basically, he's a know-it-all," said Locasta.

Takes one to know one, thought Glinda.

"If anyone can help you discover the answers to your questions, it's the Queryor," said Squillicoat.

"Please tell me you know where *he's* hiding," Locasta said.

"The Queryor isn't hiding," the apothecary explained. "His lair is in the Centerlands of Oz."

"Then it would seem the Queryor's lair is our next stop," said Locasta. "I sincerely hope the old horn-headed beast has the answer we're looking for."

Glinda hoped so too.

Because without it, she would never see her mother again.

As they prepared to set out for the Centerlands, Glinda tried not to imagine walking through the front door of Maud's cottage for the very last time. Noting the bemused look on the apothecary's face, she wondered if he was thinking the same thing.

"What is it, Master Squillicoat?" she asked. When he didn't answer, she followed his gaze to the broken window-panes and tapped him on the shoulder. "Master Squillicoat, what do you see?"

"Hmm? Oh." He shook his head and pointed to the broken glass, knitting his brow in concentration. "It didn't occur to me before, as we were so focused on the words 'Fire' and 'Independent,' but it would seem that the other two, 'Last' and 'Thought,' might also be clues. I believe they refer to one of the Gifts of King Oz."

"Gifts?" Locasta quirked an eyebrow. "What Gifts?"

"When the king was taken from us at the hands of the Wickeds, he left behind four precious and irreplaceable Gifts," Squillicoat explained, picking up his teacup and swirling the dregs thoughtfully. "Oz's Gifts were intended to live on with his spirit in she who would be born to follow him, as he had been born to follow her."

"Princess Ozma," said Glinda.

Squillicoat nodded. "Oz's Gifts were endearingly simple and unimaginably generous. They were the fiery spark of his last thought, the unbridled emotion contained in his final teardrop, the eternal echo of his confident footsteps upon this Lurlian plane, and the life-giving power of the last breath he drew from and expelled into this world."

"Elemental things," Glinda observed. "So where are these Gifts now?"

"I have no idea," Squillicoat confessed.

"*Hnnffh.* That's just what Miss Gage said about the Fairies," Locasta grumbled.

"Indeed," said Squillicoat. "Though perhaps the time has come for this particular secret to be known."

"How can that happen," asked Ben, "if there isn't a Grand Adept here to share it with us?"

In lieu of an answer, Squillicoat turned to Glinda. "Would you please go to the well and bring some fresh water for the kettle?"

Glinda hurried to obey. When she returned, she handed the dripping bucket directly to Ben, who poured the water into the empty kettle.

Squillicoat smiled at Shade. "Would you kindly stoke the fire?"

When Shade reached into the wood basket, the apothecary stopped her with a shake of his head. "No, no, my dear. Not kindling. Peat is preferable, if you please."

Looking puzzled, Shade began gathering handfuls of moss from a pail beside the hearth and arranging them in the fireplace.

"Why peat instead of wood?" Glinda asked.

"Because 'peat' is just another word for 'turf,'" Squillicoat explained. "Peat comes from the world beneath our feet. For this blaze, peat represents Lurl."

"Since when does a fire have to represent something?" Locasta challenged.

"Sometimes, Magic likes a motif," the apothecary replied cagily.

"Whatever *that* means," muttered Locasta, watching as Ben used a pothook to again hang the kettle on the iron crane in the fireplace.

Now Squillicoat indicated the tinderbox perched upon the mantelpiece. "Locasta, perhaps you would do us the honor of igniting the flame."

"Good choice." Ben chuckled. "Igniting is definitely her specialty."

Locasta grabbed for the tinderbox and made quick work of striking the firesteel across the sharp edge of the flint. Sparks sprang forth like shooting stars, lighting the char cloth; she tossed the glowing scrap onto Shade's pile of dried moss, and a sweet-scented smoldering began.

Then Squillicoat took the ancient bellows from where

they leaned against the fireplace and offered them to Ben. "Seems it wants a bit of air, son."

Ben obliged with a dutiful "Yes, sir" and aimed the bellows toward the peat. As he opened and closed them, they huffed their leathery breath onto the flame, coaxing it toward combustion.

It wasn't long before the spout of Maud's kettle produced a graceful trail of steam, gray-white and weightless, alive with purpose; an entity born of this most ordinary union of moss and fire, water and air.

As the girl who fetched the water, the boy who worked the bellows, the stranger who stoked the fire, and the girl who lit the flame stared in wonder, a slender wisp of steam wafted out of the fireplace and into the parlor.

"Even the simplest Magic has power you can scarcely imagine," Squillicoat observed as the steam billowed. "Four elements combining to tell one extraordinary tale."

Glinda wasn't sure if the four elements Squillicoat had alluded to were the items in the fireplace or the children who'd collected them. But around her, the steam was taking on substance and wrapping itself into a scene.

A scene that began just where the zoetrope left off . . .

THE STORY TOLD IN THE STEAM

Perhaps—
  Perhaps—

"Perhaps," says King Oz as he leads his brave Regents onto the terrace, "these four harridans can be reasoned with."

If they do not accept his overture of friendship, then he will fight—for the Good King Oz would never instigate a battle, but he would never retreat from one either.

A young groundskeeper who has been tending potted ivy on the terrace boldly places himself between the king and his sudden enemies. King Oz thanks him for his protection but commands the lad to take shelter in the Reliquary with the others.

The groundskeeper obeys; of course he obeys. But he will regret for the rest of his life that he could not aid his liege in this moment.

Oz and his Regents meet the Witches without their hands upon their swords. And that is their grave mistake in judgment.

Gilli is the first to go—he is tossed so mightily by the Warrior Witch that he tumbles through the air and over the side of the plateau. She bellows her name into the night as she pitches him: "Marada!"

Sir Wink is attacked by the most nimble of the Witches; she dances him under a spell, then splits him in two with a kick that is both graceful and deadly. She calls herself Daspina and pirouettes madly in recognition of her success.

The Harvester Witch who defeats Lord Quadle is strewn with flowers—thorny ones, poisonous ones, wilting ones. She force-feeds him her petals and stems until he chokes and succumbs to the toxins. She whispers her name, "Aphidina," and it carries a foul fragrance, like rotting leaves.

The most beautiful of the four by far goes after the archduke with naught but a spell, a spoken charm that first makes him weak, and then makes him gone. It is that easy; beauty has its advantages. "I am Ava, the Tyrant." She speaks this with her eyes.

Over the sacrifice of his Regents Valiant, the king is distraught. Enraged. And now the Witches begin to stalk him, coming together in a confluence of evil, pressing closer until it is impossible to discern where one begins and another ends. They have blurred into one Wicked thing. They are darkness times four.

Oz suffers a kick from the dancer, a look from the beauty, a thorny prick from the flowered one, and a good solid punch to his noble jaw from the Warrior Witch.

Weakening under their attack, King Oz drops to one knee; the Witches are quick and greedy. Even as they divest him of his fine silver armor, they are fighting with one another, haggling over these priceless pieces of silver, each claiming the prize she wants. Violently they help themselves to his gauntlets, his boots, his masked helmet, and his heavy, glinting chainmail as if they are entitled to them.

In the end, it is the mere force of their loathing that does him in. For no one—not even a king, not even Oz—could endure such profound hatred. He does not bleed, nor break, he simply draws one final breath, and cries one final tear. He stomps his foot and thinks one last thought—though only he knows what that thought contains. When his second knee hits the flagstones, there is an explosion of light. The Witches duck and stumble back from the force of it, still clutching their spoils as the king's corporeal self shatters into a thousand glowing beams.

What's left is his shadow, still kneeling in the place where he fell—a transparent remainder hovering between here and the void. The Witches ignore it and continue to admire their stolen treasure.

They do not see the four tiny orbs forming inside the shadow, spinning and glimmering. One in the center of his forehead, another in his left eye, a third in his chest, and the last beneath the sole of his right foot. These are the echoes of his final moments in the world—the thought, the tear, the breath, and the firmness of his footsteps upon the ground—turned to swirls of light.

These are the Gifts of Oz.

And they are what the Witches were sent here to

collect. But the thieves are still too caught up in their victory to notice these precious pearls of light, even as the shadow that encloses them begins to fade.

The king is gone, and the absence of him is felt by the sky, and the soil and the rivers and every single spark that exists in Oz, the home he no longer inhabits.

His departure is too much for even the castle to bear; and so it begins the violent process of self-destruction.

In the Reliquary, grief all but freezes the revelers where they stand. Even with the castle walls tumbling, the parapets crumbling, the lead tiles slipping down the pitched slope of the rooftop like rectangular tears, the party guests cannot bring themselves to move. Slivers of stone and fragments of glass from the demolished palace become embedded in the Reliquary floor, turning themselves into letters and words—an epitaph in stony verse.

Only one knight thinks to act; he does so in the scantest nick of time.

And this is a good and clever knight indeed. He shouts to the Elemental Fairies: *"Hide!"*

> *Hide—*
>
> > *Hide—*

As the scene faded, Glinda kept her eyes trained on the place where the king had been; the glowing light of his

Gifts continued to gleam, but the gray-white steam from the kettle was turning from a light vapory mist to a heavy dark cloud, bruising over first to midnight blue, then black.

"Uh-oh," said Locasta.

"We have to go!" said Ben. "Now!"

Like the frightened guests in the Reliquary, Glinda remained motionless, staring into the smoke. Instinctively she thrust her hand into the blackness, reaching first for the circle of light where the king's forehead had been, then the one near his heart. Both times her hand closed around nothing but darkness.

She felt someone gripping her arm and pulling hard: Locasta.

But from deep within the blackness something else had taken hold of her other arm. This grip was tighter, colder—a Wicked touch to be certain, and it held firm, even as Locasta tugged against it.

"The Gifts!" Glinda choked as the smoke filled her mouth and lungs. "I have to save them."

The unseen grasp on her arm gave an incredible heave. Locasta's hold faltered and Glinda staggered backward, falling into the churning smoke. Blinking it out of her watering eyes, she searched for the four Magical spheres of light, but they had faded from view. All that remained were two red blotches, like sores festering deep within the dark cloud; optic boils glaring down at her as if they would burn her alive with their hatred.

Now the invisible grip moved to her throat, squeezing until she could barely breathe—it was the same stranglehold she'd suffered on the night her mother had summoned a vision from the moon. Understanding wrenched through her: the red orbs were the eyes of the fifth Witch, glaring at her through the black cloud.

Two strong hands clamped around her ankles. With one mighty tug, Locasta dragged her out of the smoke and yanked her to her feet. "Let's go!" said Locasta.

"The Gifts," Glinda choked.

"You can't save them from here. They aren't now, they're then."

"But—"

Locasta shoved her toward the door.

Stumbling across the cottage, Glinda saw Squillicoat bent over the fire, uttering a spell:

> *"Heal now without a potion,*
> *Banish Wicked with devotion*
> *Tincture of Goodness, Mixture of Might*
> *Lead us to wisdom, set us to right*
> *Fend off the darkness, bring us the light!"*

Glinda felt the final word of the charm settle over the cottage like a spoken balm, dispelling the smoke and eradicating the burns that were the eyes of the fifth Witch.

As Glinda and Locasta staggered down the walk to the

gate where Ben and Shade waited, Glinda glanced over her shoulder and saw Master Squillicoat, watching them from behind the crackled glass. With a nod and a smile, he formed a four-fingered X and placed it over his heart—the Foursworn salute.

This, she understood, was not merely a gesture of encouragement; this was farewell.

Returning the apothecary's salute, Glinda watched as Maud's front door began to fade away; the thatch of the roof rustled once in a soft breeze and was gone. The rosieglories and razzleberries shrank gracefully on their vines, while the fence posts and pickets paled to white shadows until the whole cottage had vanished in a tender twinkling, like a dream or a peal of laughter, disappearing to a place filled with good things that used to be.

Glinda felt it go, like a wish one abandons for being too wonderful to come true. But this was not the time for wishes; this was a time for action.

With a deep breath, she took a step and the Road of Red Cobble rose up to accept it.

"To the Queryor," she said.

Her friends fell in line beside her, and they were off.

27

SHADE

They walked a long way without saying a word. Finally Glinda turned to Shade.

"Are you going to tell us anything about yourself? Other than your name, I mean."

"What do you want to know?" Shade's voice was one octave above silence; her silky hair fell over her eyes like a curtain, and her cloak swirled like a storm cloud, but she did not shrink from the inquiry.

"How about what you were doing at Maud's cottage, for starters," said Locasta. "Blingle said she found you skulking around there this morning."

"She didn't find me, exactly. No one ever does. I *allowed*

myself to be found. I wanted to get inside that cottage, and capture seemed the most efficient way to do that."

Like my mother, allowing Bog to take her to the fifth Witch in Aphidina's castle, Glinda thought. *A captive by design.*

"I knew you were headed there," Shade went on. "I wanted to make sure it was safe. Turns out it wasn't."

"*How* did you know we were going to Maud's?" asked Ben.

"Yesterday, at sunrise, I happened to be in a corridor of Aphidina's castle."

"You *happened* to be in Aphidina's castle?" Glinda echoed in disbelief. She might not have understood until just recently that the Witch's benevolence was an illusion, but she did know that no one ever just "happened to be" in the palace without permission.

Shade shrugged. "I happen to be a lot of places," she explained in her skittish way. "That morning I happened to be there. And I overheard the Witch say that she was going to arrest the Grand Adept."

Glinda's mouth dropped open. "*You* were the one who told Miss Gage about Bog?"

Shade nodded. "After the mud monster took you in the wagon, I lost you, but I caught your trail again just after the blizzard. Then I followed you to the Maker's lodge and listened outside the window. I heard you talking about visiting the old Seamstress who lived on the outskirts, so I went on ahead."

"Amazing," said Ben.

Even Locasta looked impressed. "So you're a spy."

Shade did not deny it. "I have a knack for going unnoticed. I am a Listener, and Listeners know things. Not everyone has a talent for paying attention, so those of us who do are useful to those who don't. There are many Ozians who are willing to trade food and shelter for cold hard facts." She gave another shrug. "Food and shelter I lack. Facts I have in abundance."

"Resourceful," Glinda observed.

"Sneaky," said Locasta, though it didn't sound like an insult.

"It's a long way to Maud's from the Maker's cabin," said Glinda. "How did you—"

Before she finished her question, Shade flipped back her cape and pointed to the red stones pressing up from the ruddy soil. "It comes for me when I need it. I don't know why, but it does."

It was then that Glinda remembered the counting song. *Count by four, at peace once more.* There was always meant to be a fourth traveler on their journey. And the road's acceptance of Shade meant that she could be trusted.

"Why is it you are so proficient at spying?" Locasta asked. "You don't dabble in dark Magic, do you?"

"What I do requires no Magic," Shade replied, "just a lifetime of abandonment and neglect."

This was said in such a matter-of-fact manner that it made Glinda's heart hurt.

"You can't see what you don't care about," Shade continued. "When everyone stops looking at you, it's easier for you to look at them."

"So your talent for going undetected is the result of the world's general disregard for your existence," said Locasta, her tone unexpectedly sympathetic.

"I guess you could say that."

"Well, it's an impressive skill, however you got it," Ben noted.

"Yes," Glinda agreed. "Almost like being invisible."

"Invisibility involves extremely potent Magic," Locasta pointed out. "Don't tell me you've mastered invisibility."

Shade shook her head. "No, I haven't. But then, I've never tried."

"Why not?" asked Feathertop.

"Invisibility is dangerous," Locasta explained, "even for experts. Once you disappear, there's always the risk that you won't be able to reappear. I wouldn't try it for all the gemstones in the Nome Kingdom."

"I might," Shade confessed. "Someday. I like to learn things."

"So do I," said Glinda, beaming. "And Ben, too."

Shade flicked a curious glance at Locasta.

"Oh, *she* already *knows* everything," Glinda teased, and to her surprise, Locasta laughed along with the rest of them.

With Feathertop soaring just overhead, the four companions continued on. The way was clear, and the pace was quick; it seemed to Glinda that the road was as eager to bring them to the Centerlands as they were to get there.

To the Queryor, who would tell them the secret of how to free the Fairy from the stone.

Or so Glinda did desperately hope.

At last they reached the tattering of red underbrush that marked the outer edge of Quadling Country at the Centerlands border. Rustling through the dense tangle of brushwood, they stepped out on the other side into a green pasture, a vast grassland that rolled off toward the distant greenish haze of the horizon.

As the red cobbles carried them across the sprawling meadow of the Centerlands, Glinda saw more shades of green than she'd ever dreamed existed. She'd never experienced such lushness before, not even in the South, where Aphidina prided herself on growing things. Locasta, who was used to purple, seemed as dazzled by the emerald tones as Glinda was.

The road carried them across the grassy expanse to a staircase of stone that led to a terraced garden.

The Queryor's Lair.

"It's just like I remember it," Shade whispered.

"You've been here before?" asked Ben.

"Yes."

"Have you faced the Queryor?" asked Glinda.

Shade nodded.

"You could have mentioned that sooner," said Locasta. But before she could press the dark-eyed girl for more information, a pounding noise filled the air. It was a slow, measured beat, almost musical, as if someone were banging an enormous drum.

Buh-boom . . . boom . . . boom. Buh-boom . . . boom . . . boom.

"What's with the percussion section?" Locasta said. "Is there also a marching band you forgot to tell us about?"

"It's him," said Shade. "The Queryor, banging his drum. It's part of the Searcher's Ritual."

"Ritual?" Locasta flung up her hands in agitation. "There's a *ritual*?"

"Maybe it would help," Glinda said to Shade, "if you told us exactly how this ritual works."

"It begins with the Searcher," Shade explained. "That's what those who come in search of answers are called. The Searcher approaches the Queryor and bows."

"Bows?" said Ben. "Like this?" He extended his arm and bent at the waist, just as he had done when Glinda and Locasta first met him.

Shade nodded.

"Does the Queryor bow back?"

Shade shook her head. "Not that I've ever heard of."

"Seems a little haughty to me," Locasta huffed. "He's part *goat*, for Oz's sake!"

"Even so," said Glinda. "He is wise and learned, and as

such he is entitled to respect." She nodded to Shade to go on with her explanation.

"After the Searcher bows, the Queryor asks his question, and the Searcher has to give the correct answer before the Queryor finishes drumming or else . . ." She trailed off, her words swallowed up by another round of pounding from the drum.

Buh-boom . . . boom . . . boom. Buh-boom . . . boom . . . boom. Buh-boom . . . boom . . . boom. Buh-boom . . . boom . . .

The drumming stopped so abruptly that Glinda jumped. The next sound they heard was a long, ominous drumroll.

"What's *that* about?" asked Ben.

Shade looked away and said no more.

Whatever it was, they would find out soon enough.

28

AGE BEFORE BEAUTY

The first time Blingle Plunkett misdeclared, she chose Nurse when she should have chosen Chambermaid. This, according to Madam Mentir, had come as no surprise. Even then Blingle had been far too wrapped up in what she thought of herself to give any credence to what others thought of her.

The second time she misdeclared, she picked Seamstress, and when her scroll pronounced her a Governess, no one blamed her for that error either. The fact of the matter was that Blingle would not have made an acceptable Seamstress or Governess (or Nurse or Chambermaid), for by her very nature, the child was unsuited to anything even remotely productive. Cruelty, malice, and spite were her only talents.

This had all taken place in the days when Aphidina still attended the Declaration Day festivities. The Wicked coup had only just occurred, and her reign was in its infancy. She was still new to being a queen and easily thrilled by the sensation of her own power. It was important to let the great ferocity of her presence be known to her subjects— even to those droves of pathetic little schoolgirls bedecked in hair ribbons and apron ruffles.

Blingle went on to misdeclare twenty-two more times, and on the morning of her twenty-third ceremony, Aphidina (who was by then growing rather bored with watching Blingle get Youngified), pulled the girl aside and offered her something much more valuable than a scroll.

"Let's put an end to this ludicrous charade, shall we?" the Witch of the South had drawled. "I will personally train you in the Magical Pathway of Wizardry, and when you have mastered it, you may work as my agent here at the academy ad infinitum."

Blingle was unfamiliar with the phrase *ad infinitum*, but her eyes had lit up at the thought of such an opportunity.

"You will be responsible for intimidating and tormenting anyone who shows signs of having a mind of her own," Aphidina had explained. "You shall use your Wizardry to make yourself appear forever as you do right this moment."

"Young and beautiful," Blingle had clarified.

"Juvenile and mean," Aphidina had corrected. "For

after all, what is more frightening to a good child than a bad child?"

Blingle had eagerly accepted the Witch's proposal and was thus spared the discomfort of being Youngified yet again. She reveled in the idea of being robust and dewy and (most of all) blond until the end of time.

That had been over one hundred and twenty-five Declaration Days ago.

And yesterday Blingle had been given her most monumental assignment to date. Yesterday she had been entrusted to capture the daughter of Tilda Gavaria and to secure the pendant that contained Aphidina's fiery nemesis.

But she had failed. Miserably. Epically. And unforgivably.

Aphidina knew this because, following the disaster at Maud's cottage, a disgraced Blingle had sent a buzzard to the palace to relay the details of her botched mission to the Witch. Of course, the ageless imbecile had never imagined that the buzzard would also tell Aphidina where to look for her, namely a woodsy patch near the Quadling outskirts, where she'd been dropped out of the sky by a white-headed winged thing.

Aphidina wasted no time in getting herself to the outskirts. As she glided through the straggle of red trees and underbrush, she was forced to endure the pounding of a distant drum—*buh-boom . . . boom . . . boom, buh-boom . . . boom . . . boom*—which caused her head to ache. On any other day she would have investigated, but on this day, she simply put it out of her mind and kept searching. Fury had a way of keeping her focused.

At last she found the golden-haired Wizardess cowering behind a large rock, crying uncontrollably, and minus two fingers.

Aphidina scaled the rock and perched upon it gracefully. Then she poked Blingle in the forehead with her toe and said, "I am disappointed, Wizardess. It seems you aren't much use to me outside of the schoolroom."

Blingle cried harder.

"Are those tears of regret?" the Witch inquired calmly. "Or fear?"

"Both," Blingle admitted. "What are you going to do to me?"

Aphidina laughed, and the sound echoed through the sparse forest like ominous music. "I will do that which will be the most distressing to you, of course."

"I was afraid of that." Blingle sniffled. "Would it help if I begged?"

"It would not help at all," Aphidina assured her. Then she waved an elegant hand over Blingle's head and said, "You must pay, and now . . . it's gray!"

Blingle yowled in agony as the golden hue bled from her hair like gilded paint. The spillage went on until only a limp white tangle of strands remained.

Then the Witch clapped her hands and purred, "For your mistake, your bones must ache."

Blingle doubled over in pain as her supple spine rounded into a brittle hump; beneath her skin, her skeleton withered.

"From failure comes no teeth, just gums!"

With this every tooth in Blingle's mouth began to rot. "I beg of you," she wailed, "no more, no more!"

But Aphidina's reply was a flaring of her eyes, which caused Blingle's own sparkling irises to cloud over and turn milky. "And just for spite, I'll take your sight."

From her place behind the stone, Blingle—toothless, humpbacked, and blind—wept even louder.

"I'm so sorry," said Aphidina, though she was not sorry at all, "but the time has come."

"The time has come for *what*?"

"For you to *grow up*!"

With that, Aphidina crooked her finger, beckoning Blingle's lost years to return from wherever it was that the darkness had seen fit to store them. The sky pounded from within and the ground beneath the whimpering Blingle shook. The forest erupted in shafts of light and darkness, entwined and in motion, bringing forth a past multiplied by a hundred pasts, a torrent of todays, tomorrows, and yesterdays.

Blingle had several lifetimes to answer for, and these inflicted themselves upon her all at once—days, weeks, months, seasons, all working as one to punish her for ignoring their natural passage.

As the tears spilled from her sightless eyes to dampen her

swiftly wrinkling skin, the Wizardess tried one last time to reason with her liege. "Aphidina," she croaked. "Please—"

But the Witch did not call off the fury of the years, and the aging continued, swiftly and brutally, until Blingle Plunkett stood before Aphidina at the ripe old age of two hundred and seventy-five.

And then, she didn't stand at all.

She collapsed, weak and wheezing, on the forest floor.

"Now," said the Witch, sliding down from the boulder upon which she perched, "crawl under this rock and remain there, until someone can think of a use for you."

When Aphidina slapped the surface of the stone, it lifted off the ground and hovered there, a silent invitation.

Blingle dragged her sniveling, shriveled self into its shadow and arranged her frail, ancient body in the mossy hollow.

With a snap of her fingers, Aphidina brought the rock down and smiled at the shimmer of nastiness that escaped from beneath it, where Blingle now lay.

Waiting.

With a sigh and a scowl, the Wicked Witch of the South began the long walk home to her castle.

Knowing that she, too, would have to wait.

29

QUERYING THE QUERYOR

Staring up the steps that led to the Queryor's Lair, it occurred to Glinda that something Shade had told them did not add up. "You said the Queryor beats his drum until his question is answered. *His* question."

Shade nodded.

"But I thought the whole point was for *us* to ask *him* a question."

"It's part of the ritual," said Shade. "After the bow, the Queryor queries first. The Searcher must give the beast the answer he wants; only then is she permitted to ask him her question."

"The answer he wants?" said Locasta. "You mean the right answer."

"I suppose sometimes there is more than one right answer to a single question," Ben noted. "Depending on who's being asked."

Again, Shade nodded.

"All right," said Glinda, remembering the sudden silence of the beating drum. "So what happens if you don't give the Queryor the answer he has in mind?"

"The Conundrum."

Locasta frowned. "The *what*?"

"According to my tutor at home, a conundrum is a particularly confusing problem," said Ben. "A complex dilemma, not easily solved."

"It's also what the Queryor calls his drum," said Shade. "It doubles as his prison."

Locasta cocked an eyebrow. "So if you fail his test, he traps you in a *musical instrument*?"

"Miss Gage would call that a metaphor," said Glinda. "Being trapped in your own confusion. Conun*drum*." Then another thought struck her: "What happens if you don't answer at all?"

"You walk away, twice as bewildered."

"Because you are without the answer you came for, and also without the answer to the question the Queryor asked," Glinda reasoned.

"What kind of questions does the Queryor put to the Searcher?" asked Ben.

"Some are direct, yes-or-no questions," Shade replied. "Others are complex puzzles or riddles. Some are challenges. But there is always a profound connection between who you are and what you're asked."

"I see," said Glinda. "The reward for self-knowledge is the opportunity to gain more knowledge. And the punishment for not knowing yourself is to be stuck in the confusion of the Conundrum."

"So what did the Queryor ask you?" Locasta inquired.

Shade hesitated, her eyes falling into the shadow of her shining hair. When she revealed them again, they looked even darker than usual. "He asked me if I was Good, or if I was Wicked."

These words hung in the air like heat lightning until Locasta spoke again.

"What was your answer?"

"I did not give an answer," Shade whispered. "Because I didn't know." Then, swirling her cape around her like a small tornado cloud, she began to climb the steps.

At the top was a pleasant sort of terraced garden, with privet hedges and blooming bushes marking its boundaries. At the end of a shrub-lined lane stood an elaborate archway with fluted columns and a finely carved pediment.

Beneath the arch, holding a gigantic drum, the Queryor awaited, and he was whatever came *after* gigantic. Glinda struggled to recall the definition from the Maker's book: *The Queryor. Formed of ongoing inquiry . . . desire to challenge . . . the general essence of wonder.* A being whose power came from boundless intellect, and from being in a position to use it.

But despite his size and importance, his expression was surprisingly patient and kind. He looked down at them with the gentle, wide-set eyes of a ram, glittering in a shaggy gray face. He had two enormous horns that curled off the sides of his head in a way that was appropriately reminiscent of question marks. His four-legged body, however, was not ramlike at all; rather it was gracefully feline—sleek, with silky gold-and-black-spotted fur and a tail that flicked lazily.

"Please do not be appalled by my extraordinary appearance," the beast said, his voice booming but jovial. "I am by nature ethereal, for inquiry has no solid form, but I have chosen to present myself as a symbol of that which I represent. The head of a ram to reflect the intrepid search for understanding, and the body of a wildcat to represent the miraculous swiftness with which a keen mind can absorb knowledge."

Locasta wrinkled her nose. "What about the ugly part?" she whispered. "What's that reflect?"

"Shhh!" Glinda scolded, for she didn't find the Queryor ugly at all.

When the Queryor's gaze settled on Shade, he looked

pleased. "So you've come to try again," he said. "The truly curious always do. Very well, Searcher. Step forward."

Shade did, bending herself into a clumsy but earnest bow. When she straightened, the Queryor's kindly eyes blinked slowly, as if he were allowing the proper query—Shade's query—to take shape in his mind. When he finally spoke, it was not a question but a simple command: "Tell me a secret."

Glinda wondered if she'd heard him correctly. *Tell him a secret?* There had to be more to the test than that. But he said no more, just whipped his long tail around to pound upon the taut batter head of the Conundrum.

Buh-boom . . . boom . . . boom. Buh-boom . . . boom . . .

Glinda imagined the pounding of her heart was as loud as the beating of the drum. *Answer, Shade,* she willed silently. *You have made a life of knowing secrets.*

At last Shade's voice rose above the rhythm. "I cannot tell you a secret," she said.

Abruptly the Queryor stopped drumming and tilted his ram horns in a quizzical manner. "And why can't you?"

"Because if I did, it would no longer be a secret. A secret becomes something else in the telling of it, so neither I, nor anyone else, can ever really *tell* a secret. We can betray a confidence, but that is something else entirely."

Glinda held her breath. It sounded like a wise and clever answer to her, but whether it would be acceptable to the Queryor, she could not guess. She hazarded a glance at Ben

and Locasta, who looked as anxious as Glinda felt.

The Queryor bobbed his shaggy head, pawed at the green grass with his cat claws, and proclaimed, "You have earned the privilege of asking your question. Do so, Searcher. Do so now."

"Am I Good, or am I Wicked?" she whispered, repeating the question the Queryor had put to her, the one that had gone unanswered on her prior visit. Lifting her chin from the collar of her cloak, she asked again, louder, but with a catch in her voice that made the words sound broken. "AM . . . I . . . WICKED? OR . . . AM . . . I . . . GOOD?"

With ground-shaking authority came the Queryor's unequivocal reply: "You are Good, for surely anyone who cares enough to ask if she is Wicked is, by definition, very Good indeed."

Locasta sprang forward to throw her arms around Shade, who had gone slack with relief. Ben pumped his fist in the air and gave a whoop of unbridled joy.

And Glinda—who was, of course, as happy for Shade as the others—again held her breath.

Because it was her turn to face the Queryor.

And everything . . . *everything* . . . depended on her answer.

Never in her six years at Madam Mentir's did Glinda dread being presented with a question. Today would be different. For no test had ever mattered this much.

Head high, shoulders squared, she made her way toward the Queryor.

"Don't forget to bow," Locasta whispered.

As if Glinda needed to be reminded! Going down on one knee, she reverently dipped her chin to her chest. The beast looked down at her, tilting his massive head this way and that, considering her carefully and thoroughly.

"Here is your challenge," the Queryor said at last, the deep timbre of his voice again causing the ground to shake.

Without any discernable action, word, or even thought from the Queryor, a small, fat-bellied bottle appeared in Glinda's hand.

"You have there in your grasp a measure of water," the Queryor went on. "Your task is to make of it something other than it is, three times over. First, you will fashion fire from water; next you must make lurl from fire, and lastly, air from lurl."

"Lurl?" said Ben. "He means like earth, right?"

Locasta nodded and gave a little snort. "Fire, water, lurl, and air. Is it just me or is anyone else beginning to sense a pattern to this quest?"

"You want me to use water to make fire?" Glinda asked in disbelief. "Do you mean Magically?"

"If that is your choice," the Queryor replied cagily. "I care not how you arrive at success, only that you succeed." With that, the drumming commenced.

Buh-boom . . . boom . . . boom. Buh-boom . . . boom . . . boom . . .

Glinda's stomach turned to knots. How could she make water into fire and fire into dirt without Magic?

Buh-boom . . . boom . . . boom. Buh-boom . . . boom . . . boom . . .

The more the drum sounded, the more blank her mind became. She stared at the plump little flagon in her hand, but could think of no means by which to accomplish what she had been asked to do. She glanced over her shoulder at her friends, whose faces told her nothing. Even Locasta the know-it-all seemed at a loss.

Try something, she told herself. *Anything.* She gave the bottle a shake, which caused the water to spin and slosh inside the pale-green glass, yielding nothing but bubbles. Panic rising, she wriggled the cork and tugged; it gave way with a hollow pop.

Should I taste it? she wondered. Perhaps the Queryor had put a drop of some transformative potion into the water that would give her the Magic to do what was expected of her. As she raised the tiny decanter to her lips, her hands trembled, splashing several drops over the rim. These landed as softly as teardrops in the dust around her knees.

Buh-boom . . . boom . . . boom. Buh-boom . . . boom . . . boom . . .

Glinda looked down and saw that the accidental spill had left a splatter of muddy little dimples in the dirt, slightly darker than the dry patch into which they'd fallen.

Her heart raced as a plan availed itself. Gripping the bottle, she began to carefully pour the water out, creating a damp trail of letters in the dirt. *F...I...R...E.*

When Glinda looked up at the Queryor, she saw that he was pleased. For she had indeed made "fire" out of water. Not literally, of course, but apparently, the *word* fire was enough for the beast. He gave a curt nod, as if encouraging her to continue.

"Now you must turn it into earth," said Ben. "Uh, I mean, to lurl."

Buh-boom...boom...boom...

With every beat of the Queryor's drum, Glinda drew closer to failure. Staring at the word she had written, she noticed that as the seconds pounded by, the letters were beginning to dry back to dust. The "fire" was turning into lurl.

Quickly she brushed the greenish-brown dirt from where the F-I-R-E had disappeared into the palm of her hand. She showed the lurl dust to the Queryor and was again awarded with a nod of approval.

"Water to fire, fire to lurl," Locasta cried. "Two down, one to go."

The steady thumping of the Conundrum faded into the background as Glinda struggled to find a way of turning dirt into air. Heart racing, she studied the tiny mound of dust in her hand and waited for inspiration to strike.

Inspiration. Another word for breath! (This she knew

thanks to high marks in Approved Vocabulary for Girls.) And what was "breath" if not a very special sort of *air*?

Holding her palm close to her chin, Glinda blew upon the dust; her breath carried the tiny particles into the sky, where they caught a breeze and became one with the air.

Air . . . made from lurl, made from fire, made from water.

In that moment, the pounding of the Conundrum ceased. And the beast smiled.

30

ASKED AND ANSWERED

Too numb with relief to stand, Glinda remained on her knees in the dirt.

"You may ask your question," the Queryor said with satisfaction. Glinda realized that he was not only pleased for her success but impressed by her clever solution as well.

"How do I release the Fire Fairy Ember from his hiding place?" she asked.

This too seemed to impress—or at least surprise—the beast. He stared at Glinda for a long moment, his tail flicking with interest.

"Shall I take this to mean that you—a young girl barely out of the schoolroom—have discovered the whereabouts of an Elemental Fairy, one of the greatest mysteries in all of Oz's history? Tell me, how is it that you—?"

Glinda interrupted, wagging her finger at the beast. "Due respect, good Queryor, but you have already asked me your question. The rules of the ritual, as I understand them, are that we each are allotted only one."

At this, the beast threw back his huge horned head and laughed. It was a shrill, goatlike bleating sound, not at all handsome or melodious. But it was genuine. "As I cannot argue with such an indisputable fact as that, I will indeed answer your question."

Again the beast pawed at the ground with his feline feet, as though deciding how best to phrase his response. After what felt like a thousand lifetimes, he spoke the following words:

"You must follow the arc that all heroes tread. But to achieve your goal, you must formally acquaint yourself with she who is your own spirit's likeness, cast in the permanent purity of stone. You will have but one chance to recognize her; if you miss her once, your paths shall never cross again."

"Maybe you should be writing this down," Locasta muttered to Ben. "Something tells me it's gonna be a long one."

Ben quickly reached into his knapsack for the quill and the Makewright's journal to transcribe what the Queryor had said.

"Her name has been laid low," the Queryor continued, "but her strength is Truth Above All, and this cannot be overshadowed. She resides in a castle unbuilt, the very place where your current undertaking was born. So look to the west for a falling star, and you will light upon that which she calls herself. Take all that she has to offer you, and a true friendship will be forged."

Ben hastily scribbled the enigmatic passage into the journal.

"I suppose a straightforward answer would have been too much to hope for," Locasta grumbled.

Ben's quill hovered patiently above the page as he waited to see if the beast would say more. Locasta folded her arms and tapped her toe anxiously. Shade ducked into the collar of her cape and peeked out with dark, eager eyes.

Just when Glinda was sure the beast had told them all he was going to tell, the Queryor again opened his mouth to speak.

But this time, it was not only his voice that filled the air. A borrowed one joined with his in a kind of spoken harmony, as if this second voice were tracing the Queryor's speech with light, outlining his words like an audible halo. It was an extraordinary sensation that Glinda could only liken to the sight of a thundercloud lit around the edges by the slenderest hint of a silver lining.

"*In this life we must play the hand we are dealt,*" the Queryor said in two voices.

So mesmerizing was this Magic that it was a moment before Glinda realized the voice wrapped around the Queryor's was a voice she'd known and trusted long before she'd ever heard the sound of her own.

It was Tilda's voice, speaking in tandem with the wisest creature in all of Oz.

"Some answers can only be found in the shadows."

Glinda would have liked the beast to expound on that, but somehow she knew he would say no more.

Ben closed the journal, and Locasta hurried over to help Glinda to her feet. It wasn't a hug like she'd given Shade, but Glinda decided it was close enough.

As she brushed the dirt from the knees of her breeches, she met the Queryor's quiet gaze and was caught off guard by the sting of tears behind her eyes. This, it seemed, was good-bye.

"It has been a great honor to stand before you," she said, and meant it sincerely. "I thank you most humbly."

The beast's eyes glimmered but he remained silent.

When Glinda turned to follow her friends toward the arch, she was stopped by the serene rumble of the Queryor's voice.

"One moment, if you please."

Turning back, Glinda saw that the beast had set aside the Conundrum.

In the blue-green sky the wind did not whisper, the clouds went still.

With his gentle eyes locked on Glinda's, the Queryor lowered himself to his catlike knees and inclined his tremendous horned head in a most majestic bow.

"Thank *you*, Glinda," he said, with her mother's voice entwined in his. "Thank *you*."

The red road collected them and led them away from the Queryor's lair.

"So first we have to find the place where our 'current undertaking was born,'" Locasta said. "A castle unbuilt."

"How can someone live in a place that isn't built?" Ben wondered aloud.

"On the day the Witches first showed themselves, the king's palace destroyed itself," Glinda reminded them, closing her eyes to picture the scene the steam had revealed. "There was a party taking place. I remember it was in a room with stained-glass windows, and it was filled with elegant people."

"And Fairies," said Ben. "The zoetrope told us that the Fairies were guests of the king."

"The party was at the Reliquary!" Locasta recalled. "Just before the smoke came to ruin the steam, the knight cried out, 'Hide!' Perhaps he was commanding the Elementals to conceal themselves from the danger of the Witches."

"If that's so," said Glinda, "the Reliquary of the demolished castle is also the birthplace of this quest."

"Then that's where we have to go," said Ben. "To the Reliquary at the castle of King Oz."

"The *ruins* of the castle of King Oz," Glinda corrected. "But I don't know where they are."

"There's no shortage of folklore in Gillikin about Oz's castle," said Locasta. "Once I heard some of the older miners whispering that the king had built his castle in the heart of the Centerlands, atop an enormous mountain, and adorned it with emerald stones."

"Similar fables exist in Winkie and Munchkin Countries as well," said Shade. "I've heard a lifetime's worth of stories about the king's broken castle in the very middle of Oz, but close to the sky."

"The middle of Oz and close to the sky sounds like a mountain in the Centerlands to me," said Ben, his feet in the Maker's boots tapping anxiously.

As if to confirm that their theory had merit, the red road began to rapidly unfold toward the midpoint of the Centerlands, where Glinda thought she spied the vague outline of a landform in a shimmering green mist.

They ran the whole way.

Soon they had reached the center of the rolling pasture. Locasta tilted her head upward to study the tall, craggy prominence that loomed above them. "It's a mountain," she remarked.

"Plateau," Glinda corrected, noting the flat top. She

remembered the term from a class called Natural Land-forms and Other Steep Things Girls Should Never Attempt to Climb.

"Well, whatever it is," Locasta said, "it's *big*! How in the name of Oz are we going to get to the top of it?"

Glinda was wondering the very same thing. The plateau's sides were so perfectly vertical as to be perpendicular, so there would be no hope of climbing it.

"I'll fly around the girth of it and see if I can find any manner of ingress," said Feathertop, spreading his wings. Catching the breeze, he set out to circle the enormous mountain. Given the mass of it, several long moments passed before he returned.

"Well?" asked Ben.

The eagle shook his sleek white head. "Nothing. Not even a foothold."

Glinda continued to study the plateau; scaling it would require miles of sturdy rope, not to mention some sort of grappling hook or anchor. She briefly entertained the wild notion of fashioning some sort of makeshift sail or balloon out of Shade's cloak and hoping for a stiff, upward breeze to carry them to the summit. She turned to Ben. "Is there anything in the Makewright's knapsack we can use?"

Ben took a quick inventory. There was a coil of rope that seemed promising at first but on closer inspection proved to be far too short. He flipped through the Maker's journal, but there was no advice that pertained to vertical propulsion.

Finally Ben withdrew the theodolite; the brass gleamed in the sun.

"Is there any way to put that to good use?" Glinda asked.

Ben looked doubtful. "It could help me calculate the angle of an incline," he explained. "If there *was* an incline. But as you can see, this blasted hunk of dirt and stone doesn't have any slope at all." He backed up several yards and lifted the mechanism to his eye, aiming it at the towering flat face of the plateau. Then he gasped and jerked it away, blinking in confusion. With an expression of wonder, he peeped through the lens again.

"Please don't tell me you've discovered yet *another* phantom world through that contraption," asked Feathertop.

"Not a world," said Ben. "A trail. A long, slanting path leading up the side of the plateau!" He let out a triumphant hoot. "I see it as clearly as I saw Oz from Earth. Now all we have to do is walk up the slope to the top."

"You want us to walk up a slope that isn't there?" said Locasta.

"I know I don't often agree with Locasta," said Glinda, squinting in the direction Ben had pointed the instrument. "But I'm afraid I don't see anything either."

"It's there," Ben assured her. "A natural ramp along the eastern-facing side!"

Again he bent his head to the brass gadget and looked

through the eyepiece, opening the small mirror on one side, turning the round plates. "Let me just line up these cross-hairs . . . a quick bit of arithmetic to calculate the angle of the gradient . . . rise over run . . ."

"Surveyor's terminology," Feathertop informed them with a proud bob of his head. "Young Master Clay is quite proficient at his job."

When Ben's face reappeared from behind the theodolite, he was grinning. "This won't be a difficult hike at all! The incline is roughly equivalent to a typical flight of stairs."

"I'm used to climbing stairs that I can actually *see*," Locasta pointed out.

"Then you'll just have to take it on faith," said Glinda decisively. "Faith in the Makewright's Magic. And faith in Young Master Clay."

Beaming, Ben tucked the instrument back into the knapsack and placed his booted foot onto the slope that only he could see.

"All we have to do is walk," he assured them. "The slope will be solid underfoot, I promise." He took a step, then another.

With the third, it was obvious that he was no longer trudging across a grassy flatland. He was rising higher and higher with every stride.

"It looks like he's walking on air!" said Locasta. "Angled air. Slanted air."

The others quickly joined Ben on his steady upward

climb. They saw nothing beneath them but the level ground dropping farther and farther away as they made their way up the invisible path.

"You should see yourselves!" said Feathertop, hovering along beside them. "You appear to be floating. If I didn't know better, I'd think you all had hummingbird's wings."

With every step along the unseen slope, Glinda grew more excited. She was about to see the former home of the King Uniter of Oz.

31

HEARD FROM AGES PAST

It's spectacular," said Glinda, her voice hushed, her eyes wide.

"And . . . spacious," Locasta added.

She was not exaggerating. The ruins of King Oz's castle rambled across the top of the immense plateau for acres and acres and even more acres still. The effect was both grandiose and eerie. It was clear that in its prime the castle had been a vast and handsome edifice boasting grand ballrooms, fanciful breezeways, elegant bedchambers, libraries, sculleries, and more. Glinda understood that it was not merely the gigantic shell of a castle, rather the remains of a marvelous lifestyle upon which she gazed.

Dotting the once-luxurious landscape were portions of half-toppled towers, and walls existing in various degrees— some remained at the heights to which they had originally been built, while others had broken at the halfway mark. Some of these walls still housed leaded windows with deep stone sills—the style of the casings ranged from curved at the top, to gently pointed, to straight and flat but embellished with handsome carvings.

The entire roof of what had been the great hall had long ago collapsed; all that was left of it were its rounded, rib-like rafters, with only the blue of the sky resting upon them. A few of these arced beams were still intact—which is to say they extended all the way from the east wall to the west. But most had split apart at their apex, giving the impression of a chipped-toothed smile. On the floor of the hall lay a scattering of large, leaden roof tiles. Glinda could picture these falling down like rain . . . or tears. In fact, she had seen them falling in the teakettle's tale. She'd watched the stones of the parapets throw themselves down from on high, and she'd seen the heavy wooden doors splinter on their hinges.

Everywhere vines crept, winding around broken banisters and half-smashed corbels; hanging moss made the outer walls look almost furry.

But somehow, to Glinda it still managed to look proud. Proud, but wounded.

"Do you think the entire grounds counts as the place

the quest was born?" Ben wondered. "Or does it have to be the Reliquary, specifically?"

"Reliquary," said Glinda with complete confidence. She doubted the quality of Magic she was seeking would allow for anything less than exactness.

"Let's go," said Locasta.

In a single-file line, they wandered through the bits of castle, seeing stairs that climbed to nowhere (for the second story had fallen all away) and doorways separating rooms that were not there. Floors buckled, mezzanines overlooked nothing but patches of dried grass. Outer balconies hung precariously over terraces and verandas that were hidden beneath crumbling blocks and finely formed cornerstones.

And still, it was beautiful in its disarray.

"There!" cried Shade, pointing.

They all looked and uttered a collective gasp—partly from relief and partly from awe. Because the Reliquary did indeed stand; it was located in the very center of the plateau, which Glinda understood meant that it stood upon the very heart of Oz. It was, shockingly, almost entirely intact, but for a few cracked beams and a gap or two in the gracefully domed roof.

They left Feathertop outside as a lookout and entered the sacred octagonal room through a pillared opening, the place where it had once connected to the castle.

Inside were a number of large stones—brilliant green

emerald, the whitest marble, quartz, obsidian, alabaster, and more. The far wall was dominated by two glass-paned doors, looking out over a western piece of sky. Above these was a half-moon window with the image of a setting sun leaded into it. Four arched windows were cut deep into each of the catty-corner walls, starting at the floor and stretching up to the round dome of the ceiling. These were of the most exquisite stained glass.

"It's all so beautiful," said Glinda, trying to picture it as it had been on that fateful day when the Witches appeared and the Elemental Fairies were dispatched.

"Look," said Locasta, pointing down. "Words."

Embedded in the slate floor was an eclectic mosaic cobbled from pieces of the broken castle—words, spelling out a verse of poetry—mostly obscured by dust and debris.

But Glinda spared it only a glance in favor of focusing on the four towering stained-glass windows—to her amazement, the scenes depicted in them were of the colorfully wrought moments from the king's statue-unveiling party. Her gaze settled on the etched figures of a young couple, a tall knight and his lady.

Her mother!

There was no question that the image was that of a young and lovely Tilda Gavaria. The hazel eyes, the russet-blond hair, the stately carriage and confident uplift of her dainty chin.

Locasta came to stand beside Glinda, her focus going

directly to the knight who stood beside Tilda in the glass. "He looks familiar," she said, squinting. "In fact, he looks . . . exactly like you!"

Glinda had been thinking the same thing herself. She felt a rush of warmth around her heart, because she knew that for the first time in her life, she was looking at an image of her father. In truth, she'd rarely ever thought of him, for he had been gone long before she was old enough to remember. It wasn't that she'd never been curious, but she suspected asking about him would have caused her mother sadness. She knew little of how or under what circumstances he had been taken from them, but she'd always trusted that Tilda would tell her when the time was right for her to know.

And now, here he was, *her father*, immortalized in colored glass.

How right it seemed that her parents had been friends of the king. And how tragic that they'd been there to witness his demise at the hands of the Wicked Witches.

Glinda's chest filled with a deep ache—an ache to which she could not put a name. *Yearning*, perhaps it was, though it was hard to say, since she had never yearned for anything in her life.

Admiring the artistry of the windows, Glinda couldn't help but wonder what words Tilda and her courageous knight had shared during those terrifying moments when Goodness itself was stolen out from under them. She would have given anything—given *everything*—to know.

But how did one overhear a conversation from the past?

And then, as she stared at the first of the four windows, backlit with late-day sunshine, she noticed a twinkling in the knight's eye.

With her next breath, the whole glassy scene began to move in a swirling wash of color and hue. The glass images were coming to life!

"Well, this is something you don't see every day," Locasta quipped.

The party captured in the window was now an animated celebration, fragile and one-dimensional but alive with laughing guests and clinking glasses.

If only I could hear them, Glinda thought as Shade ambled up beside her.

"His voice is deep and has the lilt of another land," whispered Shade. "He is telling her that she is surely the most Magical guest in attendance this night, and he very much wishes to make her acquaintance."

"You can *hear* them?" Locasta asked, amazed. "How?"

"Because she's a Listener," said Glinda. "Her gift makes her sensitive to the things that no one else can hear. She's *eavesdropping* on the party."

"He is introducing himself as the king's Cherished Chancellor, Sir Stanton of Another Place," Shade continued. "A place called Earth!"

Ben's face lit with delight. "Like me," he noted.

Glinda actually swayed on her feet. What a magnificent and wonderful thing to discover! "So . . . my father was . . . *Earthish*?"

"Human," Ben corrected with a grin. "Which means you're part human too."

"Your father must have been brought to Oz by the Wards," said Locasta.

As the sunlight shone against the window glass, the sounds of the party from the past continued to reveal themselves to Shade.

"Now the knight remarks that he was much entertained by the dance Tilda performed earlier in honor of the king. He notes that his favorite part was when she spun on her toes and caused the candles to burn in multicolored flames."

When the first window went still, Glinda thought her heart would break, until Shade stepped to the second one, which was now awakening into motion. The others joined her, and together they watched as Sir Stanton drew Tilda close in his arms and twirled her into a waltz. The chandelier in the stained glass threw amber light upon the sparkling red stone pendant at her throat.

When Shade frowned, Glinda's gut lurched.

"Is it the Witches?" she guessed. "Do you hear the Witches coming?"

"There is a clamoring, yes." Shade was closing her eyes and tilting her ear to the past. "A tumult, an uproar! King

Oz is steady, though, ordering his guests to remain inside while he and his four Regents go outside to confront this uninvited evil."

"So much for the waltz," said Locasta, her voice breaking with grief.

It was of course the moment revealed by the zoetrope. And as much as Glinda did not wish to witness the horror a second time, she still could not bring herself to look away.

The second window stilled and Shade hurried to the third with Glinda, Ben, and Locasta at her heels. Again the glass awoke and they saw King Oz glittering upon it, bedecked in silver armor. The glass party guests turned in the windows to gaze out beyond themselves; their translucent backs were now to Glinda and the others as they watched their king and his vassals stride out to meet the Witches.

"The battle begins," said Shade, but said no more. Glinda understood that she was keeping the worst of what she was hearing to herself—the shrieks of terror, the shouts for help. For a long time Shade just stared and listened. The others watched, but of course they heard nothing.

"The fight is finished," Shade murmured at last. "The Wicked Ones have won, and they are divesting the king of his armor."

They walked slowly to the fourth and final window. In it they saw the castle beginning to crumble, just as it had in the steam's story.

"Now we'll see what happened next," said Ben grimly. "Now we'll see the end."

"That depends on how you define 'end,'" whispered Locasta, placing a hand on Shade's shoulder. "What are they saying now?"

"The Witches are gloating over their stolen silver," Shade reported. "So involved are they in their game that they do not see King Oz's Gifts—four shimmering curlicues of green light—rising from his shadowy form. These Gifts are what they were sent for, but they are too enamored of their silver regalia to notice."

"Sent by whom?" asked Ben.

"A Witch far Wickeder than the other four combined," Shade answered. "She is watching from the shadows, unwilling to show herself. But I can hear the growl of her black heart. She is angry, watching the others fail her, and she vows never to forgive."

But Glinda did not want to hear about growling hearts. She wished only to know what her mother and father were saying. She was about to tell Shade this, when her attention was drawn to the lower left corner of the window. There, amid the glassy swirl of ball gown skirts and polished boots, a tiny form was taking shape. It seemed to be pulling itself from the depths of the glass.

As it grew more defined, Glinda felt a plummeting dread in her belly. The figure was sooty black, with pulsating red eyes.

She knew this creature.

It was the fifth Witch.

And she was appearing in the stained glass to interrupt the lesson Glinda needed so desperately to learn, just as the ink had ended the zoetrope's tale and the smoke had overtaken the steam from the teakettle.

The figure in the glass was growing larger; she was almost the size of the party guests now. And with every increasing inch, as her blackness grew deeper, the jewel tones of the other figures paled, draining away.

One of them—the knight—turned in the glass, his expression wild but determined. Feeling his frantic gaze upon her, Glinda looked up from the fifth Witch and met her father's eyes. Beyond him, through the window and into the past, the Witches were bickering over stolen silver. He opened his mouth to cry out a command.

"Shade, what's happening?" Locasta prompted. "What is he saying?"

Shade's eyes flew open, and in a voice much deeper than her own, she shouted a single word. It was the last word they'd heard in Maud's cottage just before the steam turned evil:

"Hide!"

This directive echoed through the Reliquary like thunder, and the fifth Witch clenched her dark, glassy fists in frustration—because she could not hear the knight's voice, not now and not then!

"Glinda, your father is directing the Elemental Fairies to collect King Oz's Gifts. He is instructing Ember to hide in Tilda's red pendant and directing the others, Ria, Poole, and Terra—" Leaning closer to the window, she strained to hear more of the knight's orders. "I'm sorry. I can't understand what's he's telling the other three. The reveling of the Witches and the shouts of the crowd are drowning out his voice."

Glinda saw that the fifth Witch's eyes were trained on Glinda's father, red and furious, absorbing what was left of his color, stealing away everything that he was.

With a roar that exploded from the deepest part of her heart, Glinda lifted her foot and slammed it into the stained-glass figure of the Witch.

The crash was deafening as the window split into thousands of jagged shards. The noise was amplified by the simultaneous shattering of the other three windows. Ben, Shade, and Locasta jumped back from the shower of glass.

Then, silence.

Five triangular pieces of colorful window glass lay at Glinda's feet, each containing a portion of the fifth Witch, slashed and separated, helplessly caught in two dimensions. With a sigh of great relief, Glinda kicked one of the fragments and sent it skidding across the poetry embedded in the Reliquary floor.

"My father was the one who sent the Elementals into hiding," she rasped, awestruck. "It was Sir Stanton who deemed them the protectors of Oz's four great Gifts."

Shade confirmed this with a nod.

"He *saved* them, Glinda," said Ben. "He saved them *all*. And now you're finishing what your father began."

Glinda felt both humbled and emboldened by this. Sir Stanton of Another Place—her own father—had saved the day that by all accounts should have been beyond saving. He could not defend his beloved liege, but he had succeeded in protecting the king's cherished Gifts, and thus the royal lineage of Oz. And if Glinda could become half the wise warrior her father had been, those Gifts could live on, when the time was right, in the next rightful ruler of Oz: Ozma.

Glinda took a moment to absorb what she had learned, then shook back her red hair that was so much like her mother's and strode to the center of the Reliquary floor. She had spent a gratifying, bittersweet moment in the past, but now it was time to turn her attention to the present.

In order to save the future.

32

THE ARC OF HEROES

Something's missing," said Ben, casting a glance around the Reliquary. "It was different in the glimpse the zoetrope gave us."

"Different?" said Glinda. "In what way?"

"There were statues," Ben explained. "A whole collection of magnificent statues, each carved from a different kind of stone. They were arranged in a semicircle."

Locasta lifted an eyebrow. "You saw *statues*?"

Ben nodded. "Didn't you?"

"No."

"Are you sure?"

"I'm positive!" Locasta scowled. "I would have *remembered* statues. I *hate* statues."

Ben looked bewildered. "Who hates statues? Nobody hates statues."

"*I* hate statues," Locasta assured him.

"Why?"

"I have my reasons."

When she didn't elaborate, Ben gave up and turned to Shade. "Did *you* see the statues?"

Shade shook her head.

"Glinda?"

"I didn't," said Glinda, "but I believe you did. After all, you were able to see the slope when we couldn't."

"I just assumed they were the masterpieces the king had unveiled for his guests. Odd that you wouldn't see them if they were the reason for the party."

"Where were they, these statues?" Glinda asked.

Ben pointed toward the glass doors. "Where those eight chunks of stone are. Although I only remember there being seven statues."

Glinda's eyes went wide as she made the connection. "You said the statues stood in a semicircle?"

"Yes," said Ben.

"Also known as an 'arc.' The Queryor said I was to follow the *arc* that all heroes tread. Aren't statues most often made in the likeness of heroes?"

"Not always," muttered Locasta, without further enlightenment.

"My mother mentioned something called the Arc of Heroes," Glinda recalled excitedly, "when she showed me her Magical deck of cards." She tried to remember the illustrations, and the names of the Fairies and warriors depicted in the deck other than King Oz and the child princess, Ozma. She recalled a Lonely Traveler, with a mischievous expression, a delicate Moon Fairy, and . . .

Just then a single leaf wafted down through a hole in the Reliquary's domed roof and landed softly at Glinda's feet. She picked it up and examined it, turning it over in her hand, marveling at the bright crimson color.

Locasta frowned. "What's she looking at?"

Ben shrugged.

"Don't you see it?" asked Glinda, astonished. "It's a ruby maple leaf." She held it out to Ben.

"I don't see anything," he said.

But Glinda saw it as plainly as she'd seen the deck of cards her mother had thrown into the air. In her mind's eye, she again saw the cards twirling their descent, briefly taking the shape of falling leaves before vanishing into nothingness.

Hadn't the Queryor's long-winded answer to Glinda's question included the phrase, *In this life we must play the hand we are dealt?*

Her mother had said that too.

On a hunch, Glinda held out her hands, palms up and open, ready to accept the Magic. And the Magic did not disappoint.

Eight perfect ruby maple leaves appeared in the air, tumbling downward from the dome of the Reliquary. It was as if her mother had thrown them into the air just seconds, not days before, and Glinda was watching the conclusion of their fall.

And as they fell, they abandoned their leafy shape and crimson color to once again become the beautiful cards Tilda had tossed into oblivion.

When they landed in Glinda's outstretched hands, Locasta's eyes went wide. "Where'd those come from?" she asked.

"You can see them now?"

All three of Glinda's companions nodded.

"What are they?" asked Ben.

"Statues." Glinda held up one of the stunningly illustrated cards, one of the three she had rushed over in her hurry. Glittering letters identified the image as THE TIME-LESS MAGICIAN—a lanky man of indeterminate age with an air of unmatched experience about him, as though he'd traveled farther and wider than anyone else had ever dreamed of going. In the drawing, he pointed skyward with one hand and down to the ground with the other, as if he did not conform to the same boundaries ordinary fairy-folk were forced to obey. Hovering in a twinkling around him were four tools—a Blade, a Scepter, a Chalice, and a Palette.

"My mother showed these to me just before Bog arrived to collect her." Glinda examined a card featuring a slender man in pleated vestments of red, blue, purple, and yellow, with four different faces on his head—one on the front, another on the back, and two more on either side. His title, which was inscribed in letters that rippled just like his colorful robes, was THE PLURAL PRECEPTOR. Glinda showed the card to her friends.

"I've heard of being two-faced," Locasta observed. "But four-faced?"

Ben reached for the next card in the pile. Here was another imposing Fairy called (somewhat extravagantly, Glinda thought) THE UNIVERSAL DOWAGER, ARCHITECT OF WORLDS. Her regal posture gave the impression that she could easily hold said worlds upon her shoulders and not buckle beneath their weight. Shade leaned in to admire the artistry of the drawing before Ben handed it back. Locasta just looked eager to find out what in the world Glinda was getting at.

"I think the statues Ben saw are of the once and future heroes of Oz," she told them, "and the drawings on these cards are meant to represent them. That's why I didn't see them in the scene from the zoetrope. To me, they existed only as I had already seen them—in the form of playing cards, not statues."

"That makes sense," Ben agreed. "Once you've seen something in a certain light, it requires a conscious adjustment of perception to imagine it in any another version of itself."

"So perhaps it's not just what is being perceived but who is doing the perceiving that determines what is seen," said Glinda. "Ben was able to see the statues because he's a sculptor, and always seeking a glimpse of the artistic." She gestured to Locasta. "You didn't see the statues because you were afraid to see them."

"Hey!" Locasta pouted.

"I'm sorry, but it's a fact," said Glinda. "You said so yourself: you hate statues."

"Hatred," Locasta said stiffly, "is not the same as fear."

"I disagree," said Glinda with a solemn shake of her head. "I suspect those two feelings are much more alike than you'd think. But that is a conversation for another time."

Locasta rolled her eyes.

Glinda turned to Shade. "I think the reason the statues weren't visible to you is the same reason you were the only one who could hear the windows."

Shade nodded. "Statues are silent. And I am a Listener. I heard what was meant for me to hear, just as Ben saw what was meant for him to see."

"Exactly," said Glinda with a grin. "I think the Queryor was telling *me* to look to the Arc of Heroes for the answer to my question about Ember because there will be something there that only I can understand."

"Soooo . . . ," said Locasta, "you're expecting to get your answer from a bunch of statues . . . that *aren't even here*?"

"What makes you so sure they aren't here?" said Glinda with a coy smile. "The party was an unveiling, remember? But the zoetrope never told us what was being unveiled. Except for Ben. Ben saw the statues even though we didn't."

"Then where are they?" Locasta asked, motioning around the Reliquary.

"We know the castle destroyed itself to avoid the agony of watching its king's passing," Glinda reasoned. "Perhaps his artwork could not bear to look upon such loss either. What if the statues retreated to a place where they wouldn't have to see?"

Glinda crossed the Reliquary and stopped in front of the largest of the seemingly haphazard stones. It was a vibrant green, flecked with black; it gleamed in the rays of the sun that filtered through the doors behind it.

She crouched down, placed the slender stack of cards on the floor, and flattened her hand upon the top one. Then she swept them into a perfectly arcing fan—just as her mother had done.

"Now what?" Locasta asked.

"Be patient," said Glinda. "I know you like your Magic to happen quickly, but this Magic has art mixed in." Glinda motioned for Ben to join her. "Will you read the cards please? Out loud."

"Me?" Ben blushed, flattered to be trusted with such a noble task. "But I'm not Magical. I'm from New York."

"You are also a sculptor," Glinda reminded him with a knowing smile. "We have stones but are in need of statues. As your wise friend Michael once told you, it is your job as the sculptor to *free* them."

Ben laughed. "Michelangelo. And he isn't exactly a friend of mine."

"Nonetheless, the counting song told us, 'Count by three to set them free,'" Glinda reminded him. "Your arrival made us three, so it only stands to reason that you are here to set the statues free." She pointed to the cards. "Just read the epithets on the cards, and invite the enchantment of this sacred room to guide you."

Ben cleared his throat and read the first inscription aloud. "The King Uniter."

As the words rang through the chamber, a tiny chip appeared in the smoothness of the emerald stone. The chip announced itself with a puff of stone dust, then gave way to a deep crack that became a gouge. Pieces broke away in smooth slivers and splintery fragments, spilling down the sides of the stone like pebbles sliding down a mountain. And precisely as the mysterious Michelangelo had promised, the figure inside the stone began to emerge. Ben was sculpting it, not with a chisel and mallet, but with words.

"It's working!" cried Locasta.

"The Queen Ascending," Ben read from the second

card. And sure enough, the gleaming pink quartz stone beside the emerald one began to chip away at itself from within. Glinda caught a glimpse of a plump cheek and a high, smooth forehead buried in its rosy depths.

"Ozma," she whispered to the princess in the stone, as if she were greeting an old friend.

Ben continued reading the cards, pronouncing every title with the proud resounding eloquence of a seasoned orator: "The Light of Night . . . the Priestess Mysterious . . . the Timeless Magician."

And as he named the stones, their statues began to break their way to the surface. The hunks of granite, marble, and obsidian again revealed from their depths the statues they had once been.

"The Plural Preceptor, the Architect of Worlds, the Lonely Traveler," recited the boy from New York. Faces, torsos, and limbs seemed to climb out of the travertine, alabaster, and limestone. Masterpieces one and all, each sculpture had an aspect all its own—one was a figure poised for battle, another was tranquil in repose, yet another struck a playful pose, while all around them a shimmer of multicolored stone dust billowed and sparkled in the gingery glow of the softening afternoon light.

When the last detail of the eighth statue in the Arc of Heroes had been sculpted, the sweep of cards on the floor vanished.

Ben whirled to face Glinda. "Do you see them now?"

Glinda's smile affirmed it, and he turned to Locasta. "Do you?"

"Oh, yeah," Locasta murmured, taking a cautious step backward, then another. And another. "I see 'em plain as day." Her eyes went to the window, where the sun was slipping lower in the late afternoon sky. "What's left of it, anyway."

The eight stone effigies stood in a gently curved line with their backs to the glass doors, facing the mosaic of poetry embedded in the slate tiles, giving the impression that they were reading the words on the floor.

Glinda felt a thrill remembering what the Queryor had said: one of these magnificent pieces of artwork was a reflection of her own spirit, a kindred being with an essence and a life force that mirrored her own.

But which one?

Despite the distance Locasta had put between herself and the statues, she seemed to sense what Glinda was thinking. "So which one do you think knows the secret to freeing the Fire Fairy?" she asked.

But Glinda was not about to give a hasty answer. These eight figures were the hand that she'd been dealt, and it was time for her to make her wager.

In the entire history of Oz no gamble would ever matter more.

33

SHADOW OF THE SORCERESS

They huddled around the Makewright's notebook to consult the Queryor's answer, which Ben had inscribed there.

Follow the arc that all heroes tread.

To achieve your goal, you must formally acquaint yourself with she who is your own spirit's likeness, cast in the permanent purity of stone.

You will have but one chance to recognize her; if you miss her once, your paths shall never cross again.

Her name has been laid low but her strength is Truth Above All, and this cannot be overshadowed.

She resides in a castle unbuilt, the very place where your current undertaking was born.

Look to the west for a falling star, and you will light upon that which she calls herself.

Take all that she has to offer you, and a true friendship will be forged.

In life we must play the hand we're dealt.

Some answers can only be found in the shadows.

They congratulated themselves on the parts they'd deciphered thus far: they had correctly discerned that the place where their quest had been born was the Reliquary, and from the phrase, *play the hand we're dealt*, Glinda had been able to make the connection between the cards and the arc of heroes.

Ben dipped the quill into the tiny (yet seemingly bottomless) pot of ink he'd toted from the Maker's cabin and crossed out these points.

"I think the most important part is here," he said, pointing to the line that read: *You will have but one chance to recognize her; if you miss her once, your paths shall never cross again.* "It seems to be a warning."

Glinda agreed. "If I approach the wrong statue on my first try, I won't be given a second chance." She looked to the newly carved statues, which were going pearly in the waning sunlight, and she felt a charge of realization. "We can eliminate four possibilities right now!" she said. "The Queryor repeatedly uses 'she' in his answer. So all the male beings can be eliminated."

This immediately took King Oz, the Timeless Magician, the Plural Preceptor, and the Lonely Traveler out of contention, simplifying Glinda's choice by half. As she examined the four female statues, she saw that each pedestal bore not only the title from her card, but her name as well. The Queen Ascending, of course, was Ozma. The Light of Night, as Glinda had recognized upon first seeing the illustration, was Elucida the Moon Fairy. The Priestess Mysterious claimed the name Mythra, while the Universal Dowager, Architect of Worlds, was Lurline. Glinda was suitably impressed, for Lurline was the Queen Fairy who had created Lurlia. That would certainly qualify her as a hero.

Ben tapped the quill against the page and said, "Look. It says you must 'take all that she has to offer you.' But only three of them are holding objects that they could give to you."

This was indeed a sage observation. The statue of Ozma carried a dainty circlet crown, the same headpiece she wore in the illustration on her card. Mythra—whose craggily carved but dignified face indicated her to be the eldest of the heroes—had a sword raised in her marble fist. The detail of the blade's beautifully wrought handle was particularly exquisite, encrusted with faceted jewels that would have

twinkled with color and light had they not, like the priestess herself, been rendered in white marble.

The creamy alabaster figure of Lurline held in one
of her pale hands a wand—or at least Glinda guessed it
was a wand, for what else could the slim baton-like item
be? Around her wrist was looped a wreath of leaves and
boughs, pulled from the endlessness of Nature and fashioned into a perfect infinite circle. Even in the stillness of
alabaster, the dowager exuded a powerful creative force,
for the great purpose of her Magic was to build, to bring
about from nothing everything.

The Light of Night—Elucida—had been cast in gray granite, heavily flecked with gleaming silver mica. This gave the
statue an outward sheen, making her appear as if she were
emanating light from within. But Elucida's hands were empty.
She had nothing to offer . . . not in the literal sense anyway.

Glinda surmised that Elucida was not the statue she was
looking for.

"We're down to three," said Locasta as Ben crossed the
"offer" clue off their list. Then he handed the journal to
Glinda.

Her eyes raked the words, reading and rereading. So
much of so little, it seemed. Words that meant nothing until
you discovered how to hear what they were not saying.

She gave a little jump when Shade appeared from out of
nowhere beside her.

"This," said the dark-eyed girl, her finger tracing one of

the phrases Ben had scribbled: *cast in the permanent purity of stone.*

Glinda raised an eyebrow at her.

"Purity," said Shade, her hand disappearing back beneath her cape. "White."

"She's right!" said Ben. "White is often considered a symbol of purity."

"So that leaves *her* out of the running." Locasta pointed to the statue of Ozma, which was sculpted from pink stone. "With no disrespect to the Ascending Queen, of course. Pink's nice too."

Glad as Glinda was to have narrowed the field by one more, there was a pang of disappointment in learning that Princess Ozma was not the one to whom her spirit was bound. She felt faintly ashamed for even entertaining the notion. It was overreaching to think she might one day walk in the slippers of a queen. And yet deep down she had a powerful feeling that someday she might earn the chance to walk, if not *in* Ozma's shoes, then closely beside her. Proudly, and with great responsibility.

Now Glinda stepped back to observe the two statues carved from white stone—one of pure snowy marble, the other of pale alabaster.

She remembered how, on the playing card, the artist's trick of forced perspective had made the Priestess Mysterious look as though she'd been submerged beneath the papery surface.

But here, in three dimensions, she did not shrink away; rather she stood tall, looming larger than even Lurline, who had been carved in a restful state, reclining. Glinda imagined the Dowager Architect taking a well-deserved moment to catch her breath after the laborious task of inventing the Lurlian world, which her stony eyes seemed to be admiring and adoring even now.

Looking back and forth from statue to statue, Glinda recalled the Queryor's words. "Her strength is Truth *Above All*," she quoted. "The clue says she cannot be *overshadowed*. Do you think that could mean something as simple as we're looking for the tallest one?"

"Seems logical to me," said Ben. "And listen . . ." He read from his notes in the Maker's journal. "'A true friendship will be *forged*.'" He nodded eagerly toward the statue of the priestess. "Look what she has to offer you."

"A sword! Swords are *forged*." Glinda clasped her hands over her heart, which was racing madly. "It has to be her! Mythra, the Priestess Mysterious, is my spirit's likeness!"

A hush settled over the Reliquary as the magnitude of this set in.

"What do you think 'formally acquaint yourself' means?" Locasta wondered.

Ben shrugged. "Maybe it wants Glinda to, you know, introduce herself. To the statue."

Glinda quirked up one eyebrow. "Introduce myself?"

"Formally acquaint," Ben repeated, pointing to his notes

for emphasis. "How else would you interpret it?"

Having no better idea, Glinda sighed and stepped up to the statue of the priestess. Feeling silly, she cleared her throat, curtsied, and said, "It is an honor and a pleasure to meet you, Mysterious Mythra, Hero of Oz. I wish to introduce myself. I am Glinda Gavaria, of Quadling Country, and, it would seem, a kindred spirit."

Glinda's cheeks burned. She knew she looked ridiculous, talking to a statue. But nonetheless, she held her curtsy and waited.

"I don't think it's working," said Ben at last.

"Neither do I." Glinda straightened up. "But how else does one formally acquaint oneself with another?" She felt a surge of dread, because the Queryor had been clear about no second chances.

"I'm not used to making acquaintances," Shade admitted. "But I have seen others do this." Her cloak fluttered back, and Glinda saw that she was extending her right hand.

Extending it for a handshake.

Locasta gasped. "Of course!"

"It has to be," Ben agreed. "It's polite to shake hands with someone when you meet them in a formal setting!"

Filled with hope, Glinda again approached the statue of the Priestess Mysterious.

And reached out her hand.

34

ILLUMINA

The sword came away from Mythra's grasp even before
Glinda touched the cool stone of the statue's hand.

It was the purest of offerings, given and taken in the
same breath. Generosity and gratitude executed in a single
gesture, a promise of hope for the future of Oz, in the form
of a marble sword.

But it was not marble for long. As soon as Glinda's
fingers closed around the handle, the blade turned from
cold white rock to gleaming metal; it was set in a braided
golden hilt, encrusted with colorful gems.

Glinda's mouth dropped open at the sight of that which
had come so easily into her keeping. Turning to her friends,

she whispered, "Do you see the sword in my hand?"

Ben began to reply. He got as far as the "Ind—" in "Indeed," but then said no more.

Similarly, Locasta managed to execute the downward half of a nod, but did not complete the gesture.

Shade may have intended to answer "Yes," but didn't. Or couldn't. She'd just begun to twirl her cape, when the heavy gray fabric ceased its motion mid-sweep and went still. Still as stone.

"Shade?" Glinda prompted. "Ben?" When she got no response, her voice rose to a frantic shout. "*Locasta!*"

But for once, Locasta did not shout back.

She had frozen in place. The girl so filled with fire was chilling away, not so much like a statue of stone as an artifact formed of halted time. Stopped, like a clock.

Beside her, Ben and Shade were in a similar state.

"No!" Glinda cried out to the Magic of the Reliquary. "Please bring them back!"

As she pleaded, she sensed a flicker of movement from one of the statues. A glance at the name on his obsidian pedestal told Glinda that this was Eturnus, the Timeless Magician, who seemed to be awakening from a long but fitful sleep.

He was *alive*!

Glinda stared as Eturnus stepped from his platform to stride toward her. He had a ready smile and a pair of snapping eyes and was dressed in what was surely the strangest

garb Glinda had ever seen. In fact, his apparel was alter-
ing itself even as he walked, tailoring a strange new
ensemble out of the robes that had, just seconds before,
been chiseled in stone. This new clothing was tightly fitted and made of a shining fabric Glinda had never seen
before. Along the sleeves and down the sides of his trousers pulsed slender panels of glowing light—pink, pale
blue, and a vibrant light green!

Before she could ask what he'd done to Ben, Shade, and
Locasta, he shook his head and grinned more broadly, as if
he found the whole situation wildly entertaining.

"Don't worry about them," he said with a careless flick
of his long chin in the direction of Glinda's friends. "They'll
be fine. And I only need a minute of your time."

Glinda was clutching the sword in both hands, gripping
the handle so tightly her knuckles had turned white. "A
minute to do what?" she managed to croak.

"A minute to show you how to operate that incredible
piece of hardware you're now clinging to for dear life," he
explained with a chuckle. "Oh, and by the way, if you're
thinking about using it to run me through, well, I'd strongly
advise against that." He gave a smug little toss of his head.
"I'm basically un-smite-able."

"I have no intention of smiting you! You're a Hero of Oz."

"Wellll," Eturnus drawled out the word and waggled
one hand dubiously, "*that* sort of depends on who you ask.
Not to mention *when* you ask them. That is the trouble

with wandering the coiling caverns of constancy ad infini-tum, ad nauseam, and in perpetuity: you open yourself to a multitude of opinions, based rather unfairly upon the mode of the time in which these opinions are formed. Which is why I have also been accused of being a besotted romantic fool"—here he cast a smitten glance at the Prin-cess Ozma statue—"a mad scientist with a mystical bent, a tragic figure too smart for his own good, a pompous dare-devil, a tortured soul, a brash manipulator of time"—he paused to take a breath—"and last but not least, a royal brat with a disarmingly crooked smile and a charmingly roguish manner."

He finished by demonstrating said smile for Glinda.

"And which of these conflicting opinions is accurate?" she inquired.

"All of them," said Eturnus, unfazed. "I am a skilled and extravagant practitioner of the Magical arts, both good and Wicked, though I only skew Wicked when the situa-tion absolutely calls for it." He wrinkled his nose, shaking his head disdainfully. "Wickedness . . . not really my thing."

Eturnus snapped his fingers, and the four items from his card appeared, hovering in the softly sunlit air around him: a Scepter, a Chalice, a Blade, and a Palette. These he casually began to juggle, as though he were some traveling minstrel, entertaining an audience of little children.

"Now then," said Eturnus, tossing his wares from hand to hand and back again in a graceful four-part loop, "I'm thinking you don't have a whole lot of experience with weaponry, am I right?"

Glinda made to reply, but he cut her off.

"Of course I'm right. Ya know why?" He caught the Chalice, leaving the other three items floating in midair while he spun it on his index finger. "Because I've been here before, many Ages of Oz previous. Previous for me, that is, but currently for you. I've come back expressly to speak to you, in this moment, which of course is the very thing for which I will be famously infamous one day. Actually, at certain points along the ongoing forward pitch of history, I already am."

"Famous?"

"Infamous mostly, but what's a fellow to do?"

Glinda's mind was spinning. The lights on his clothing were making her head throb and her eyes bleary. "I don't understand."

"It's simple, really. I've perfected the Magic that makes time malleable. I've plied it, reformed it for my own purpose, and now I have the power of doubling back, retracing the footsteps of my own life. The point, Glinda, is that I am back to where I've been: not *here* but *now*, in this Age of Oz, and I've come intentionally in the course of *your* magnificent lifetime so that I may once again see you and your Illumina in action."

"My *what*?"

He motioned to the sword. "Illumina. Your weapon. It's . . .

um . . . let me see, how did you describe it to yourself when you first dreamed it up in that pretty little head of yours? Oh, right . . . Illumina is 'a sword of smarts, a blade of brilliance forged of vision without vengeance.'" He gave her a teasing look. "Don't tell me you would have rather had a spadroon?"

The memory came back to her like a thunderbolt. The Mingling in the Woebegone, the Quadling with the spadroon, the Munchkin with the saber. It was there that she'd imagined a weapon exactly as this peculiar man described.

And now—her head turned slowly until she was staring at the sword—here it was! *Illumina*.

Glinda's eyes fluttered, then rolled back. She felt the Reliquary waver and shift as she swayed in her boots and realized that although she wasn't the least bit tired, she was overwhelmed with the need to fall into a deep, sound slumber. And as she slept, the Timeless Magician spoke to her in a voice that was suddenly solemn.

"Do you wish it, Glinda?" he asked. "With all the Magic that is in you, do you wish to forge with the heat of your heart and quench in the cool of your intellect this singular sword of enlightenment, which henceforth will be known and revered as Illumina?"

Her sleepy reply carried the soft sibilance of hot iron being plunged into water: "Yes."

"So shall it be," Eturnus intoned. "Let the alloy from which this blade is born be the steel of your intelligence."

He held out his hand for his Scepter, which fell into his grasp. This he passed first over the sword, then over Glinda's head. "Give to this blade the radiance of your wisdom," he instructed. "Temper it with your own benevolence, so that it will yield to nothing except justice."

From deep within a dream Glinda wholeheartedly offered these gifts to the sword; and in the dream she saw its blade dissolving from solid metal into a dazzling presence of light dancing above the gilded hilt. That which was, was no more; no edge, no point, no substance. What remained was a luster, bright beyond white, pure beyond gold, strong beyond silver. It was so vibrant, so brilliant, that Glinda believed she was holding all the light there ever was, and ever would be, right there in her own two hands. Drinking in the gentle force of its incandescence, she deemed it equal to the glimmer of a trillion moonbeams, and as warm as her mother's smile.

"You are not one to battle in the darkness of ignorance," Eturnus proclaimed. "Knowledge, Glinda, will be your call to arms, and soon all of Oz will look to you for protection. For you are Glinda the Good. And Goodness does not court destruction. Goodness makes of itself a fortress, it readies itself in defense, but it does not march out; it resists the urge to inflict harm, even when harm is sorely warranted. Goodness is vigilant, it is protective, but most of all, it is the light of wisdom that will lead us to right."

"Wisdom and right," Glinda whispered. "When does it all begin?"

"A million years from now," he replied. "Tomorrow. Yesterday. Now."

Glinda frowned, tilting her head, wanting to understand.

"It will happen when it is meant to happen," the Timeless Magician explained. "There is a saying in the future, where I have been: time will tell." Here he laughed his scoundrel's laugh. "It is true, of course. Time is where the answers lay in wait. Some will ambush us, but most will greet us like a pleasant surprise. Time keeps its secrets until we are ready to know them, and that is both the Magic and the authority of Time. It has a hand in everything, no matter how we attempt to twist it to suit our wanting. But here is a lesson for you, one I've learned at great peril: if Time advises patience, then patience you must employ."

He bent down so that they were eye to eye. "One day, Glinda, you will walk beside the one I love, and secure her in her rightful place as ruler of Oz. She is fragile, but she is also boundlessly strong. It will be you who teaches her to keep the promises Time demands of us. And I am grateful to you for that, even now, before you've done it."

With that, Eturnus kicked up his heels and spun, his laughter echoing through the Reliquary as he returned to his pedestal to stand again among the Heroes of Oz.

"What of the Fire Fairy?" Glinda asked eagerly. "Can you tell me how to free Ember from the stone?"

"Time will tell," said Eturnus, the gleam of his clothing fading, his voice softening to a whisper as the obsidian slowly claimed him back to stone. "In its steady passage, it eventually shines its light upon all the answers we seek." He sighed a stony sigh. "Such a shame that so many of us are not looking when it does."

35

TIME TELLS

Glinda felt the pressure of a fingertip against her throat; the slight roughness of the skin told her it belonged to Ben.

"Her heart still beats," he declared, relieved.

"I'm all right," Glinda assured them, slowly lifting her cheek from the cold slate of the floor and blinking at Locasta.

Locasta threw her arms around Glinda and squeezed for all she was worth. "I thought you were gone from us," she whispered in Glinda's ear.

A vision of Locasta looking as stony as a statue had Glinda whispering back, "I thought I'd lost you, too."

"What do you mean?" Locasta cocked an eyebrow. "We were standing right here watching when you collapsed."

Ben helped Glinda to her feet, and the four of them eyed the exquisite weapon in her hand. Metal and gold, studded with jewels.

"It's gorgeous," said Locasta, running her finger along the blade's fuller groove. "If I'd known someone would be presenting you with a sword, I'd have whipped you up a scabbard to go with those trousers."

Shade examined the weighty gold of the handle. "It would bring a fortune on the dark market," she observed, then blushed and lowered her eyes. "I mean, I *imagine* it would. Not that I know anything about that."

Locasta grinned. "Don't apologize for being wily. I like that about you."

Ben, who had turned away from the blade to frown at his notes in the journal, sighed heavily. "I suppose I don't need to point out that we are still no closer to solving the mystery of how to release the Fire Fairy than we were before the sword."

No, he didn't need to point that out. They were all painfully aware.

"Maybe I'm supposed to use the blade to *strike* the pendant," said Glinda, feeling the heft of the weapon in her grasp. "Crack the stone open, or break it to bits."

"And risk slicing the final thought of the king to smithereens in the process?" Locasta said.

She was right; the answer to freeing the Fairy was bound to be more elegant, more *poetic* than simply hacking at the pendant with a blade. Even if that blade were Illumina.

"We can't just give up," Locasta said, beginning to pace. "We have to *do* something."

Glinda glanced at the sword . . . a *sword of smarts*. "Or maybe we just have to wait."

"Wait?" Locasta sounded as though both the word and the concept were completely foreign to her. "Wait for *what*?"

"For Time to tell," she said. "I know that Time has a hand in everything, no matter how we attempt to twist or cajole or even outsmart it. Sometimes it is up to Time to decide, and the difference between one minute and the next can turn out to be the greatest difference of all."

Locasta stopped pacing and looked at Glinda as though she'd just sprouted a tail. "Waiting is the same as doing nothing."

"I don't think it is," said Glinda. "Patience is the most difficult demand Time makes of us, but it's also the one for which it doles out the most significant rewards."

"At home we're taught that patience is a virtue," said Ben, trying to be helpful.

"It's a definite advantage in spying," Shade offered.

"It's *boring*!" Locasta sulked.

"Trust me," said Glinda. "If we just give the world a moment to turn and let Time move at its own pace without trying to hurry it along, something may change in the course of that moment, if only just a little bit, and that something will give us our answer."

"Then we might as well get comfortable." With a loud rush of breath, Locasta dropped to the floor in front of the Arc of Heroes, pointedly propping her chin on her hand. "This is me waiting," she huffed. "Happy?"

Glinda bit back a smile when she saw that Locasta had inadvertently positioned herself between the statues of the now empty-handed Mythra and Queen Lurline. This was precisely where a fiery-spirited rebel like Locasta belonged: flanked by Oz's two greatest examples of wisdom and action.

Slipping the sword into the sash of her tunic, Glinda sat down beside Locasta. Ben sat as well, and Shade leaned against one of the cracked pillars at the entrance to the Reliquary.

To wait.

Several minutes later, Glinda noticed something utterly ordinary. But supremely important! "It's getting dark."

"Yes, that's what happens when the sun sets," Locasta teased. "It's how day turns to night."

"It is, isn't it?" said Glinda. "And in between, the shadows fall."

Ben anxiously handed the journal to Glinda; her eyes pored over the Queryor's clue.

She found the phrase she was looking for and read aloud just as a golden deluge of sunlight came pouring through the curved window above the doors behind the statues. "Look to the west for a falling star! What is the setting sun but a star . . . falling behind the horizon?"

Sure enough, the hazy rays of sunshine were causing the statues to cast long, sooty shadows over the words of the mosaic on the floor.

Glinda quickly reached into her pocket and withdrew the cross-stitch she'd taken from Maud's cottage, the one Maud and Tilda had sewn under the ruby maple so long ago, when the shade of the leaves had fallen over their shoulders and dappled the cloth with patches of sunshine and darkness. Glinda recalled that this had left some of their stitches visible while others were hidden in shadow.

Some answers can only be found in the shadows.

"Look," she said, hastily flattening the sampler on her lap. "The poem in the mosaic on the floor is the same one my mother and Maud embroidered on the sampler."

"How did we miss *that*?" said Ben.

"Well, we've been a little busy," Locasta noted. "And not exactly in the mood for a poetry reading."

Glinda scrambled to her feet, her grasp going to the handle of the sword as if she'd been carrying it all her life. As she ran to the far side of the Reliquary, she noted that with every passing second, the shadows cast by the heroes were shifting and deepening, skittering across the floor to obscure some words of the mosaic, while ignoring others and leaving them visible in scattered patches of light.

She brushed away a coating of dust.

And in the mix of light and shadow, she saw:

A HERO IS HE WHO AS IN A **MYTHRA** LLIES ON FIELDS OF BATTLE

HIS SPIRIT EVER STEADFAST **A SWORD SHE WIELDS**, AND TAKES

THE LO **STONE IN HANDLE** AVES WITH A HEAVY HEART.

SO SOLEMN IS THIS AF **FAIRY** ET REM **EMBER**:

A RIGHTEOUS FIGHT CAN SOON **IGNITE**

TO YIELD THE LIGHT WHEN THOSE

FAR TOO LONG **INDEPENDENT**

AT LAST

UNITE.

Glinda let out a ringing shout of joy, for she understood beyond all doubt—beyond *the shadow* of a doubt, to be exact—that the means by which to release the Fire Fairy was quite literally within her grasp.

Tingling with excitement, she snapped her eyes up from the mosaic to meet the astonished and thrilled gazes of her friends. "Mythra's sword is more than just a gift from her spirit to mine," she told them breathlessly. "It's the key to freeing the Fairy. Not by attacking the stone with it, but by *uniting* the stone with it."

She lifted the sword, cradling the gilt handle in her hands. The jewels of the grip twinkled back at her, as if they

were smiling upon her success. One was a blue sapphire for Munchkin Country, one a yellow topaz for Winkie, and the third a deep violet amethyst for Gillikin.

All that was missing was a red stone for Quadling.

Heart thumping, she angled the sword to examine the pommel—the small knob at the very tip of the handle. As she expected, the pommel contained a tear-shaped indentation, an empty fitting for a missing jewel that was the same size and silhouette as the red beryl pendant in which the Fairy of Fire had so long been concealed.

By now, Ben, Locasta, and Shade had joined Glinda, and she pointed to the depression in the gold. "I must return the stone to the sword," she said. "Like in my mother's song: a perfect fit must be achieved."

As she spoke this phrase, the last shimmer of pinkish sunlight lit the dainty shoulders of the Ozma statue. The power to save her mother had come to her at last, and she knew now what lay ahead:

She must defeat the Witch Aphidina after releasing the Fairy by securing the stone in the pommel of Mythra's sword.

A sword that bore the name *Illumina*.

And in that moment, the Haunting Harvester Witch of the South would meet her doom.

When the others stepped out of the Reliquary and into the dusk, Glinda lingered behind. She wanted to stay just a bit longer in the place where her parents had first met.

Glancing through an empty window frame at the cobalt sky, she caught a glimpse of the newly risen moon, plump-ish and bright against the twilight, though not quite full.

The night the moon had shared her secret with Tilda, she'd graced the Grand Adept with the full beauty of her celestial face. But tonight a sliver of the moon's rounded edge had already slipped ever so slightly into shadow.

Glinda pulled her gaze from the sky to admire the statue of the Moon Fairy in the Arc of Heroes. In it, Elucida's pretty face had been carved in profile, like a cosmic coquette, peek-ing over the shoulder of night to flirt with the world below. As Glinda studied her, Elucida's eye began to twinkle, but not with charm or mirth . . . with warning!

Glinda followed the Fairy's stony gaze across the Reli-quary.

And there in all its dark majesty was the horrible vision from her dream-that-was-not-a-dream; the premonition Elucida had conjured for Tilda on the night before Decla-ration Day had returned.

Where the Reliquary's domed ceiling had been, Glinda now saw the black canopy of some future sky, holding a moon swollen with light. Around it twinkled four celes-tial bodies, to which Glinda could put names. Directly below it loomed the same four ghostly figures she recalled from her own backyard. They were now as they'd been then—surrounding a trio of unwilling participants.

Glinda repeated the words her mother had spoken to the first vision: "Identities." Because she already knew who made up the outer circle, she was careful to aim the spell at the three frightened captives huddled at the center.

Slowly the gloom that cloaked them receded. The first of the three began to shed its shadow, emerging feature by familiar feature, until Glinda's heart clenched in her chest. It was her mother! Tilda was making a shield of herself against the Wicked Magic, defending the smallest captive, who now began to materialize from the dark haze. Green eyes, coppery hair.

Glinda was looking at herself.

Before the third figure could reveal itself, a silver spark burst forth from the future moon in the counterfeit sky, a spark so bright it looked as if light itself were being born. As it had in the earlier vision, it fell slowly from the sky, growing larger in its descent. The shadows of the Witches reached up to seize it.

"Elucida!" Glinda screamed. "Elucida, look out!"

The sound of her voice ruptured the Magic as violently as if she had sliced at it with her sword. With a thunderous clap, the four sinister figures and their three captives exploded in a glare of broken light. The echo of her own voice burned in Glinda's ears.

"What are you yelling about?"

Glinda whirled to see Locasta, standing on the threshold of the Reliquary with Ben and Shade beside her.

"Nothing," said Glinda. Glancing upward, she saw that the domed ceiling had returned and the night sky was once again outside where it belonged.

"It seems the moon will be bright enough to travel by tonight," said Ben.

Glinda's thumb found the empty hollow of the sword's pommel. "Good," she said. "I don't think I'll be able to rest until we've retrieved the red beryl and put that stone in the sword."

"The *stone* in the *sword*," mused Ben. "Where I come from, there is a famous legend about a *sword* in a *stone*." Guiding Glinda out of the Reliquary, he smiled. "I must say, I am finding your adventure to be far more exciting."

36

LILIES

The invisible slope took them down the side of the plateau, and the Road of Red Cobble met them at the bottom. Elucida's gift of moonlight turned the green pastures of the Centerlands a silvery blue.

Shade and Ben walked side by side, while Locasta galloped ahead. Glinda shuffled along behind them, quietly gathering her thoughts.

In the cool of the night, she tried to take comfort in the sounds that days ago would have been strange to her, but were now as familiar as the thrum of her own heartbeat—the soothing swish of Shade's cloak, the muffled thud of Ben's boots, and the haunting-sweet lilt of Locasta's humming.

But the sight of her mother and herself surrounded by the Witches under a future moon was simply too disturbing. The more she thought about it, the more tense she became. She could feel her shoulders tightening, and her mouth turning downward into a scowl.

Glinda was so focused on the vision that she didn't notice Locasta had stopped walking; she crashed right into her, sending her sprawling across the red cobblestones.

"Hey!" said Locasta. "Watch where you're going."

"It's not my fault," Glinda snapped. "You're the one who stopped for no reason at all!"

"I had a reason!" Locasta shot back, scrambling to her feet. "I needed to buckle my boot strap!"

Glinda pushed past her and kept walking.

"The least you can do is apologize!" Locasta shouted, coming up behind her.

Glinda pressed her lips together and said nothing. In her mind, she saw her mother wrapping her arms protectively around her, her eyes wide with terror.

"What is *wrong* with you?" Locasta demanded. "Did you suddenly forget all those fancy manners you learned at Madam Mud Bucket's School for Featherheads?"

"Nothing's wrong with me!" Glinda hurled back. "What's wrong with *you*? Besides *everything*!" The shrieking of the Moon Fairy as she fell into the Witches' grasping hands rang in Glinda's ears.

"Glinda," Locasta said in a warning tone, "I don't know

what happened back there in those ruins, but—"

"That's right, you *don't* know!" Glinda roared. "You don't know anything, except how to roll your eyes and boss people around and cause trouble! You don't even know what *really* happened to your brother, do you? No wonder he ran away!"

Ben let out a low whistle. Shade dipped her chin into the collar of her cape.

Locasta's purple eyes had gone cold. For a long moment they remained locked on Glinda. Then she turned and took off, stomping along the red stones as they hurried to press themselves up from the ground to accommodate her.

The others ran after her. Not until she'd trudged through the tangled underbrush of the border and returned to the outskirts of Quadling Country did they catch up to her. She was curled on a patch of the red road with her face in her hands, her shoulders heaving.

"Locasta," Ben said, "I'm sure Glinda didn't mean to make you cry."

"I'm not crying about what she said," Locasta muttered. "I just . . . I twisted my ankle on a loose stone and it hurts."

But there were no loose stones on the Road of Red Cobble, and everyone knew it.

Shade and Ben turned to Glinda; but she was still so overwhelmed by the vision that even their disappointed faces could not coax an apology out of her. "We'll rest here for the night," she decided coolly. "And take up the journey at daybreak."

Shade sighed and unclasped her cloak, arranging it over Locasta like a blanket. Ben offered her the Makewright's knapsack to use as a pillow.

"You shouldn't have said that," Shade whispered to Glinda, shaking her head.

Glinda frowned. "You don't understand."

"We might have," said Ben. "If you'd just trusted us enough to tell us what was bothering you."

As they settled in for the night, Glinda wondered if she should tell the others what had set her nerves on edge and caused her to behave as she had. She decided against it; the sight of herself and her mother encircled by the Witches would just worry them. There was no point in frightening her friends, when she was already frightened enough for all of them.

She removed her sword from her sash, sticking it upright in the soft dirt, where she could reach it quickly if need be. Feathertop promptly perched atop the handle, tucked his head under his wing, and fell asleep.

Watching the moonlight play upon the jewels of the handle, Glinda imagined the same moon casting pools of silver light upon the Arc of Heroes in the Reliquary.

And on Aphidina, enjoying a luxurious night's sleep under the same moon, dreaming her Wicked dreams.

Dream on, Aphidina, Witch of the South, Glinda thought. *For this night's dream shall be your last.* Then, swallowing her pride, she turned and whispered to Locasta, "Good night."

Locasta grumbled something sharp and angry that Glinda couldn't quite make out; that, she figured, was for the best. Drifting into a fitful sleep, she was unaware of the cobblestones shimmying and dipping beneath her, slipping swiftly and soundlessly away.

When the first rays of sun kissed the horizon pink, Glinda awoke to find Locasta already up and pacing in the dirt.

"Locasta," she ventured softly, "I'm sorry for what I said about Thruff. It was awful of me to—"

"Leave me alone."

"Please, let me explain. I was upset because—"

"I'm not interested in your explanations," Locasta barked, her strides kicking up trails of red dust. "I just want to get this quest over with so I can go home to Gillikin and you can go back to playing with dolls."

Ben sat up, rubbing his eyes. "Are you two arguing already?" he asked through a yawn. "The sun isn't even up yet."

"It's up enough for us to set out," said Locasta. "So let's go. The sooner we get to Quadling to smite the Witch, the sooner I can stop listening to Glinda."

Shade looked as if she might say something to encourage a truce, but the frown on Locasta's face seemed to change her mind.

"Why can't you just accept my apology?" Glinda snarled.

"Why can't you just shut up?" Locasta stamped her foot

and a small cloud of dirt rose up, stinging Glinda's eyes.

"Hey—" she began. And then she realized.

Locasta had stamped her foot in the *dirt*. *Not* on the red road.

Shade noticed it too. "Arguing! It's the arguing!"

"What are you talking about?" asked Locasta, whirling away from Glinda.

"That's the quirk," cried Shade. "The road doesn't want you to quarrel. Whenever you do, it disappears."

Glinda knew that Shade, whose presence made them four—*count by four, at peace once more*—was right. Just as Ben had been the one to set the statues free, Shade had recognized that *peace* would keep the road from vanishing!

Locasta rolled her eyes. "That's the most ridicu—"

Before Locasta could utter another argumentative word, Glinda jumped up to clap a hand over her mouth. Then she looked down at the soil in the hope that the road would return. But where the cobblestones should have been, a manic profusion of flowers was sprouting up around her feet. Large pink-and-white trumpet blossoms were growing quickly enough to reach her knees.

Lilies, she thought, breathing deeply.

"What's with the flowers?" asked Ben, for it seemed as if hundreds more had bloomed in the time it had taken him to ask that question.

"I've never seen lilies grow so quickly," Glinda noted,

removing her hand from Locasta's mouth. "Or so many all in one place. A most unusual type. I never saw their like before, not even in Horticultural Expressionism."

"The last thing I'm in the mood for is a gardening lecture," Locasta huffed, shuffling away from the impromptu flower patch. "Now let's get going."

As Ben shouldered his knapsack, Shade plucked her cloak from the ground and swung it around her shoulders, prepared to march.

But the scent of the unusual blooms was so pleasing that all Glinda wanted to do was revel in it. "What's your hurry?" she asked, rubbing her cheek against the velvety petals. "Let's just linger here for a bit and talk."

Feathertop tilted his white head. "I was under the impression that there was a degree of urgency to this quest."

"There is," said Locasta, frowning. "Now let's move it!"

Glinda ignored her. The lilies had such a friendly look about them, tipping their petals toward her as if they were eager to hear anything she was willing to tell. Bending close to a particularly robust blossom whose leaves trembled with anticipation, she whispered, "Here is a secret for you, lily. I am on my way home to retrieve a very special stone." She twirled the stem between her thumb and forefinger and gave a careless shrug. "It's not quite a jewel, but is priceless nonetheless, for contained in its depths is the Elemental Fairy of Fire!"

"Please come out of there," Shade begged. "Something isn't right about those flowers!" She dipped her chin into her collar. "They remind me of something."

"Of what?" asked Locasta.

"Of *me*!"

"Enough dawdling," squawked Feathertop. "Glinda Gavaria, you have far more important things to do than lounge around in a flower bed. Remember?"

Glinda blinked at the eagle as if she had no idea what he meant. "What could be more important than chatting with these convivial blooms?"

"The quest!" Ben exclaimed. "The Fire Fairy. Aphidina. Your *mother*!"

"Oh, that!" Glinda sighed. "Of course I remember that. In fact, I'm having the most delightful conversation about it with this lily. I was just saying how I needed to fetch the stone from my house in order to—"

The next thing Glinda knew, Locasta had trounced into the flower bed and was hauling her out. She felt as if she were awaking from a dream. "What in the world was I doing sitting there in those flowers?" she asked.

"You were talking to them," Ben informed her. "And what's stranger is I could swear they were listening to you."

With a sigh of relief, Shade pointed down to the fresh length of red road that was erupting from beneath the dirt. "I think this means we should be on our way."

Without another word, they set out on the Road of Red Cobble.

None of them noticed the gust of wind that swept over the lily bed, plucking the pink-and-white petals from their stems and carrying them off to the Witch's castle.

37

HOME AGAIN

The road seemed to be propelling them even more quickly than usual, as if the cobblestones were as keen as Glinda was to see the business with Aphidina successfully concluded.

As they drew closer to the heart of Quadling, they found themselves on the road that wound through the Woebegone Wilderness. Around them the scenery became more scarlet. Even the blue of the sky was streaked with garnet clouds. Soon enough the road would deliver her home to find the red beryl pendant. And then they would confront the Witch.

The Road of Red Cobble brought them to the bustling

main street of the village, the same street Glinda had traveled every day for the past six years on her way to Madam
Mentir's.

Never in trousers, of course, with a sword swinging
from her sash. And never under cover of Magic.

The red road rose ahead and fell behind, winding
through town like a secret whispered in the wind. What an
unsettling sensation it was for Glinda to be crossing paths
with her neighbors, unseen, hearing the fleeting ripple of
their conversations as they went about their midday business thoroughly unaware of her presence.

The shops and houses, with their red-painted shutters
and red-stained porches, stood in their same neat lines
along the streets. The bakery, the potter's studio, and the
grocer's stall looked just as they always had, and on the
corner, Mr. Blauf's Wagon Wheelry smelled, as it ever did,
of fresh sawdust.

At the end of the street loomed the old library, with its
thatched dormers and heavy plank doors, offering only the
books that Aphidina deemed appropriate for Quadling citizens to read. That had not changed; it was just that Glinda
understood it now.

The presence of Aphidina's soldiers and guards milling
around with muskets on their shoulders and broadswords
on their hips was as it ever was—the only difference being
that now they were looking for Glinda.

The road wound them uncomfortably close to one

hideous plant guard with a horrible traplike appendage growing out of its back; this growth consisted of two enormous oval lobes fringed with stiff hairs, hinged at the soldier's spine like a vicious, insatiable mouth.

"The botanists at home call that a Venus flytrap," said Ben, his face wrinkling with revulsion. "Of course at home, they don't walk. Or have faces."

"It's hard to believe we Quadlings thought we'd been spared the tyranny that ruled the other countries of Oz," Glinda said glumly. "Now that I know it was all a lie, I don't know how I didn't see it."

"Well, you were probably too distracted by all those ruffles on your pinafore," Locasta joked. "The important thing is that you know now. And you're taking action."

They tramped on until the bustle of the town gave way to the quieter lanes of the Gavarias' neighborhood; soon the road brought them to the gate at Glinda's front walk. She stood quietly, staring at the splintered planks that remained of the front door.

"Interesting," said Shade.

"What's interesting?" asked Ben.

Shade pointed downward. "Road's still here. It hasn't gone back into the dirt."

"She's right," said Ben. "It usually goes underground the minute it brings us to our destination." He wiggled his toes in the Makewright's boots. "Maybe it thinks we need to be protected a bit longer."

"Protected from what?" asked Locasta. "No one's about. There aren't even any guards posted at Glinda's door."

"Also interesting," Shade murmured. "Maybe best not to go inside."

"I have to find the stone," Glinda pointed out. "So you three wait out here. I'm going in."

As she spoke, the road did something it'd never done before: it began to vibrate beneath Glinda's feet, pulsing, as if in warning.

"Well, that's new," said Ben. "Perhaps you should delay going in until we've considered the situation more closely."

"What's to consider?" Locasta challenged. "Just because Aphidina hasn't posted guards yet doesn't mean she's not planning to. I say she goes in while she still can. I say we all go in!"

"No," said Glinda. "Just me." But when she lifted her foot off the road, the cobblestones pulsed with even greater force.

She drew her foot back sharply, just as three armed soldiers came thundering through the place where the front door once had been. "Plundering is thirsty work," said one, admiring the silver candlesticks in his grasp. One of his fellow guards was clutching Tilda's favorite porcelain teapot like a prize.

The guards stomped down the walk. When they stopped at the gate, one came nose-to-nose with Ben; another was close enough to reach out and pinch Locasta if he could have seen her standing there.

The tallest of the three turned to the one changeling among them, who seemed to be on the verge of transforming into a fat, prickly cactus. His face was the dull green of a desert plant, sprouting sharp yellow spines.

"You stay here," the tall one barked, poking a finger into the changeling's chest.

"Witch's orders," said the third, who had fleshy jowls and a bristle of brassy red hair poking out from the brim of his tricorn hat. "Someone must stay behind and keep watch." He pinched a petal from the cactus flower that was the changeling soldier's ear, and the cactus winced.

"Watch for what?"

"For the Grand Adept's offspring, you stupid succulent," the tall soldier hissed. "A daughter, 'bout this high, red hair, green eyes. Goes by the name of Flindo. Or Plindum."

"Glinda," said the third distastefully.

The cactus soldier turned and clambered back up the walkway to stand guard on the front steps.

The other two marched off in the direction of the tavern.

"That was close," said Ben. "Glinda, are you all right?"

Glinda shook her head. Because the sight of those soldiers in their scarlet coats and shining boots had filled her with a heart-wrenching realization:

It's over.

The thought turned her cold inside. By their own admission, these soldiers had *plundered* the house!

"We've failed," she said, her voice sounding frayed

around the edges. "They must have found the red beryl stone on the floor. Any idiot could have spotted it."

"Maybe not those idiots," Locasta said.

Ben dragged a hand through his hair. "Then we'll just have to find another way to destroy the Witch."

"There *is* no other way!" Glinda exclaimed. "We can't destroy Aphidina without the Fairy. And if we can't destroy Aphidina, we can't save my mother."

She watched the cactus soldier pluck one of the pointy spines that jutted out from his forehead and use it to pick several gnats out of his teeth.

"I'm going inside," Glinda announced. "Even if the stone is gone, I just want to stand in the spot where I last spoke to my mother."

Locasta pointed to the stoop. "I'm sorry, but did the fact that there is a pricker-faced Witch minion standing outside the front door somehow escape your notice?"

Glinda shrugged off that remark and again made to step off the red road.

But Locasta boldly placed herself between Glinda and the gate. "You're not going anywhere."

Glinda let out a growl of frustration and dropped her face into her hands.

That was when she heard a voice, calling out to the soldier.

"Officer," it said, "I require your assistance."

38

THE PROTECTOR OF OZ

Who's *that*?" asked Locasta.

Glinda looked up but was too stunned to answer; she stared at the girl who was rushing across the front yard.

The soldier greeted the girl with a frown so deep it threatened to snap most of the spines on his cheeks. "Good day," he said as formally as a guard with the face of a cactus could manage.

The girl planted her hands on her hips. "I am the Governess Ursie Blauf, presently in the service of the Hitherinyon family, who live just over the next rise. One of my charges—the middle boy, Gertzsplatch—is such a disobedient rascal that he's gone and locked his sisters, the twins, Immavinth and Wurlitzoo, in the root cellar."

"Immavinth and Wurlitzoo?" Locasta echoed, cocking an eyebrow. "She's *got* to be making those up."

"She isn't," said Glinda, bemused. "Although, since it is widely known that Gertzsplatch Hitherinyon is the sweetest child in all of Quadling, and also happens to be half the size of his sisters Imma and Wurli, I suspect that what Ursie *is* making up is this preposterous tale of Gertz holding them prisoner in the root cellar."

Ursie was now tapping the toe of her boot impatiently on the Gavarias' walkway. "I insist, Officer, that you do your duty and come with me to the Hitherinyon homestead *right now* to free those poor frightened little girls from the cellar."

It was clear that the soldier was befuddled over receiving a direct order from this wisp of a Governess. "What if the Sorceress's spawn returns in my absence?" he fretted, glancing left and right, causing his spines to quiver.

"You mean *Glinda*?" Ursie gave a careless wave of her fingertips. "Oh, I wouldn't worry about *her*. She and I were classmates, and I never knew her to be anything but a timid little coward. She'd *never* have the courage to venture back here. And she'd certainly never attempt to storm the castle!"

The soldier looked confused. "Who said anything about storming the castle?"

"Oh, I thought *you'd* mentioned it," was Ursie's off-handed reply. "I thought you pointed out that it would be reckless of Glinda to try such a thing, since Aphidina has posted her most ferocious minions along every available route to the palace grounds, and doubled the number of guards in the watchtower."

"I'm sure the soldier is aware of all that," Locasta observed. "Why is she telling him what he already knows?"

"Because she's not telling *him*," said Glinda, a slow grin curving her lips as understanding dawned. "She's telling *me*. She knows I'm here! She can see us!"

They all watched, astonished, as Ursie gingerly took hold of the guard's prickly arm and guided him to the gate. There she paused, her shining eyes meeting Glinda's.

"Believe me, Officer," said Ursie. "There is no need for you to worry about Glinda. She was never capable of much. In fact, I was forever having to remind her of the simplest little things, like, for instance, the fact that fireflies *love* the taste of roses. Now, come along, sir, as you are duty bound to assist me in this dire emergency!"

With that, Ursie Blauf swept the soldier past Glinda and rushed off toward the Hitherinyon homestead, where Glinda was certain he would find no one locked anywhere. What Ursie would tell him then, Glinda could not imagine, but she was confident her friend would think of something.

The moment the soldier and the Governess had disappeared over the hill, the stones of the red road fell away beneath Glinda's feet.

For the second time, she said, "Wait here."

Then she hurried up the walk.

Silence welcomed her as she slipped through the broken door, like a cruel hostess inviting her in to share the emptiness. There was a chill in the parlor Glinda had never felt before, not even on the frostiest of winter mornings. Gloom touched every corner; she shivered.

In addition to the damage Bog had done, Aphidina's soldiers had given the place a thorough trampling. The spinning wheel was broken into a hundred pieces; the embroidered curtains had been yanked from the shattered windows and now lay bunched on the floor, torn and soiled with muddy red boot prints. Even the crockery mugs from which Glinda and Tilda had sipped their tea on the morning of Declaration Day were crushed to powdery bits. On the floor lay the pewter vase in which her mother had arranged the rosebuds.

Glinda had never felt so wretched in her life.

The Witch had won, of that there was no doubt. In the name of power, Aphidina had taken Glinda's mother and destroyed their home. In the name of Wickedness, she'd gathered the future of Quadling into her frigid hands and crushed it between her bony fingers like so much dried grain. Now all that remained of what the

Foursworn had set in motion eons ago was the dust of a glittering promise.

A promise Glinda Gavaria had not been strong enough to keep.

It's over.

A wail of grief escaped her and an ache settled in her chest, a weight that pressed itself against her heart until her spirit felt too heavy to hold. Staggering to the hearth, she crumpled herself into the only chair that had not been smashed or over-turned. There in the fireplace, amid the cold gray ashes, was her Declaration scroll; the fire must have gone out before it had fully caught. Only the corners were singed.

With a shaking hand, Glinda took the scroll from where it lay across the andirons.

The crackle of the parchment sounded like fireworks in the silent room. She recalled with a wave of humiliation that it had been blank when she'd received it in the Grand Drawing Room, and Madam Mentir had been forced to write a substitute future upon it.

How long ago that seemed now. And how meaningless.

She was about to return it to the ashes when, of its own accord, the scroll unfurled in her hand.

The word SEAMSTRESS (which the headmistress had snapped out as if she'd been handing down a life sentence) was gone. In its place was a phrase written in glittering emerald letters, each as perfectly wrought as if it had been inscribed by Quadling's most talented calligrapher.

Glinda the Good, Protector of Oz

Glinda stared at it. The brilliant green of the inscription was the same color as her eyes, which blinked in disbelief.

She read it again—*Glinda the Good, Protector of Oz*—then, with a shudder, she tossed the scorched scroll back into the damp cinders of the hearth.

"I am no such thing!" she said aloud. "I was entrusted with everything and able to deliver nothing."

She stood on wobbling legs and stumbled toward the door. But in her haste her boot heel caught on the toppled vase and sent her sprawling. Her cheek hit the wooden floor so hard that she was momentarily blinded by the pain.

Blinded . . .

The world spun behind Glinda's eyes. Her cheekbone throbbed and she could already feel the sting of its swelling, but she pushed away her discomfort and focused on the memory that was making itself known.

In it, she saw Bog, pulling the necklace from her throat. She heard him roar and watched him fling the pendant across the room.

The image was so vivid in her mind it was as if it were happening all over again—she saw the pendant flying toward the vase of rosebuds, the chain catching itself on the stem of the one blooming rose in the bouquet.

The rose that had opened in the same moment that Glinda had been given the Gift of her mother's Magic.

In the memory Glinda heard the clattering of the pewter

vase crashing to the floor, spilling water and buds every-where.

And one blossoming rose.

Ignoring the throbbing in her cheek, Glinda lifted her-self to her hands and knees and crawled to the toppled vase. Around it the scattered buds lay dry and shriveled.

All but one.

One bud, fresh and alive. Despite having been deprived of water for three long days, it was alive and ready to burst into bloom, just as plump and as lush as it had been when Tilda had placed it on the Magical trunk.

Glinda felt her heart quicken.

Because this bud had already bloomed once before. Something had caused it to close again.

Ursie's voice suddenly filled Glinda's head: *Fireflies love roses.* Ursie had told the soldier that Glinda could never remember this fact, when in truth it was Ursie who'd always gotten it wrong. This time Ursie had remembered. She'd been giving Glinda a hint. Fire*flies* . . . Fire *Fairy*?

She took the stem between her trembling fingers, ten-derly cradling the fragile bud in her palm.

"Bloom," she whispered.

Like a dancer executing a graceful twirl, the bud began to unfold itself, opening into a ruffle of velvety petals until it had revealed its heart, nestled in which was the red beryl stone, still on its chain.

Safe. Not lost, or stolen or seized by the guards who'd

plundered the house, but shielded inside a Magical flower.

Glinda removed the stone from the blossom and found it warm to the touch. Ember, making his presence known. The sudden sound of her own laughter rang through the house as she gazed down at the treasure in her hand.

"Well, hello again," she said to the pendant.

But it was not the pendant that answered her. It was a voice that came from the kitchen door.

"Hello again yourself."

Glinda whirled to see the soldier closing the back door behind him. In only a few confident strides, he was standing in the parlor beside her.

Unable to speak, she closed her fingers around the red pendant.

And in the next moment found herself wrapped in the comforting arms of Leef Dashingwood.

Glinda stepped into the daylight where Ben and Locasta waited, leaning against the gate. Feathertop sat perched on a fence post.

"You'll never guess who I found," she announced.

Ben looked hopeful. "The Fire—?"

"My old friend, Leef Dashingwood!" said Glinda abruptly, cutting Ben off. "He just came in through the kitchen door." She smiled at Leef, who was exiting the house behind her.

Locasta stiffened and Ben's mouth dropped open at the

sight of Leef gallantly placing the red beryl pendant around Glinda's neck and fastening the clasp.

"Leef has been very worried about me since the . . . *incident*." Glinda's voice was so cheerful she might have been ordering a slice of cardamom cake with orange zest icing—frosted left to right—from the baker's shop.

Locasta planted her hands on her hips. "Would that be the *incident* in which the Wicked Witch sent a stinking splat of swamp scum to drag your mother to the castle dungeon?"

"Yes, that incident," said Glinda.

Leef, who was absently brushing a stray lily petal from the shoulder of his scarlet coat, grinned.

"He had a hunch," Glinda went on, "that I'd be returning from . . . well, from wherever it was I'd run off to in my fear and confusion. As one of Aphidina's most trusted soldiers, he understands how precarious my situation is, so he's offered to arrange an audience with the Witch to plead my mother's case."

"An *audience*?" Locasta spat the word out like it was something with bones in it. "Is that what he's calling it? Because it sounds to me like he's planning to deliver you right into the Harvester's hands like some kind of criminal!"

Glinda was utterly unruffled. "He's going to escort us along the route to the castle, past the doubled guards in the watchtower, through the reinforced gates, and across the moat with its tripled growth of poisonous water hemlock."

She gave Locasta a pointed look. "Isn't that thoughtful of him?"

Locasta's response was silenced when Ben jabbed a quick elbow into her ribs.

"I'd say it's extremely thoughtful," Ben agreed with a smile.

"Then let's get on with it," said Leef, beaming as he gestured to the walkway. "After you, Miss Gavaria. After you."

They made their way along the road that wound through the Woebegone Wilderness toward Aphidina's palace. Soldiers dotted the path, with swords and muskets at the ready. Locasta's glittering purple eyes shot threatening looks.

"I wouldn't provoke them if I were you," said Leef with a chuckle. "These are the fiercest of Aphidina's troops." He turned to cast Glinda a warm look. "By the by, that's quite a fine-looking sword you have there. You've certainly come a long way from the curious schoolgirl who begged to borrow my *Particulars of Pointy Combat* textbook."

Glinda smiled. "Well, it's not really the blade, but the handle that intrigues me."

"Ah, the jewels. Of course. Girls like you do enjoy a shiny bauble."

"Yes," said Glinda, her hand resting on the hilt. "Girls like me."

At last they arrived at the Witch's castle, which was enclosed within an immense wall overhung with masses of tangled vines. On closer inspection, Glinda realized that it was not a wall, rather a squadron of the Witch's homegrown Lurcher monsters, standing shoulder to shoulder with their vine-arms linked together at their twiggy elbows. Sticky green sap dripped from their fangs as they stared down at the new arrivals.

"Looks like they're preparing to do a song-and-dance number," Locasta quipped. But there was a tremor of fear in her tone.

The questing party followed Leef across the moat bridge, and two tall cabbage-leaf gates swung open to allow them entry. As Ben gaped at the agricultural marvel of growing turrets, buttresses, and parapets, he seemed to have trouble keeping the Makewright's boots from beating a quick retreat. "We're going in there?" he asked with a gulp.

"No," said Leef. "The Witch has asked to receive you there." He pointed across the garden to a gravel lane flanked by two lines of towering trees.

Studying the grouping of trees, Glinda was impressed to see that every one was pruned to perfection, and in precise alignment with the one that grew directly across from it. They looked less like trees and more like soldiers mustered for inspection, each a flawless mirror image—branch for branch, leaf for leaf—of the tree that stood opposite. The entrance to the lane was marked by a handsome wrought-iron sign:

THE GRANDE ALLÉE OF SYMMETREES

Glinda frowned, for she'd never heard of such a genus before. However, in A Smattering of Geometry Is More Than Enough for Girls, she had learned that "symmetry" meant "exact correspondence or equal proportion," and the sign, like the trees, reflected that definition. Just as each branch and twig grew in perfect alignment with the one that mirrored it, the sign's letters were all perfectly measured and matched.

And then . . . they weren't.

The questers watched as the tidy, uniform letters began to squirm, bending and twisting from their orderly arrangement into a harsh and irregular pattern of zigzags and curlicues.

"I don't like the looks of that," Ben whispered.

"Neither do I," Locasta snapped. Grabbing Glinda's arm, she hauled her away from the gate.

Leef's hand shot to the dagger at his belt. "Where are you going?"

"Nothing to worry about," Locasta called over her shoulder. "Just a little girl talk between me and my bauble-loving friend here."

Leef let them go but watched with narrowed eyes as Locasta towed Glinda just out of earshot.

"All right, I get that you and soldier boy have a history," Locasta hissed, "but this is a bad idea. He's the enemy. And you've willingly put yourself into his hands!"

"I know that," Glinda whispered. "But look around

you. This place is impenetrable. The only way we could have gotten near the castle would be if they dragged us here in chains, and then, even *with* the Fairy, we'd have been helpless. Leef walking us in like invited guests puts the element of surprise on our side."

"That would be perfect," Locasta retorted, "if we were throwing Aphidina a *birthday party*! But this is a *siege*! And right now our entire army consists of me, you, Ben, and Sh—" Locasta stopped short. "Where's Shade?"

"I don't know. Last time I saw her, she was waiting outside my house with you."

Locasta let out a grunt of frustration. "Some spy! Disappears when we need her most."

Leef cleared his throat, prompting Glinda to speak quickly. "Leef is very ambitious; he would have arrested me if I hadn't gone willingly."

"If that's true, why were you so happy to see him?"

This time Glinda rolled *her* eyes. "Don't you know a charade when you see one? I had to make him believe I was prepared to surrender to Aphidina. Once we're inside, all I have to do is place the stone into the pommel and Aphidina will be vanquished. We can save my mother and—"

"Girls," Leef interrupted, waving them back, "Aphidina doesn't like to be kept waiting."

"Neither do I," said Locasta. "Good work, Gavaria. Now come on! Let's go vanquish ourselves a Wicked Witch!"

39

CONVERSATION OVER

Aphidina had heard nothing from the Krumbic one since her brief and flamboyant appearance three days before.

Ordinarily this would be a source of relief. But Aphidina knew from reports brought by the Listening Lilies that the daughter of Gavaria was fast approaching and the confrontation between herself and the Fire Fairy was imminent.

Shouldn't Mombi be present to see the Harvester best the Elemental in battle? To relish the moment they had so long awaited?

Or, if things got complicated, to lend her terrifically powerful Magic to the fight?

Mombi. An enigma, to be sure. And a mighty one at that.

Strumming her fingers impatiently on the throne's armrest, Aphidina thought back to the day Mombi had led her and the other three into a deep cavity in the Lurlian world, where the waste of the realm's birth had concealed itself for longer than even the seasons themselves could reckon.

The ceremony in which Mombi had anointed them with Wickedness had been harsh and irreversible, and when it was concluded, Aphidina had left her miserably aimless childhood in that hole and begun her Magical initiation at the Krumbic one's filthy hands.

So where was she now? Now, when Aphidina would at last have a chance to prove that she was worthy of Mombi's expectations?

She stood and paced the throne room in long strides; she could think of only three possible places where Mombi might be.

"Daisy, fetch me the speaking things!"

Daisy, with her sweet face and thorny spine, scampered from the chamber and returned soon after, lugging three cages.

One was fashioned of webbed wire and contained a burly spider. One was made of golden bars, and within it a serpent bobbed its head to and fro as if dancing to music only it could hear. The third cage was covered with a flowing scarf of pink silk.

Trailing behind the maidservant on a heavy chain was an ox, broad and shaggy with long, bent horns.

Aphidina stood beside the covered cage and sighed, motioning for Daisy to pull back the scarf. Beneath it was a delicate structure of finely woven twigs. Inside this cage was a bird that looked as if it had been grown from flower seeds, a piece of paradise. The creature boasted a sweep of downy white and yellow tail feathers and a crownlike growth of red plumage adorning its regal head.

When the Witch nodded to the pretty bird, it spoke, loudly and clearly, in Aphidina's own voice. "Marada?" it called. "Daspina. Ava Munch!"

The snake wriggled, the spider skittered, the ox threw back its bulky head and lowed. Clearly, none of the other three Witches wanted to engage in this conference any more than the Harvester did.

"It is Mombi I seek," the bird said for Aphidina, turning its piercing eyes to each of its three companions. "Who among you has seen her recently?"

The spider spoke in Ava's breathy tone, a reply that traveled all the way from Munchkin Country in the East. "She has not paid me any visits of late, I am happy to say."

"Nor me," sang the snake, twisting and darting as Daspina's musical voice filled the chamber. "She dislikes my parties and revels, and therefore keeps her distance."

"I have heard nothing from that Krumbic menace," the ox droned deeply.

Aphidina shuddered, for the ox's voice was Marada's voice, and Marada's voice was the voice she hated most of all. It was a warrior's growl, filled with rusted thoughts of battle and rock-hard cruelty. Glad she was that Marada resided far up in the North of Oz and that Quadling and Gillikin shared no borders.

"Why do you ask?" Daspina said through the snake, her wispy voice hissing between its fangs.

"Because of the Grand Adept and her missing calf, of course," the ox chortled on Marada's behalf. "We have all heard the rumors, Aphidina. Your bounty beast had the Sorceress's child in his grasp and he lost her. And the Fairy as well! Idiot!"

Aphidina could picture Marada in her Silver Gauntlets, clapping her hands with brutal delight. She could see Daspina celebrating in her Silver Shoes, and Ava, a smug smile hidden behind her shining Silver Mask. Collectively, they believed she had already failed.

Well, they believed wrong!

The exquisite bird shook out its feathers in a show of Aphidina's indignation. "As it happens, I have recovered both the child and the Fairy! And you would all do well to remember that three more Elementals remain unaccounted for."

This quieted all but the ox, who snorted mightily, blowing the foul stench of his breath into Aphidina's scowling face.

"Flowers versus Fire," the ox sneered. "Doesn't sound like much of a fight to me."

Aphidina motioned to Daisy, who quickly covered the bird's cage with the silken scarf, striking the spider, the snake, and the ox dumb.

Conversation over, Aphidina told herself, tromping back to her throne.

Without being told to, Daisy removed them from the chamber.

And still no word of Mombi.

So be it. She would face the Fairy alone.

That's what her Magic was for, wasn't it? That's what Wicked was for.

Of course, the Fairy would have the girl—that *Glinda Gavaria*—on his side. But she was only a child. And although Aphidina's childhood had been unspeakably grim and unnaturally brief, she did recall pieces of it, bitter memories that did not include much in the way of strength.

No strength at all, in fact, until Mombi had gotten ahold of her.

This realization comforted her. Glinda was young, and young was akin to weak. And stupid. According to the lilies' report, the empty-headed Glinda had all but surrendered to Leef Dashingwood and was, at that very moment, preparing to deliver the Fairy right into Aphidina's waiting hands.

And Aphidina would be ready.

And she would win.

A moment later she was startled from her thoughts by Daisy's voice. "They have arrived, Your Weediness. The soldier has delivered them to the Grande Allée."

Aphidina gave a curt nod. "Bring the book," she directed. Then she smiled. A pleasant stroll in her favorite lane was just what she needed.

A pleasant stroll and an epic battle.

A battle she had no intention of losing.

After all, she told herself, *this is Quadling. And all is well.*

40

THE STONE IN THE SWORD

They followed Leef into the allée, their boots crunching on the gravel path as they made their way to the midpoint. Glinda stood with Ben and Locasta on either side and Feathertop hovering above. Leef snapped his fingers and two flytrap soldiers crept from opposite sides of the allée to flank the trio.

From the far end of the lane, a willowy figure glided toward them, regal in her gown of pomegranate-colored silk and elegant headdress. Draped over the gown, somewhat incongruously, she wore a vest of Silver Chainmail; Glinda recognized this to be a piece of the armor the Witches had stolen from King Oz, and anger roiled within her.

Behind Aphidina a tiny creature—part girl, part flower—scampered along, toting a heavy book bound in a cover of dried leaves.

As they approached, streamers of sunlight filtered through the Symmetrees, glowing briefly upon the Witch's face, then just as quickly falling to shadow; the effect was that the Witch was somehow walking through both darkness and light at the same time.

The illusion, Glinda thought. *The lie.*

Aphidina halted, leaving several yards of gravel path between herself and those who had come to destroy her. Tilting her chin up and striking a stately pose, the Witch considered her guests, her cold eyes boring first into Locasta. Taking in the riot of purple curls and snapping jewel-toned stare, she gave a disgusted little laugh. "Gillikin filth! How dare you present yourself in my garden? You are a step below manure, in my opinion."

For once, Locasta said nothing.

Next the Witch pointed her nose in Ben's direction and inhaled, her nostrils flaring with distaste. "And you!" she drawled. "An even stranger stranger! Not homegrown, that is certain. I can tell by your stink that you are the harvest of a foreign field. There is no Magic in you at all."

"Better no Magic than Wicked Magic," Ben muttered. The comment earned him a kick from the flytrap posted beside him.

At last, the Harvester turned to Glinda. "So you are the

Sorceress's seedling," she drawled, the mulchy scent of her breath filling the air. "You are not a wholly unimpressive specimen, I must admit; but you are just a tender hothouse blossom. Weak, fragile . . ." As her gaze swept to the red beryl pendant, a smile of pure triumph spread across her face. "And not nearly as clever as you think."

Glinda's stomach lurched.

"You thought you would catch me unawares, didn't you?" Aphidina taunted. "You thought sneaking the Fairy in would give you the advantage and my ignorance would be my undoing." Again her piercing glare went to the stone.

She knows, Glinda thought.

Locasta understood at the same moment. "Now who's got the element of surprise?" she snarled, slicing a sideways look at Glinda.

"Dashingwood!" Aphidina commanded. "You know what to do."

Glinda's hand shot to her throat to protect the red beryl a split second too late. Leef's fist was already there, closing around the stone. The Witch's laughter filled the allée as he ripped the chain from her neck.

"Did you think I would not discover what I needed to know?" Aphidina cackled. "You told the lilies exactly where I could find the stone, and I knew if I sent young Dashingwood to collect you, you'd come willingly. Now it is I who will surprise Ember. And win!"

Frantic, Glinda turned to Leef, sickened by the sight of the precious pendant dangling from his grasp. "Don't do this!" she implored, her voice wild with hope. "Leef, please! Give me the stone."

"Give her the stone!" Locasta echoed through gritted teeth.

Instead Leef reached into his coat and withdrew a perfect pink cherry blossom. This he offered to Glinda.

As he did, it shriveled before her eyes.

Then he marched across the room to stand before the Witch. "Your Mercilessness," he said, presenting the pendant. "As you commanded, the red stone is yours."

"Leef!" cried Glinda, her voice breaking. "No!"

Leef returned to Glinda's side, his face blank and cold. Clutching her arms roughly behind her back, he said, "I hereby arrest you, Glinda Gavaria, in the name of Aphidina, the Haunting Harvester, Queen Witch of the South."

The Witch nodded to her handmaiden. "Daisy, bring me my book."

Scuttling forth, the flower girl held up the tome. Aphidina opened to a blank page, reached into the pocket of her gown, and withdrew a handful of plump black seeds. These she sprinkled over the book, reciting an incantation:

> "Seeds I sow, words I plant,
> To reap the Fairy, I grow a chant."

The Magic took hold and the seeds sprouted into words that ripened into phrases, which became the lines of a Wicked spell.

Holding her hands above the book, palms down, fingers splayed with the chain dangling from them, the Witch read the words the seeds had produced.

> "Element of fire, so long sought
> Release yourself and Oz's thought
> Beryl break so I may claim
> The life of Ember, and douse his flame."

With a hiss, Aphidina dropped the red stone onto the book. Greedily the words loosened themselves from the page and wrapped around it, as if desperate to strangle the Fairy hidden inside. But the stone began to rise up slowly, shirking the wordy tentacles until it dangled in nothingness, rising higher and higher, hovering in the space between the book and Aphidina's grasp.

Glinda went numb. It had never occurred to her that Wicked Magic could drag the Fire Fairy out of hiding. She'd been certain that only the reunion of stone and sword could release him. But it was clear from the way the pendant was now floating in midair that the stone was reacting to Aphidina's spell.

Or was it?

It began as a shimmer; a trembling of the air behind

the Daisy girl. Glinda was sure she was the only one who noticed it—the form taking shape, at first a silhouette that then began to fill itself with presence, substance, not quite color or matter but something more indistinct, like the palest of shadows. Or a patch of shade.

Shade!

She was a flicker at best, a fleeting whisper of herself, standing across from the Witch with her barely visible arms outstretched, her hands poised above the book.

Grasping the stone.

It was not Aphidina's Magic that was acting upon the beryl . . . it was Shade! She was holding the pendant, lifting it with her invisible hands, fooling Aphidina into thinking she had control.

Before Glinda could blink, the shimmer that was Shade vanished. But the stone continued to hover. Aphidina repeated her incantation, unaware that the beryl remained safe in Shade's hands.

Leef looked on with wide eyes, so in awe of his liege's Magic that his grip on Glinda faltered.

With a mighty jerk, she wrenched herself free of him at the same time that Ben surprised the Venus flytrap with a well-landed punch. Then he dove for Leef, tackling him hard.

"Shade! Throw me the stone!" Glinda cried.

At the sound of her name, Shade materialized, startling the Witch, who roared and grabbed for her. Shade tossed the pendant in time, vanishing from view before it even left her hand; Aphidina found herself clutching nothing but air.

Glinda reached out to catch the stone sailing toward her. It danced on the tips of her fingers for one second, then fell to the ground, skipping over the gravel and stopping beside the tussling Ben and Leef.

Aphidina dashed for the stone. Locasta dodged the other befuddled flytrap guard and leaped into her path, only to be slapped away by the Witch as if she were no more than a piece of dandelion fluff. Aphidina stormed on in Glinda's direction.

"Feathertop!" Glinda hollered.

Feathertop swooped down with an ear-piercing cry, his talons outstretched to catch the loose weave of Aphidina's Silver Chainmail. Flapping his wings, he managed to yank the heavy mail vest up over her face.

The Witch shrieked, swinging blindly at the bird with one hand, grasping at the heavy mail with the other.

As Feathertop fought, Glinda lunged for the pendant on the ground. But Leef gave a fearsome grunt and shoved Ben aside, scrambling for the stone just as Glinda's hand was about to wrap around it.

Her gaze met his and she let out a cry of horror. Leef's brown eyes, once so gentle and familiar, were solidifying into lifeless tree knots. His golden hair turned to dead yellow leaves.

Leef lifted his arm—now a thick tree branch—to attack

but stopped mid-punch when a firm kick, seemingly from nowhere, connected with his midsection.

He doubled in half, clutching his gut, unable to breathe.

Above him, Shade materialized once again, her booted foot pressed to his ribs.

Quaking with relief, Glinda again reached for the stone, at the same second that Aphidina's fist connected with the eagle's chest. The bird released the mail, squawking in pain; he fell to the gravel with a sickening *thumppffff*.

Locasta gained her feet and chased after Aphidina, who was again bearing down on Glinda. This time Ben threw himself in front of her, but she pitched him aside and thundered onward.

Glinda drew her sword, slid the red beryl off its chain, then held the stone near the hollow place in the handle. "I call upon the Elemental Fairy of Fire! For Oz! Forever! Truth Above All!"

Heart racing, fingers trembling, she slammed the stone into the pommel and pointed it at the Witch.

41

THE FAIRY AND THE WITCH

The Grande Allée filled with a light beyond light, a brilliance more dazzling than a thousand Lurlian suns. It poured from the red stone and became a whirling twister of radiance, exploding into a column of flame from which burst a colossal fiery physique—brawny torso, powerful arms, sturdy legs . . . and wings!

Ember!

Free from the stone in all his blazing magnificence, the Fairy and the purity of his beauty were in stark contrast to the Witch, whose stunning face was distorted in an expression of rage. The heat of his appearance wilted the flytrap guards instantly.

The Fairy spread his enormous arms; the tips of his fingers touched the rows of trees, scorching them as he speared toward the Witch.

Glinda thought Aphidina might turn and run, but instead the Harvester raised her arms, waving her hands like weeds in the wind and chanting in a guttural tone; the Magic was so intense that the words pulled the Witch into a trance. She now seemed oblivious to the Fire Fairy, singeing the gravel as he sped toward her.

Leef logrolled out of Ember's way just as a massive tree branch swung into the lane, twisting itself into something misshapen and grotesque and blocking the Fairy's path. The tree across from it, no longer its perfect twin, thrust out an even larger branch, which bent itself in the opposite direction, impeding the Elemental Fairy from the other side.

Leaves shook on their stems; thick roots bucked and rumbled in the ground. Aphidina slipped deeper into her trance, letting loose another, eerier string of Wicked words, which had all the trees stretching and contorting across the allée, extending and entwining their limbs until the Fire Fairy was surrounded by a snaggle of gnarled boughs and branches.

And it wasn't just the Fairy the trees were attacking.

Whifffphhh. A limb wound around Ben's leg, knotting itself like a rope.

Whumpfff. Another branch swung out to trip Shade,

who went rolling across the gravel path, bits of rock biting into her cheeks and arms.

Fwwzzzztttt. A springy shoot flicked hard at Locasta's face, and a fat root lurched up from the ground, knocking Glinda off-balance. She leaped over it just in time to avoid being thrown into the trunk across the lane.

"What's happening?" cried Ben.

As the dazed Aphidina rasped on, swaying and gesticulating, Glinda realized that the more disfigured the trees became, the more ferocious their attack. "She's taking away their symmetry. It's not natural for them to be unbalanced! That's what's making them vicious!"

Ember was now completely penned in by the disfigured branches. As the wood and vines grew denser and more contorted around him, he struggled to flare brighter and hotter, his flames licking desperately at their jagged bark. But the fire wouldn't catch.

Glinda, Locasta, Shade, and Ben did their best to elude the branches curling and crooking from every direction. Limbs slithered and slapped; one wrapped around Ben's throat as though to strangle him.

"Glinda! Help!"

Glinda wielded Illumina, hacking at the branch until it gave way. Ben fell to the ground, just as a stubby limb landed a punch to Locasta's jaw and sent her reeling into a thicker one, which encircled her ribs and squeezed.

Again, Glinda swung the sword; with a sharp crack the

bough split. Out of the corner of her eye, she saw Shade sidestep a whipping vine.

"We have to free Ember!" Locasta shouted. "Now! Before the branches smother him."

Gripping the sword handle with both hands, Glinda chopped and sliced at the blockade, but for every bough she destroyed, another one grew to take its place. The Elemental Fairy was suffocating before her eyes.

"Why can't he just burn through the wood?" cried Ben, eyeing the smoldering tangle of limbs and shoots that held the Fairy prisoner.

"He's trying," said Glinda. "It's the Magic of his nemesis he's fighting, and the effort is exhausting him."

"I think you mean *extinguishing* him," Locasta said.

It was true; Ember's frantic efforts to ignite the fresh wood and thriving greenery had caused him to die down considerably. The once gigantic Fairy made of heat and flame was now little more than the size of a cozy hearth fire. And the branches were closing in more tightly.

"I need another blade!" Glinda hollered. "One sword is not enough. We need . . ." She spun around and chopped at a branch that was tangling itself in Shade's hair.

Chop!

"We need . . ." Another spin, a swing, and a *chop*!

"We need an *ax*!" Locasta finished. "*That's* what we need! An ax!"

And as she said the word, the ax appeared.

In the able hands of a boy in blue.

Glinda was so stunned to see him that for a moment, she stopped fighting. The tip of a twig took the opportunity to snap at her forehead, bringing up a welt; she hissed at the pain and carved through the twig with zeal.

"Nick Chopper! How did you get here?"

"I don't rightly know."

"He's here because I summoned him," Locasta snapped. "Didn't you hear me say 'We need an ax'?"

As Glinda swirled the sword behind her back to whack an encroaching branch in two, she caught sight of the Witch, who was far too entranced by her hexing to notice the addition of the Munchkin and his ax.

"What are you waiting for?" said Ben, slamming his boot down on a squirming vine. "You have an ax. Use it!"

When Nick made no move to swing his blade, Glinda recalled with a wave of dread what he'd told her in the prison wagon. "If he uses it to prune the trees, he'll chop himself to pieces. Right?"

Nick shrugged and nodded, helpless.

Helpless, except for the brilliant sword he held.

A sword just like Glinda's; in fact, an exact replica.

She blinked, confused, until she realized that what she was seeing was the reflected image of Illumina in the gleaming tin of Nick's arm.

Just as her mother had been reflected in the surface of the scrying mirror.

Just as each perfect Symmetree reflected the one that stood across from it in the Grande Allée.

"Nick, put down your ax," she directed. "And hold out your hand."

Nick did not question, just did as he was told.

Closing her eyes, Glinda let the memory of her mother's Magic book flood back to her. Seeing the words inscribed on the pages, feeling the soft leather of its cover, she called upon the power of all that ever was or would be written there, and felt the words of an incantation form on her lips:

> *"Blade of brilliance, sword of smarts*
> *Double the strength of these true hearts*
> *Forged of vision, spirit of light,*
> *Be twice yourself for just this fight*
> *Sword Illumina on my command*
> *Place your twin in the Woodman's hand."*

As Glinda squeezed the jeweled handle, the blade began to glow from deep within itself. Rising out of it—as once, long ago, four Gifts had freed themselves from within the king—came a spectral shape, a glittering ghost of a sword, a trembling sweep of light honed to a lethal edge.

"The spirit of the sword," Locasta murmured. "You made it two."

"Now you make it his!" Glinda instructed.

Locasta spread her arms and twirled, just as she had when she'd danced Glinda's tunic into existence; the sword essence mimicked her motion and went spinning across the lane to settle easily in Nick's waiting hands.

With renewed fervor Glinda went after the trees, and Nick followed suit: Glinda chopped through a branch on her side of the lane, and then Nick slashed the corresponding tree on his side of the allée to match it. All angles were precise, all lengths exact. Cropping, slicing, sawing, Glinda wasn't sure if she felt more like an arborist or a mathematician. But it was working!

Again and again, the twin swords whistled through the air. Wood chips flew, and limbs shattered. Branch after branch fell upon the gravel until, finally, every tree was in perfect alignment with the one that stood across from it. Their balance renewed, the violence drained from them like warm sap. The Symmetrees were Symmetrees once more. And the attack on the questing party was over.

But even as the cage of branches fell away, it was plain that the fight had taken much from the Fairy. Glinda saw with alarm that he had been smothered down to the size of a candle flame.

And Aphidina was slowly coming out of her trance.

With a wave of her hand, Glinda called the twin sword back to her; like a streak of lightning it returned to Illumina's core, glowing even more brightly than before, as if it, like Ember, were made of fire.

"Locasta, can you hold off the Witch?"

"Way ahead of you!" Locasta replied, snatching a branch from the ground and gesturing for Shade to do the same, indicating a piece from the tree opposite. When she touched the end of the broken limb to Glinda's sword—*hisssssss*—it lit like a torch. And because Shade was using a piece of its symmetrical counterpart, the branch in *her* grasp did the same.

Both girls ran toward Aphidina, poking the burning branches at her. Leef made a move to assist the Witch, but Ben caught him in a chokehold and pulled him back.

"What do you think of this Gillikin filth now, huh?" Locasta jibed, jabbing the torch at the Witch.

Aphidina shrieked, ducking away from the flames.

Glinda ran to Ember, who was fading to a flicker. With a deep breath, she placed the tip of Illumina into what was left of the Fairy's flame and repeated the word her mother had said just before Locasta had carried Glinda off into the Woebegone:

"Unite!"

Whooooooosssshhhhh. The brilliance of Illumina lent itself to the Fairy, who blazed up into an enormous conflagration. A searing dazzle filled the allée as again he spread his giant wings and charged the Witch, licking toward her like fire on a fuse, his toes leaving a charred trail along the gravel where they brushed against it.

Shade and Locasta jumped out of his path.

"Noooo!" Aphidina shouted, as if such a pathetic command might actually extinguish the very fire that gave birth to fire. "Be gone! Snuff thyself, smother." But the words seemed to melt on her lips, useless against the Fairy's burning might.

The air was nearly too hot to breathe as he closed the space between them.

Closer . . . hotter . . . brighter . . .

The Witch recoiled from her enemy, weeping tears that boiled on her cheeks. "No!" she croaked. *"Noooooo!"* Then she heaved one final piteous sob as Ember enfolded her in his blistering wings and incinerated her in his scathing embrace.

The Witch of the South went silent.

Aphidina, the Haunting Harvester, was no more.

Ash.

That was all that was left of her when Ember opened his wings—a dusting of dull gray ash and the chainmail vest.

When Glinda met the Fairy's gaze, his fiery eyes flared in a way that made her understand he was offering her his thanks.

"We did it," Locasta rasped, her expression a mixture of

disbelief and shock. "We actually vanquished the Witch."

The sword in Glinda's hand was once again a thing of metal and jewels, not fire and light. Slipping it back into her sash, she gazed up at the fiery being hovering in the air before her.

"Is the final thought of King Oz still safe?" she asked him.

In response, Ember raised his flaming hands in front of him and rubbed them together. The friction produced a crackling shower of sparks, which danced and swirled until they had formed the outline of a sphere, a fiery shell. This spun slowly in the air before the Fairy's face.

When Ember closed his eyes, Ben asked in a hushed voice, "What's he doing?"

"I'm not certain," Glinda whispered. "But it looks like . . . he's *thinking*."

Sure enough, another spark—this one shimmering green—appeared within the fire that was the Fairy's forehead.

"Is that what I think it is?" Locasta asked.

Glinda nodded, for it could be nothing other. King Oz's final thought. One of the Gifts that were to be bestowed upon a grieving kingdom by its rightful ruler long ago.

The spark emerged from the Fairy's forehead and entered the spinning sphere, filling it with its emerald light and changing it to a glistening orb.

"Astounding," said Ben.

Ember took the orb gently into his hands and gazed at

it with both affection and pride, for this treasure had been his to guard and protect for almost as long as there had been history.

When he leaned down and offered the orb to Glinda, her eyes went wide. "Oh, I couldn't possibly," she protested, shaking her head. "It's far too precious, and much too important."

Ember smiled and offered the orb again.

"Oh, go ahead," Locasta urged with a grin. "Take it."

"I agree," said Ben with a wink of encouragement. Even Shade nodded.

Glinda cupped her hands to accept the glowing sphere that was King Oz's last thought. It felt vibrant against her skin, alive and tingling, as if it were being thought anew, right there in her presence.

She closed her eyes and saw an image of the good king, lying defeated on the stony ground. Around him, the Wicked Witches celebrated their victory, selfishly helping themselves to his silver armor, unaware that his essence had left his body in the form of four sparkling Gifts, one of which now glowed in Glinda's grasp.

The image vanished from her mind and was instantly replaced by a thought—a thought not born of her own senses, but resonant with the wisdom of a fallen king:

That moment in which all is lost is the same moment in which begins the battle to regain it.

When Glinda opened her eyes, her hands were empty, but the beryl stone in the pommel of the sword had gone from red to bright, glimmering green.

"Thank you," she whispered to Ember, "for sharing the king's last thought. I will never forget it."

The Elemental Fairy inclined his head and vanished in a blaze of fiery light.

As the heat in the allée burned off to warmth, Ben sighed heavily. "Something tells me that after being in Oz, life in New York is going to be awfully dull by comparison."

Glinda laughed, and the joyful sound echoed down the path. Her heart felt indescribably light as she smiled around at her friends. "Let's go find my mother," she said.

"Yes, let's," said Locasta, stomping to where Leef still lay sprawled on the gravel. "Tell us where the Grand Adept is being held," she commanded, her purple eyes boring into his knotty ones as she clutched the Symmetree limb.

Leef was silent.

"You'd better talk, Dashingwood," Locasta warned, twirling the branch she'd used as a torch. "With *this* stick, I only have to hit you *once* . . . but you'll feel it *twice*."

Again, Leef said nothing.

"It's a big place," said Ben, glancing through the trees toward the castle. "It could take hours for us to find her."

To Glinda's surprise, the Daisy girl came forward, stepping over the scattering of Aphidina's ashes.

"The Sorceress, your mother, is being held in the root

dungeons of the palace. I can show you." As Daisy spoke these words, the ridge of thorns that ran the length of her back fell away, leaving only her lovely smooth stem.

"I would be most appreciative," said Glinda.

"Come, then," the flower urged. "We must hurry or else—"

There was a terrible creaking sound. Glinda turned to see that the castle had begun to sway and shudder. And, if she wasn't mistaken, *sink*.

"*Now* what?" groaned Locasta.

"This castle was the greatest symbol of Aphidina's power," said Daisy. "Now that her power has been destroyed, the castle can no longer stand."

Indeed, as they watched from the allée, the Lurlian ground seemed to be sucking the castle back into the depths from which it had grown.

"I have to get inside," said Glinda. "You three, cross the moat and wait on the far side."

"If you think," Locasta began, planting her hands on her hips, "that we came all this way to let *you*—" Another crashing sound from the castle cut her off.

"Just go!" Glinda commanded. "Get off the grounds, now. The whole garden may get pulled under." She took two steps to follow Daisy, then spun back. "And take Leef with you."

"*What?!*" Locasta's eyes nearly popped out of her head. "Not a chance!"

"He used to be my friend. And we can't call ourselves Good, then just leave him here to die!" Glinda shook her head. "That's what Wicked would do."

"She's right," said Ben. "We have to at least try to save him."

"Uh, I don't think that's going to be necessary," said Nick grimly. "Look."

Leef's face had gone completely wooden, and his legs—now curved into spiny roots—were planting themselves deep into the soil.

Glinda felt a choke of sadness that might have turned to a sob if the castle hadn't shuddered again, causing the allée to rumble beneath her boots. "All of you, go! Now!" she directed.

This time Locasta didn't argue.

Ben lifted the wounded Feathertop into his arms as Nick retrieved his ax and Shade scooped up the Silver Chainmail.

And Locasta Norr of Gillikin pulled Glinda in for a powerful hug. "Be careful in there, Glinda the Good. Ours may be a fiery friendship, but something tells me it's meant to last."

Count by two, with hearts so true . . . , thought Glinda, returning the squeeze.

Then Locasta whirled on her heel and sped after the others through the cabbage-leaf gates, which trembled and swung wildly as the wall of Lurchers, too, began to sink.

Daisy grabbed Glinda's hand and tugged. "Hurry!" she said.

And Glinda did.

They were halfway through Aphidina's throne room when the floor cracked and yawned into a wide, sucking gap. Glinda jumped back from the edge just in time and watched with a racing heart as huge chunks of the audience chamber were pulled into it. The Magic of Lurlia seemed determined to reclaim the castle, swallowing it in hungry mouthfuls, as if the world regretted giving it to Aphidina in the first place.

Skirting the sinkhole, Glinda and Daisy ran down a dewy green corridor and through the Hall of Hollyhocks.

"How much farther?"

"The entrance to the dungeon passage is at the far side of the palace," Daisy said. "But it is treacherous and dark in the depths. We won't be able to see without a torch."

"I have something much better than a torch," said Glinda, raising her sword.

She followed Daisy through room after room of the sinking castle until they came to a winding stairway that led downward, branching off in several different directions.

"The castle's roots," Daisy explained as she picked her way along the twisted mass. Glinda was right behind her, holding up the sword; this time, it was not the blade but the handle that pulsed with just enough light to guide them.

Around and above them, the ground continued to shake, loosening the dirt so that it fell away in clods, or showered down like thick red rain. Glinda spit it from her mouth and blinked it out of her eyes as she descended along the jagged pathway. The roots fought bitterly to hold on to the soil, but the suction was formidable.

"There!" called Daisy, pointing with one of her leaves to a gigantic brown cocklebur, lodged in the dirt. It was oval in shape and covered in hooked spines. "Aphidina put them in there."

"Them?" Glinda feared the flower girl had brought her to the wrong place. "I'm only looking for my mother."

But since there was no time to debate, Glinda ran for the burr. "Mother!" she shouted above the swooshing din of the sliding dirt. "If you can hear me, stand back. I'm going to cut you out of there."

She gripped the sword tighter and raised it high above her head.

Just then the root on which she balanced jerked beneath her, throwing her sideways. As she swayed dangerously, the world heaved again, dislodging another surging torrent of dirt.

Glinda felt her heels sliding off the edge of the root.

With dazzling speed, Daisy jumped forward, catching Glinda and pushing her back onto the root, out of the angry path of the underground landslide. Glinda's boots found purchase and she steadied herself, but Daisy had misjudged the force of her leap and tumbled over the edge of the root.

One of her leaves caught hold of a narrow shoot. She clung to it.

"Daisy! Hold on! I'm coming." Slowly Glinda picked her way along the shuddering root toward the brave little blossom dangling above the abyss. She reached for the flower girl, but again the castle shifted overhead, dislodging a fresh stream of dirt.

"Don't let go!" Glinda cried, watching in horror as the shoot in Daisy's leafy grasp began to tear away from the root.

"It's all right," said Daisy, her sweet voice filled with conviction even as her grasp faltered. "I was sown from Wicked Magic, but a daisy's spirit is perennial. I will spring up again, and this time I will grow Good. Look for me, Glinda, when next the shoots awaken. Thanks to you, it will be a gentler Quadling then. Now you must go back and save your mother! For Oz."

"Daisy . . . !" Glinda reached again.

But it was too late. With a horrendous ripping noise the shoot tore away.

And the Daisy girl disappeared in the deluge of dirt.

Glinda tamped down the shriek that threatened to escape from her throat and made her way back to the cocklebur cell. Again she raised the sword and brought it down upon the prickly prison, slitting it cleanly down the middle.

A sprinkle of giant seeds spilled from it.

And two beloved faces looked out at her.

She would have collapsed in tears of joy if the root hadn't shuddered again. Without a second to waste, she helped her mother and Clumsy Bear out of the burr.

Clumsy had the hardest time of it, but they managed to climb their way upward through the dirt slide, barreling through the remains of the sinking palace.

Ahead, Glinda could see daylight through the archway that was the castle's entrance. The bridge was in sight. She grabbed her mother by the elbow and sped toward it, with Clumsy loping along behind.

Glinda's boots hit the bridge just as it broke away from the castle. She could feel the great force of the suction behind her, but they ran harder and kept running until they reached solid ground.

There Glinda turned back to watch as the castle sank away, disappearing into the rich red soil of Quadling. An enormous cloud of crimson dust billowed around Glinda, Tilda, and the bear, rising into the sky, rolling toward the Perilous Pasture and the village beyond.

It was through this haze that Glinda saw her friends.

Safe, and eagerly awaiting her return.

"Thank Oz," she whispered. "They made it."

42

FOR OZ, FOREVER!

"They made it!" Ben cried as Glinda, Clumsy, and Tilda joined them safely at the far end of the bridge.

"Thank you all for your part in this courageous rescue," said Tilda, her eyes shining with emotion as she patted Clumsy's silky fur. "That includes you, of course, good bear."

"Yooboo arb wubellcum," Clumsy rumbled.

"Grand Adept," said Locasta, bowing deeply, "I am so glad to see you safe. My name is Locasta, of Gillikin. My father, Norr, spoke of you with great affection and regard."

"The regard was mutual," said Tilda, pushing a stray purple curl from Locasta's forehead.

Glinda nearly fell over when Locasta blushed. "Mother, I'd like to introduce Benjamin, Shade, and Nick Chopper. Oh, and the one with the wings, he's Feathertop."

The eagle, who had by now fully recovered from his altercation with the Witch, preened.

Tilda curtsied to her rescuers; when her twinkling eyes fell upon Ben, she remarked, "You have quite a familiar way about you. Have we met before?"

"No, mistress," said the boy from New York. "But I, like Sir Stanton before me, hail from Another Place."

At the sound of her husband's name, Tilda's eyes welled with tears. "Ah! Well, that explains it, doesn't it?"

Tilda reached out a gentle hand to touch Shade's cheek, then smoothed Glinda's red hair, sighing with tranquil delight. "Look how young our future is!" she said, her eyes shining. "All promise and energy. Youth is a kind of Magic, for it is the most wondrous harbinger of progress and change. And hope."

Glinda noticed that a crowd was fast approaching. The noisy destruction of the castle must have alerted the townsfolk. They were hurrying toward the once-forbidden grounds of the Witch's palace, pointing and whispering, curious and confused. More troubling was the sight of several battalions of Aphidina's soldiers, marching forth from their barracks in town.

Instinctively, Glinda positioned herself between her mother and the troops.

"It's all right," Tilda said.

"But Mother . . ."

"Watch, darling. And trust."

To Glinda's shock, when the soldiers reached them, every last one went down on a knee (or stump, or root, depending) in thanks to those who had vanquished the Witch.

Ben was the first to recognize this. "They're honoring *us*!"

"As well they should," said Tilda.

"But they were so loyal to Aphidina," Locasta pointed out.

"Loyal is not the same as bound," said Tilda, indicating the rusted manacles encircling Locasta's wrists. Then she waved her hand over the shackles and whispered, "Golden, please."

With a jangle and a puff of gilded smoke, the hideous iron manacles turned into beautiful gold bangles.

Locasta gasped, but Tilda went on speaking as if nothing even remotely extraordinary had occurred. "These soldiers had Aphidina's Wickedness thrust upon them; they did not choose it for themselves. Those who were naturally inclined to darkness will have likely already scuttled over the borders into Winkie, Munchkin, and Gillikin," she predicted, "to hide among the evil that dwells there. But these soldiers before us now are genuinely grateful for your courage, and they are placing themselves willingly in our command."

Now she turned her attention to the restless crowd.

"Good fairyfolk of Quadling Country! Today we find ourselves liberated from the Wicked Witch of the South."

A murmur of amazement rippled through the assembly.

"This glorious victory is a great stride toward our noble goal of restoring a rightful ruler to the throne of Oz. This goal has long been a secret, wrapped in a wish and nurtured by a dream. But today, my friends, it has matured into something even more powerful—a *promise*. A promise that Wickedness shall never again prevail."

The clear confidence of her mother's voice, and the beauty of her words, had Glinda tingling with pride.

"But since it is my firm belief that until *every* Ozian is free, *none* of us are, we must prepare to fight. In the days ahead, we will join with Winkies in the West to topple the regime of Daspina, we will band with the Munchkins in the East to bring down the vicious reign of Ava Munch, and we will wage war beside the Gillikins in the North against the brutality of the Warrior Marada!"

Applause thundered from the crowd, as Tilda drew Glinda to her side.

"To lead us in these worthy pursuits, I present to you my daughter—Glinda the Good, Protector of Oz."

A rousing cheer rose up among the spectators. "All hail Glinda, Protector of Oz!"

Glinda drew her sword and held it aloft; it glowed in the last rays of the late-day sun. "For Oz, forever!" she cried out.

"For Oz, forever," the crowd erupted.

"Return to your homes now," Tilda concluded, "to make ready for that which will come. None of it will be easy, my friends, but all of it will be right!"

When the crowd had dispersed, Glinda spied a familiar buckling in the ground; she smiled as the Road of Red Cobble appeared, and on it stood Miss Gage, who swept Glinda into her arms and spun her around. "You've done it! I knew you would."

On the road behind Gage stood three distinguished-looking beings—a Winkie, a Munchkin, and a Gillikin. They all stepped forward and bowed to Glinda's mother.

"My fellow Grand Adepts," said Tilda. "It is a pleasure to see you again."

"If I may, Grand Adept Tilda," said the Winkie, tossing back his short yellow shawl, his fingers going briefly to the handkerchief that peeked out of his breast pocket. "Can you tell us what has become of the Gift that was entrusted to Ember? Was it safely recovered?"

"Indeed it was, Dallybrungston," Tilda replied.

Glinda held out the sword and pointed to the green stone in the pommel.

"Excellent," said the Munchkin delegate, doffing her blue bonnet. "And now that Aphidina has been undone, there is no longer any need to keep King Oz's final thought hidden."

The other Adepts responded excitedly, chiming their agreement.

Turning his purple eyes to Glinda, the Gillikin Adept gave a solemn nod. "And so it falls to you to commend the king's last thought to time and space."

"Where it will remain until Ozma's return," Dally-brungston added.

Locasta frowned. "But if we release the thought into the atmosphere, won't we be endangering it all over again? Won't that be undoing everything the Foursworn have done to protect it all this time?"

Tilda smiled and shook her head. "Until today, that would have the case, but you and your friends have brought about great change."

"Before the Wickeds attacked," Dallybrungston explained, "the Elemental Fairies roamed free. They had no enemies, and no fear, for who could ever dream to harm that which is responsible for bringing about the world in which we live?"

"Now that Ember has destroyed Aphidina, he can once again enjoy the right and luxury of freedom. He will have the power to watch over and protect the thought wherever it may be, which is everywhere."

Glinda was relieved to hear this. "How do I release the thought?" she asked, hoping there wouldn't be another grueling series of puzzles to solve. Right now, all she wanted was to go home and share a cup of tea with her mother.

And a popover, perhaps. A popover would be nice.

Gage draped an arm around Glinda's shoulders. "How do you release any thought into the world?"

"You think it?"

"Exactly," said Tilda. "You think it."

"Can you think it out loud?" Locasta suggested. "I just risked my life to save this particular thought, and I'd really like to know what it is."

"I believe we all would," said Dallybrungston, grinning.

So Glinda placed her hand upon the green stone and spoke King Oz's final thought aloud: "That moment in which all is lost is the same moment in which begins the battle to regain it."

Gage wiped a tear from the corner of her eye and nodded.

The Winkie murmured, "So true. So wise and so true."

When Glinda lifted her hand, the stone was as clear as a diamond, and into the sky trillions of tiny green orbs were rising. Higher and higher, like fireflies at play. The awed little gathering watched until the flickering lights had all disappeared from sight.

"I thought it was only one thought," said Glinda.

"One thought can become a million thoughts," said Tilda sagely, "when it is shared with the world and embraced by the like-minded."

"Certainly encourages one to think carefully, doesn't it?" said Gage with a hint of a teacherly smile.

"But what did it mean?" asked Ben. "What the king thought?"

"I think," said Glinda, "it meant that when something you cherish is taken from you, you mustn't let even the space of a moment go by before you begin the fight to get it back. Even if the beginning of that fight is just waiting and planning until the time is right to fight in earnest."

"In other words," said Locasta, "be vigilant, be ready, and never give up."

"Well said!" exclaimed the Munchkin Grand Adept, returning her bonnet to her head. "Well said indeed. Now then, shall we be off?"

"Yes," said Dallybrungston, adjusting his shawl. "There are Minglings to arrange and spells to write and all manner of rebellions to attend to and revise, now that Glinda has defeated the first Witch. Magic may be patient, but let us not keep it waiting overlong!"

"Good luck," said Locasta.

"And to you as well," said the Gillikin, whose wrists, like Locasta's had been, were encircled in rusted iron. "One day all of us in the North will cast off Marada's chains," he predicted. "Perhaps sooner than you think!"

With that, the three delegates turned on the Road of Red Cobble and headed back in the direction from which they had come.

Glinda watched until they rounded a bend and disappeared from sight. Happy and exhausted, she sighed, slipped her hand into her mother's, and said, "Let's go home."

43

TWO WINGS THAT FLAP

It had been ages, perhaps even longer, since there had been such a hullabaloo in the palace Reliquary.

But of course the little monkey could not have known that.

He had been swinging contentedly from a rafter of the ruins when he heard the commotion. It had begun with excited voices and breaking glass and was followed by the sound of crumbling stones and a beautiful swelling of light.

From a safe distance, he'd watched with bright, inquisitive eyes, his tail twitching, the fur around his young face standing on end from the thrill of such activity.

And when it was over, when they were all gone, he crept over to investigate.

Statues! Eight of them, and all perfect for climbing. Chattering with glee, he scaled first one, then another, his narrow fingers gripping at shoulder blades and collarbones and corners of armor where none had been before. They felt heroic underfoot as he danced upon their heads and slid down their smooth backs.

On the Reliquary floor, he scampered across a mosaic of poetry, being careful not to cut his tender small feet on the slivers of colorful window glass that littered the place.

Five shards in particular caught his notice. These he approached eagerly, tilting his head this way and that at the dark smudges contained within them. He touched one with the wrinkled tip of his tiny finger and spun it. He took up a second and placed it beside the first, just so.

A puzzle!

Whooping happily, he slid a third piece into place below the first. The fourth he had to rotate in several directions before he could make it fit.

The final shard frightened him a bit. It was dominated by two red circles. To the monkey, these looked like hateful eyes glaring out at him from the lifeless glass.

But he was not the sort to give up on a task, especially one so entertaining as this. So he used the tip of his lithe tail to push the last piece into the spot where it belonged.

Pleased with himself, he blinked at the form he'd so cleverly assembled, wondering what it was.

As he studied his work, the glass pieces melted into a pool of slick liquid, smoldering with thick black smoke that molded itself into a dark shape. Tall, slender, confident. A Witch! Her eyes were the worst of it. They burned down at the monkey, and a voice as sharp as shattered glass said, "You saved me, tiny beast."

The monkey let out a shrill squeal, frantically shaking his little head. He did not want credit for accidentally restoring this shadowy presence.

As if to reward him, the figure reached down and used her smoky fingers to inflict a violent pinch upon his back. He yelped at the pain.

"Oh little thing of tail and fur
Be no longer that which once you were!
To you I tip a Golden Cap
And here shall spring two wings that flap."

The Monkey looked over his shoulder and saw two pointed, bonelike nubs pushing through the silver-blond silk of his fur. As he watched, the gnarled nubs expanded into wing-shaped skeletons, which covered themselves first with a film of Magical flesh, then layers and layers of iridescent feathers.

His little monkey heart sank in his chest and he placed

his tiny face in his hands, for she'd done the worst she could do—she'd made him one of *them*.

Already the wings were flapping of their own accord, stirring up a small wind at the Witch's feet. Satisfied with her work, she turned to look out over the Centerlands, the red sores of her eyes sweeping the skyline to the south.

The monkey looked too, and saw the great cloud of dust that billowed up from the land there. An explosion of dirt! Leafy debris, twigs, petals, and roots tumbled within it. And although the monkey was young and untaught, he understood this much: something had come to an end.

Something in the South was over and gone.

If the Reliquary windows had not already been broken, the roar that ripped from the throat of the window-turned-to-Witch surely would have shattered them.

The monkey cocked his head in the breeze of his own wings, his eyes asking why she was so distraught.

"Because I can feel the absence of the Harvester from here," she growled. "Engulfed in flames, that was the last sensation she knew. Do you feel it, monkey?"

The monkey, who was beginning to admire the harsh beauty of his new appendages, *did* feel it—fire and loss. He gave a shriek—*eeet-eeet-eeeeet, ooo, ooo, oooooot*—hoping his tone matched the fury of hers.

"See how the land of Quadling shines now," she snarled, "there in the far-off and away? That is the glow of Goodness! That is the light of victory."

The monkey shook his head in disgust, loving his wings and hating the Good. He stamped his minuscule feet on the stony floor and wailed, joining his screeching voice with hers as together they watched the dust settle.

Then, to his surprise, the horizon glowed green and the distance danced with the glimmer of a thousand emerald orbs.

The Witch stretched her arms southward, reaching helplessly as if to snatch the bubbles of gleam right out of the sky. "One Gift!" she lamented. "Free and safe!"

The monkey did not know at all what she was referring to, but his wings made him feel reckless and strong—and a touch Wicked. He wanted only to assist her. Mombi, that was her name; he knew it now, for suddenly he could sense the power of it. Hopping up and down, he tugged at the smoky drape of her black robe, his eyes imploring her to allow him to help.

She scooped him up and, with cold fingers, pinched the tips of his wings.

"For this deed
You'll need great speed.
To North, West, East
Fly, tiny beast!
Tell the Wickeds what they must know
To see for themselves to the South they'll go!"

When she flung him to the ground, the monkey took off like a shot, his skinny legs pumping into a run, his untried wings beating madly, lifting him off the ground only to plummet down again and land hard on his face.

Undaunted, he again darted across the floor of the Reliquary, his scrawny feet scraping over the mosaic poem. This time the air rushed under him, and his wings knew what to do with it. He sailed upward, somersaulting once but shaking off the dizziness.

This was a mission of great darkness and immense cruelty, and the young monkey knew it. But her Magic had given him wings and made him immune to caring.

To North, West, East! He would deliver her message.

And she, alone in the ruins, surrounded by the echoes of Goodness and of her own ancient attack, would wait.

With her eyes on the sky.

44

YELLOW BRICKS

Tilda gave Glinda's hand a squeeze. Then she let go. "Glinda, my darling, I cannot come home. Not now."

Glinda lowered her brows. "Yes, you can. Of course you can."

"No," said Tilda, shaking her head. "I can't."

"But Mother . . ." A tightness swelled in Glinda's chest. "I worked so hard!"

"And I could not be more thankful or more proud. You've found loyal and capable friends to assist you, and you have taken my cause—the cause of the Foursworn—into your heart as your own. You found out for yourself that the only path worth following is the path to Truth

Above All. But I must leave you here. Not forever, just for now. You have a very specific path to follow now. As do I."

Glinda threw her arms around her mother's waist and held her tight. She knew it was a childish action, but she did not care; she would allow herself this brief moment of childishness, since she doubted the chance to be childlike would ever come again.

"Where will you go?" she whispered into Tilda's shoulder.

"I will follow the Road of Yellow Brick," she whispered back. "It is the road of discovery, and that is what my first task must be—to discover the identity of the fifth Witch. She is the most vile and dangerous of them all."

Glinda knew her mother was right. There was no question in her mind that the evil of this elusive being transcended the Wickedness of the other four combined.

"Nick Chopper," said Tilda. "You seem to be a lad with much still to discover. I invite you to join me on the yellow road. It will require great daring and fortitude." Her eyes sparkled as she studied him. "Do you think you have the heart for it?"

"Oh, I most certainly do!" said Nick, hoisting his ax onto his shoulder and giving it a twirl. "Heart is the thing I have most."

Pulling back from the hug to look up into her mother's serene face, Glinda tamped down the ache in her own heart to ask, "What am I to do while you are gone?"

"You will ensure that the momentum we've gained is

not lost," said Tilda, bending to press a kiss to Glinda's forehead, then kissing Shade, Ben, and finally Locasta on their foreheads as well.

Absently, Locasta reached up and touched the kiss, plucking the tingle of it from her skin, and slipping its memory into the pocket of her knee breeches.

"From affection, comes protection," Tilda said. "Don't despair, Locasta. You'll master it, soon enough."

Locasta all but glowed under the Grand Adept's praise.

"Glinda, my darling," Tilda went on, "you have done beautifully thus far. You have answered the questions. Now it is time to question the answers, to learn beyond what you have learned and lead the way. Be as brave as you've been, and as wise as you are. Though our plan has been thrust into action far sooner than we had anticipated, there is still every chance that it can succeed. And so, to that end, I must tell you about—"

A sudden, panicked look flashed across Tilda's face, and she tilted her ear to the sky. With a gasp, she turned frantic eyes back to Glinda. "You must *find Mythra*!"

At this command, Gage looked shocked.

"*Mythra?*" Glinda echoed. "The ancient Priestess? From the statue? Mother, I don't—"

"I'm sorry," said Tilda. "There is no time to explain further." Again she listened to the sky.

"I hear it too," said Shade. "Hurry! Go!"

Without another word, Tilda took off toward the

boundary of the Woebegone Wilderness. Nick dashed along beside her, his tin limbs clanking. When they reached the shadowy edge of the forest, Tilda turned to give Glinda a wave. Then the two travelers slipped into the thick cover of the trees and were gone.

Glinda was staring so intently at the woods that the sensation of a huge paw against her back came as a complete shock. The shove from Clumsy Bear sent her stumbling forward onto the red road. He did the same to Locasta.

"Quickly!" Gage commanded, herding Shade and Ben toward the cobblestones. "Everyone on the road. Now!"

"Why?" asked Glinda.

The answer came from the sky, which was suddenly filled with the sound of snapping jaws, blaring horns, and a deafening drone.

"Because," cried Gage, "the Witches are coming!"

ACKNOWLEDGMENTS

A Royal Adventurer requires an extensive network of support, and it is with the most heartfelt gratitude that I, Gabriel Gale, hereby acknowledge my compatriots in this quest to chronicle the Ages of Oz:

The first and most emphatic thanks must go to Lisa Fiedler, whose gift for words is matched only by the majestic truths told in Glinda's Book of Records.

Ruta Rimas and the team at McElderry Books, our Publishers and friends at Simon & Schuster, and Sebastian Giacobino and Craig Howell have made this book a joy to create and a pride to share with the world. This book series would not have happened without the guidance and magical matchmaking of Judith B. Bass, Esq., and Susan Cohen along with the team at Writers House.

Royal Historians of Oz George Makrinos and John Bush have contributed tireless research in uncovering the myths and truths of Lurlia and Oz. As Royal Cartographer and Architect, George has charted the course and laid the groundwork for many adventures to come. John, as Royal Bard and Headmaster of Fireside Institute, has lyrically immortalized facts long forgotten and turned history into poetry.

Royal Artist Arthur Jedrzejczak has captured the forms of the most elusive magical creatures both Good and Wicked. Sylwia Filipowicz, Eugene Jedrzejczak, Sebastian and Michael Khorched, Kevin Hamilton, Karina Chu, and Ronnie Debbs have come to his aid in that thrilling and most dangerous endeavor.

Royal Trustees Ralph, Joanna, and Karina Succar guard the hallowed Royal Vaults of Emerald City. With their help, the riches of the Magical world can now be shared with this mortal one.

Thanks also go to the noble Lord Greg Angelides and the illustrious Lord Anthony Lolli, who are ever willing to provide mentorship, friendship, wisdom, and advice, and to the brightest members of their respective Courts, Lady Matti Angelides and Lady Love Lolli, who are both surely bound for the stars.

Regents and Viceroys Vincent Aparo, Brian Hathaway, Chris Zias, David Schwartz, Charles Capetanakis, John Lignos, and Michael Zoumas have opened their doors and guided my course.

Grand Masters of the Oz High Council John Fricke and Willard Carroll are incomparable in their knowledge of

Oz. The wisdom they gave me early on continues to reap rewards.

And thanks to Royal Adventurer-in-Training Liam Dempster and Royal Gamer Corey Tettonis, honorary Princess Isabella Anderson, Emerald City Chef Angelique Tettonis, Emerald City racing champ Baxter Johnson, and the youngest Minstrels of Oz, Noah and Joseph Hochman. And to Royal Builder Vasili, Royal Politico Kosta, and Royal Keeper of Records Dean Tettonis, I continue to be proud of your accomplishments.

Thank you to the schools and people that helped prepare me for my adventures in Oz: The Dimitrios and Georgia Kaloidis Parochial School, Cooper Union for the Advancement of Science and Art, Columbia University, PS/IS104, Hellenic Classical Charter School, Fort Hamilton High School's Dr. Alice B. Farkouh and David Whitebook, and Royal Educator Christina Tettonis gave this adventurer his love for cartography and math, opening his eyes to boundless Magical realms.

The extended families that offered their hospitality during my travels: Stamatis and Irene Makrinos, Succar, Tettonis, Tsatsis, Karavolos, Poniros, and Luccioni.

My deepest thanks go to Rene and Dean Makrinos, who help this adventurer when he strays too far from the safe and narrow. I am forever indebted to you for your love and protection.

And finally, it is through the kindness and generosity

of Queen Ozma of Oz, Glinda the Good, and our dearest Princess Dorothy Gale, that we are able to share their story with new generations around the world. I offer my sincere hope that we have made their most legendary Royal Historian, L. Frank Baum, proud with this endeavor.

TURN THE PAGE FOR A SNEAK PEEK
AT THE NEXT BOOK IN THE AGES OF OZ SERIES,

A DARK DESCENT

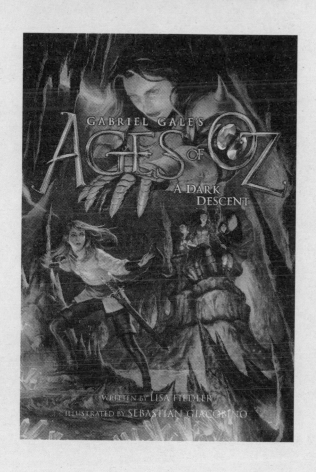

The tumult overhead was nothing short of Wicked.

Clatter and motion, fury and speed. Dark Magic seemed bent on tearing the sky to pieces in its desperate race to the south. Underfoot, the solidness of Oz felt close to crumbling.

The Witches are coming.

Miss Gage's warning rang in Glinda's ears, colliding with the sound of the enemy's approach: croaking and hissing from the West; a droning buzz from the East, and a deep lowing groan from the North.

Where moments ago the air had sparkled with the pure emerald light of King Oz's final thought, there was now a vicious melee of stingers and wings. The ground shuddered under a violent stampede of trampling hooves and swiftly slithering things. Billows of scarlet dust rolled forth as the menacing armies of the Witches advanced.

"*Why* are they coming?" Locasta asked, her violet eyes focused on the fracas above their heads, her fingers fidgeting nervously with the new gold bracelets on her wrists.

"To see for themselves that their rival in the South has been vanquished," said Miss Gage.

"Will they attempt to avenge her?" Ben rasped, his face pale.

Gage shook her head. "More likely they've come to celebrate her defeat."

As the commotion drew nearer, Clumsy Bear whimpered and covered his face with his paws. Glinda and the others watched as Ava Munch, the Royal Tyrant of the East, touched down. She was riding an insect of uncommon proportions—a weevil as large as a lion, with jagged legs and waving antennae. Swarming around Ava was a platoon of bulging-eyed creepy-crawlies: oversize wisp-wasps, mosquitoes and fruit flies, beetles and tumble-bumbles with iridescent wings. Out of the din they swooped, stirring up a small cyclone of dead leaves as they landed. Dressed in a sheath of blue satin, Ava hid her face behind her Silver Mask, as though she were ashamed to be seen in the hideous company of her own army.

Daspina the Wild Dancer of the West arrived next,

gracefully astride a spiny-tailed skink lizard. Flanking her was a legion of warty toads and scaly snakes, all of inordinate size. Draped in yellow scarves, the Wild Dancer shimmied in her saddle, her Silver Shoes catching the sunlight.

Finally, from the North roared Marada, the Wicked Warrior; her army was a careening herd of draft animals, each ridden by a Gillikin soldier armed to the hilt. The beasts—yakityaks, buffalopes, oxen, and bulls—came snorting and bellowing. The Witch used her Silver Gauntlets to yank back on the reins of her mount, and the gigantic yakityak skidded to a halt. Its pointy horns missed impaling Ava's weevil by less than an inch.

"Watch it!" Ava warned, removing her Silver Mask.

Marada growled and raised a gloved fist in a warning of her own.

Glinda spied a small, white-faced monkey scampering about. His presence among these creatures was inexplicable to her, and his wide eyes surveyed the scene, as if he, too, wondered what ugly twist of fate had brought him here. What Glinda found most stunning was that he had *wings*.

Sliding down from the skink, Daspina sashayed on dainty silver heels—first a few steps to her left, then a skip back to her right. "The Harvester is *quite* vanquished," she declared, as if there had been any doubt. "Gone to seed, one might say!" At this, she laughed and turned a pirouette.

"She was worthless," Marada spat. When she leaped

from her yak, the spurs of her heavy sandals left deep gashes in the dirt. "Ruling by delusion and trickery is not ruling. It is merely deceiving. She was as weak as the flowers she grew! I could have crushed her with one blow."

"And she was a terrible hostess," Daspina observed with distaste. "She never once threw a ball or cotillion, not even a pitiful little tea party."

"Still, her Magic was potent," Ava admitted in a grudging tone. "And there was an elegance about her. Handsome features. Good bones—"

"Good bones are the best kind to crush," Marada noted.

"—but she was more vain than she had any right to be."

At this, Marada whirled on Ava with raised brows. "*You* dare to call another vain?"

"*My* vanity is warranted," Ava insisted. "Aphidina was merely pretty. I stun."

"In more ways than one," Daspina conceded with a nervous giggle, eyeing Ava's mask.

Marada grunted; it might have been laughter. The sound made Glinda queasy.

Now the three Wickeds fell silent, looking out over the ravaged castle grounds, each with a glint of longing in her eyes. The monkey, who as far as Glinda could tell had no particular connection to any one of them, sped anxiously from steer to insect to amphibian, none of which paid him any mind.

"Surely I could collect immense amounts of taxes were

I to lease this land to the Quadling farmers." Ava's fingers twitched as if she could feel the gilt coins being pressed into her hands.

"And I could erect dance halls and bowling greens and gaming fields," Daspina twittered. "There would be garden parties and carnivals every day and every night if this were mine."

"The lists for training would go there," Marada planned aloud, pointing to where the Grande Allée of Symmetrees had stood just that morning, before Aphidina's defeat. "And there, rows of sturdy barracks for my soldiers."

"Don't you mean 'barns'?" scoffed Ava, gesturing to Marada's cattle grazing on what was left of the Haunting Harvester's grass.

"I would put my herd up against your pests in any battle!"

"Oh, would you?" Ava's eyes burned. "One well-placed sting on the rump would have your mount galloping back to Gillikin with his tail between his shaggy legs."

"*My* soldiers have fangs," Daspina boasted, her hips swaying with pride, "and venom."

For a moment, the three harridans stood motionless, hurling lethal glances at one another. Glinda shivered at the nearness of the Wickeds, thankful for the protection of the Road of Red Cobble beneath her feet; she was close enough to reach out and pull the mask from Ava's hand.

"This is a little too close for comfort," Locasta whispered. "I know they can't see or hear us, but I wish they'd just go back to where they came from."

"So do I," said Glinda, ducking back from the whipping hem of one of Daspina's scarves.

It was then that she felt the tickle—a soft, fuzzy graze against her trembling hand.

Startled, she looked down and saw that the monkey had crept to the edge of the Road of Red Cobble. The fluffy top of his head, swiveling from side to side as he took in the patch of road with great curiosity, was brushing against the tips of Glinda's fingers. Tilting his face upward, he met her green eyes with his enormous round ones. He blinked, as if trying to determine what her purpose was, there upon that patch of road.

Then he turned to Marada, and Glinda held her breath.

The monkey's wings fluttered slightly as he snapped his gaze to Ava, then Daspina. Glinda knew it would take no more than a single screech for him to alert this rancorous triad to her invisible presence, and she sensed he knew it too. But after a moment of eyeing the Witches, he seemed to decide against raising the alarm and returned his attention to the cobblestones.

Expelling her breath in a grateful sigh, Glinda watched the monkey tap his slender toes onto the red bricks, holding there a moment as if waiting to experience some sensation. But when nothing occurred, he simply shook his head in disappointment and trotted off. Glinda's eyebrows furrowed. The road had accepted him. But weren't these cobbles only welcoming—not to mention visible—to those who were worthy to travel them?

Her thoughts were interrupted by the words of the Royal Tyrant: "Perhaps I shall claim the South as my own so it will belong to me now and evermore."

"That simple, eh?" Marada let out an inelegant snort. "You think just because your lineage is noble you can claim lands at will?"

"You *are* quite the saucy former princess, aren't you?" Daspina snipped, gliding toward Ava. "Why should such a bountiful country as Quadling be *yours* for the taking?"

"Because," Ava drawled, returning the Silver Mask to her face, "*I* can do this!" A bolt of blue fury burned through the slit eyes of the mask, heading straight for the Witch of the West. But the Dancer was keen and graceful, and Glinda watched in horrified awe as Daspina quickly knocked her heels together. Three quick clicks of those Silver Shoes and she'd moved faster than sight or sound to the far side of the Tyrant.

"What was *that*?" Locasta asked.

"Those stolen shoes," Gage replied with a foreboding look. "It seems they allow the Dancer to skip from place to place without the bothersome inconvenience of utilizing the moments it would ordinarily take to do so."

"Well, they did belong to King Oz once," said Ben, who

was still holding Aphidina's Chainmail. "No wonder they carry such power."

"Power corrupted by the Witches," Shade added softly. "King Oz would never cheat time."

Glinda knew Shade was right; whatever Good Magic these pieces of silver contained before the Witches ripped them from the fallen king had been converted to Wicked long ago.

Now Ava turned the mask on Marada, but for all her immense bulk, the Wicked Warrior was agile; she dodged the blue bolt, then crouched low to hammer her heavy Silver Gauntlets against the ground. The terrain bucked up like an angry stallion, throwing both Ava and Daspina off their feet to land hard in the red Quadling soil—Ava sprawled on her back, and Daspina on her hands and knees. Fortunately, the red road beneath Glinda and the others remained steady. They all turned to Ben, clutching the chainmail.

"Careful with that," Locasta muttered wryly, and Ben slipped the silver mesh cautiously into his knapsack.

"Enough of this!" sang Daspina, executing another trio of heel clicks; this returned her instantaneously to the skink's side. "We were not sent here to battle among ourselves."

"More's the pity," Marada muttered, but she stood and swept the red soil from her gloves.

"Much as I hate to agree with the dancing fool," said

Ava, tucking the mask under her arm and frowning hatefully at the place where Aphidina's castle once stood, "she is indeed correct. We all know who will decide what is to become of Quadling. She ordered us here only to show us what Glinda Gavaria has done."

Hearing her name on the lips of the Wicked Witch of the East made the hair on the back of Glinda's neck prickle. But the true import of Ava's statement was not lost on Miss Gage. "*She* ordered them? Who's 'she'?"

The elusive and terrifying fifth Witch, thought Glinda, *that's who.*

Marada punched the knuckles of one gauntlet into the palm of the other. "Hah!" she barked. "I for one do not fear *children*. They are small and weak, scrawny and stupid. They cower and cry and have very little intelligence."

"This may be true of your little slavelings in Gillikin," Ava averred (and Glinda instinctively grabbed hold of Locasta to prevent her from bounding off the road to attack the Witch for her insult). "But children do grow up. They learn things. I realize that Glinda is presently no more than a pupa—"

Glinda's jaw dropped. "*What* did she just call me?"

"An insect," Ben clarified, "in its immature stage."

"—but once she is trained, she will surely be a force to be reckoned with." Stroking her weevil's glossy shell, Ava clung a little tighter to her Silver Mask and looked concerned.

"That is a most unsettling thought," Daspina remarked with a pout. "I believe I shall double the guards along my Winkie borders."

"I will do the same," said Ava. "It is in our best interests to keep the Sorceress larva out, for with the proper tutelage, there is no telling how powerful her Magic might become!"

Marada glowered and again surveyed the emptiness of the Harvester's grounds. "Perhaps we should teach this youngster-beast, this *Glinda*, a lesson ourselves. Let us not wait to hear the Krumbic one's plans for Quadling. Let's annihilate it!"

On the red road, the four friends, the bear, and the teacher froze. Even Feathertop, hovering over Ben's shoulder, stiffened in horror.

"Can they do that?" asked Ben. "I thought Ember would protect Quadling Country now that he's free."

"He can only protect the final thought and its power to birth Goodness," Miss Gage explained. "Quadling and those who dwell in it will never be completely invulnerable until Wickedness is abolished entirely."

"Great." Locasta rolled her eyes. "No pressure."

"Destruction is always an excellent idea, Marada," said Ava, returning the mask to her face. "Even if it was *yours*. I say we begin by torching the village."

Daspina twirled and clapped her hands. "Oh yes! A bonfire! How lovely. And how Wickedly injurious."

Marada clasped her big hands above her head in a gesture of certain victory. "And while the village burns, I shall capture as many Quadling prisoners as my soldiers can carry and bring them back to Gillikin as slaves."

Locasta went ashen. "We have to do something! The Quadling citizens will be caught totally unawares. They can't possibly defend themselves against three Witches."

"Neither can we," Glinda murmured, feeling helpless and afraid.

Until her eyes again fell on the little monkey, whose curious face was now turned skyward.

She followed his gaze, and her heart filled with hope.

Just overhead was a twinkle of green—a piece of King Oz's final thought, glowing emerald against the blue and red of the sky. Suddenly Glinda's whole mind echoed with the king's wise words: *That moment in which all is lost is the same moment in which begins the battle to regain it.*

And *that* moment, it seemed, was *this* moment!

Heart racing, Glinda reached into her sash and drew Illumina.

"What are you doing?" asked Ben.

"Beginning the battle," Glinda replied. "I think I can infuse the ground with Oz's last thought."

"Excellent plan," said Gage. "It won't keep them out of Quadling permanently, but with any luck, it might shock them enough to send them scurrying now."

"Hurry," Locasta advised. "They're preparing to ride."

Indeed, Daspina was prancing past in a flurry of yellow silk, the toes of her silver slippers a mere inch from the Road of Red Cobble. "I shall collect every crystal punch bowl and silver candlestick in the South," she announced, as she slipped into her saddle. "These will be the spoils that adorn the tables at my next banquet. And I shall kick the teeth out of the mouth of any Quadling who attempts to stop me."

Glinda aimed Illumina toward the bobbing green orb overhead.

"More to the left," Locasta coached.

"Now higher," said Ben.

"Gently," Shade advised in a hushed voice.

Glinda guided the tip of the sword toward the orb until the ball of light balanced upon it, quivering like a green flame on a candlewick.

"You got it!" Locasta cried as Glinda lowered Illumina cautiously out of the sky.

Just then Marada came marching past them with such gusto that the road shook; Glinda stumbled and nearly lost her grip on Illumina. Ben gasped; Shade ducked into the collar of her cape. But Glinda held fast and the orb remained perched on the point of the sword. Gage, Locasta, and even Clumsy Bear shared a sigh of relief.

"Are you sure this is going to work?" asked Locasta.

Glinda wasn't sure at all. But if all were to be lost, it would *not* be because she failed to take the chance.

Plunging the tip of Illumina into the dirt at the edge of the red cobblestones, she sank the green orb into the soil. Blazing streamers of green light erupted beneath the hooves and underbellies of the Wicked armies, and the surge of Goodness threw the Witches from their saddles. Daspina twirled in the air; Ava shrieked and Marada flailed. All three hit the ground with a sickening *thud*.

"Good Magic!" Ava howled, slapping at her satin sleeves as if they were engulfed in flame.

Lumbering back toward her yak and leaping into the saddle, Marada bellowed, "Retreat!"

"Retreat?" cried Daspina as she scrambled onto the skink, blowing on her singed fingertips. "So . . . no punch bowls, then?"

"Not unless you are willing to pay for them with your blistered skin!" Ava shot back, leaping onto her giant weevil. "Fly!"

"Slither!" Daspina commanded, snapping the lizard's reins.

Marada spurred her yak so violently that the animal grunted in pain. The rest of the draft beasts followed, thundering northward as Daspina sped west and Ava and her flying creatures veered east. With the monkey flapping frantically to keep up, the three armies formed a thrashing mass that briefly covered the setting sun.

From below, on the safety of the red road, Glinda, the Protector of Oz, watched their escape. She knew they could not feel her furious gaze upon them.

But they will, she vowed silently.

And soon.

When the Witches were out of sight, the Road of Red Cobble sank back beneath the grass. Glinda wasted no time; she spun on her heel and headed for town.

"Wait!" called Ben, galloping along beside her. "Where are we going?"

"To find Mythra."

"Mythra?" Locasta echoed. "But you already found her in the Reliquary."

"That was a *statue*," Glinda corrected, doubling her pace. "This time I need to find her for *real*. You heard what my mother said before she ran off on that yellow brick road. 'Find Mythra.' And that is exactly what I'm going to do!"

"Glinda," began Miss Gage, who, along with Clumsy Bear, struggled to keep up with Glinda's speed.

But Glinda had already climbed over a stone wall and leaped across a narrow creek, marching faster and more furiously as she went. Ben, Shade, and Locasta stayed close at her heels, while Feathertop soared just overhead, causing Glinda's coppery hair to flutter in the breeze of his broad wings.

"I'm still not entirely clear about who Mythra is," Locasta panted. "Besides being a hero of Oz, that is." She glanced at Shade. "Have you heard anything?"

"Only a whispered mention here and there," Shade replied. "It's said she was the king's Mystic, the one who ushered him to his place as rightful ruler. And because no one was more knowledgeable in the ways of Magic, it was she who trained the Regents Valiant to lead the four countries of Oz while Oz himself ruled from the Centerlands."

Glinda listened to Shade's insights and kept her eyes trained on the armory in the distance. The village was not far off, and in the center of it was Madam Mentir's Academy for Girls. As she hurried on, a plan began to form in her mind. She would commandeer the school as a base for the Foursworn Rebellion, and from there she would begin her search for Mythra, the Priestess Mysterious.

"Shade, please go to the academy," she instructed. "Find Madam Mentir, Misty Clarence, and any other faculty member who remains loyal to the Wicked regime. Until we can decide what to do with them, we'll hold them in the school's cellar."

"Like a dungeon?" Locasta let out a chuckle. "Impressive."

"Feathertop and I will help with that," Ben offered, and the three of them rushed ahead, disappearing into the falling twilight.

"Clumsy," she called, "go into the forest, and apprehend any Wicked sympathizer who might be attempting to flee."

The bear gave an affirmative wuffle-snuff, tripped over

his front paws, then righted himself and loped off toward the trees.

"Glinda!" Miss Gage shouted. "Please, wait . . . there's something you should know." Catching up at last, she clamped her hand around Glinda's arm and dragged her to a stop. "I'm sorry to have to say this, but no matter how hard you try, you will never find Mythra."

"Of course I will," said Glinda.

"No, you won't. You *can't* find her, Glinda. No one can."

Glinda's stomach clenched as the words sank in. "Why is that?"

"Because," the teacher whispered, lowering her eyes. "Mythra . . . is *dead*!"